Under the Poppy

Under the Poppy

a novel

Kathe Koja

Small Beer Press
Easthampton, MA

Small Beer Press
150 Pleasant Street #306
Easthampton, MA 01027
www.smallbeerpress.com
info@smallbeerpress.com

Distributed to the trade by Consortium.

Library of Congress Cataloging-in-Publication Data

Koja, Kathe.
Under the poppy : a novel / Kathe Koja. -- 1st ed.
    p. cm.
ISBN 978-1-931520-70-6 (alk. paper)
I. Title.
PS3561.O376U53 2010
813'.54--dc22

                                    2010025912

First edition 1 2 3 4 5 6 7 8 9

Text set in ITC Caslon.

Printed on 30% recycled paper in the USA.
Cover design by Base Art Co.
Cover photograph by Jonas Jungblut.
Author photo © Rick Lieder 2010.

To Chris, for the trade

And to Jane, who gave me the room.

But suddenly he disappears,
As so much else has down the years . . .
Until I feel him deep inside
The emptiness, preoccupied.
      from "Mercury Dressing," J. D. McClatchy

ACT ONE

THE FLOWERS OF THE STREET

1.

The room is small but chilly, the coal grate piled low. At the table together, scarlet damask and black tea, her shining pince-nez, his cheroot: Rupert with the night's receipts, Decca the month's accounts: "Adderley was here again?" Her pen's steel nib makes a disapproving sound, *scratch-scratch.* "Was it for Lucy? Sometimes I think she tries to fall ill, tries to ferret out the most diseased—"

"Not Lucy." He dwarfs the dainty duchess chair, its carved arms and wan petit-point roses: long legs, tight-squared shoulders, the sober frock coat and glass-polished boots of a prosperous undertaker. Black hair to his collar, a deep groove between his eyes, at odds with his young man's face. "Omar. An abscess."

"Then Omar can pay for the doctor himself, next time. Or switch to the spoon." Fox-colored hair piled high, secured with silver combs; on her violet silk breast are several pins, pinked topaz, opal, silver-gilt, and, pinned inside her bodice, a miniature blue eye in a circle of gold, a lover's eye, far more opulent than the others. "More tea?" She pours without waiting for an answer. He takes the whiskey glass instead, he rubs his forehead. "Your head.... Call Vera, let her see to you."

"Fucking doesn't ease a headache."

"It relieves tension."

"I am not tense."

Lips parted to dispute this, she closes them again. *Scratch-scratch.* "The fire screen in the parlor wants replacing, the carpet there is fairly scorched through."

"Mmm."

"Did we do well tonight?" She glances briefly at the door. "It seemed a thin crowd when I was on the floor."

"Well enough, considering."

She glances toward the door again. "Redgrave was in early, I saw him sporting with Pearl."

"Yes.... What do you look at?"

"Nothing." And then both hear it, the noise of commotion past

1

the muted hum and thump of the dwindled downstairs crowd, the
upstairs rooms: a girl's voice, Pearl's voice, high in protest—"No, sir!
Stop! *Sir!*" Not playacting—the heat of actual distress as Rupert stubs
out his cheroot, Decca half rising: "Let Omar deal with it. Rupert, let
Omar—"

—but bald Omar is already at that door, half-bandaged arm, rapping
with the truncheon's handle: "Hey! All square in there, Pearl?"

A smothered cry from within as another door opens, a vexed and
peering guest from the Blue Room across the hall, the whore Lucy
behind him, trying to jockey him back inside. Decca arrives, hand
outstretched in futile warding, as Rupert turns the knob, Omar at his
shoulder—

—to peer through the guttering darkness, no candles, just a dim
and flickering tallow light, and see the whore Pearl, wide-eyed and bare,
trying to claw up the wall and away from a lean-muscled man in a white
plague mask and a lumpy, determined dwarf, still half-dressed, who
appear to be assaulting her simultaneously: the dwarf's arm is aiming up
her back passage, the man is pounding at her front and "What harm?"
Omar says, looking to Rupert stilled a step past the threshold as "They
didn't pay for two!" cries Pearl. "The little one, he didn't pay!"

Rupert nods, one step closer through the cloaking dark as Omar
grasps the dwarf by the neck—"Hey, messire"—but "No!" shrieks the
dwarf, a high and terrible voice, though his ugly head lies flaccid in
Omar's grasp, black hair and rolling eyes staring backward at the three
of them, like a felon pursued to ground. "No, no! Don't make me stop,
she's tight as a virgin!"

"Let's go, messire!" as the masked man still pounds busily away,
long hair slapping his naked back, Omar tugging at the dwarf, tugging
harder and "Jesu!" Omar's shout as the dwarf's head pops loose into his
hand, pink blood spurting across the sheets, he throws the head from
him with a curse and Pearl goes mad, the hideous half-clothed body
still attached to her by its arm, its hand still jammed inside as Rupert
reaches, grabs a leg and pulls—

—and stumbles backward from the force as the masked man
shouts with laughter, as Rupert flings the body to the floor, stares at the
bed, at the man on the bed, who tugs aside his mask and "Shhh," he
says sweetly to Pearl, who is retching now into the sheets beside him.
"Shhh, it's just a toy."

"It's a God damned puppet," Omar cries.

"Hello, Rupert," the naked man says.

Silence, blank and dead until the boom of Omar's laugh, aghast,
relieved, Pearl wipes her mouth on the sheet as Rupert stares at the

man, a stare like a blow, turns viciously on his heel and leaves the room and "All's well," Decca says to the watchers in the hallway, half a dozen peering and unnerved, Vera and Jennie and Vladimir, their tricks and johns—until Lucy starts laughing, Lucy from the Blue Room laughing and clapping and "Bravo!" she cries, and the others relax into shrugs: Why, it was just a joke, a show, just another peculiar amusement at the Poppy, no cause for anyone's concern.

Decca turns, peremptory, to Omar: "Go fetch Velma, have her change the linen in here. Take her too, yes," as the nude and trembling Pearl climbs to her feet. "And *you*," sharp in their departure, as the door shuts decently behind them, as the unmasked man retrieves his fallen accomplice, setting the head politely on a chair, "oh you imbecile," helpless and smiling, crossing the room to gather him into her arms.

Lucy

So I am working this man, you see, watching the little clock by the bed frame, I aim for just six minutes and no more to do the job. Which is what they pay for really, those six minutes, no matter how long the business really takes. *Umphf-umphf -umphf*, he's a fat one, fat jelly roll underneath me, I don't like the fat ones usually, they're much harder to bring on. But sometimes you get lucky, sometimes they swoon, and you can go through their pockets while they catch their wind. Sometimes they even die. Last month one died on Vera, she was milking his prick and boom, he fell right over on his face. Their hearts give out, you see, because of the fat.

This one, he wants a fairy tale, he wants me to pretend I'm an angel from heaven, whistle like a canary and wear little white wings on my back. All right, I don't mind, the feathers itch but he pays extra so I get extra. They always want you to pretend to be something, act out some sort of play; that's why they come here, to the Poppy.

So there I am, an angel fucking a fat man and thinking maybe I'll be lucky and he will die and I can pilfer him before Omar or Decca get there, especially Decca. Omar I could bribe, he's still friend enough to take money or a handful of snuff or dope to keep his mouth shut. But what he really wants is to be a manager, stop sleeping in the back rooms, start sleeping *With Decca?* I say to him, *you want that cold cunt wrapped around you at night?* And he laughs. I think what he wants mainly is to be Mr. Rupert, but that'll never happen. Omar works hard, yes, downstairs and upstairs, but he likes the drink and the snuff and even, sometimes, the needle, he likes to take Pearl, or Jennie, or both of them together. He likes his fun, does Omar. So he could never run a place like the Poppy, not the way Mr. Rupert does.

UNDER THE POPPY, it says on the sign, with the picture of the poppy flower, dark red painted but to me it looked black when I first came here, and I wondered, What kind of flower is it that grows black? I didn't stand wondering for long, though, it was freezing, snow up to my ankles, leaking into the cracks of my boots.... I remember those boots, they were Katy's, I had to stuff them up with paper just to keep them on my feet. Katy, my sister, who had the only pair of whole boots

4

in the house, the only new dress, the only bed. Because she shared it with our father. Not long after I came to bleed, he started in looking at me, too. I told Katy that if he ever touched me I was going to kill him, but she said *No, Lucy, he'll hurt you. Just go. Go to the city, you're a likely girl, you can get some kind of work there for sure.*

What about you?

I'll be fine. I know how to handle him. Handle him! She had already had one of his whelps, thank God it was born dead. Dead and ugly. *Come with me,* I said, I begged her, but in the end I went alone, wearing Katy's boots, carrying Katy's coins wrapped up in a bit of wool under my dress, and the little silver mirror she gave me to ward off the evil eye. Sometimes at night I still wake and think, *I should have killed him anyway, I should have killed him quick before I left.* Did he punish her, because I ran away? I don't know. I don't know what happened to Katy. May be she had another baby. May be she is dead. She used to braid my hair, when we were little, and put flowers on the ends, and sing me songs about the fairies in the trees: *Watching out for you/ And watching out for me.*

So I went to the city, and started in whoring: first on my own— that didn't last—and then for Mr. Angus at the Europa. It didn't take me long to see that he was cheating me, cheating all of us girls, charge ten and give us half a dollar, but when I complained he hit me: *Every day I see a dozen like you,* he said. *You don't like it here? Go back to the Alley.*

The Alley was where they gathered, the girls without pimps, the ones right from the country, or too old for a house, or stuck hard on the needle, or whatever. Cigarettes rolled in newspaper, sleeping where they stood, wiping themselves with their hands—no, no Alley for me. But I won't be hit, either, not just for talking. So I went to the Palais, and Miss Suzette.

"Miss"! She must have been forty if she was a day, a hard forty too, grooves all over her face, her tits like bags of old rags, carnelian earbobs and that rose sachet, ugh, like someone's grandmother in a coffin. She never hit anyone, her punishment was to starve: get smart, no dinner for the day; steal, or fight with the other girls, or try to cut yourself, no dinner for a week. I got along with her all right, especially when she found out I was lettered. She used to have me in her rooms with the newspaper to read the advertisements to her, the news of the day. At first I thought she meant to try to touch me, which would have been all right, I don't mind that. But what she really wanted was to learn to read! Isn't that funny? She knew a little of her letters, how to spell her name, and she could cipher perfectly. But she could barely put two words together.... She wasn't happy, when I figured that out. She didn't starve me, but she started giving me the worst of the customers, the ones no one else wanted, the ones who never wash or who took forever to bring on, then complained afterward that you were too quick. She let that go on for a week until I went to her rooms—dust everywhere, mice in the featherbed stinking of rose sachet—and *Miss Suzette,* I said, *you can keep giving me these bastards from the bottom of the barrel, and I can leave. Or you can let me help you with your letters, and I can stay.*

She didn't say anything at first, let me wait for a day or two, but I watch people quite carefully, you know, and when you watch them, you get to know about them. It was how I knew when a man was going to be troublesome, waiting in the parlor. Or which girls you could make friends with, and which not to bother with. Or that my father was going to try with me. So I knew Miss Suzette was going to come around, and I started planning how it would be, how I could get her to a certain point in her lessons and then ask for things, ask not to have to fuck so much, or at all, may be even ask for money.

But then she caught the scarlatina, caught it hard, and the house closed up like a fist because Faulk put himself in charge, that greedy, high-nosed, gutter-bred prick. He locked her in her room with a spoon and some laudanum, and put us to work around the clock, receive from noontime till nearly dawn; only Sunday afternoons were we free, and then we were supposed to clean the grates and sweep the rooms, empty the slop jars, peel spuds for Sunday supper; ridiculous. *I won't do it,* I told Faulk, *I'm a whore, not a housemaid.*

You're not a schoolteacher, either, but you were ready to act that part quick enough. So you can take your turn at the mop with the rest of them.

But I didn't, I stole away, out into the streets to take the air. It is a big place, and the avenue is long: up and down the vendors selling everything you could think of, pomade and fruitcake, boot-blacking and smelling salts, picture puzzles of the palace and the White Gardens, walking sticks with ivory heads of birds and dogs and tigers, silver ribs for silk parasols, blue crayons to make your skin look whiter. And all sorts of little food shops and wine parlors, it made your mouth water just to see them, but I had no money for those kinds of things. And theatres.... Do you know, I never even saw a theatre before I came here? Once or twice a year a drummer would come through, and Katy and I would give him a penny to crank the concertina, and once there was a puppet show, a little man with a hook nose and a slapstick, and his wife and baby, and a toby-dog. We laughed so much! The drummer could make all the puppets talk with different voices, and he even barked, for the dog. They were called Punch and Judy, they were in the book that Katy had, called *Droll Tales*. It had a story about Cinder-Ella, too, who lived among the ashes until she found her rightful prince, and one about the Mouse King, and the people who live underwater and talk by bubbling, one bubble to another; it was how I learned to read, that book, until our father found it.... I should have killed him, really.

At the Gaiety Theatre there are plays, and dancing, you could hear the music from the street: a real band, with a fiddle and piano, and the ladies bright as butterflies in spangles and lace; I saw it on the sign and I thought, If I could only dance, or sing! Wearing lovely costumes, not going with the men unless you wanted to, unless they bought you roses or scent or jewelry, what a life that would be. But I am not so pretty, and I cannot sing or dance. I couldn't even afford a ticket to go inside and watch.

But that Gaiety, it was how I ended up at the Poppy, really. Omar was there—I didn't know him then, of course, but it was Omar, with his bumpy bald head, standing outside the Gaiety having a smoke and *Hey,* I said. You could tell he wasn't a trick. *Hey, messire, you work in there?*

Why? You need a job? And in the end it was as simple as that, what Jonathan calls the kismet. Omar told me about the Poppy, how it was a kind of theatre, with a stage, and costumes, and plays, private plays for one watcher at a time. *Mister Rupert is always looking for likely girls,* Omar said. *Are you likely?*

I put my hands up under my tits and jiggled them. *You tell me,* I said, and he laughed, and I went back and told Faulk to go fuck himself, and I walked in under that black-flower sign, I walked in Under the Poppy, and I never left. I hate Decca's guts and she hates me, but the rest of us get along fine, and Mr. Rupert treats us very fair. And the shows, the little plays—the ones downstairs, where there is music, Vera and Pearl and Laddie, and Spinning Jennie, she used to be in a circus somewhere, she can hang from the ceiling up-so-down like a bat. And Jonathan plays the piano like an angel. And Puggy can declaim lines and lines of verse, he can read French and English both. Anything you give him, he can read.

And upstairs—well, sometimes the feathers tickle, and the fat bastards won't properly die, but they finish anyway, six minutes is six minutes. And things happen at the Poppy that would happen nowhere else. Like Mr. Istvan. And Pan Loudermilk. Even the Gaiety has nothing like them.

❧❦❧

"And this one?" Guillame lifts a louche blonde puppet, lips painted primly pink, wires threading its blue brocade skirt and "That's Miss Lucinda," Istvan says. "She sings. And cries real tears," milking a tiny secret bulb so a drop of glycerin oozes from her eye socket and rolls, slow glass, down her cheek. "Although I try not to make her."

On the narrow bed beside him, Lucy claps her hands. "Lucinda! That's my name, almost." She fingers the bright brocade. "This is so lovely."

They have gathered, the four of them, like curious circling animals, drawn like animals by instinct unspoken to this narrow room at the end of the upper hallway, Istvan inside like a creature in a den, dozing among his things: a meager bag of personal accoutrements, crocodile-toed boots beneath the bed, narrow razor and steel hand-mirror, a clean shirt hanging wrinkled from a peg; all the rest of his luggage is cases and traps for the puppets, *les mecs* he calls them, the *farceurs*: made of wood and sacking-cloth and glue, muslin and plaster, carven eyeballs and hair of silk or boiled wool, strings and wires and levers intricate and odd: a level of cunning construction, fabrication, that the players of the Poppy have never seen before. And Istvan is generous with his secrets, displaying the tear-bulbs and the blood-drips, seeming pleased to answer everything they care to ask.

Guillame has the most questions, proper in a stage manager; he keeps shaking his head in admiration, that pudgy head he has lately begun to shave a la Omar. Now he points to the largest puppet, horse's head and man's body, standing tall as a man in the corner: "Now, who is this gentleman?"

"His hair is like yours," Lucy says, noting the dark chestnut mane.

"His hair is mine. Some of it.... That's the Chevalier. He is French, I believe. His favorite is riding, but he can do all manner of things."

"I'll bet he can," says Omar, parting the Chevalier's black morning coat to show a thick wooden penis, detailed as a man's. "He must put on quite a show. You put on a good one yourself, yesterday, you and, what is it? Dan?"

"Pan," Istvan says. "Pan Loudermilk. We met in Paris. Or possibly it was Antwerp? He is a citizen of the world, is Pan."

"You had me fooled, I'll tell you that. I thought the little man was arm-fucking Pearl for certain. That voice... And then his head came off! With blood and all. How in the world did you do that, messire?"

Istvan squeezes Miss Lucinda's tear-bulb again. "Glycerin and rose water," he says. "One can use it for anything, almost."

"You had me fooled."

Lucy laughs. "Pearl too—she had the nightmare last night, I had to wake her. 'Get him off me!'" she mimics, eyes closed, legs cantering against the coverlet, as if caught in deadly embrace, then looks around the room, this smallest receiving room, called the Cell for its narrow bed, its barred ceiling-window; it faces the privy yard. Above, the roll of glum afternoon clouds; it will rain soon, or snow. "Where is it, that Pan puppet?"

"Sleeping," Istvan says, nodding to the case against the wall, more coffin than carrying-box, sized as if for a dwarf, or a largeish child. He rolls over, leans his body across Lucy's lap, his long hair brushing her breasts and "That fellow there," pointing to what looks like jumbled sticks, "wants stringing. Lift him up, messire," to Guillame, who digs his fingers in the pile to draw forth a mournful skullface, eyeless eyes blank and dire, and a wobbled xylophone of bones, some correctly connected, most not and "The Bishop," says Istvan, "had a delicate time of it, in the countryside. He used to be the Arch-Bishop, but some yokels demoted him. They take their hymn singing seriously in the countryside," and "'Rock of Ages, cleft for me,'" groans the Bishop, a bass croon so instant and harsh that Guillame, startled, nearly drops the head, laughs in nervous surprise. "'Let me hiiide myself in Thee.' Is it not so, Bishop?"

"They struck you with my thighbones," the Bishop says, seems to say, it is uncanny how the voice draws the eye, even though one knows it is Istvan speaking. "Biblical precedent, mayhap. Or should it have been the jawbone?" Jonathan laughs through closed lips. "Though I am dead, I can yet feel pain at the baseness of Man."

"As did I." Istvan lifts his shirt to show the bruising; Lucy puts forth two fingers to touch his yellowed ribs.

"I've arnica. In my room."

Omar chews the end of a bent cigar. "The Poppy's got a higher class of clientele, at least they won't pummel you. Much... So, you are here to perform, then?"

"That's up to your master."

"Who'll be wanting me directly," says Omar, checking his pocket watch, fat silver carapace jingling with cheap-looking fobs. "You too, Puggy," to Guillame who rises, Jonathan behind them and "Take the *Merchant*," Istvan says to him, skittish Jonathan who starts at being addressed, widens his eyes and "You were looking," Istvan's nod toward the small stack of books, a Greek travelogue, a vampire penny-dreadful, Shakespeare's *Merchant of Venice* and *Titus Andronicus*, a Latin copy of Cicero's Catiline orations. "*Tolle lege*. Take it, read it. But not in the jakes, hmm? The smell gets into the paper."

Jonathan smiles, slips the book into his pocket, gives an awkward bob of a bow. Lucy nods after him, once the three have gone: "He never speaks," she says.

"Too shy?"

"No tongue," opening her mouth to waggle her own. "Someone cut it out for him, he's never said who."

"It would be surprising if he had. So it's rough trade, here?"

"Not like that. More like this," touching his ribs again, stroking the bruises. "In my room—" .

"Is it only in the rooms, the acting? Or is it downstairs, too?"

"Oh every night. Puggy is in charge of those shows, they choose the players from among us girls."

"Are you on the stage, then?" but almost immediately "No, or that is, yes. You *are* the stage, yeah?" and Lucy laughs, she has not heard it put that way but yes, she supposes she is. And they talk of the theatre, the private shows and the ones onstage, how they are different and how so much the same; and of other performances, the Gaiety down the street, the great theatres of the world and "Have you played many places?" Lucy wants to know, sitting up straight now, like an eager schoolgirl. "Where have you traveled?"

"Well," thoughtful, "since the leaves fell, we've played the Capitalia, and the Phoenix, and the Theta Grande—*that* was a disaster—and the one in Syracuse, what was it called?"

A muffled voice from the coffin-box: "It was called the Syracuse."

Lucy's eyes gleam with the glamour of the list. "And then you came here?"

"Then we came here. Sub rosa. Under the Poppy. Whorehouse, playhouse, flophouse. Do you like it here, Lucy-Belle?"

She dimples at the name. "It's a likely place. Better than any other house in town, I can tell you that. And Mr. Rupert treats us all very fair."

"Mister Rupert," Istvan says. "Is that so."

"It is so. He never beats us, or cheats us, or fucks us—"

"No? Who does he fuck?"

"I don't know for sure. Some people say that he and Decca—"

"People are so base."

"Sometimes that happens," says practical Lucy, "when there is no one suitable, sometimes a brother and a sister—"

"Well," as the door swings open to show Decca on the threshold, "here's the very image of the idle whore. How have you time to sit and gossip, Lucy, while the rest of us toil? Go on." Blue silk, black combs, arms folded to watch the girl slide sullen off the bed, the door slammed behind her and "You'll catch a dose off that one," Decca says. "Runny cunt. She has the doctor here twice a week."

"You're sour, aren't you."

"No, only concerned. About you... Have you spoken to him yet?"

"Who? Herr whoremaster? Your 'brother'?" His whole manner has changed since she entered, as an actor changes coming offstage: he is looser, coarser, he slumps, he yawns. "Not yet."

"Did you sleep, at all?" He shrugs. "You look wretched in general.... Why are you here?"

"To make magic," says the muffled voice from the box.

"Stop that." She takes a seat on the bed, close to where Lucy sat. "In your letter, you said—why did you come, truly?"

"If you wish me gone, why did you let me in?"

She sighs through her teeth, a soft and painful sound. All night she heard Rupert up and pacing, up and pacing, smelled the constant dry smoke of his cheroots. "I thought you would arrive—differently. Your letter—and that prank with Pearl! What on earth possessed you?"

He is looking at her, only that, but suddenly she laughs, muffling her face in her hands, and he laughs, too, one arm around her, his gaze on the door, attending to what? The sounds of the house around them? Footsteps passing in the hall? Whose?

Finally she drops her hands, cheeks flushed; she looks younger now, like the street-girl she once was and "Oh," she says, "that nasty puppet—and how she squealed! But I thought—"

"You think much too much, Ag." She does not react to the name. "I said I was coming, well, here I am."

In silence they consider one another, his arm about her, her hands clasped in her lap. Tears rise to her eyes that, if she blinks, will fall; she does not blink. Finally, in surrender, her near-silent sigh and "Whatever you came to do," she says, "you must stay invisible tonight. We're to have a thorny time of it, Jürgen Vidor is entertaining—"

"Who's Jürgen Vidor?"

"Never mind. I'll have Velma bring up a bottle, some food, whatever you would like. Only do not cause a disturbance, please, just stay quiet in your room. *Please.*"

His arm is still about her shoulders, now he holds her slightly off from him, gives a sweetly solemn wink and "As a mouse," he says. "All right? Now send me that little whore again, what is her name? Pearl?"

Warily, "Why?"

"I want to make it up to her."

"You're lying, doubtless," but half smiling in defeat, Pearl appearing a few moments later, skittish and lovely in a red-ribboned camisole,

eyeing Istvan from the threshold as "My dear young lady," his tender
half bow, "I must utterly apologize for yesterday's confusion. You are an
actress yourself, you understand, sometimes the play simply gets away
from one. But shall we," easing shut the door, "tête-à-tête now, just us
two? And keep the toys out of it?"

The latch clicks, a figure pauses in the hallway: Rupert in shirtsleeves, silent and cold. He looks deliberately at the door—murmurs
rising from within, Istvan's soothing tenor—then turns to Decca, who
waits in the shadows with folded arms.

"This is what you want?" he says, very quietly.

"Throw him out," she says, as cold. "His hateful puppets, too."

Jürgen Vidor

This is not by any measure a city, nor even a cosmopolitan town. Many who visit me here find it scarcely bearable, and wonder aloud that I stay, accustomed as I am to Venice and Paris and London, the conveniences and comforts of true cities, their soothing anonymity and bustle. But what distinguishes a gentleman is the ability to accommodate, no matter the circumstance. If one seeks *divertissement* in Paris, one visits the Objet d'Art. Here, one goes Under the Poppy.

It is a sort of vulgar wordplay, "poppy" being gutter slang for a woman's female organs, though a somewhat grimmer version of *Papaver orientale* is indeed painted over the door. One recalls the delicacy of the door-knocker at the Pale Ophelia, that lovely nude form meant to be caressed as much as grasped, or the naughty devil winking from the wall at the Roxy…. I digress. The true poppy itself, opium, is not on open offer at the Poppy, though one can certainly obtain it there; the majordomo—a rough fellow name of Omar—is familiar with all intoxicants. And the whores, while not especially beautiful, are as skilled as one can reasonably expect, and very fairly priced.

What most distinguishes this brothel from its lower-caste brethren in town is a certain gaiety of intent and execution. Believing the erotic arts already twin to the theatrical, it marries the two, both onstage and in the private rooms: that is, one may watch, or dally with, an angel or a costumed beast, a mermaid from the sea, King Cophetua's saucy beggar-maid, the barefoot Little Cora; or, if one has certain stories of one's own devising, the whores will enact them, though this becomes more costly. Especially if it involves the receiving, or giving, of pain.

Permit me to digress once more, for it has long been my philosophy that pain is a sadly misunderstood phenomenon. In our lives we flee it by a thousand troubled routes, but does it not find us, always, no matter where we may hide? Its very ubiquity argues for our respect, and a closer scrutiny. Yes, certain grosser pangs, those of hunger or cold, are certainly to be despised, and may be successfully avoided with the application of some little industry.

But the sterner, more refined, most passionate pangs: do we not reach heights of immediacy, depths of contemplation, eternal instants of, yes, stern bliss, when by those pains we lie tautened to our very limits? And is this not happiness? Submission is the key, but not in a fearful or despairing way, as a broken brute gives over to the club: rather we throw wide the doors of our *sanctum sanctorum*, not only allowing but inviting the pain to enter, and, by giving such invitation, retain our mastery of self and situation, as well as divining more about both in the process.

Even so at the Poppy.

So, when business beckons me here, as it often does in the current and unstable situation, I do not drag my feet, I go willingly: into rooms kept chilly with too little coal, to bloody beef instead of foie gras, bouquets of feathers and prairie rose, the nightly parting of the somewhat shabby velvet curtains by a backwoods D'Oyly Carte, to reveal a mute who plays the piano like Monsieur Chopin himself, and the sensual acrobatics of girls who cannot spell their own names. And there is Omar's pharmacœpia, of course, and the occasional afternoon concerto coerced from that mute, one forgets his name since he never speaks it, but certainly he could have a fine career were he not so maimed, and were he elsewhere: in Paris they would overlook his silence, or even find it piquant; the French are perverse, after all. And there is conversation, too, with the brittle proprietress, Miss Decca, she who sells every vice while tasting none for herself, and time spent with the Poppy's owner, Mister Rupert Bok.

We met last winter, as I was traveling through the area, and found myself benighted by a hopelessly snowbound train and a taxi coachman who seemed to speak no human tongue; instead of pressing on to Archenberg as demanded, he brought me here, where boredom drove me from the first, musty embrace of the Europa Hotel—a third-rate hostel, even by local standards—to seek my evening's entertainment elsewhere. I saw the swing of the black bloom, I accepted a light from a fur-hatted Omar, and smoked my cigar in the Poppy's lobby, where the mute's music beckoned me deeper inside. I recall being charmed by the rude vigor of the show, surprised by the decent tang of the brandy. Miss Decca offered me the bill of fare. And then I met Rupert.

Rupert—is a unique individual. He could easily move among the great, in the highest circles of society, any society anywhere, such is his natural refinement and innate courtesy. He possesses a rare quickness of mind, a brilliance, really; I do not know his equal, even in Paris. Even in London. And his wit...Well. I am by nature somewhat of a solitary, preferring my own company to that of others who neither share nor comprehend my views; and those with whom my business yokes me are often not to my taste, to put it mildly. But

Rupert—suffice it to say that, from the start, I lacked no stimulation in his company.

Which is a true boon, since I find myself called here more often than formerly, as the civil situation continues to decay. Commerce is, or ought to be, a thing apart from politics, above it; no matter our individual affiliations, men must buy and sell, that is how the world spins. To complicate that necessary spin with needless disputes of border and tribute is a kind of evil, one that we, as men of business, must confront with all the weapons at our disposal, not the marching armies of czar and general but the subtler soldiers of the pen and the mind. I will touch only on the present crisis by noting that its escalation is marked by powers much greater than my own, men whose vision I share, beside whom I have toiled for many years; to build takes time. In this time, now, we are doing all we may to bring remedy, before the region's circumstance deteriorates past all recall. Already there is talk of secession, already there are shortages in the shops—

At any rate, to go Under the Poppy at such a time is more comfort than concession, and I hesitate not at all to host my cosmopolitan colleagues when travel sends them this way. I am in fact employing the staff and players of the Poppy for a private celebration for a gentleman from Brussels with whom I am in ongoing consultation, regarding some interests we share. He, and I, and several of the local *haute monde*—Colonel Essenhigh certainly, and the mayor, and, alas, the mayor's dunce of an attaché—will gather there for supper and entertainment. I am hopeful that Rupert will join us, if only for a while, but he is chary of much socializing, a reticence I respect and understand: after all, one does not pour the finest wine into a shallow trough. It is quite enough that he gives his time to me.

"Laddie," Guillame says, "you're the Light of Love, you'll be here with the candelabra. Vera on the chaise, yes, just so. And you, Jen, up there, I want you dangling like a grape. A ripe grape about to fall into a hungry mouth—"

"The straps hurt my back," says Spinning Jennie. "I can't do it." Lucy, kneeling beside her on the stage, hemming her costume, pinches Jennie's long white thigh through the cheesecloth skirt; Jennie makes a sluggish gesture as if to chase a fly and "You're so dosed," says Lucy, "a hammer couldn't hurt you. Puggy, look at her eyes."

"Shut up, Lucy!"

"The harness, Jen. Go on," chewing a cigar like Omar does; if it is true that Omar wants to be Rupert, then Guillame wants to be Omar, or at least look the part, bald head, cigars, and all. He has none of Omar's imposing physical presence, being rather comically short and round, but when Guillame is in his element, bringing life to this stage, he possesses an undeniable energy, a human dynamo in boiled wool and old blue spats.

His title is stage manager, which means a thousand things on a hundred different days: direct and wrangle the players, cadge the props—such as the harness, a refurbished cast-off from the livery; conjured diamonds from paste, Triton's trident from a hayfork, a paper dove that flutters into life—and construct and assemble the sets, school Lucy into a seamstress, make sure Jonathan has piano enough to play. Some nights he works the doors with Omar, vetting the lustful from the drunks. Most nights he stays up past dawn, reviewing the evening's playlets: what brought applause or indifference, what roused the crowd, what roused them too much. *The verge,* he likes to say. *That's where we want them, the utter, utter verge.*

Guillame tells a thousand stories of his advent at the Poppy, his life before he came: in some he is the hero, some the villain, some just a winning young lad with a wonderful gift to share. There is no telling which story might be true, if any, though portions of the tale persist in every telling, so perhaps the factory father is real, and the consumption that killed him; certainly the scars on Guillame's legs are real, from riding on the trains, any trains, as long as they were headed east. *The theatre was calling me,* he likes to say.

And it is true that he has a gift for it, the spectacle, the glitter and dash; he can make do with few resources, though he agitates always for more: as now, Decca passing through, a passing pince-nez glance and "Wax candles," he implores, pointing at the candelabra held by a yawning Vladimir. "This fucking buffalo tallow, it's all smoke, no one will be able to see a thing."

"I can see her tits," Decca says. "So will they."

"If that's all we mean to offer, we might as well change our name to the Sloppy. Or set up next to that cesspool on the corner." First strident, now wheedling; he is a bit of an actor himself, Guillame. "Decca, have mercy. To spin gilt-paper to gold, and cheesecloth to silk, I must have the proper light."

"The tables will have wax candles. We cannot afford—"

"We cannot afford to skimp for Jürgen Vidor, his one night will bring a year's worth of business." This is an exaggeration, but close enough to truth that Decca frowns, and fiddles with the pins on her breast, topaz winking between her fingers until "All right," she says. "But save all the ends, mind…. Lucy, why are you here? No one wants you in the show."

Lucy looks up from the skirt she is pinning. "Puggy wants me."

"You belong upstairs."

Slowly, Lucy draws the pins from her mouth. The others— Guillame, Jennie, Vera, Vladimir, Jonathan sitting quiet behind his keyboard—take a waiting breath, cut their eyes one to another. There are various theories as to why Decca so implacably hates Lucy; it is Guillame's private opinion, shared only with Omar, that there is some jealousy involved.

Now "Upstairs," Decca repeats and "That's all you think I'm good for," snaps Lucy. "You think I'm just tits and two holes."

"Three." Decca taps her lips. "Now go and ready your room."

"Decca." Guillame steps forward, into the sightline between Decca and Lucy. "If I might—"

"You might remember who is in charge here. Every hour Lucy spends prancing onstage is an hour stolen from the lockbox. Why do you flatter her into thinking she can do more than suck prick?" Her voice grows louder. "Why does she—"

"Stop." Rupert in overcoat and gloves, the cold still on him, a princely apparition at the back of the house; his voice is calm but it carries. "In this room, Puggy is in charge; if he needs Lucy he must have her. When she must, she will be in her room, yes?" to Lucy who nods, replaces the pins in her mouth, straightens the hang of the cheesecloth with an angry tug. "Where's Omar?"

Decca's voice is even. "Seeing to the wine."

"More guests are due than we expected—half the garrison it seems. Have him buy double. Puggy, tonight's show will be exceptional?" as Guillame bows—"Exceptionally so"—and "It had better be," striding up the aisle with Decca in his wake, into the empty lobby where she stands before him, en garde, at bay and "If she's an actress," low, "I'm a Dutchman. Have I no authority at all, here?"

"Why must you meddle where you're not needed?" He stuffs his gloves into his pocket, rubs his forehead. In this brighter light, his overcoat looks scuffed and slightly shabby, his hat in need of brushing: the pauper prince. The whole lobby wears that same declining air, brave enough by candlelight, by day just a bedizened box smelling distantly of damp wool, cigars, and ancient sperm. "Christ knows there's plenty else for you to do this day."

She knows the truer source of his agitation; she bites her lip. "And what of you? You were abroad early."

"Vidor sent for me this morning. Apparently he must have Redgrave and that idiot Franz attending, as well as the colonel and his retinue. And the man from abroad, all expecting our *ne plus ultra*, he says." He rubs his forehead again. "Kippers and bacon fat, Jesu. And swilling tea by the gallon."

"Did he—"

"What," flat. "Did he what."

"Will he," carefully, "be returning to the hotel, after the show?"

"How the devil should I know?" although Decca knows that he does, knows that she knows, as well. She and Rupert never discuss Jürgen Vidor except in business terms—his river of money first a bonus, now a lifeline for the Poppy as times grow darker and rumors escalate—but this is the heart of that business, the wizened byzantine heart of an aging man, aging out of everything but wealth and acid need so "Let it be," Rupert says now, and "Yes," she says. So much of what she wants to say, longs to say, can never be uttered, ever. Especially to him. "So, you breakfasted, then?"

"On fucking kippers, yes.... What about that other?" nodding upward, the merest motion of his chin, face a forced blank, as Decca shakes her head: "Tomorrow," she says softly. "Let him bide for the evening, this day has trouble enough."

Watching them both, seen by neither, is Jonathan, sheet music in hand, paused at the lobby door he has opened as he does everything, quietly. Thin shadow waiting until they separate, Rupert up to the parlor office, Decca down to the kitchens and the yard, making sure they have safely gone before he climbs the stairs himself, past receiving rooms empty in dim daylight, past Velma on her knees with a bucket, toward the half-open, beckoning door of the Cell.

Guillame

I always knew it would be the theatre for me. It was all I wanted, even before I had a name to put to it: the miracle of make-believe, the astonishing power of pretense. What you believe—what you *make* believe, yes—it can put you right where you most want to be.

As an urchin boy outside the factory gates, waiting for my old da, I'd do a bit of a dance, a buck-and-wing, water dribbling through my boots, to see if I could make them stop and watch me, the heedless passersby: whistling shrill and villainous through my teeth the *Vive le Monde*, or "Madame By-Your-Leave," anything with a gleeful melody. First one would pause, then a few more, then a biggish crowd; they'd clap for me, or sing along, sometimes they gave me pennies. My da would come trudging out with his beer bucket, grime to the eyebrows, and he'd say *Are you a poofter then, son? Dancing like a woman in the street?* And then take the pennies. It was a good lesson for me.

Other lessons I had little of, and wanted less: I was more or less lettered on my own stick, and I could cipher, and who would have spent tuppence on the curate to teach me any more? Any coins I kept, I used for mugs of milk, or buns. I'd have had to save them all for a theatre ticket, the high-type theatres, but there was nothing like that where I was, so I learned from whatever I saw in the streets: the corner opera, and the Punch-and-Judy man, the blackface boys with the trained larks.... It was a sort of theatre, too, when my da fell ill, and the fever settled in to stay: coughing and babbling, eyeballs rolling as if to catch death coming on, like a bad actor overdoing the role, and nothing for me to do but sit and watch, sponge his mug and tell him stories to put his mind off it. With small success, I suppose, but between the stories and the wine the landlady gave us—the Missus Potts' special, wine with who knows what mixed in, Godfrey's Cordial or some other dope—he entered eternity rather peacefully, poor old geezer, wrapped up in the coverlet he and dear Maman once shared.... If there was a dear maman; actually I never saw her, my fabled maman, whoever she might have been. He and Missus Potts, lord knows I saw plenty of *that*.

And tears or no tears, she sent me packing from her lodging house just as soon as he was cool: *This is no place for a boy alone*, blotting

20

her eyes with a bit of rag, a new renter in the room by sundown and me and the bucket out in the street where I sang the heartbreakers, "The Last-Flying Sparrow," "Only a Bit of a Girl," and let the tears trickle down: oh, people stopped, and a few of them sniffled along with me, but not so many pennies came my way. Why should they? Life makes us weep for free. So that was a good lesson, too.

There were many paths I could have trod, from there. Stay on the streets, and find a protector: the city was full of them, all cities are; in the city, the weak need the strong, and vice versa. Or seek out a different kind of master, buckle down and learn an honest trade. Or hie myself to the ever-damned factory, like my dead old da: furious at sunrise, drunk by nightfall, trying to drown the one in the other…. Instead I consulted myself, grubby little orphan on the corner, tuppence in his pocket, and said, Guillame, messire, you're free and clear now. What do you want to do? And the hunger gave me my answer.

You see, that hunger inside us, that ambition, or whatever you may choose to call it, is a compass really, a compass of true desire. And if you will be happy, you must follow that desire, no matter which way the needle points. For me it was the train-yard, I don't like to say what I did to get onto those trains! and banged-up, too, I've still got some lovely scars. Going east, always east, because I had heard in the lodging house that that was where the theatres were. I had never seen a proper theatre, never even seen anyone who had, but in my mind they were like the Ottoman's palace, you know, velvet curtains and twinkling candles, lovely ladies with diamonds and low-cut gowns. What I found was something rather different, in my long apprenticeship—I am almost eight-and-twenty, after all, and have played, or stage-managed, or set up booths in many a city and town. What people will pay money to watch—why, you'd not believe it if I told you.

But it was to me quite amazing—it is still amazing!—that one may conjure what is from what is not, crack an egg and make a pair of gilded rings appear, take wool and wire and paper and voila! a knight, a king, a fairy princess, alive and living for as long as the lights are low. The stage is not only a world apart, it is a myriad of worlds, and in those worlds a man can have anything he fancies, if only he believes in what he sees.

One sees it here at the Poppy, every night: That Pearl can be a seraphim, or Laddie a Spanish grandee, that Spinning Jennie can make a man compete to spend money he barely has for the chance to stick it in her, lazy doped-up Jennie whom he would pass on the street for free! Or Jonathan Shopsine, poor mutilated bastard, hunching down at a spavined piano and calling Wolfgang Mozart back from the dead, how is that not miraculous? If there is any God in this world, He lives in a theatre. And it may as well be the Poppy as anyplace else.

So when people say to me—and there are those who will say it, you'll see them at the tables on Saturday night grasping after a bouncing tit, and on the Sunday streets with the missus in her walking-out suit—*You seem, sir, very nearly a gentleman. How can you bear to toil in such an establishment?*—wrinkling their bourgeois noses at the whores, the liquor, the utter baseness of it all.

And I bow to them, a dancing master's bow I learned from a man in Philadelphia, Pennsylvania, who was gaoled there for venery, and I smile a smile I made up myself, the one I used on the penny-throwing crowd, the one I'll wear in my coffin, and I say *Ah, but the spirit moves where it lists, messire!* And then I offer the missus my primrose boutonniere, and she accepts it, every single time.

"Mister Arrowsmith," says the mayor, "you have quite the continental taste." His cigar smolders like burning punk, he sports an extravagant tie, red as a poppy. "For Champagne, I mean. I would have thought you was more a whiskey man."

"When in Rome," says Mr. Arrowsmith pleasantly.

"Is that where you hail from?" asks the colonel. He has three teeth missing, at times it makes him mumble, but his gaze is clear enough, his bearing stiff. Beside him Jürgen Vidor smiles a sketch of a smile, pours again for the three of them and "Commerce," says Jürgen Vidor, "is at home in all locales. Much like the military, eh, Colonel? Did you try the elk, Mr. Redgrave? Shot just this morning, in the forest, they say."

"Shot at dawn," says Mr. Franz, the attaché; he giggles. No one acknowledges his remark.

Champagne and elk and rye whiskey, cigars and cheroots, five seats filled at a table for six. Onstage, Jonathan in a gravedigger's suit plays a Chopin etude; the stage curtains are drawn primly behind him. At the outer door Omar adjusts his cuffs, shakes his head at the looming queue of disappointed revelers: "Private party tonight, sorry. Come back tomorrow."

"Tomorrow I'll be broke!"

"Then come back when you're not…. Private party, sorry, gents."

At the head of the aisle, Decca, in a lemon yellow silk that in no way becomes her, jet combs like horns in her red hair, mutters instructions to Velma, herself an overseer tonight, the two hired hotel servers her domain so "Watch them every second," Decca says. "Every fork that goes missing comes out of your pocket. Now, what of the wine?"

"Fine for now," says Velma, resplendent in unaccustomed bombazine. "It'll do."

"Don't give yourself airs, just do as I say…. Where is that ass Puggy?"

"I don't know, miss."

"I'm not speaking to you," though no one else stands with them, Decca distracted, gaze up and down the room, the four tables bright

23

with wax candles, unthinkable expense, that and the champagne, will they notice how poor it really is? Puggy says the show will overcome all defects, but where is Puggy? or Lucy, neither there when she needs them most so "Get back on the floor," she says to Velma, her roving gaze now seeking Rupert, who had agreed, had he not, to dine with them, Jürgen Vidor and his guests? At least Istvan is where he promised to be, she has just checked, knocked, eased open the door on darkness to see him swaddled and sleeping, face thrust deep into the pillow, long hair fanned on the coverlet, a rind of meat and whiskey nearly empty on the floor. Pearl maintains that she gave him quite the frolic, so fucked, fed, and bottled, he should slumber like an infant, thank God.

And now, thank God again, or someone, here is Rupert, unsmiling, his linen immaculate, signet ring gleaming on his left hand, bloodstone and gold; up close she can see the sallow pallor of the headache but in the candlelight "You look so handsome," Decca says, then winces inside, O the wrong thing to say but "Shall we greet our guests?" he says as he offers his arm, down the narrow center aisle, isthmus to the revelry, the five at the center surrounded by three satellite tables occupied by the colonel's men and a few of the Poppy's regulars much aware of the signal honor, less boisterous than on a normal Saturday, more refined, their pricks are still covered at least. The men at the center ignore them, ignore everything but the bottles on their table, their own lurching conversation as the colonel is not one for talk, and Mr. Franz is a giggling idiot, so Jürgen Vidor, who thus far has drunk only sparingly, must direct and prompt the flow, keep the mayor from making a fool of himself, keep Essenhigh and Arrowsmith on cordial terms, while shielding from each, as per instructions from his faraway master, the true reason for the other's presence. Usually this is a game he enjoys, or can tolerate, but tonight his attentions are focused irresistibly elsewhere, he can feel Rupert nearing before he sees him, smell him as an animal might and "Ah," says Jürgen Vidor, when the tall form pauses, Miss Decca unfortunate in yellow beside him, no redhead should ever wear such a shade. "Our charming hostess." Rising, one hand to take, and shake, Decca's own. "And our host."

"Mr. Vidor," says Rupert. "And gentlemen. We are honored to have you with us this evening."

"Thank you, Rupert. Will you join us for a glass of champagne? Miss Decca, your bill of fare is exquisite tonight."

Rupert does not move. To Decca it is as if he stands in his own weather, a high wind he must brace himself against; she can feel the resistance coming off him like heat from an oven, cold from a grave so

"You're too kind," she says to Jürgen Vidor, noting the pomade on his thinning hair, the faint shine of elk fat on his lip. "I only hope all is sufficient for your enjoyment. Is there anything else you might require, gentlemen? You have only to ask."

"Tell the piano man to play a waltz," says the mayor. "Or a polka, something a little more merry, eh?"

"Certainly," says Decca, rustling off to murmur in Jonathan's ear, Jonathan who gives her an odd look, thin shoulders tight beneath the ancient coat, but whose hands fall at once into an easy pattern, "Miss Marigold's Lament," about the beautiful girl who simply can't say no. Rupert takes his seat at the table's empty chair. Jürgen Vidor pours him champagne, and offers a toast: "To companionship.... I believe you will enjoy the show, Mr. Arrowsmith. Something different, here at the Poppy."

"I always enjoy novelty," says Mr. Arrowsmith, with a cordial nod to Rupert.

Behind the curtain, Guillame and Lucy attend to the last of the last-minute details, tugging a sleeve there, a strap here, adjusting the candelabra "Just so," murmurs Guillame. He is almost breathless, his round face is grinning pink. "Lucy, are they dining still?"

One eye to the curtain: "The plates are on the tables, but most are smoking, now. Mr. Rupert has sat down."

"Then tell Jonathan—no, I'll tell him myself," edging past her in the air of make-up and tension, more so than normal, this is no normal night and "Puggy," Lucy whispers, catching his arm as he passes. "Shall I go now?"

"Yes. Go on," and she is gone, melting into scenery's shadow as Decca appears stage left, face pinched pale in the darkness—but Guillame waves her off because it is time, now, for Jonathan to play the overture, for the noise on the floor to dim, time to light the candles and pinch the nipples and let the play begin.

As the curtains part, "Miss Marigold" becomes a different tune, more intimate but still recognizably a waltz, appropriate for dancing and they do: the dark boy and the fair girl, Vladimir and Vera, as Jennie stands apart, harness concealed by her bouffant gown, ruched and spangled for a princess though no princess surely ever showed such rash décolletage. Vladimir stands in for the watching men, cupping and pressing where they would cup and press the lovely Vera, whose playful gestures seem to put him off while daring him to go further still; the men enjoy this, the soldiers whistle and shout. At Jürgen Vidor's table the mayor grins; Mr. Arrowsmith's narrow face is calm but attentive. Rupert reaches past the champagne for the whiskey bottle.

The men begin to clap along with the music that quickens seemingly to urge them on, a sharper tempo as another pair of dancers takes the stage: a tall masked gentleman, a small languorous blonde in blue brocade—

—as Rupert's shoulders jump, a swift tremor unseen by all but Jürgen Vidor, whose sharp gaze moves from Rupert to the stage to Rupert again—

—as the new couple onstage waltz in place like well-matched lovers, lovely to see, but the lady is disinclined, unwilling to kiss the man who seeks her prim pink lips, turning her head again and again as if in negation: *No, no I don't want you, messire, try howsoever you might.*

The first couple, perhaps infected by this discontent, now drift apart, the boy to the spangled princess, who greets him willingly, the girl to drape herself over the chaise and pout—until another gentleman appears, a small strange man seemingly self-conjured from the candelabra's shadows, nestling down beside her as the dancing couple grow more vigorous in both pursuit and refusal, the man frankly groping beneath the brocade skirt, seeming ready to ravish his lady onstage, right there before the watching men who loudly approve, shouting comments and suggestions: insistence despite denial, who is she to say no to him anyway, the whore? Pretty she is, pliant she ought to be so "Give it to her!" bawls one of the Poppy's regulars, forgetting his company manners, "stick it in!" as Mr. Franz hoots like a boy, and Mr. Arrowsmith leans forward with a little smile. The colonel's soldiers stamp their booted feet. Jürgen Vidor, beating time on the tablecloth—one-two-three, two-two-three—murmurs in Rupert's ear, Rupert with one hand on his whiskey glass, the other a cold fist on his knee.

Now Jonathan flows smoothly into yet another tune, sprightly yet melting, and the strange little man, lying back in Vera's arms, caressed by her willing hands, opens his little dark mouth and begins to sing, a cracked beguiling voice that cuts nicely through the clamor:

"Your light of love has briefly shone
On other hearts, dear, than mine own—"

Decca, quietly berating Velma at the back of the room, stiffens to silence, turns her full and shocked attention to the stage. Guillame, in the wings, watches everything at once, can this work? It is working. Beneath the chaise, cloaked all in black, Lucy sweats and smiles.

"You may have dreamed that their love was true," sings the little man; as sentimental and melodious a voice as it is, still there is something antic and cold beneath, as if he is secretly laughing at all of them, laughing at the very idea of love. "But none were destined, dear, for you."

Now the spangled girl lifts her overskirt, sheds her overskirt, as, watched rapturously by the dark boy and all the men, she begins to rise: clad now only in leather straps and spangles, wee mirrors twinkling in the candlelight, the candelabra held high by the boy shows her dangling, pink and sparkling, her bare breasts depending like ripe fruit, herself a juicy morsel there for the picking as the soldiers roar, as the dancing couple abandon all pretense of the waltz and devote themselves to erotic battle, Jürgen Vidor's murmur very close to Rupert's ear, Rupert who stares fixedly at the stage as the masked man roughly bends his partner over the chaise, right next to Vera and her small suitor, throws the blonde's skirts up from behind to finish the job where she stands—

—as the little man worms his way deeper into Vera's arms, head back between her breasts like a pasha on pillows, singing all the while— "Through this dark world I sought your light/Beaming, gleaming, ever-bright—" in a kind of ecstatic cackle, his troll hands disappearing into her skirt-band and she jumps, the watching men confused into sudden laughter, a heated, hectic mirth, and Vera laughs, too—*O you naughty boy*—

—as in her harness Spinning Jennie begins, glittering, to spin: her princess face slack, her arms outstretched to grasp at legs equally extended, she opens herself, splits herself, pink cheeks aimed at the audience, as the troll on the chaise reaches crescendo—

"This shining light of love has shown me true:

I love no other man, my dear, than you!"

—as all freeze in breathless tableau, the utter, utter verge: the masked suitor in mid-thrust at the stiff resistant blonde, Vera's humping skirt, Vladimir staring upward at Jennie, who, of course, continues to revolve with her own momentum, ass and tits and spangles as the piano pounds fortissimo, the men lurch stageward, the mayor thumps on the tabletop, the curtains swish grandly to meet—

—and a little head pops out, lank-haired and grinning, the cracked hilarious voice: "Thank you, messires, for your so very kind attention! The players will be out directly for your pleasure!"

And *finis*.

"Eh," says Lucy, fingering the salve pot, still in her pale wrapper, its ragged piping loose about her neck. "Those soldiers—don't they have women where they come from? Or whores? I was up till dawn with the, what you call it. Surplus."

Omar blows on his tea, little blue cup seeming smaller still in his large hand. Velma has left out teapot and bread in the understairs kitchen, a bowl of slightly wormy apples and pears. "Surplus is the word. We made our fortnight's quid and then some.... Save some of that liniment for Laddie, poor boy. Velma had to carry him his breakfast."

Lucy makes a sympathetic face. A pearly noon, Jonathan yawning in the hallway, the rest of the house still deservedly abed: it was a monumental night at the Poppy, the lavish dinner repaid fourfold, even the candles and "When he left," says Omar, "the mayor thanked me." Jonathan rolls his eyes, takes a chair. "And that Mr. Franz tried to shake my hand. Jesu. I'd as soon stick it down a snake hole."

"You don't know the half of it," Lucy says. "Jen says he's a rare biter.... There you are," with pleasure as Istvan, sedate in parson's blue, enters smiling, bows to the assembled company and "Felicitations all round," he says. His hair lies loose around his shoulders, he looks well-rested and his eyes are bright. "We tickled their nuts for them, yeah?"

"You're quite the showman," Omar says, with a tribute nod. "Puggy told me you worked up that bit, lyrics and all, so's to fit with Jen on the harness, in just an hour or two?"

Istvan points to Jonathan, who beams. "I had expert aid."

"But the singing—"

"A minor *coup de glotte.* You," to Lucy, "you were simply invisible. Better than any actress. I believe Pan may be in love with you."

Lucy laughs softly, sliding into the chair beside him, sideways to leave most of her shapely legs exposed. "Vera said his hands in her skirt felt funny, even if he is just a doll."

Istvan plucks a pippin apple from the bowl, reaches into his waistcoat pocket for a little white-handled knife, applies one to the other. "'Just a doll'? Some people say puppets must be possessed by spirits, that is, if the show is any good.... I once knew a fellow who told me that puppets were as old as man himself. He was a slippery old bastard with a silver ring he wore on his thumb, and he claimed that the leftover makings of Adam and Eve, the dust and scrapings ignored by God, were swept up by Lucifer and breathed into a crooked sort of life, not true souls like Man and Woman but nearly as immortal, desiring to move amongst their human brothers and find love—or, denied that love, make mischief. So how different, really, is a man from a mec?"

"I'd rather fuck the puppet," says Lucy, "than some of those soldiers. They all smelled like gin and—"

"That big one," Guillame entering, reaching for tea; his face is puffy. "What-you-call-him, the Chevalier, with the big rod. 'Course he'd probably pay in wooden nickels, eh?" and everyone laughs, Istvan winks and "That rod," he says, "was carved whole out of a mandrake root by a giggling witch who told me she had tried it for herself: 'Better than any man,' she said. But no, the Chevalier was elsewhere engaged." He tucks an apple slice into his mouth. "In jail once I met a man who said he had watched a statue of Christ Crucified bleed real blood over the sins of man at a roadside passion play. He swore that he had seen this, and beat me with his boot when I explained how the thing was done." Guillame laughs, as if this story is no news to him. "That same man offered me a franc to fondle one of my old mecs, and when I said no, asked was I fool enough to believe in my own magic."

Guillame grins. "How else shall the magic work?"

Lucy plucks up one of the apple slices, thumbs off a brownish spot. "Which old mec?"

"An operatic lady, her name was La Duchessa. I don't use her any longer."

"Why not?"

"She came apart at the seams. There was a man, I believe he was a priest—"

"Oh how *dare* you," venomous and stealthy as a viper from the floorboards, all of them, even Istvan, startle, Omar almost drops his little cup. "How dare you all sit there and cackle over what you have done?"

"Decca," Guillame the swiftest to recover, awkward to his feet, a supplicating, warding hand. "Decca, we made money—"

"Don't speak." Hair dragged back in a frightful bun, her face a study in mottled red and whey, she stands in the doorway as if to block their communal escape. Too overrun last night to punish them, she has been roiling inside, a brew of outrage and terror and relief. "Every single one of you, lying to me—even you," one finger leveled like a duelist's at frightened Jonathan, "you who cannot speak a word, yet found a way to lie. Did you think I wouldn't know you brought him the music? Or you," to Guillame, "who engineered the whole mad enterprise? Or you," last and angriest to Lucy, "who birthed his ugly toy out from under your skirts? Well, you can find yourself another house to tarnish, or go rot in the Alley with the rest of the muck. You'll not stop here another evening."

"Mr. Rupert—"

"Mr. Rupert is amazed that things grew no worse than they did! Do you not understand that this was a private party, a special evening for the elders of the town, and for their guests? You could have ruined us all with your capering! There was a military presence—"

"I know!" Lucy shouts. "I fucked most of them!"

"The colonel of the garrison—"

"I fucked him too!"

Istvan laughs, calm again, plying his little knife. The smell of apple is sharp and sour. Decca does not even look at him, addresses a spot on the wall as "You ought to go," she says, "tonight. Pack up your traps and go."

"What of Pan? Is he allowed to linger?" but "Quiet," says a very quiet voice. "Decca, Lucy, you can be heard all over the house." Rupert in shirtsleeves, unshaven and pale to the lips; he looks at no one but Istvan. "You. Come with me."

No one says a word, not even Decca, as Istvan, knife and apple follow Rupert up the stairs. Behind Decca's back, Guillame raises his eyebrows at Omar, who shrugs minutely. Jonathan disappears like smoke in a breeze, Lucy glares at Decca whose gaze is aimed at the ceiling, the parlor office upstairs, the closed door behind which Rupert stares at Istvan who stares back without a smile.

"Hello, Mouse," he says.

Mouse! *the hiss, the reaching hand from the sliver of dark, black space between two crooked buildings, shit stench, an impromptu pissoir with no exit save the street but* Take a breath, *the breath against the skin, one boy whispering to the other.* You're all in.

They—followed—me.

I know. I saw, I followed them.... Just breathe. *One arm warm around his neck, thin ropy arm in the ragged greatcoat, silver braid on the collar, Lieutenant Flat-Boy, rent boy, from behind with his hair in braids he can be a rent girl, too. He can be whatever you want, whatever you pay for, for as long as you pay, or until he decides to be something else. Like mercury on glass, Mercury the patron of thieves and travelers, feathers on his helmet, wings on his feet.* Air enough, now? Come on, then.

Where? *but already he's climbing, swift and vertical on the bricks, his toes and fingers finding purchase to clamber up, up, up to the sway of iron, less balcony than chamber-pot perch but* Up here, *he says,* we can get to the roof, *and they do, hand over hand to crouch at last shivering and safe, one coat for the two of them; they share everything, these feral boys, on the street where no one else cares except to fuck or rob them, make slaves or toys or servants of them, dispose of them like rubbish when the service is done.*

The fox and the wolf, the other children call them. The mercury boy is twelve, perhaps, or slightly younger; he is a general favorite, a joker, a liar, a prankster, he can make an onion cry as he peels it, he can change or throw his voice. The older boy keeps himself to himself, dark melancholy mouse in a hole. He came from an orphans' home run by monks, or priests, he forgets, it was a long time ago. Men in skirts who spoke a funny tongue, they called him Tacio, the silent one, or in French farouche, *half-savage and half-shy. But they taught him to cipher, spell his name, even read; now he is teaching his friend. His friend is teaching him things, too.*

And helping him, with the help of a little girl, the boy's sister, half-sister, it is not certain how they are related but certainly they are, the buttoned-up girl in the foundling's dress who worships the boy, and

31

the boy who visits her on the sly, brings her paper dolls and pilfered ribbons, takes from her coins and woolen hats and wrapped packages of food; she is a clumsy thief, and often beaten, but she never yields. He has taught her how to spell out her name, AGATHA, and FUCK YOU, a useful phrase. He promises one day to take her with him, them, but not just now; not yet.

Now he settles closer to his older friend inside the coat. Got a smoke?

Wait. The light, *nodding toward the street.* If they're still down there, they'll see. *Instead he takes from his pocket a packet of rye bread, a shriveled knob of cheese, and a fierce little flick knife, butterfly knife white in his dark hand, and slices the food, half for each. The knife is scarred, beautiful, and* Real old, *the younger boy says admiringly.* May be a hundred years?

May be... He said that it came from a unicorn horn. That makes it magic.

What kind of magic?

You can't lose it. Always it will find its way back to you.

Where you get it, Mouse?

He shrugs one thin dark shoulder. The fat man had had a case, and the knife was one of the things in the case; the others are sold, or in the river with the man. You keep it, *he says, folding the other's hand around the hilt.*

The other slips the knife into his pocket. Wish we had some wine, yeah.

Don't.

Don't what?

Don't wish. Only the devil hears wishes.... Anyway they don't work.

The younger boy laughs, loops his arms around his friend, pressing close and closer in the cold; is he cold? You still a monk, *he says.* Are you?

Don't laugh at me.

I'm not.

Istvan—

The younger boy's lips are soft and cold; his kiss is a smile, too.

"Sit," Rupert nodding to a chair, cracked leather and hobnails, a hideous thing; Istvan makes a face. The whole room is like that chair, dreary and unwelcoming: no windows, stagnant wallpaper printed with martial fleurs-de-lis, its furniture meant for stern usage: the dire armchairs permit no lounging, the table is bare, the lamps plain, the spittoon dry. The most abundant article in the room is the writing cabinet, with its piled papers, black inkwell, tufted pigeonholes and spring-locked drawers, steel keys dangling from a chain. This office-parlor opens onto a smaller, even more forbidding room; a bedroom? Rupert closes that door.

"Quite the dungeon," Istvan says pleasantly. "I prefer the whores' chambers, on the whole." He sets aside his apple and knife, shifts, trying to sit comfortably, tries again, then sighs and reseats himself on the edge of the table, close by Rupert who leans back in his chair, away but not far enough to elude Istvan's touch, two fingers lightly brushing the stubble on his cheek: "No silver, yet?" Both can feel how he stiffens at this contact, see how swiftly he stands and steps away, missing Istvan's smile, a small and very tender smile as "You look just the same," Istvan says.

"You don't," Rupert arms folded, the table between them now. "Why did you come here?"

Istvan tilts his head, links his fingers on his knee. "Why not ask my dear sister?"

"Decca only sings the song you taught her."

"And you don't credit her? Your charming partner in whoredom?—And when did *that* begin?"

Rupert ignores his question. "How she credits you is a wonder, you lie as easily as you breathe. You and your puppets—she's your puppet, too. And a terrible actress: 'Throw him out,' with tears in her eyes—"

"Don't let her hear you say that."

"That you came at all—" Rupert stops; he rubs his forehead. "That you decided to play one of your fuckwit tricks—you could have brought disaster to us all, your trusting sister too, did you realize that? That man—"

"The one who sat with you? The old masher? About to cream himself, wasn't he?"

"He, and Arrowsmith, and that stiff-necked cunt of a colonel—they could close this place down, you understand? Any one of them could close it down in a day."

Istvan picks up knife and apple, slowly slices a sickle of fruit. "Would that be the worst thing?"

"You never change, do you?" Rupert's eyes widen. "You can hurt a great many people, messire, with your artistry. Is that why you came?" Istvan does not answer. "Why are you here?"

"Why are you? When there are so many other places to be? Like Paris. Or Hammersmith—"

"Stop it."

"Or Petersburg—"

"Stop!" so hard they both stop, then. The room is quiet. Finally, "I have people, here."

"And I have people everywhere I go, in my little trunks. And more people out front, watching. There are people people people everywhere, Mouse, all over the fucking world, and all of them will pay to see what they want to see. You of all people should know that." Another pause, then more quietly, "What did you think of my song?"

Again Rupert looks away, this time at the floor, at his feet in their mended boots. When he speaks, it is not in answer.

"He wants to meet you. He thought your show was 'piquant.'"

Istvan smiles then, another kind of smile, it might remind a watcher of Pan Loudermilk's icy grin. "Who, the masher? By all means. Is it to be a private showing?"

"We're dining with him this evening," Rupert says, and steps away, toward the door, holds it pointedly open and "Don't mistake me, Istvan," using his name for the first time, looking directly into his eyes, darkness into darkness. "You can bolt whenever things get sticky, but I have a house to run."

"A *house*." Softly as a lover, a murderer come face-to-face, mouth to mouth almost, they breathe each other's breath. "What kind of house? A second-rate brothel in a third-rate town, catering to the hoi polloi, the slippery pricks, any bastard with a dollar can shine his shoes on you—"

As softly: "And what you do is better?"

"What I do is mine. And you, you could be—"

"Enough. We leave for the hotel at half-past six. Wear a smile, messire, or I'll break your fucking neck."

He shuts the door on Istvan, closes his eyes. When he opens them again he sees the apple remnants on the table, the little white knife that he takes into his hand, fingers curled so tight they turn white as the bone it is carved from, horse bone maybe or maybe a deer; *a unicorn horn. That makes it magic.* He slips the knife into his breast pocket, seems to find its weight hurtful, takes it out again. The desk has a tiny drawer, perhaps the width of two fingers, opened by the smallest steel key on his watch chain. He tucks the knife into this drawer, and locks it shut again. His hands are trembling.

Javier Arrowsmith

It is a failing to be dainty, but truly, I dislike it here. The climate does not at all agree with me, being both damp *and* dry, and the hotel is somewhat vile: this morning there were silverfish in the bath, many silverfish, as if a thriving colony had been disturbed. I am no aesthete, I have slept in the fields many a night, but when my business here concludes I will not be sorry.

Others have business here as well, differing steps in the same dance, though not all dance to the same tune: my associate Jürgen Vidor, of course, as well as the foolish little mayor, and the bewhiskered colonel who measures me, man-to-man and eye to eye; he is predictably hardheaded, I think, that Essenhigh, but it is never too early to cement local alliances, the town will be annexed by the military very soon. The shops are still open, there is still meat and fuel to be had, but this will not last the winter. And as ever, carrion will bring the ravens. I will have returned to Brussels by then, or at least that is my modest hope, but our holdings in Archenberg will continue to require protection, and here is where the garrison is housed. No matter the civil shortages, the town lies close enough to a railway that our resupply will pose no lasting problems; certainly the General is sanguine. Whatever disorder awaits the region, our interests will finally prevail: order is the true handmaiden of commerce, always. It is why I left the diplomatic corps.

Though I am but an agent of commerce, still I strive to see beyond the horizon imposed by the demands of that commerce. And as a man and a citizen, it is surely one's duty to participate in the widest world possible to one's station in life. Therefore, I have closely observed several of these "revolutions," these periods of flux, and always what intrigues me are the patterns one finds.

Men are, at bottom, most predictable creatures, with predictable rages and woes. The majority of the citizenry pose no threat at all to our interests: one may soothe them with promises, or bully them forward with the fist, much like driving cattle. But always there are the few who act, and react, according to their own inner lights. I have lately read some interesting theories as to why this should be so: does a man's inner spirit drive his actions, say, or do the actions form the spirit, as a glass shapes the liquid it holds? My own belief is that we see a man most clearly in his wants.

Consider my current colleagues. The mayor, Redgrave, is purely cattle, he wants only to be fed and cosseted and kept from real harm. On the wants of his disgusting attaché I will not speculate; they do not signify, as he finally does not. The colonel—I do not know the colonel well enough, yet, to say what it is he most desires, other than what all military men desire, power over others. No one becomes a soldier for the rations, after all.

Now consider Jürgen Vidor. By his will, we must meet here, in this barren little town—instead of in Archenberg, where the General visits weekly, where the accommodations are, if not lavish, at least more civilized—because of this Rupert Bok, the brothel keeper, to whom Vidor is plainly attached. Now why this man, and not another? and to a degree unmatched in Vidor's history? Always before, he has prized variety, and anonymity, and discretion most of all. It is a very curious thing.

The mayor does not mark this, though that attaché is more thoroughly in the know. The colonel also is unaware, but our evening at the theatre must have shown him something, if he has eyes to see.... I myself enjoyed that evening very much, especially the fine surprise of seeing Dusan onstage—I had last seen him perform in Brussels, he was calling himself something different there, and something else again here. But there is no mistaking true artistry. Those puppets! They are just like little men, though spared the dullness of death and the rigors of conscience. Very entertaining. And what a clever stroke, to mix them with the whores—Dusan did something similar in the Grand 'Place, once, though nothing like so elaborate....The little pianist is quite talented, too.

Tonight Vidor dines tête-à-tête with his *amour potentiel*. Tomorrow he and I will meet with the colonel, if he returns in time, and the wire from Brussels agrees. Until then I take the air, I read the local broadsheets, I harry the silverfish, I attempt to buoy my spirits with spirits and conversation. If the redheaded young madam was amenable, I might ask for her, she reminds me not a little of my own sweet Liserl. But that drink, I'd warrant, is sour all the way down.

"Lovely," Istvan's wink as he and Rupert enter the hotel to the smell of boiled beef, horseshit, and horsehair glue. A hulking man in brown clodhoppers sits as if planted on the bench by the door. One ill-potted tree lists at drunken attention, the sullen clerk does the same, watching them approach the front desk. Istvan is groomed and clean-shaven, boots freshly blacked, faultless in midnight blue. Beside him Rupert, in his black and shabby hat, looks like a beadle or a jailer, stands watchful as both and "One jape," he murmurs, "one funny joke.... Not tonight."

"My thoughts were purely pious, till you spoke."

"For Mr. Vidor," says Rupert to the desk clerk, who stands marginally more erect, though his expression does not change, suspicion and grime and "I thought," the clerk says, "you was maybe here to hire some more whores for your dancehall."

Istvan gives him a wink. "Are you looking to change professions?"

"Quiet.—Mr. Vidor," says Rupert. "Is he in?"

"I am, and I am here," summoned seemingly out of the air, resplendent in bottle-brown velvet, impeccable boots, a dandy's shimmering tie. His genial hand offered first to Rupert, then to Istvan, the clerk's quick and counterfeit grin as "Mister Vidor," he says, too loudly, "gents to see you. Will you be wantin' the guard, sir?" nodding to the hulk in the corner; Jürgen Vidor shakes his head. "And you was dinin' in your room tonight, is that right? With these gents, is that right?"

"Yes, dinner in my rooms. But we'll have the wine now," nodding toward a little alcove, green-striped curtains and a table set for three, a brown-haired maid with a bottle and a nervous smile and "Whiskey," Rupert says to her, though Jürgen Vidor raises his eyebrows: "We've a quite acceptable Bordeaux," he says. "The General sent it with his compliments. You will have a taste, at least, Rupert?"

Istvan looks down at the green needlepoint chair, watching through his lashes; Rupert feels his gaze. "I'm not much for wine, Mr. Vidor, as you know."

"Just a taste."

Three glasses are poured. Jürgen Vidor offers a toast: "To Caliban and sawdust," nodding at Istvan. "I felicitate you, sir, on your performance. And your artistry. It is not often one sees such wit in such a lonely place."

"Many thanks," says Istvan. "I felt myself inspired."

"By—?"

"Erato. Or is it Euterpe?" He sips his wine; he appears to be in vast good humor. "I confess I've been known to confuse them."

"Sisters sometimes look alike," says Jürgen Vidor. "Even Melpomene…. I understand you come to us from abroad?"

"This vintage is excellent," Istvan says; he taps Rupert on the wrist. "Try it, go on.—Yes, I was on the Continent awhile. A poor player like myself must go wherever the winds take him."

"I think you are too modest. I am sure you have had many patrons."

Between them, Rupert sits silent, the wine stem in his fingers. Jürgen Vidor's gaze never leaves Istvan, who leans back in his chair and smiles, a sunny smile and "The theatre," he says, "finds friends wherever it goes. Or makes them. I am fortunate enough to stop here for a time—"

"How long are you with us?"

"Until the muse beckons me elsewhere. And yourself, Mr. Vidor? Do you stay?"

"Whiskey," says Rupert to the maid. Both men look at him; he offers a thin smile and "I'll have my wine with the meal," he says, but leaves his glass behind when dinner is announced. The three of them move together, past the benched and watchful bodyguard, through the lobby that has become more crowded, now, as night comes on, trunks arriving, carts departing, men calling one to another, people passing on the stairs and "Ah," says Jürgen Vidor, pausing to halt a narrow-faced gentleman on his way down. "Mr. Arrowsmith, good evening. You're acquainted with Mr. Bok—"

"Indeed," a bow pleasant and correct. "Good evening, messire." His gaze touches Istvan, is there the slightest flicker in his eyes?

"And this is—"

"The *maître de marionette*," says Mr. Arrowsmith; his smile is genuine. "Of course. Sir, I much enjoyed your programme."

"Many thanks," Istvan says. His bow is luxurious. "You are too kind. I was but one of a talented troupe."

"So many talents, at the Poppy," says Jürgen Vidor, with a genial air. To watch the four of them, one might think he, Istvan, and Mr. Arrowsmith are old friends, Rupert a conscript or a mute valet, so much does he angle himself apart, so silently does he stand.

But as one they move aside when a fifth descends: Colonel Essenhigh, his springy whiskers doused in some spicy scent, his uniform buffed and brushed and "Good evening, Colonel," says Jürgen Vidor; he seems mildly surprised. "I understood you to be in Archenberg tonight—?"

"No," says the colonel. "I'm not."

"You know Mr. Arrowsmith. And Mr. Bok—"

"Yes," nodding first to Mr. Arrowsmith, no nod for Rupert, who returns the look, the two of them expressionless as wolves on the steppe, dogs in the alley until "You," says the colonel abruptly to Istvan. "That was your show, at the whorehouse, eh? With the dolls?" Istvan gives an agreeable nod. "I don't care for that, sir. Dolls, and other things. A man ought to fuck a woman and no one else, that's what I say."

"Pan Loudermilk would agree with you."

"Who's that?"

"A doll."

Mr. Arrowsmith's lips purse minutely. Jürgen Vidor nods toward the stairs. "Will you join us at dinner, Colonel? Mr. Arrowsmith?" who shrugs graciously, he is otherwise engaged but "I don't care to eat with masquers," the colonel says curtly, "with people who hide what they are."

"You must often be lonely, then, Colonel," says Mr. Arrowsmith, with affable regret. "Come, have a drink with me before my appointment. I don't know that I can subdue that villainous brandy alone."

The colonel shakes his head. "I'm going to the whorehouse. The real whorehouse," stolid down the stairs, the others watch him go and "He lacks imagination," says Mr. Arrowsmith, in a diagnostic tone. "Endemic in the military, I'm afraid."

"I could teach him to waltz," says Istvan. Mr. Arrowsmith smiles openly. Jürgen Vidor motions ascent: "Shall we, then? Good evening, Mr. Arrowsmith."

The first impression of his rooms is of an overstuffed pocket: red velvet curtains deeply drawn, every surface cluttered with books, maps, inkstands, wax flowers and other ephemera of *vertu*, a large rosewood teapoy, opera glasses, a brass telescope, a silver cigar-lighter shaped like a nude Greek god. Two wardrobe trunks stand open, hung with waistcoats, lined with neckties and cravats. By the shrouded window, a round table is set for three, with ugly, heavy china. A chipped teak bed tray is half laid with a hand of cards creased with much usage, the kings and queens furtive and Italianate. Istvan nudges them with one finger: "You play patience, messire?"

Jürgen Vidor shrugs. "In the small hours, I am often wakeful."

"You have many cares," Istvan says, with sympathy. "A man of business such as yourself." Rupert, by the dining table, gives him a

glare; his whiskey glass is empty. When the brown-haired maid brings
their dinner—rare beef and mashed turnips, heavy cream and cheese,
the fine Bordeaux—Rupert sends her back down for the bottle, sits
drinking all throughout the meal as the other two watch him covertly,
measure one another, eat and pretend to enjoy a chat: about the theatre,
about the continent, about the stickpin worn by Jürgen Vidor, a golden
snake shaped like a question mark, a fat black pearl caught in its fangs:
"The Questioning Serpent," he says, touching it fondly. "Disraeli had
one just like it, I understand, brought back from the Ottomans."

"Oh, I love the Bosporus."

When the meal is finished at last, Jürgen Vidor invites them to take
the air, offers cigars but "An early night for me, I'm afraid," says Istvan.
"My puppets took a bit of a beating yesterday—they need refreshment,
like any actors. And a sponging."

He makes a comic face, and Jürgen Vidor smiles: "I very much
look forward to seeing them again. Seeing you, that is, upon the
boards.... Please," proffering from an ebony card case a snowy calling
card, beautifully engraved. "Henceforth consider me a patron of your
work, messire."

"Too kind," says Istvan, rising with an actor's grace, a grave and
courteous bow. He tucks the card carefully into his pocket. "I am
deeply aware of the honor you do me, and can hardly hope to extend
the same to you, but," taking from his waistcoat, what? a bead? no, a
button, no, a wooden eyeball, dry and staring and terribly blue and "I
shall keep an eye upon you, sir," he says, and bows again, "in the hopes
that I will see you again."

"A—singular memento. Many thanks."

Rupert rises, now; Jürgen Vidor's gaze flicks from him to Istvan
and back again, a serpent's tongue. His smile widens, overripe. "You
retire early as well, Rupert?"

"I wish that were so." Rupert's voice is flat and too precise. He
seems to be staring at a grease spot on the wallpaper. "Duty calls."

"Ah, the happy demands of industry. And Miss Decca. Tender her
my best regards, yes?" and they all shake hands, the two out the door
and down the staircase and "When the devil falls in love," says Istvan.
"It's the whip, am I right?"

"Don't speak to me. Don't say another word. You and your fucking
toys."

Together in silence they cross the lobby, step into the chilly muck
of the streets. The main avenue lies dark beneath guttering street-
lamps, torches tossed and flickered by the wind that blows straight from
the forest and the hills, spooking the waiting carriage-horses, rattling

the thin tin signs. The doors of the livery are stoutly bolted, as is the cooperage, and the greengrocer's, the wine parlors and the bakery; the seamstress' shop sits abandoned, its curtained window cracked to the sill.

The avenue vendors have disappeared until daylight, taking their cups and sandwich boards, their trinkets and trays; the streets have emptied into the taverns, piss-puddled and hectic with smoke and noise, a hurdy-gurdy grinding out an ancient drinking song. Soldiers loiter everywhere: by the hotel and the mercantile, the silent bank, abusing the beggars who flee their approach, clustering outside the Europa and the Palais, trying to see inside: dirty hands and young faces, weapons bright and new. At the Alley's mouth a small band of immigrants, round hats and grubby work boots, take muttered counsel, perhaps pooling their resources to hire one of the flock of tired whores; they smell of beer and field-tobacco. At the door of the Gaiety Theatre two men in top hats argue loudly, while a third, older, stoop-shouldered, stands waiting with folded arms.

Just beyond the doctor's storefront, shared with the midwife who lives above, two shadows, boys loitering in the windbreak corner, jump out like jacks-in-the-box upon Rupert and Istvan in their silent passage. One sticks a knife to Rupert's neck, a hunter's short-bladed gutting knife, the other stands tense before Istvan, palm out.

They say nothing, nothing need be said. Istvan's hand dips into his pocket, slides out empty as "Wait," he murmurs, "I have something for you—" then with scornful force cuffs the first boy, the taller, so hard that the boy falls sideways like a sapling to an axe, as Rupert clamps the knife-wielder's arm, spins then knees him, once, twice, kicks him to the ground and into his fallen accomplice, kicks that other in the ribs, kicks him again for good measure; then he and Istvan walk on. One of the boys burbles and vomits, the other lies still.

Istvan glances over his shoulder—no stealthy third—as Rupert tugs his coat back into place, makes to pocket the hunting knife but "Give it to me," says Istvan, "mine's gone missing.... Did he cut you, that little prick?" tilting Rupert's chin to check for hurt but "No," says Rupert, smiling, a very faint smile.

"It's wet."

"May be a scratch. Fuck it."

"Let me—" Istvan reaches with his handkerchief, Rupert halts him, hand on his wrist; and they stand so, in the wind and the dark, Rupert holding Istvan's wrist, staring at one another.

At the Poppy, each turns his own way through the bustling lobby, this evening's show has drawn last evening's crowd as well. Jonathan's piano chants a cheery alehouse rhythm, Laddie and the girls will soon be on the floor, so Omar is busy, Guillame is busy, but both converge on Rupert as he slips off his coat, Omar's frown instant at the sight of the blood—"What's this then, what happened?"—but Rupert shakes his head, lights the first of a nightlong chain of cheroots.

"It's nothing," he says. "Nothing happened."

Meanwhile Istvan reaches the stairs, Decca and Velma descending and "Go on," Decca orders Velma as soon as she sees him, "wait for me in the kitchen," waiting until Velma has gone to ask, "So?" tense and low. "What happened?"

"Nothing. The meat was bad, the wine was passable. He has a strumpet's taste in ornament. What did you expect?"

She glances toward the lobby, then motions him determinedly upward, the quiet heart of the staircase and "I have money," she says, low. "Enough to send you back to Brussels. Or even Paris, if you—"

"Little girl, I don't want your money."

"Oh what do you want?" Her voice is hard, her eyes, yes, are filled with tears. "Don't play your games here! That man—you don't understand, he will kill you. He and Rupert—"

"No," says Istvan, kindly but firmly, he could be correcting a wayward child. "The old masher, yes. Yes indeed. But Rupert—"

"There is more there than you imagine." She is whispering, now, her fingers tight on his arm. "How do you think we live, here? He loathes it, but he does it. For all of us."

Istvan says nothing. She holds him, he watches her, chin lifted, gazing down through his lashes, until voices rise, men's voices, the tricks beginning to gather so she turns, dark silk rustling like dead leaves, and Istvan climbs to the landing though not to the Cell after all: instead he heads to the Blue Room, Lucy alone in a corset and a frown, cleaning her nails with a pair of embroidery scissors and "Miss Dolly-mop," he says, in an old man's high-pitched wheedle, "Miss Judy, have you time to give an old gent succor? How about just a suck?"

Lucy laughs, then frowns again and "I'd do it for free," leaning back to show herself, smooth legs, pink sex, "but I'm on duty. The show is 'most over, the tricks'll be up here directly—"

"Ah," his murmur, "don't fret about that. Put your dress on, darling. We're going to have some fun."

Omar

So I say to the gent, this trick from Madagascar, or Borneo, or wherever the fuck he hails from with his swarthy skin and his two-inch prick, I say, "Sir, messire, your honor, things may well be different elsewhere, but this is how we do it at the Poppy." And then I throw him out on his ass. As soon as he could stand he was back inside, laughing. He even bought me a whiskey.

You have to know how to treat them, the gents, in a way that keeps the peace *and* keeps them coming back. You have to understand that what they seek here, all of them, no matter what shape it takes—if it's Jennie hanging from a strap or Laddie bent over a chaise, drink or smoke or dope or whatever-may-have-you—it's relief they're after, right? They have an itch, or a pain, or a broken heart, or a stiff prick, so you get 'em scratched, or soothed, or fucked or sucked or petted on—Pearl is best at that—and you take their money, and you thank 'em. And they always come back. Some gents still come who were here the very first night; I remember them. I was here, too.

I had come down from Victoria, where my sisters were, and my wife—I was married, yes, and happy, until she died, my Annie, the cholera got her and the little baby, too, and afterward I didn't care to be married again so much. And my sisters, well, one of them was wed to a soapy churchman, he was always on and on about the torments of the flesh. We get a few like that here at the Poppy, pure tit-mad but always scowling in the morning. The girls don't like them. And they're cheap, that type, they don't want to pay for their sins.

Anyroad I left Victoria, and since I didn't care to rob I fought my way up the river instead, bare-knuckling it for a few dollars a bout, for anyone who'd pay to watch. I learned to shave my pate, then, so's there would be nothing to grab on to; it kept me cleaner, too. And I learned I could take a deal of pain and come back shiny. Bad thing was, it made me a bit of a brawler—and I was a youngish chap, already I thought I could whip anything in shoe leather, right?

So when I came here I fought all the townies, and beat 'em, and was casting about for something else to beat on when I met Rupert. Now, to look at him, lean as he is, and dark as a diddakoi, you wouldn't

44

think he could box it up man-to-man. But Jesu, he destroyed me. Not that he could hit so hard—although he can—but that he never quit, just kept on and on until I was on the ground and crawling and *Stop*, I said, *I'm all in. You win.* And then he gave me one more, just to think about. And then he hired me.

Men need refreshment, he said to me, as we sat drinking in the Four Cups; nasty place, the ale reeks like bilge water. But he was talking about the Poppy. *If all they want is to dip their wicks, fine, they can go to Suzette's, or to that mongrel Angus. Or the Alley, and stop in at the sawbones on their way home for the clap they just caught. But we can offer them something more.*

He's a deep, deep thinker, you know, Rupert, and Miss Decca, too; she was in it as much as he was, and in a way the building's hers, right, since it was her old man who had it first. So she could do as she liked with it, and didn't we work to tart it up! They were both tickled to find that I could sew—as I can, a fine, neat seam, my sisters taught me. So Miss Decca and I made the costumes, and the curtains. And Rupert used the hammer and the broom.

It was my idea to have the dope, mostly because I enjoy a taste myself now and again. It's better than drink, leaves your belly alone, and you can mark up the price however high you like, because those who want it'll pay no matter what. Same as some of the gents' desires, you know: they can get plain-fucked any place, even their own wedded wives will do that. But to fuck the girl you carry in your mind, you know, the one who wouldn't have you, or the one you'll never have, the one you shouldn't have—or the boy, there are those who like it that way, too—to have just what you want, as you want it, served up private and discreet: well, who wouldn't pay for that? However much, it's always worth the cost.

And for the gents without daydreams, well, we give 'em the show to think on, the girls dressed up so pretty and fine, Jen with her needle-tracks covered, and Vera, and Pearl with her moony smile. And wily Puggy always thinking of new things for them to do, pretending to be princesses, or rubbing themselves with feathers, or the Roman Candle—the gents always go for that one—while our Jonathan plays so high-class you'd swear you were in a concert hall with the queen. He's a good lad, Jonathan, does his best and never complains, not that he can, you know, but still. I'd like to catch the gent who cut him, I truly would.

That first night we didn't have Jonathan yet, nor Puggy, nor any of these girls—only two girls did we have, Lorraine and, what was it, Nora or Dora—Dora, yes. We didn't even have the sign yet, only the name, Under the Poppy chalked mysterious-like on the wall outside. It was me on the door, Miss Decca the hostess, and Rupert the host and barkeep and coin-changer and everything else, telling the girls what to do, how to stand, how to flutter their fans: *You're the Queen of Sheba,* he told Lorraine, sitting there with her tits out so you didn't notice her face so much. *And Dora, you're her slave girl, you're there to satisfy her however she likes. Understand?* They didn't really, but they were glad to be in out of the wet, and they would have done anything for Rupert; the ladies have always fancied him, not that he fancies them back.—Well, shouldn't've said that, perhaps, but who cares anyroad? especially in a place like this? It's his own affair who he fucks or doesn't. Poor Miss Decca, she's in love with him, you know, straight-up, and that's not telling tales because anyone who spends a tick with her can see it. There's some talk about them being sibs, but people only say that 'cause they live here together and aren't wed or bedding, and people have to say something.

That other's her true brother, the showman, the puppet man from overseas, or wherever he says he comes from: they have that same foxface look, and the same air of, what you call it, secrecy. Like they both know something you don't. But he wears his easier than hers, like for him it's a sweety tucked into his pocket, and hers is a bone stuck in her throat…. Wish we'd had him in the old days, with his dolls, what does he call them? The mecs, right? They put on quite a show, quite a show, I was flummoxed as a trick myself, watching. I can't get past how he makes one talk while he's diddling with the other, I bet he could do three at once if he'd a mind to. That bony one, the Bishop he calls him, that's a spooky toy, don't think we'll have much use for it here. The one thing the gents don't like is to be scared.

That very first night, I think we were the scared ones, were any gents going to come to us? Was the Poppy a good idea or not? But after the two queens of Sheba got done petting each other, and giggling around with their roostertail fans, the five men who were there stood in line for them. And the next night it was ten, and then thirty, and we were in business proper. We've never had to worry about the lucre until recently, all this commotion with the soldiers. They say there's going to be a war, or something like. I imagine that's why Rupert spends so much time with that Jürgen Vidor, keeping us out of harm's way.

We've had a shiny time of it here, most of the time. Vera and Velma showing up just as Lorraine was falling ill, and Jen getting tossed out of her circus act…. Puggy was a stroke of luck: if he hadn't wanted a bit of smoke he might have wound up at that penny-gaff Gaiety instead! He says he was just passing through, and maybe that's so, but he settled down quick enough. I like Puggy. He has ten bad ideas for every good one, but his best ideas are better than anyone's. He found us Jonathan, for one.

And I found us Lucy, I'm proud to say, just picked her out right on the street. She's a very likely girl, Lucy, always pulls fair and never has a bad word to say about anyone, except for Miss Decca, and who can blame her there? It's Puggy's belief that Miss Decca's jealous, she sees our Lucy's got some talent for the stage, more than a little, more than the other girls for sure—hear her sing, she's got a very true voice—and that's why Miss Decca's so dead-set against her. Puggy says Miss Decca wants to tread the boards herself, but that's just Puggy talking nonsense. Miss Decca could no more perform than she could fly.

No, she's Rupert's left hand, and I'm his good strong right, and us three together are the heart of the Poppy, or I guess we were, until this Istvan's come. But that's the way of it, right? I don't believe he'll stay, he doesn't look the staying type, but he's brought a new kind of life to us for sure. Not that we were asking for it! But that's the way of things as well. And those puppets are well worth having, I'd like to learn to work a few of them myself. Make that Pan Loudermilk jig, eh? Not bloody likely. He looks like he'd bite off your fingers if you tried.

"The girls are mostly hale," says Dr. Adderley to Rupert. They sit together in the parlor-office, the doctor enjoying a morning glass of whiskey while Rupert goes over the bill.

"Mostly?"

"It's that Jennie." Dr. Adderley rubs his eye, the one without the little golden monocle; he privately believes that a monocle gives him more stature as a physician. Adderley is generally assumed not to be his true name, he is a mulatto from somewhere he cares not to mention, and his doctoring degree is perhaps self-conferred. But he is skillful and thorough, the whores' conditions have improved under his care, all but recidivist Jennie: "Her arm's going to drop off, Mr. Bok, she's got to get away from that needle. I've advised Miss Decca about it, and Omar, too, to put him on the watch."

"Miss Decca's not much of a nurse," says Rupert dryly. "And Omar's got his troubles, too, in that department."

"Oh, he's healed up nicely, very nicely. *He* knows to stay away from the needle." Adderley swallows the last of the whiskey. "Now, that Laddie's got to have a few days off." Rupert raises his eyebrows. "Well, he can suck, or, or whatever, that's fine. But I had to do a bit of stitching, and he'll need to rest that area for a bit."

Rupert nods, folds some bills into an envelope, raises the whiskey bottle—"Another?"—but Dr. Adderley shakes his head in thanks, takes the envelope, and departs, monocle a-shine. Rupert heads for the whores' hallway, knocks on the door next to Lucy's Blue Room, where Laddie reclines, up on one elbow and "Adderley was in to see me," Rupert says, closing the door.

"Yes," says Laddie glumly, "me, too." His English is accented still, a faint chuffing aftertaste of Berlin, perhaps, or Moscow, his name is Russian though no one ever calls him Vladimir. A lean, dark, slightly mournful boy, yet not at all girlish, one would never mistake him that way. Though by certain lights, in certain lights, he might be taken for a man somewhat older, a man resembling, say, Rupert, or someone very like him, if he cut his hair, or tucked it into a collar or cap. "I'm hurting some, Mister Rupert, I am."

48

"I know you are. Why don't you take the evening off? Tomorrow, too, if it pains you still. Just stay in your room and rest, or watch the show, whichever. I'll tell Miss Decca."

Laddie's smile is pleased and surprised. "Why, many thanks, Mister Rupert. You're good to me."

Rupert shrugs, looking not at Laddie but at the door, the floor; is he thinking, perhaps, of that resemblance, of the heat it rouses, the pain it might cause? but "Just rest," he says again, hand on the doorknob when his glance is caught by something bright, gold and gleaming black: a black pearl, a stickpin stuck between the coverlet and the slats, it is in his hand and *Take it*, he wants to say to Laddie, still smiling on the bed, *take it, break it, sell the pieces* but of course nothing this fine, this distinctive, could be fenced with any safety in this town. Instead he slips it into his pocket and goes to Decca, pince-nez and scowling over the books, and "Give Laddie a little something extra," he says. "And a day or two off the floor."

"Extra? Why? Are we paying them not to work, now?" but "Do it," he says, not loud, not unkindly, but her lips tighten and she nods. From Decca's room he enters his own, to extract the stickpin from his pocket and lock it in another of his desk drawers, another narrow chamber bound by the steel key on his watch chain. Then he frees and retrieves the little white knife, and holds it in his hand, his curling fingers, as if it is a key of a different sort, an amazement to remind him just how wretched one can be.

The children sit together, boy and girl on a low wall in the mist of earliest morning. The foxface boy holds the puppet on his knee, a fantastical concoction of wire and scavenged wood, coarse black string for hair, nutshells painted blue for eyes that it, he, Marco, rolls just like a real boy's, if you pull a certain thread at the back of his neck.

Last night he made five dollars, *the boy says.* Dancing for the ladies and gents.

The ragged girl leans closer, the better to see. Her aching fingers are jammed into the pockets of her skirts; she has no gloves. Around her neck is a cord of plaited "silver," gilt-paper woven cleverly into a chain: her brother made it for her, draped it on her like a coronation. Can I make him dance?

No, Ag. He's not a toy, yeah? He won't do it for anyone but me.

The girl sighs, but does not protest. She has learned that protesting does no good, that the thing to do is bear down and wait. Wait until he changes his mind, if he changes his mind. Wait out the whippings from Mrs. Segunda, wait for the day to turn to dusk, wait by the window for this brother, half-brother, son of the same mother who sleeps now with the holy angels, who, like an angel himself, always appears from the darkness, bringing hope, however short-lived.

At the asylum the windows are bolted at sundown, Mrs. Segunda is most insistent about robbers who slip through open windows to steal the silver and threaten the householders' lives. Agatha has been punished many times for undoing those bolts, letting in the night air itself a hazard, and who can guess what other dangers as well? The milky vicar sadly importunes his wife: The poor child is striped from neck to knees. Can you not reach her by some other means, my love? *but* Naught else will serve, *insists Mrs. Segunda,* this one is nigh incorrigible *and in this, unlike most other matters, she is correct and the vicar is not. Privately she considers her husband too soft to deal effectively with children. Observe the dry unwinking stare of the girl Agatha, with her pockets full of candy floss and flimsy-dolls, paper chain about her neck, where did she come by such trifles? She will not say. She is disciplined, to bring an answer to her lips; still she will*

50

not say. Very well, if she refuses to open her mouth for the truth, she shall have no food, either, as the spirit is superior to the flesh.

Thus Mrs. Segunda toils tirelessly in the care of these unwanted girls, who like wayward vines will grow crooked, wicked, unless they are trained strictly, and with strict resolve. They come from no proper family or parentage—such as this Agatha, self-deposited one cold morning at the turn, waiting stiff and silent for the morning doors to open—and, without aid, destined to starve, or perish in the work-houses, or descend even lower to theft and prostitution, producing more orphans while still children themselves. It is a dreadful life for the girls on the streets, and Mrs. Segunda obeys with vigor her Christian duty to rescue them from lasting harm. She has had some success—one of her girls is in service in the household of the Lord Mayor himself—and thanks Providence for the chance to be of continuing aid.

Vicar Segunda has a different method with the children, gentle smiles and sweet hymn singing, dandling them as if they were his own, tickling them until they weep from laughter; all but Agatha. "Sad Agatha" he calls her, taking it as a failing that he cannot make her smile as he does the others. Why do you grieve, child?

Why does she grieve? Does she grieve? or only swallow grief as she swallows her hunger, her loneliness, her resolve to wait for her brother to free her if it takes the world's end to bring about. He has promised, many times, nearly every time he comes, to take her away someday, away from the hymns and the whippings, the sewing lessons stitching shrouds for pauper babies, the everlasting slops and chores. For now it is only a precious few hours at a time, running beside him while he roams with his dark twin, silent Rupert whom he calls "Mouse" (though only he can call him so, once she watched another boy attempt it as a jape and get beaten toothless for the try). Together they dash and scatter, stealing, larking, watching the city from a thousand hidey-holes, depositing her at the window or the gate to await the next time: when? She is never sure. She can only wait.

Rupert the Mouse loves her brother, she can see that, but in a way very different from her own worship; some of it may have to do with bumming, the way the boys do with one another, but there is more to it than that. It is a kind of love that sleeps with one eye open, brooding over the chosen other, the kind that wraps around like a cloak in the storm, that finds fierce little knives made from magic that can never, ever be lost or left behind.... And her brother loves Rupert, too. Much more than he loves her, or their mother who died calling his name; even more than his puppet Marco that he made with his own hands and carries everywhere he lodges, sleeping in a special box. *No, this love is a kind of need for Rupert, a requirement: he must have Rupert to be happy. What would that be like, to be so needed by someone else, to be essential? She has no words for these ideas, cannot even frame the question; all she can do is keep close to their love, the way one hugs the grate in the cold, whatever is extra seeping outward to where she bides. She can make do with very little, with almost nothing; it is both her strength and her doom.*

Now she reaches to touch the puppet's blouse, brown velvet soft as kitten's fur. Did Rupert watch him dance, too?

Her brother gives a fond nod. He sang "Paddy's Lament," and "Lady Angela Takes the Air," and whacked a masher's knee when he got too disputatious. *Funny.* He makes Marco's eyes roll. Funny, yeah, Marco?

The puppet gives a little shake, as if in remembered mirth. His paper boots, painted to look like leather, kick against Istvan's lap, as though he might start up jigging directly. To Agatha he seems a mean little boy, the kind of boy who tries to snatch up her skirts in the streets, the kind she hits and pinches as she longs to hit and pinch this doll, this dummy, this creature beloved of her brother, whisked off by him and singing Rupert to dance for mashers and curry coins and travel the wide world while she herself is left bereft at the asylum door. Pinch him, yes, she would like to pinch him, pitch him head first into the kitchen stove, velvet shirt, nutshell eyes and all. He is all dry wood, he would make a jolly fire.

She smiles to herself; Istvan smiles, too. I might make a lady for him, *he says musingly.* To dance with. Think you can get me some of that pink muslin, again?

She can and she does, the very next midnight, absconding the entire rag-bag, muslin, shroud-scraps and all, is tumbling it over the sill when she is unhappily surprised by the vigilant Mrs. Segunda, whose caught glimpse from the window of the waiting gang—three boys, though one is apparently a cripple—convinces her that Agatha's vice-raddled soul merits sterner corrective measures than even she can provide: I have done all that Christian love may warrant, *she tells her sad husband, as Agatha stands silently by, furious with herself for being caught, frightened white as Mrs. Segunda goes on to decree that* The girl must go directly to the lock-hospital, *a true gaol where there are bars on every door, and no outside windows at all. If she ever wept, Agatha, she would cry as her few possessions are gathered, as she is led to the warder's wagon: how will her brother and Rupert ever find her, ever free her, now?*

But from disaster comes sudden rude salvation: the warder's driver is somewhat less concerned with Christian virtue than with having his thin prick diddled, and what is it to the yawning turnkey if eight girls arrive when nine were promised? Perhaps there was a mistake on the papers that at any rate neither of them can read. So a swift figure drops from the wagon and loses itself in the darkness, incorrigible Agatha who by the time the sun rises has chopped her braids with a fruit-seller's paring knife and changed her name: she is Decca, now, a jigger and singer, for half a penny she will give you "Paddy's Lament" and "Lady Angela Takes the Air."

"The first one," says Istvan, carefully thumbing a glued eyelid, keeping it from sealing shut, "was called Marco, after a lad we—a lad I knew. After that, I let circumstance name them for me."

"What about Miss Lucinda?" Lucy asks, and Istvan smiles: "A comely whore in Paris, who fed me pea soup and let me sleep between her tits on chilly nights.—Hold this, darling," proffering one end of the twine while he twists the other: together they labor quietly in the Cell, their intercourse intent as any whore's and customer's but with creation as its aim: they handle the puppets as tenderly as parents with their young, Lucy giving Istvan her memories of the drummer with the concertina, she and her sister clapping for the toby-dog, *Droll Tales* and "Yes," says Istvan, "I've a droll tale in mind myself," a new show using again the players of the Poppy alongside his own troupe but "I've no title for it yet," he says. "Perhaps 'An Interlude with the Oracle'? That's what she was, that Delphic lady: a voice-thrower, a ventriloquist. Puppets are very very old, darling, did you know that? and their handlers classed always as the vilest of men, down there with gypsies, Jews, and prostitutes," winking, linking bone to bone, the Bishop restrung for possible use though "Maybe I ought to change his name," Istvan muses. "What say you, my lord of the church?"

From the shuttered box, a dry voice proclaims, "Name us Legion, for we are many."

Lucy starts, then laughs and "I still can't feature how you do that," she says, her fingers nimble in the snarl of strings; all the tools of his kit—the winking sharps and small steel hammers, the buttonhooks, the snips—lie easy in her hands, she is a marvelously quick study, as if she were born for the work. "I know it is a trick, I mean a dupe, but still—Do you ever make him talk to you, alone? the two of you? No, that's silly, isn't it."

"Not at all." Istvan pauses, considering, smiling, Rupert or Decca would recognize that smile. Finally "He sleeps," says Istvan, "with a black cloth across his face. It keeps his soul primed.... Does that give you your answer?" and before she can give him hers, continues:

54

"They *are* toys, philosophical toys, as we are puppets really, to our base desires. Don't you see the same, in that Blue Room of yours? What man owns his soul in there? Does he not instead give it into your hands, to manipulate as you do his prick?"

"Turn it like a crank," says Lucy, suddenly grinning, a funny wolfish look Istvan has never seen her wear: it surprises him into laughter, both of them chuckling as "We are so much alike, you and I," he says, bending to kiss her cheek. "Both of us vendors of the art of the moment, the impermanent pleasure, the will-o'-the-wisp that lifts a man from the prison of time, and for just that moment sets him free—"

"Why, it's poetry," says another voice, Puggy's voice, Guillame a-grin in the doorway, a bolt of dusty blue velvet beneath his arm. "A shame to cut in, but may I borrow your apprentice just a tick, messire? I need a lady's touch with this rag."

"Must you pay for her time, as I do? Decca ought at least give me a discount."

Lucy bites a thread, makes a face that makes her look much older, lines sprung sharp around her lips and "That's Decca's daily labor," she says, "to make me into her. That's why she won't let me play onstage, and sets me to everlasting scutwork, like *she* does, the evil cunt."

Istvan raises his eyebrows, looks to Puggy, who shrugs in eloquent mock-surprise, and "I suppose she may leave me," Istvan says, with reluctance equally counterfeit, "I've got an errand or two to run this noon. Lucy, love, will you find the time to finish the Bishop on your own?" and Lucy smiles, delighted as a child to be so trusted, bundles the bones and threading into her own room for later employment as Istvan winks Puggy to the door, closes it to dress in careful blue and black, boots and hat and cravat tied as they do on the Continent, a dandy's flounce and flourish appreciated not at all by the surly clerk at the hotel where Mr. Arrowsmith sips his tea with a solemn face behind the grainy broadsheet and "Alas," Istvan's bow beside the table. "Is the news then so vastly grim, messire?"

"Not yet as grim as the tea," says Mr. Arrowsmith, "but the wind is blowing, yes.—You come again to visit...?" letting it trail as Istvan waits, a moment's test for each, of each until "May I invite you to join me in more palatable refreshment, sir?" as they then ascend the stairway, watched by the clerk who spits on the floor, marked by the chambermaid as they enter the suite just to the left of Jürgen Vidor's, unseen by that man himself busied with communiqués from various sources from which he attempts to tease some usable truth; as Lucy, draped like Venus in moldy velvet, teases out the threads that worm and tickle beneath her damp armpit as Puggy, on his knees with the shears, chops the skirt down to mortal size and "What's the new show to be," he asks Lucy, "has he hinted?" as Mr. Arrowsmith asks the same of Istvan, who replies with a teasing smile.

It begins with a tinkling tune, sweet and sinister both, with just the slightest breath of heat, the prickling, serious sweat of real desire: and a girl's dreamy voice, humming, musing to herself: Vera, blue velvet on a black swing, back and forth, alone on the stage as Jonathan, curtained off, plays the melody:

"I want to meet a swain
Who wants to meet me, too,
Who wants to do with me
The things I want to do."

And here enters just such a one, Laddie tricked out as a toff in high hat and curling whiskers, an exaggerated hands-to-heart discovery when he sees luscious Vera, positioning himself at once behind her to set the swing in wider motion, as she continues to sing—*is* it Vera, singing? or another's voice, Lucy's voice so much richer and sweeter, Lucy cloaked in black again at the back of the stage, obscured by two tall figures, one with a definite horse's head. At the far reaches of the house, beyond the tables and the watching tricks, Decca, in red from head to toe, a bloody, rosy, field-poppy red, pinches Velma viciously for some failure in service, Velma's yip of pained surprise lost in Lucy's voice rising into the second verse:

"He must be very handsome
And upright, too, of course.
But first of all he must possess
A large and healthy horse."

—as the two men advance from the darkness, Vera swinging more lustily now, Laddie stepping back to give place to Istvan who is dressed as a rustic stable boy, breeches and slouch cap, leading the silent, impressive, priapic Chevalier, whose appearance creates a moment's quiet in the audience, then a hearty laugh; even from Jürgen Vidor, in his seat up front between silent Rupert and gently smiling Mr. Arrowsmith, who has a certain advantage over the rest, having had a private preview of the piece in his hotel room some days before:

But may they not take a bit of umbrage at the subject matter, your audience? How many have themselves found some comfort in the barnyard, do you suppose?

Oh, they'll laugh, messire. All but our upright friend the colonel, who won't be there.

No, he is en route to the capital with General Georges, some dilemma of logistics, soldiers are much easier to move as markers on a map than real men on muddy roads.... You are acquainted with the General, I believe?

We've met.

"We mustn't tell Mamma,
For she would not endorse
Her precious virgin daughter
A-cant'ring on a horse."

Vera rolls her eyes in perfect rhythm with Lucy's bantering soprano, as the Chevalier approaches, bears down upon her in the swing, morning-coat, carved mandrake root and all: and Istvan the stable boy plays it purely for comedy, rolling his own eyes in shock as Vera hikes her pretty velvet dress to show herself knickerless beneath, as the Chevalier tosses his chestnut mane and mounts, neighing with such enthusiasm as to set the watchers howling, many are up from their chairs now, pressed beside the stage.

Brussels was kind to you, I surmise. Many times I heard your name mentioned among the fashionable ladies and lords. Your performances were well-attended, the Grand' Place, the Place Royale—and the private shows, as well. Why, I myself heard, from the Misses van Symans—

Brussels was good.

Yet you chose to come here, to shit and silverfish and war. I realize Art is a capricious goddess, but—

The theatre's not only art, messire, it's magic, too. Sometimes the best magic is made in the dark.

Black magic? Well. It will soon be dark enough for any sorcery, once the full complement of troops arrive. You will want to be just a fond memory, here, when that day comes. I plan to be.... Your friend Mr. Bok is very fortunate.

How so?

In your friendship.

The men hoot more loudly still as Vera's heels dig into the Chevalier's sides, her dress hiked up to her waist, Istvan shielding his eyes with one hand and miming self-pleasure with the other, Lucy's voice ringing out with swoony glee:

> "The paddock gates are open
> The gallop has begun!
> What man alone could ever be
> A centaur's-worth of fun?"

The piano leaps into a driving tantivvy-tantivvy, the rhythm of the hunt, as, in a true coup de théâtre, the Chevalier rears backward, Vera still merrily aboard, and "canters" around the stage, with scandalized Istvan—breeches agape, tugging the useless bridle—seemingly towed along as well. The men roar their approval, perhaps as much for the illusion as the sight of Vera's pink thighs and buttocks, which in any case they have seen many times before.

The trio circles back to the swing at center stage as from both wings new equestriennes emerge, eager Pearl and loose-limbed Jennie slightly green around the gills, pantomiming clamor for their turns in the saddle while Vera, spent, slides almost gracefully to the floor, props herself on an elbow as Lucy, expert on the cue, sings out:

> "Perhaps Mamma was wiser
> Than I had thought before.
> I had not dreamed that one could be
> So awf'ly saddle-sore!"

Laughter, applause, more applause. From behind his creation, Istvan gives a modest bow, Laddie steps up to escort the Chevalier offstage; Istvan bows again, flanked by the girls, Vera flushed and smiling, Pearl beside Jennie who blinks like a bat at bay. Mr. Arrowsmith's applause is vigorous, as Jürgen Vidor notes: "You're a horseman at heart, then, Mr. Arrowsmith?"

"I admire sport in all its forms, Mr. Vidor. Especially when executed so well as that. What say you, Mr. Bok?"

"I don't ride."

But what of Mr. Bok's other friends?

You mean the folk at the Poppy?

No—though they must be some consideration for him as well, he does not look the man to shirk his duties. No, I meant some others, here in town.... It is called kukolnost, *is it not? The state of being a puppet?*

Kukolnost, *"puppetness," yes. Is there something you wish me to know, messire?*

Only what you must surely know already: that your Mr. Bok has his own debts to pay. May I be very frank with you?

I'd assumed you were nothing but.

Since my advent in this unhappy place, I have noted two things about Jürgen Vidor. One is that he maps his own course here, beside his charge from abroad, and his alliance with General Georges, who himself has more than one master, as always do we all. Which, to my mind, may unnecessarily complicate what ought to be a simple situation. And the second is that, even in the midst of this tangle, Mr. Vidor finds ways to indulge himself, ways that war may threaten, that may then render him—unpredictable in his dealings.

He's a trick. Tricks are always predictable.

Ah. Have you much experience with war?

Money plus blood makes war: a simple situation, as you say. I know blood and I know Rupert. I'll run when I have to and take him with me. Is that frank enough for you, messire?

Admirably so. You lodge with him, then, not to ply your gift, but to oversee Mr. Bok's?

You think his is to keep house in a brothel? Every skill I have, I had from him. I lodge there for many reasons, war or no war. And in the meantime, the mecs will continue to play.

Capital! Art and conflict are no strangers, sometimes the best grows from the worst. I will look forward even more avidly to your presentations. And it is my sincere hope that however long you linger here, Dusan, you will consider me a friendly and useful patron.

Mr. Arrowsmith, I already do.

It is to Mr. Arrowsmith that Istvan bows first, as he arrives beside their table, still clad in his stable boy's weeds. He takes the chair beside Rupert, nods affably to Jürgen Vidor seated on Rupert's left, who returns his nod with apparently equal affability before asking, "And where is your crooked little man tonight?"

Istvan's smile is positively sunny: "Limbering up for Act II, I'd warrant. Eh, Rupert?" He reaches past Rupert's unused wine goblet for his stout little glass of whiskey, drains it, winks at the trio, and leaves, after using Rupert's shoulder to lever himself upright, to disappear once again past the curtains. Mr. Arrowsmith looks thoughtful, Rupert's gaze is fixed on the tabletop. Only Jürgen Vidor smiles, cordial and very cold.

Jonathan Shopsine

When you are silent, no one sees you, that is what I know. Onstage the audience never looks to me, they only hear the music, Monsieur Chopin, and Mr. Mozart, and all the bawdy parlor-songs; I never mind that, the music always comes first. But people think that because I cannot talk, I cannot hear. Or that I'm stupid. But I am lettered, I can read, and reason out what I read, too. Like that *Merchant of Venice* that Mr. Istvan lent me: "Hath not a Jew eyes?" I like that. It is like me. A Jew, a mute, a whore, we are all down there on the bottom.... I can read music as well, any music written down. And I can read faces.

Miss Decca watches faces, too; she watches everything. There at the back of the house, studying the men who come in, and Lucy and the girls, and Mr. Rupert always; or down in the kitchen, counting the potatoes, measuring out the coal in the coal-bin. She is worried, I know, all she talks about downstairs is money, and the war. Omar says not to fret, that a whorehouse makes lucre even in bad times. Puggy just shrugs, all he ever cares for are the shows, especially now that the puppets have come.

But I go into the streets and I see those soldiers, they are not from cities, or towns, they are from holes and dens in the countryside, where the people are more like beasts than men. They cut a whore in the Alley two nights ago, cut her to the ground, they burned out a tea-seller's stall for no reason, except that they like a fire. I believe that Miss Decca is right to be afraid. The girls are growing frightened, too. I try to cheer them, Vera, and Pearl, make them laugh if I can. Especially Pearl. She's not a stout trouper like Lucy, or set on her own chart, like Vera. She is different.... I wrote a little tune for her, Pearl, it said, *We will fly away, like birds we will fly away, birds can fly through the storms and so shall we.* It seemed to ease her.

But I know they are wondering, as I do, what will become of us here. David, the bootblack at the Gaiety, told me he is going to Archenberg before long, he said that I should flee, too. The man who makes the picture-puzzles has left already, and the seamstress has closed down. The streets are looking like an old crone's mouth, gapped and black: it shivers me to walk out, now.

Instead I stay in, and practice. You can never practice too much, and I love the sound the piano makes when the theatre is empty. It rings like a bell, or trickles like water, or crashes like rude thunder: I can make it sing, or talk, or say whatever I want to say.

When I first came here, I used to make the piano cry, it was all I wanted to do. All the sad songs my grandpapa taught me, beautiful songs, "Under the Willows," "Until the Trump Shall Sound." I missed my grandpapa so much. But Papa was gone, and there was me, and Alexander, and Charles, and all the little ones, the girls to feed and keep together: we were many, too many, and my grandpapa was so ill. Poor Mamma. We three were the big boys, we could take care for ourselves. I believe Alexander made for Vicksburg. Charles was a blacksmith's apprentice when I saw him last, he worked beside a livery and was wanting to marry the blacksmith's girl. May be he did, and has little ones of his own by now. I hope we will meet each other again someday. I wish they could see me here, playing the piano up on stage. I wish Grandpapa could hear me. May be in Heaven he can.

I was his favorite, he always said; he taught me to play. He said, *Music has charms to soothe the savage breast. What does that mean, Jonnie? It means that folk will heed music when they heed nothing else. You watch and listen, see what power the music has.*

And Grandpapa was right, music has power. Right from the start, it fed and kept me: When I played in the kirk, the pastor gave me pennies, when I played at the lodging-house, I earned my room. I liked it there, that lodging-house. It was down by the river, I used to walk out of a night and catch the breeze. And Mr. Carstairs was a kindly fellow, he tried to keep a good house—to keep safe—he tried—

From the start Puggy was good to me, because of—of the way I cannot talk. He even got Miss Decca to bring the doctor, to see if aught could be done. But Omar used to tease, and the girls, too: make fish-mouth at me, or pretend to be hard-of-hearing, cupping their ears: *What's that you say, Jonathan?* Mr. Rupert put a stop to that. And when they found that I could play, Miss Decca gave me to Puggy, and let me out of the kitchens, though I was fine with Velma; Velma is much sharper than anyone may think. She cleans all of the rooms, she knows all the tricks, she sees everything that goes on here, top to bottom. Miss Decca should listen to Velma, and stop pinching her and calling her names. Velma could help her the way Omar helps Mr. Rupert, because even Miss Decca cannot be all places at once.

She tells me things, Velma, secrets, some because we are friends, and some, I think, because I cannot talk and tell others: such as how hard it was for Omar to drop the needle, that he sweat and bit the sheets for three nights running. Or how much money Vera hides in her necklace box, and how Jennie steals from her, cunning as a midnight rat. Or which of the tricks likes to hit, or be hit, or be tickled, or dress up like ladies, and which like to do other things, unclean things, it gives me the shivers sometimes, what she tells me. To look at them they all look like fine honest gentlemen. But they are not, no. That Mr. Franz— and he works for the mayor, too!

And that Mr. Jürgen Vidor: Velma sees him, what he does with his jewelry-pins, what poor Laddie has to bear, and how Mr. Rupert has to stand and watch it all. At first I did not credit it, but she showed me through a chink in the door, the three of them there; it made me very sad. I am kind to Laddie, always, and now I try to be kinder. He also is like a Jew or a mute, the boy whores have it worst of all.

I would be kind to Mr. Rupert, but he lets no one close to him, not even Miss Decca. Mr. Rupert is worried as well, but why, I don't know, nor Velma, either. She says his writing desk is full of secrets, but those rooms he tends to himself, she has no key to that door. Mr. Istvan is the one *he* watches, whenever they are in the same place, he cannot take his eyes away.... Mr. Istvan is so clever with those dolls, his "mecs" as he calls them. His mecs speak for him, I think, the same way the piano speaks for me.

"Mr. Franz to see you," says Omar, eyebrows raised as high as they will go, his tone courteous and noncommittal as the mayor's attaché steps into the parlor-office, bowing to "Miss Decca, Mr. Bok," beaver hat in hand, seating himself without invitation. There are little red blotches on his cravat, breakfast remnants perhaps, or dinner's. His boots leave wet spots on the carpet, his coat is damp. "Many thanks for this opportunity."

At their table, account books set hastily aside, Rupert and Decca share a glance; it is she who answers, removing her pince-nez as Omar gently shuts the door, stands outside with folded arms, to listen, and ward away. "Opportunity, Mr. Franz?"

"To deliver the mayor's message." His gaze crawls the room, touching everything—the furnishings, petit-point and damask, the weary potted ivy, the plaster statue of Athena with her chipped breastplate and owl—before returning to the two at the table. "The mayor felicitates you on your shows, he enjoys your shows very very much. But the mayor is not happy with the—horse." Mr. Franz's lips twitch; it seems he is suppressing some emotion. "I need not speak of it more fully before Miss Decca, need I, need I explain what the horse is doing to that girl up there on that stage?"

This time it is Rupert who replies. "What exactly is the mayor's concern with the performance, Mr. Franz?"

"He doesn't care for it, not at all. Not at all." Mr. Franz seems to be struggling internally. "It is not—Christian."

"It is not a real horse," says Decca dryly. "Perhaps the mayor was unaware of that fact, having not been in attendance. It is merely one of the puppet players, operated by—"

"The mayor is not a lackwit, Miss Decca."

"I never suggested that he was, Mr. Franz—"

"Perhaps," says Rupert, overriding them both, "I ought to speak with the mayor myself."

Mr. Franz draws back in his chair, nostrils wide; for that moment he looks like a horse of a sort, a beast about to kick or stampede. "That is very unnecessary, Mr. Bok, and very uncouth. I am here to speak for the mayor. You must speak to me as if I was the mayor himself."

Decca's lips part; Rupert makes a minute move, one finger tapping softly against the table; her mouth closes. Rupert turns slightly in his chair, so he is facing the attaché head-on, and says, in a mild, reasonable voice, "Well then, if I were addressing the mayor personally on this issue, I would propose that a horse-puppet pretending to diddle a whore is somewhat less a threat to community standards than those drunken soldiers who broke up the Four Cups last night, one of whom was shot for his antics by a constable, but not before causing considerable uproar and distress to many citizens. I might then go on to invite the mayor to a private showing of the performance, so that he might judge for himself how—"

"I do not care for your tone, Mr. Bok."

"I don't give a fuck, Mr. Franz, what you care for or don't. I do know you like to have your prick yanked, hard, while you bite my whores on their arms, leaving bruises and occasionally drawing blood. Which is none of the mayor's business, or that of anyone else. I only mention it to illustrate my point: that the Poppy is a place apart, and things happen here that have nothing at all to do with the workaday world we all inhabit, in a sane, generous, and Christian fashion. Do I make myself clear, Mr. Franz?"

The attaché's face is a curious shade of yellow, a cross between bile and beer. Decca sits very still, her fingers steepled against her lips. As no answer appears to be forthcoming, Rupert rises, calling for Omar who swings the door wide as Mr. Franz rises as well, his motions somewhat stiff, as if he himself were a puppet, a marionette and "Good day, Mr. Franz," says Rupert. "Please give my kind regards to the Mayor, and Miss Decca's as well. Show Mr. Franz out, Omar."

"This way, messire," says Omar, as Mr. Franz pushes past him; the door swings shut again. Decca looks as if she cannot decide whether to clap or cry; finally, she laughs, an airless little noise. "Was that— entirely wise?"

Rupert rubs his forehead. "Do you think that ass Redgrave dreamed up this foolishness for himself? As if the waters weren't shit-murked enough." He turns for the door again. "We can finish with the books later. I must step out."

Where? but she does not ask because she knows he will not answer, believes at any rate she knows the answer, if not the final outcome. So she says nothing, only rises behind him, his dark, contained, and troubled form, one hand out helplessly, secretly, where he will never see—

—but he does see, turning to surprise her, that empty, reaching, supplicating hand, surprises her even more by taking her hand, taking her into his arms for a moment, a brotherly embrace as she, shocked, holds to him, her head tucked beneath his chin and "Trust me," he says, "will you trust me? Things are getting darker here, I am doing the best that I can."

For that moment she cannot answer, cannot speak a word: inhaling the scent of his waistcoat, of his body beneath, feeling the beat of his heart. Once, long ago, they slept this way, curled up on a quay, his arms around her like safety, his heart like the sound of the sea in her dreams. Finally "Yes," she says on a breath, a tremulous exhalation. "Yes, I trust you."

"All right, then. Good." He releases her, slowly, slowly she steps away. "I'll be back directly.... And tell your jester brother I want to see him."

"He adores you," she says.

Instantly his face pales, her eyes open wide with alarm—not at all what she meant to say, not at all what he thought to hear—and then his gaze goes flat and he is gone, slamming the door as she strikes the table, horrified at herself, has she lost her mind entirely?—as the teacups wobble, splashing the ledger, her hand creeps towards her throat but finds instead the lover's eye inside her breast, circle of gold and blue, and her fingers seize it blindly through the silk, curl about it like a dying insect's legs—

—but after a rigid pause she reaches, instead, to right the tipped and dripping cups, move the stained ledger, find something to blot the mess. From down the hall come nearing voices, Omar and Vera; she clears her throat, she takes a breath to call.

"Will the gentlemen be wantin' wine, then? Or whiskey?" The clerk smells strongly of raw chicory, he is apparently having trouble focusing his eyes on Mr. Arrowsmith, who shakes his head: "Have someone bring tea," to the rooms upstairs, not his, not Jürgen Vidor's but another, dimmer, emptier suite, drawn curtains, one table, three men, four chairs and "It is barely noon," says the colonel in a disapproving mumble, as the serving maid departs, "and that yokel at the desk is already bottled."

"Perhaps he drinks to lubricate his wits," suggests Mr. Arrowsmith. "Or quiet his fears. Tea, General?" to the third man present, who sits at his ease, a raptor's gathered calm: black uniform fastened in gold, long silver hair, silver ring on his left thumb, black tea for General Georges who nods with the *politesse* of long acquaintance, waits with the same until Mr. Arrowsmith has poured for himself and then "The weather is against us," the General says. He has an unexpectedly musical voice, a poet's voice, an orator's. "But things will go very quickly, even in the snow. We will not have the passes, we haven't yet the troops for that, but I am not persuaded that we need them, the railway should suffice. And Essenhigh has the town fully secured, yes, Colonel?"

The colonel is not a small man, but next to the seated General he seems diminished. "Yes, sir. The men have settled in well."

Mr. Arrowsmith sips his tea. "But there was some unpleasantness…? The staff downstairs was all a-buzz."

The general leans forward; the colonel scowls: "What unpleasantness?"

"Apparently a few of your more feral forces amused themselves poorly at a tavern, and were shot dead for their trouble, but not before—"

"No, it was a commotion at that whorehouse, Under the Poppy: some ill-minded bastard brought in a horse to fuck the girls. First dolls, now a horse! We ought to close that place down."

The General blows softly on his tea. "A horse?"

"From whom have you that intelligence?" asks Mr. Arrowsmith of the colonel, who returns him a level stare and "My men," he says. "They advise me of everything that passes in town."

67

"A cavalry unit, perhaps?"

The colonel flushes. "You're forever defending that cesspool, Arrowsmith, who are you shielding really? The puppet-maker? Or that queer, Bok? I know that you're friendly with Vidor—"

"We are all comrades here," says Mr. Arrowsmith, unsmiling, "all in hopes of a successful outcome, Jürgen Vidor as much as—"

"Javier," says the General, with immense courtesy; Mr. Arrowsmith falls silent. The General turns his gaze to the colonel, whose martial stance softens substantially. The room is so quiet one can hear the mantel clock tick, hear the maids passing by in the hall. The silence continues. Finally General Georges asks, "How many of your men were shot, Colonel?"

"Two."

"How many dead?"

"One."

"Any civilians?"

"No. But they were not my men, sir, they were hill-men, they—"

"The mercenaries are yours to control as well. Do so. And remember that both Mr. Vidor and Mr. Arrowsmith are essential partners in our efforts, and merit all your courtesy and respect." There is a knock at the door. "That would be Mr. Vidor now. Admit him, Colonel," but instead it is the mayor, Redgrave, his attaché quivering in the background, asking for "General Georges, I must see the General. Is he in?" but it is Mr. Arrowsmith who steps into the hallway, the door closing prudently behind as "You motherless idiot," the General says without emotion to the colonel. "If this was Ghent I'd shoot you myself."

"I am sorry, sir."

"I have twenty ready and eager to replace you. I have only one Arrowsmith, one Vidor. Do you understand?"

"Yes, sir. I am sorry, sir."

The General looks him up and down as if he were faulty ordnance. "Go to the telegraph, see if my wire's been returned. Then wait for me in my rooms."

The colonel's face is red, he stands, he salutes, he waits for the door to open: on Mr. Arrowsmith only, the hall is empty now. The colonel bows, stepping stiffly aside as "What passes?" the General asks Mr. Arrowsmith, whose shrug is graceful: "Local color. Not to worry. More tea?"

"What did that fool mean, a puppet-maker?"

Mr. Arrowsmith smiles. "Ah, it's Hanzel. From Brussels."

"What, our boy with the prick-puppet?" When the General smiles, odd lines spring up about his mouth. "Well! What does he here, in this sorry place?"

"He is performing, I'm pleased to say, at one of the brothels. Very droll, Vidor's a regular there." He drinks the last of his tea, sets the cup aside. "Yourself and Vidor, now—that rift's fully healed? And the man-mountain who attends him mainly superfluous? I assumed that since our last unpleasantness—"

"You mean London? Or Prussia?" The General shrugs. "One can't hold a grudge forever."

"And lucre is a marvelous antidote."

"As long as it flows," as the door opens again, this time on Jürgen Vidor, smiling and nodding to both men, a soft tube of paper tucked beneath his arm: a map. In the hallway beyond, a heavyset man, a hired bravo, waits with folded hands, as two maids—the brown-haired girl who brought the tea, and, in smock and tented kerchief, Velma—wait together for the door to close, then hurry off, each in her own direction.

There is dirt beneath his nails, dirt on his borrowed finery, the noble-man's cravat and shirt; he is filthy as any urchin, crouching there in the stables beside the cabriolet, the dented coffin of puppets at his feet. He is stabbing the straw with a little white knife, crying the way a child cries, the silent tears of absolute fury until What's all this? *asks a quiet gentleman, walking stick and fragrant cigar, halted mid-stroll by the tableau.* Are you ill, young man?

He wipes his face, it smears the dirt. No.

The gentleman considers. Were you recently—upstairs?

No!

Here, proffering a chased silver flask, fleurs-de-lis and peacocks, a lovely artifact and the brandy inside is even better, it warms the heart, it dries the young man's tears as he drinks but does nothing for the fury, the gentleman can see that in his eyes, remarkable eyes and I must not smoke in here, *says the gentleman, indicating the flammable straw, the restive horses.* Will you walk with me, outside?

I don't suck, *says the young man coldly.*

I do, *says the gentleman pleasantly, and despite himself the young man smiles.* But all I asked was if you would walk, *and they do, out into the sweet chill of the evening, the green lawns and gravel pathways between trellised pink roses, lilies white as the ghosts of flowers in the dark though it is early yet, barely midnight after* A supper so dull, *sighs the gentleman,* that I traveled so far to attend, it is a pity. Ste.-Gilles sets a fine table, but I do not care for his amusements.

The boy retrieves the flask without asking, drinks a long draught, hands it back. I was meant to be one of them, messire. *Now the brandy has reached his eyes.* But I was delayed, and ruined.

The gentleman indicates his dishabille. By robbers?

By my—comrade. And then some burghers, God curse them, I think they broke my Marco. And now I am here alone, the Comte Ste.-Gilles will pay nothing, and—

You were to present at the dinner?

After dinner, *says the young man, pausing on the path as the gentleman pauses with him, takes a puff on his cigar that suddenly* squeaks, "Ow! C'est chaud!" *so he gives a start, almost drops it, looks sharply at the young man, then laughs.*

You're a conjuror, then.

The young man makes a lovely bow, and they walk on, lilies and cigar smoke, up and down the quiet paths. Upstairs, in the chateau, the dinner party continues without its evening's central entertainment, causing disappointment amongst the guests, and distress in the comtesse: They played at Marie-Elaine's birthday fête, they were too quaint! The dark one sings and tells stories, and the one with the puppets acts them out, it was marvelous. And they are so handsome, too, those boys, boys of the avenue, you understand? Such pretty boys, I am really put out…. Pierre, go check the courtyard again, perhaps they have arrived—

—*but they do not arrive, in tandem or separately, they perform nowhere onstage together ever again. If you asked the young man on the gravel paths, he might tell you it was due to his partner's fierce intransigence, his lunatic's insistence on certain modes of payment and behavior; if you asked that absent partner, he would very likely tell you nothing at all, only look at you in such a way that made the question itself seem a hazard, swiftly and prudently withdrawn. If you had been present at the time of the rupture, you might have glimpsed the tussle, might have heard the shouting, might have seen the young man seize his taller friend and insist that he not go, no,* you can't leave, you mustn't, Mouse, God damn you! Where will you go?

What difference to you? Our shows mean nothing to you, I know that now. You whore your toys, you whore yourself—

Stop this, why do you want to do this! We can make fine wages, steal from them if we like, do just as we please—

As *you* please. I won't watch that again, I told you. I'm sick to death of watching.

You watch nothing! It means nothing!

That man, that—bourgeois—splayed out like cooling beef—

What I did has naught to do with you, with us. How can it? He was just—

Fine. Do whatever you want, you cur fox, you—cumbox—

—*as from that point all deteriorates to violence and tears, one in flight, one on the tiles with his family of toys, soon overtaken by the drunken sons of local merchants who find it fine sport to fling his wires and tools around the cobblestones, toss the yarn and thread, abuse the puppets until the young man manages to poke out an eye or two, gather his torn children in the following confusion, and flee, weeping, furious, and bereft, heading toward the grand estate where perhaps his mate is waiting, perhaps having reconsidered his obdurate stance, perhaps stands in that very stable now, ready to extend his hand, his arms, make all as it was and should be, must be, must always be between them—*

But instead the long, dusty trudge, the empty stable, the impossibility of continuing versus the equal impossibility of, what? Not continuing? Should he lie down in the straw and die because Rupert is a fool and a jealous fool, who still seems not to understand that no one, no one, not even Decca who would gladly die for either of them, no one who lives or ever will could ever be so close or dear or necessary as Rupert, why is he so criminally mulish, so entirely in the wrong? And thinking thus, the white knife in his hand, there sat the young man until arrived the gentleman with the cigar, to suggest certain easements of mind, and provide as well as the brandy and a wash a way into the next city, a restful ride in a pleasant cabriolet during which the gentleman pointed out monuments of interest and was taught, in turn, how to make a paper flower appear and disappear, a longish ride in which Istvan became Hanzel, alighting with if not a lighter heart then a mended case full of those over which he broods, his toys, his friends, his children, in the foul rented rooms over the butcher shop, the butcher's wife an avenue to the kitchens of the bourgeoisie who, he finds, are more than pleased to pay him for what he can do, and free him, finally, from both his unfortunate lodgings and the butcher's more unfortunate wife, whose silly tears he has grown, in these short weeks, to loathe.

Within a few more weeks, pockets full, he is riding back whence he came, not, this time, in a carriage but a fruit-wagon, making three lean children clap and shout while their older brother drives the crop to market, the marketplace where Hanzel searches without reward for his friend, who has disappeared more thoroughly than any paper flower or magic dove or puppet through a trapdoor, he is simply gone. Gone. Not even Decca knows where he is, or will say if she does, though he has no choice but to believe her after the hateful scene he causes, during and after which she holds, sobbing and stubborn, to her tale: she has not seen him, he has sent no hint or note or letter, she does not know, Istvan, please, stop shouting at me! How many times must I say it, I've no idea where he's gone!

Fine. Then I'll stay with you, and wait for him to come.

Wait, yes, all you like! I hope he does come, I hope—

You hope what? Ag *where is he!*

Please! Stop!

He stops. She hopes. But Rupert never comes.

Lucy bites the thread with a nip as neat as a mouse's, holds up her handiwork to admire: Miss Lucinda's new fascinator is taking capital shape, it will look a treat when she is done. All the practice with the costumes has made her an excellent seamstress, the struggle was to find suitable supplies: half the vendors of fancies have disappeared, the lace-ladies, the button-man with his trays of jet and bone, even the ribbon-clerk is down to green twill, white, and parson's black. And Puggy has become so very stingy: *Lucy, stop, you've no idea. I'm pinched to the bone, Decca won't let me spend a farthing—*

Just a handful of feathers! was all she took, and a swatch of that moldy blue velvet, the blue thread from her bedroom hangings is nearly the same shade, and she will have all of that as she needs. The needle is Istvan's, from restringing the Bishop, and wasn't that a project, her fingertips are prickled still, and sore, she can barely pull pud for those beastly soldiers, Jesu knows there are so many of them now. Pearl says that one of them told her that they will be running the town soon, and she had better learn to love the taste.... And afterward, running anxious to ask Lucy *Is it really the foreign Hussars, like people say, coming for to take things over? Hussars, or is it Huns?* As if she would know, or it would make a penny's difference either way. *Just fuck them,* she told Pearl. *Fuck them, and don't listen.*

The tallow throws uncertain light, matching the gloom outside, the cold noon sun still buried by clouds. Vera says before the snow falls, they will all be out in the Alley; she is very glum these days, Vera. Laddie drinks gin and tries to be cheerful. Jennie tries to stay upright inbetween tricks; she is getting worse, Jennie, on the nod most of the day, lost by dawn to dreams she cannot master, Lucy can hear her, whining and groaning in her sleep. The tricks have started to avoid her, always an ominous sign.

Now Lucy loops a hairsbreadth of thread around a tiny black quill, fixes it in place with stitches tinier still, carefully loops up another; the work is a pleasure for her. She has hinted that she would like to become more involved in the making of the shows, in planning as well as performance, but so far Istvan has put her off with a smile:

73

I fear my mecs would eat you, darling, if I left you in a room with them alone.

If only she were Istvan's true apprentice! or even Puggy's, she could do a better job with the stagecraft than Jonathan, as willing as he is to fetch and build, he has no eye for it; he is an ear…. The idea makes her grin. Jonathan the ear of the Poppy, yes, as Puggy is the hands, as Omar is the fist, as Velma is the cooking pot. As Decca is the purse, as she and Laddie and the girls are, what, the holes…. And Mr. Rupert is the mind. An anxious mind, truly, see those furrows dug between his brows, even worse since Istvan came—and yet he is far more alive, now, his movements swifter, his eyes troubled and alight. Those two strike sparks from one another, anyone who looks can see that—

—though Decca is quick to deny it, quick and fierce and perhaps she, Lucy, ought not have said what she said yesterday, though everyone has a snapping point and the Lord knows Decca has trod hers times past counting. But still… She and Velma and Vera in the downstairs kitchen, sifting through the daily oatmeal for weevils, Vera complaining about the soldiers, they are too rough, too quick, not quick enough—until Decca, counting coal, flew down her throat: *You'll take what walks through the door and there's an end to it! Or try your chances on the road!* Vera crumpled into silence, Lucy flicked a weevil to the floor and, consolingly, *Oh the road's not so bad,* with an eye to Decca, *Mr. Istvan's told me all about it. May be he's on his way soon anyway, and he'll take you along if you ask him nice.*

And of course Decca swallowed the bait, hands on hips and *Shut your mouth about Mr. Istvan* which gave Lucy the chance to go on, ostensibly to Vera—*May be he'll take Mr. Rupert with him—they're thick as thieves, those two. Why, Mr. Istvan's the only one who can ever make him smile, have you noticed?—Ow!* as the iron ladle struck her shoulders, what a smart but worth it to see Decca brought low: so she knows, too. Of course, how could she not—though it seems hidden, still, from Omar and Puggy. But then, they are men, they pay attention only to what's right below their noses. "May be that's why they worry so about their pricks, eh, Miss Lucinda?" as she twirls the fascinator on her fingers, checking the spotted veiling, the pale feathers that should hang right above the lady's eye, so: just down the hall into Istvan's room, pop the hat on the puppet to check before she does the final stitching—

—but checked, herself, by voices from the Cell, Rupert's voice: "—deaf as well as heedless? I told you, come and see me."

And Istvan back, flat, no more sunny drawl: "You told me nothing of the sort."

"I told your sister to—"

"My sister is not I, perhaps you've noticed."

Your sister? Oh she should leave, she should not listen this way, what they say together is private. She takes a step back, Rupert's voice become a murmur, then "—offstage—your puppets from now on." The mecs, offstage? She steps forward again.

"What? Why?"

"Because the fucking mayor's up in arms, that's why." How hard Rupert sounds, a stranger's voice almost, it gives Lucy a chill to hear it. "Your horsemanship is not admired."

"What horsema—oh, that? That was just a little frolic—"

"Frolic enough. Leave off, I haven't come to argue—"

"Only to, what? Give orders?" They are right beside the door now, Lucy dare not move, cannot move. "Listen, Mouse, you can't be spooked, now's the time we must—"

"Must? I must keep this place intact, that's what I must do. You've no idea, you don't know—"

"Then tell me. Trust me."

"Trust you, messire?" Not loud, but a cry, one can hear the pain of it—and now the door bangs open and she is caught, pop-eyed guilty with silly hat in hand, but Rupert barely sees her, brushing past as if he flees, Istvan bow-strung tense in the doorway, he does not see her either until she moves, he blinks, then "Ah," the drawl halfway resumed, the smiling mask reaffixed. "Lucy-Belle. You startled me."

She offers up the hat. "I just meant to, to see how it sits on Miss Lucinda. I didn't mean to listen—"

"Listen?" He is barely listening himself. "Why, step in, miss, let's have a look.... We need something better than tallow," as the door swings shut behind them, "it's so dark in here today."

The crowd is mixed this evening, a decidedly segregated crush. Up front are the regulars, though thinner than most nights; the mayor is pointedly missing, and his coterie, as well as the more prominent local businessmen, publicly siding with Redgrave in the tiff. Several constables sit with this group, but whether to enjoy the show as private citizens or observe as public defenders would be hard to discern.

In back, nearer the liquor, is the military presence, not foot soldiers—though there are a few of those, their noise out of proportion to their numbers—but quieter lieutenants; Essenhigh is not among them, but men who report to him are. Omar stands watch over this crowd, Guillame beside: "Jesu," his wary murmur, "piss and gunpowder, I don't like how it smells in here tonight. Make a nice play, Puggy, eh? But keep the roof on."

"Oh, we'll be dull as ditchwater, never fear." The showman in him sighs. "It'll all be tits and spangles, the mecs are in their coffins, Istvan's out on the town tonight."

Off to one side, close to the stage but set off by a Japanese screen—fading scarlet dragons, black matchstick frame—sit Jürgen Vidor, Mr. Arrowsmith, and Rupert's empty chair. The two men are drinking wine, have been drinking for some time, a bottle each as the dinner was slow, the show delayed, why is the show delayed? "Perhaps," suggests Mr. Arrowsmith, "the marionettes are capricious. Or tangled in their strings?"

"I believe," says Jürgen Vidor, "we shall see the young ladies solo this evening." Tipping the dregs into his glass, he signals Velma for another bottle. He is resplendent tonight, slick pomade and snow-white linen, the town's last tailor worked around the clock to finish the shapely new fawnskin waistcoat that *Sir wears so well,* said the tailor, his lips thinned with pins, *Sir is quite a handsome figure, yes;* had he said "yes"? Or "yet"? Silk cravat red as the ruby in his stickpin, a griffin's glowing eye, red as the poppy-headdress worn by a drooping Jen who dangles, topless and unspinning, from her swing, as the curtains open with a sentimental etude: Jonathan's playing seems to lack a certain verve, or perhaps that is just fancy, or foreboding. Surely the girls

76

do their best, Vera and Pearl waltzing together, shedding their gowns as they go, Laddie seated at a table downstage mimicking the watchers who clap and cry out, the regulars good-humoredly, the foot soldiers with a crude impatience—"Let 'em fuck!"—that the girls, waltzing, pretend not to hear, that Jonathan tries to override with strident chords, and keep the show afloat.

Still the shouts grow louder, uglier, more confused; some of the regulars bellow back for quiet. The girls grasp one another, Laddie tips his chair as a spoon bounces off his onstage table because now they are throwing things, the soldiers: another spoon, an empty glass, a half-chewed tobacco plug, a crumpled hat catches Jennie full in the face. Omar takes a step forward, resigned to force, but Rupert quells him with an upheld palm; Rupert who has been waiting at the back of the house, smoking one cheroot from the next, one eye on the door.

Now he moves toward the loudest of the soldiers, a pair grimy and riotous, and tries courtesy first, would the two enjoy another drink? On the house? but "We came here to fuck," the shorter one grunts, while the other takes Rupert's measure with one glance—lean man in a fancy coat—then plucks a candle pot from the nearest table, and flings it flying toward the stage.

It lands far short, splashing burning tallow wax, as men leap aside cursing, glaring back to see which fool to fight, while Puggy, bald head sweating, springs to stamp out the fire. Jonathan's piano is pounding, now, the girls twirl in broken circles, ready to bolt, Laddie rises to his feet but "Not to worry!" Omar cries in a ringing, falsely hearty tone, just below the stage, truncheon loose in his belt. "Ladies, keep a-dancing!" so they do, Laddie resuming his nervous seat as Rupert escorts one of the soldiers to the door, overcome by drink perhaps or perhaps a broken neck, it is hard to be sure in the tallow dimness and at any rate his comrade is uncomplaining, draped over a bottle at the back of the house as the show reaches a hasty crescendo that concludes in a tableau, the bare girls swarming over Laddie who mimes erotic glee, but they all look so happy to be heading offstage that the effect is somewhat spoiled.

The curtains close, Jonathan falls into a moment of silence in which the mutterings are clearly heard, half the crowd cheated by the tameness of the show, the other half angry at the soldiers, and "Where's the puppets?" someone asks, loud enough to be heard by Mr. Arrowsmith, who shrugs to Jürgen Vidor, who beckons to passing Puggy wiping his head with a napkin, saying, "Your master, a moment." It is not a request.

Mr. Arrowsmith pushes back his chair, pleading an early evening: "Please tender Mr. Bok my farewells." Jonathan strikes up a merry barroom tune as Omar wades watchfully through the crowd, Rupert reentering just in time to pass Mr. Arrowsmith who pauses to shake his hand and murmur, "'Ware, messire. Your friend is on the boil tonight," as he departs.

Rupert continues to the table, rubbing his forehead, to pause without sitting, half a bow as Jürgen Vidor greets him with the bottle: "A splash of the grape, Rupert?"

"Not just yet, if you please. The floor—"

"Your men are capable, they can spare you. Please take your seat." Again it is not a request. Rupert's hands knead against the chair back, an unconscious pressure; then he pulls out the chair and sits down.

Istvan has not visited the Gaiety Theatre before, and after brief perusal does not seem to find it particularly gay: the street-corner fiddler leading a grog-shop band, the backwoods cancan onstage, where did they find these girls? On hooks in the butcher shop? The crowd is not much more inspiring, including as it does the disgruntled mayor and his maggot of an attaché, as well as a thin sampling of the town's more virtuous whoremongers, and the usual corset-sniffers and drummers passing through. Or perhaps it is Istvan's own foul mood that fouls his impressions so.

"Drink, sir?" asks the barman, a whiskey that has, like most supplies in town, been affected by the climate of shortages: it tastes vaguely like lamp-oil, whale-oil, Istvan can barely swallow it down. "Care for another, sir?"

"No."

"You've missed 'most the show," the barman shrugs, "but not to worry, they'll start up again in a tick. Freshest young ladies in town, sir, and none of them too fine not to have a nice drink afterwards with a gentleman, if you see what I mean."

"You mean they'll bend over for me?"

The barman's gaze turns opaque. "That's not what I said, sir. These young ladies are tip-top stage actresses, not sidestreet judies. You'd want to go Under the Poppy for that kind of show."

"The Poppy? These crows aren't fit to fatten the Poppy's bedbugs." Istvan thumps down the price of the whiskey as his gaze roams the room—cigar smoke and wilted green damask, the brass pots of browning ferns—searching for what? An older man, hard-faced and stoop-shouldered, catches his eye, approaches to palm the offered coin and lead the way to the stairs to the private rooms, where a coughing little maid hauls up a load of coal. Istvan helps her with the hod, dusting his hands discreetly on her skirt before he pauses at the corridor's end, three quick raps on a door opened by Colonel Essenhigh, whose distaste is intense and instant: "You. What business have you here?"

"None of yours. Step aside."

"I don't take orders from a queer-loving dollmaker. Get back down the stairs before I kick you down."

A murmur sounds from behind the colonel, laconic with command: the colonel stiffens. Istvan brushes past to make his bow—exquisite, and exquisitely polite—before General Georges, who sits at ease at a map-strewn table, jacket shed, drinking port and "Monsieur Hanzel," says the General; again that curious smile. "Well. Greetings, young man. Arrowsmith said that you were in town."

Between the corridor and the threshold Istvan's voice, his carriage, have altered, gone cool and fey, fluid as mercury on a mirror; he could be in a Paris salon, a bedchamber in Brussels, he could be playing a role. "I am that, sir. Although one can't call it much of a town."

"And you've brought your puppets along with you, *les mecs*? Amusing yourself whilst you amuse the yokels?"

"I try."

"As well as stirring the pot a bit, hmm? Adding your own seasoning to the stew."

Istvan laughs, a silvery little chuckle. "Very well said, sir. But you overrate my poor influence."

"You forget, I've seen you deployed…. Have some port," pouring for him, the little leather cup from the General's own flask, while Essenhigh stands rigid at the door, radiating disapproval until "Colonel," the General says, "step out into the hall," to stand resentful sentry to a meeting of old acquaintances, where impressions are exchanged and opinions offered—on the town, the military, the current state of the lively arts—and more drinks poured; a performance mounted and accomplished, a certain debt recalled, a local compensation proposed and accepted, to the benefit of both parties. Capping his flask, "You are a shrewd campaigner, Hanzel," says the General approvingly. "If you should ever wish to enter the military, I would gladly sponsor a commission—"

"Alas, I lack the discipline, sir."

Laddie's room is tidy and pleasant, his few clothes hung neatly on pegs, a picture on the wall, framed in blue, of a white boat a-sail on a vast and sparkling sea. Laddie himself lies stretched across the bedstead, its iron lines wrought to look like curling leaves of ivy, with his wrists strapped, eyes bound blind by a strip of yellowed cotton. Above him is Jürgen Vidor, pasty and humid and "You like this?" he asks Laddie, pin in hand, then glances back over his shoulder, to make sure that Rupert is watching, Rupert who stands silent, arms-crossed, his taut back pressed against the door. He wants to rub his forehead, to try to chase the throbbing pain; he wants to go downstairs and see what the fuck passes with the soldiers and Omar, if there is breakage, wreckage, if Puggy and Decca and the girls are faring all right. Most of all he wants to be anywhere but in this room, at this moment, watching Jürgen Vidor wield his pin.

"You like this?"

Laddie groans against the straps.

It is far after midnight now, closer to dawn; yet the night seems to have lasted forever. Where is Istvan? On the town; on the road? *Trust you, messire?* His face, then; his eyes. *He adores you.* Does he? Jürgen Vidor seems to think so, Jürgen Vidor in a frightening mood, a peculiarly ugly and avuncular mood, enthroned there at the screened-off table as if the place was his: *Your welfare is of the greatest importance to me, Rupert. This unfortunate* contretemps *with the mayor—*

A tempest in a teapot. Mr. Redgrave was badly advised.

Whatever else he may be, he is the mayor still, and holds civil authority that we must respect.

Do you respect it, Mr. Vidor?

I do not like to see you compromised.

Always with him is that odor, that sour, ether whiff; does it come somehow from the man himself, his very skin? Rupert breathes through parted lips, carefully, so as not to smell it now.

Compromised in what way?

In any way. But especially where it concerns the military. Our situation here is soon to grow acute, and I would have you on safety's side, always; you and the Poppy. But how can I promise this when your—colleague is so reckless? Hand on his forearm as rigid as wood, as one of Istvan's puppets. *The General and his men will be seeking lodging, a local headquarters. The Poppy could be that place, and how better guarded than by housing the guardians themselves? No one would trouble you then, you or your girls. And you would be more than fairly compensated, I would see to that myself.* That canine flash: his teeth are brown, like old ivory. *But in the current atmosphere, the General and the mayor would be at public loggerheads, embarrassing to both. So your puppeteer friend must first move on.*

The straps creak with strain, Laddie whimpers like a child. Blood spots the sheets. "You like this? Eh? *Eh?*" as Rupert breathes through his mouth, stares at a stain on the wall, just above the picture of the boat on the sea.

He is not—mine to direct.

Not yours? Would he say that? Those teeth again. *I think not. And Miss Decca agrees, his presence is disharmonious to the functioning of your house.* Decca? What the devil has she to do with it? or to speak with Jürgen Vidor at all? Yet troubled as she is with Istvan present, watching the both of them, feigning to want him gone, she might have said something foolish or untoward, something that Jürgen Vidor can make a weapon of, the way he does with everything, with everyone in his path—

Your house, Rupert. To do with as you decide.

—as his head turns, now, thin hair lank with pomade, gaze fixed on Rupert's as the pin digs in, saying as plain as words with both instruments *This, look at this, this is you.*

The moon is low; the Poppy is dark. A wind like a dying man's sigh rises, pauses, falls to rise again. Istvan, hatless, brandy bottle in his pocket, investigates the lobby, the hallways, the silence behind the stage: only Velma there, patient with her mop, with whom he shares a weary little nod. Upstairs there are noises, a door closing on Omar's mutter, Decca's answer; Istvan turns his back, back out into the darkness, the sorrowful moonlight more sorrowful still in the noxious little alley so close to the jakes, below his own Cell, just beside the iron fire-ladder bolted to the bricks, extending only to the second floor but he is nimble, he has done this kind of thing many many times before, hand over hand like the boy he once was—

—and his boy's instinct is correct, for there sits Rupert, shirt-sleeves and whiskey, head sunk between his shoulders like a gargoyle's on a church and "Hola, messire," Istvan calls, softly. "What do you up here so late?"

"Not a God damned thing." Rupert sounds drunk. "Want a drink?"

"I was about to take the temperance pledge, but if you insist." Istvan sits beside him on the shingles, knees up, close enough to touch. From this vantage the view covers much of the town: the newly empty buildings, the trash fires in the streets, the soldiers clustered like roaches, hiding in cracks from the cold and "One needs whiskey," Istvan breathes, after wiping his mouth, "for a sight like that. Not so very tidy, outside our little cocoon. Hey!" as Rupert's arm swings backward, flinging, what, a stone into the street, at the closest clump of soldiers who swear and scatter, fire clumsy into the darkness at an enemy they cannot see. "What you doing, Mouse? They'll plug us by sheerest luck."

Rupert laughs. "Whose luck?" He *is* drunk, that stage of drunkenness where the compass swings from calm south to stormy east in a heartbeat, a minor puff of wind. "Theirs? Or yours?"

"Ours... Jesu," tugging his coat closer. "It's arctic up here."

"Is it?" Rupert laughs again. "Have you been there, those frigid polar regions?" He takes back the bottle, drinks a punishing swallow. "Or should I ask, where have you *not* been, messire, in your long and illustrious career, with all your beloved fucking theatrical puppets?"

"I wasn't here tonight."

"No you were not. Although I looked for you." He closes his eyes. The wind tugs at his hair. "I'm always looking for you, you fox. Cur fox..."

"You're reversed, it's I who look for you. Always. Everywhere." Istvan's voice is very low now. "It's why I'm here."

"Is it? Is that why you came to our charming shithole hamlet? For me?" Due east now, his fist white around the bottle's throat. "Did you take one step out of your path for *me*, messire? Your trek across the Continent, playing for the crowned heads? Hanzel, and Dusan, and, what was the other? Marcel? The *bouffon du roi*, Marcel, yes. What other names are there, for all the things you did? Answer me!"

"Names are for armor. Or camouflage. Ask Ag." They stare at one another in the darkness, two men, two boys. Rupert raises the bottle again, Istvan takes it from him: "Wait. Listen to me—"

"No, you listen to me," but then says nothing more, eyes wide, staring at Istvan as if he has never sought another sight, as if he is blind and "I see many things, out there," Istvan says, still more softly. One hand reaches, fastening on Rupert's wrist. "One of them is war."

Rupert is trembling hard, as if from the cold; he cannot feel the cold. "What war."

"Here. They're going to make war here, they're going to burn this place to the dirt and trample the cinders without even taking notice. Because it is in the way, of Archenberg, and Gottsburgh, and all the places they mean to go. Because it is nowhere. And I want you nowhere fucking near it when that happens, you understand? I want you with me, out there—" pointing with his free hand, a gesture neither sees, they are staring into each other's eyes.

"'Out there,' how? As before? When you—"

"I want—"

"What do you want," shaking and helpless, now, as a puppet unstrung, all the old love rising up unstoppable as war, as the moon rolling cold above them, as the dawn on the cusp of that moon and Rupert says it again, he whispers, "What do you want of me," but it is not a question and there is only one answer, given mouth to mouth, breath to breath, the taste of whiskey, of brandy impossibly sweet, crushed so close that they could be one skin, one beating heart in the cold that takes no notice of them, the cold they learned so long ago to defeat by the simple strength of heat, one body to another in the all-consuming dark.

Sun in the Cell, morning's chill yellow light, Istvan wrapped in a grayish sheet, coaxing water from the ice crusted in the bedside jug. He drinks, then nudges with the cup the long body on the cot, Rupert rising on one elbow to swallow the rest. Their eyes meet, silent still with the normal enormity of intimacy so instantly resumed, as if no time at all has passed, nothing at all has changed, the two together in the piled detritus of strings and coffins and wooden eyeballs watching without comment, ready to resume the rigors of the day; even the talk resumed, last night's murmured argument, whether to stay or "Leave?" says Rupert, voice rough, his hands clasped now between his knees. The lines at his eyes have gentled, his gaze is wide open, nourished and exhausted both. "You can; no doubt you should. For many reasons. But I have—"

"People, yes, I know. Like Omar, who'd make a capital man-at-arms in any man's army, including his own. Or Jonathan, I could get Jonathan work in London tomorrow. In Brussels today! Or Lucy-Belle—"

"Or Decca. What will you do with Decca, messire? Set her up at a field hospital in this war you see coming? Put her in charge of the orphans?"

Istvan gives him a sour look, then, softened, sits beside him on the cot, brushes back Rupert's hair with one hand. "All right then, stay. We stay. The merest while."

"Stay how," not asking so much as seeking, casting a way on cloven paths, that deep-set gaze on Istvan saying *I have known you, messire, for so very long, oh how I know you*—

—as Istvan's smile in return is playful, rueful, joyful, reveling in that knowledge even as he marks its reach and "If you're going to drown," he says, "do it in deep water. So we must play our way out of this ditch, yeah?" Smiling lips against his ear, a whisper, a murmur as familiar as the mind's own voice: "Mouse. Play with me."

Rupert's eyes close, his hand goes out. "No more now. No more of this—"

"Always more. Of this. This—"

By the time Rupert steps into the hallway, loose-limbed, it is late enough that Vera and Pearl are awake and quarreling, the wet smell of oatmeal rises from the kitchen, Velma, skirts tucked close, climbs sweeping up the stairs. She sees Rupert—did she see his advent as well?—and returns his nod, stolid and friendly, is she friendly? Silent with her broom and pan, more silent somehow even than Jonathan, at least with Jonathan you can see what he is thinking, his eyes hide nothing; hers show the same. Rupert continues down the hallway, down the stairs. Vera's door slams hard, Pearl starts weeping. Velma tucks up pan and broom-handle, and rustles quietly away.

2.

It is by sheerest chance that he sees her at all, bedraggled stray peering out of her bolt-hole into the evening's air. Evicted from the tailor's backstairs lodging, the tailor's common-law wife screeching You fuck that mutt! I know you fuck that mutt! *for the fortnight past she has been biding instead in this alley, hoarding what scant coins her work has gathered, knowing they will not outlast the coming cold. She has reached a point, Agatha, Decca, where each day melts into the next, one long morning of sour hunger, one longer evening of scuffling and failure in the dark. Sing, dance, play parlor tricks in the parlor of the streets, where the passersby fling stones or ignore her, or watch for free then walk away, or watch and then suggest other tricks and dances, other modes of more personal employ; and more and more she must sink that low, her dress stained brown to the knees, coin-purse fingers pinching at the pennies they let fall. Sometimes she fears dying, there in the alley, sometimes she thinks she is dying, and will never see her brother, or Rupert, again, though she has remained in this hateful place for that sole reason, that it is the last place she saw either, that either saw her. In the cold hours she wonders if they have ever looked for her; in the coldest hours she is sure that they have not.*

But then her name, spoken in surprise: Ag? *All in black, wool cap and seaman's rucksack, she can barely believe what she is seeing, scrambling to her feet and into his arms before he can disappear, Rupert the miracle there before her in the street and* Ag, *he says again, gently setting her back an arms-length.* Jesu, don't cling so, all's well.... Are you well? *Looking at her more closely, now.* Are you hungry?

He feeds her, sausage pies and fried sugar-cakes, all she wants, and cup after cup of scalding tea; they walk together around the town square, so close to the lock-hospital that one can almost hear the shouts, then all the way to the road by the river that leads out of town, the road Rupert has just traveled coming in, coming back, why? She tries to think of how to safely broach the subject, him here alone, no

Istvan, no puppets, could any of their quarrels be so final? but in the end he simply asks, himself: Have you seen him? Is he here?

His voice so offhand, dry, his eyes so naked, twin to that other cry, Istvan's howl, Ag where is he! *but* I do not know where he is, *she says, which is partially the truth: she does not know where Istvan is now, only where he said he might be, and who is to say that he would be there still? or where he might have landed?* He took Marco, and is gone.

Rupert says nothing for a moment, a long moment. Then blackly, bleakly: And before he left—did he ask after me?

Before she speaks, she stares down at her hands, her chapped, cracked, slavey's hands, dirtied from the alley, ground-in filth beneath her nails. No. He did not.

Silence, then, as he looks away in such a way that she knows she must not speak again, the raw wound is bleeding, her own heart bleeds for him but what else can she do? One day she will explain, but now, today, this instant she is dying here, drowning in the cesspool of these streets. Together, they cannot need her; these empty years have taught her that. Apart, there is use for her, and sanctuary. And it is not as if she drives them from one another, they have done so, it seems, impossibly, themselves. Her brother will no doubt reappear someday as he always has before, in his own good time. In the meantime, she can help Rupert, be of aid to him, in ways her brother never could.

So when Rupert walks on at last, silent, she walks beside him, equally silent, together not into town but down to the quay, a shabby vessel called the Queen Maritsa *of Cathay and* Did you go to Cathay? *she asks warily, the first words spoken in an hour, dreading the bob of the boat on the water but* Not so far, *he says.* Wait here a moment, *and back in the same with a larger bag her heart sings to see, shouldering that bag as he steers her back toward town but after a few steps* You're all in, *Rupert says, with distant pity, the distance of shock, the shock of great pain, but dizzy with her own pain's relief she does not see, does not want to see, wants only to rest as he bids her, there on the quayside, tucked in a corner out of the wind, his heart against her back like the mothering sound of the sea. She sleeps then as she has not slept for ages, soundly, utterly, like an animal gone to ground at last. Holding her, Rupert does not close his eyes.*

Of where he has been, he says almost nothing: no sailor after all, and no performer, either, just "traveling," he says, and she must be content with that. Of Istvan they do not speak again, not even his name, though he is present, ghost as he is, far more thoroughly than Rupert himself, as their traveling now is less journey than mere motion, his attempt to outpace the loss, her determination to keep at his side, a shadow's shadow tending his needs, bargaining and badgering for their food and lodging, as he provides funds in other ways. Once he returns from a day's foray masked in red, fresh blood that she wipes away in silence, dressing the gash on his scalp, the hard scrapes across his cheeks; that night their pockets are full.

By the time they near Victoria, near penury again, she understands that she loves him, not only as Rupert who saved her from the alley, Rupert the Mouse she has known since her girlhood, but as a man. When he is busied with other tasks, she studies him, his face when he reads, his hands when he counts coinage or sharpens his knife: the line of his jaw, the gypsy pelt of his hair, the way he rubs his forehead when the headache comes upon him. Twice she has tried to take that office, gently stroke the pain away, but he puts her off, less kindly the second time. Other remedies she dare not offer, as she dare not offer her love for him; he will never want her that way, no. In his eyes, she is dressed in Istvan's luster, valued mainly as a reminder; this she understands as well. Some nights in the depths of her troubled dreams they meet Istvan on the road, a princely Istvan robed in gold and motley, wooden Marco his lieutenant at the head of a puppet army; or a black-clad Istvan flying fleet and secret as a cuckoo, swooping down upon them from the sky. In every dream, his eyes accuse her. From every dream, she wakes with a little cry.

Whom they meet in truth, in a buggy ale shop just outside of Archenberg, is another kind of fortune: A man short and massive as a badger, an older man called Mr. Mattison, who is searching, he says, for a temporary bravo, a man-at-arms for his fancy-house since My old fellow's gone sour with the clap, diddling too much with the fancies; he's no use to me just now. You look fierce enough, young sir, are you clean also? With your pretty young lady there at your side?

*Rupert does not even smile—*You may trust that I am clean that way, sir—*and goes to work that very evening, vetting the callers at the Rose and Poppy, as Decca installs in the kitchens of the house. If the girls there are clannish and disagreeable—and they are—still Mr. Mattison is a fair if slovenly master, both to Rupert and to herself, and, as the old bravo seems unlikely to recover, mayhap Rupert will decide that they shall stay for good. Winter has taken hold in earnest, and here is a warm place to sleep, food to eat, one could almost call it safety—*

—until the quiet afternoon that Rupert comes to the pantry-room off the kitchen where she sits scraping potatoes, to sit sideways on the

little cot and tell her that he is going, declining to say exactly where as Mattison sends you? *she asks, guessing this is not the case, certain when he does not answer.* Do you—will you—*search for Istvan, go to Istvan, ever come back? but she can never ask those questions, can only perch stiff on the stool with her paring knife as* Mattison will look after you, *Rupert says; already his gaze is distant.* I've paid up your board until spring.

And what then?

For that one moment his stare is hers, the darkness of it, the truth: that he has truly been elsewhere all along, worked only to weave her a nest and I have to go, *he says.* I have to know. *A kiss on the cheek, brief and fraternal, grip-bag in hand and he is gone, as she sits on the stool, peels curling dry at her feet, sits on the stool and stares at the knife in her hand. Late that night Mr. Mattison finds her weeping, face turned toward the wall and* Ah, *he says, stout and warm and smelling of brandy,* don't cry, child. 'Twill all resolve, you'll see. There are more things here for you to do than scour spuds, eh?

I can sing, *she sobs.* I can sing and dance, and play onstage—

Hush, *says Mr. Mattison, taking her into his badger arms.* I know you will do capital. Hush, child, you'll see.

Arthur Redgrave

To govern a municipality such as this town, sir, you got to keep an open mind. I say this often, I've always said it, and Mr. Vidor agrees. Not everything you want can always be had, and not everything you dislike can always be avoided. And everyone's his own idea of what's right and what's wrong. So truly, you got to keep an open mind.

Mr. Vidor and I see eye-to-eye on many factors, even though he's traveled a bit more of this old earth than I have, and we both understand certain things. Such as that a man wants a little bit of warmth on a cold night, a bit of drink and a bit of fluff, and what could ever be the matter with that? I am a staunch supporter of the church, of course, and of Christian morals, I seek to live them out every day of my life, as a mayor as well as a man. Did I not pay with my own funds to have the churchyard cleared and weeded, and marble stones brought in for them who wanted to purchase, and mark the resting bones of their sacred dead folks? And do I not sponsor the Little Misses' milk breakfast every Eastertide? A man has got to have a strong moral compass, or what's to become of him in the end?

So this business with the Poppy is a conundrum. This business with the horse, that is. I needn't say more about it except that it is a, a barnyard type of act, something that men ought not to watch, or not to pay to watch, at any rate.

And I will say, I am very disappointed in Mr. Bok. I have had many dealings with him previously, business dealings, that is, and he has always been a very sound fellow, a supporter of the town, kicks in his share of lucre when it's needed, keeps his house nice and quiet. I don't believe we've ever had to send the constables out there, what with Mr. Bok himself and that big Omar, they keep the peace quite sufficiently and well. Although Elwin—Mr. Franz, that is, he's my deputy-mayor— Mr. Franz says that Omar was a tick hasty with his fists the other day, when he came to call. And on official business, too.

What we'll do about it next, the horse business and all, I'm not yet sure. In Elwin's opinion—well, he is a bit disputatious on the issue, he feels the whole place ought to be shut right down, and its trade split up three ways, with Miss Suzette, Angus, and the Gaiety, and mayhap a donation to the coffers from them who are pleased by the split. Which is a nice touch—Elwin tries to think in the town's best interests, always.

Mr. Vidor has a different idea. His thinking is it's not Mr. Bok at all behind this behavior, but that vagabond from France, that long-haired popinjay who brought his dolls and his vices to town, and that if we drive that one out, the Poppy will be right as rain again. I lean somewhat toward this view myself. Although I did like some of the new playlets, I must admit. The little troll-type puppet, singing his songs— why, I laughed fit to split. One knows it isn't real, that funny ugly little man, but when he starts humping at Vera, you feel the tickle anyway! And singing at the same time, pert as a jaybird—

Well, as I say, it is a conundrum. And the army being here as well makes things much more difficult, and it all moves along quicker, too. From what the colonel tells me—he's quite a good fellow, that Colonel Essenhigh, likes his gin and faro, and a bit of fluff like any man does, in fact Angus says that his girls are quite taken with ... Well, as I say, the colonel tells me that the army's on the march now, up there in the hills, and we'll have to bolt the shutters sharpish. He's even brought that General Georges to town, to lend some aid. Now *there's* a gentleman I'm not sure of, that general. Shakes your hand and speaks squarely, but you're never quite certain what he's said when he's finished. Just like that Mr. Arrowsmith, cut from the same bolt, those two. All smiles and courtesies, but when they walk away what have you got in your hand?

And now I'm hearing from Faulk, over at Miss Suzette's, that they're thinking of closing up shop altogether, moving the young ladies up to Archenberg or even Victoria, to keep them out of harm's way. Miss Suzette is very poorly, she never did get over that scarlatina she had so long ago: it sapped her heart, Faulk tells me, and she is not a young lady any more. So if they go, that leaves us Angus and the Alley for all those soldiers. And the Gaiety, although that crowd fancies itself real players, you've got to cuddle and cozy up the girls to get them to do anything, buy champagne and whatnots, and no soldier's going to do that, not in the midst of a war! There'll be no champagne to buy at any rate, already it's getting difficult to bring in certain foodstuffs, this winter's going to be a rouser. And if we can't get liquor, or enough coal... My uncle Arthur, who I'm named for, why, he was caught in a siege years and years ago, and according to him things went dire fairly swiftly, they were burning up the floor planks, and eating the wallpaper for the horsehair glue. Awful, what people get down to when they're hungry. And the hungrier they are, the worse they act.

So I've much to think of, these days, much to keep on my mind.

And even though Mr. Vidor's urging me to act strong and swift with that Frenchman—and even though Mr. Vidor's been more than generous with the town, spending as freely as he does—his bill at the livery, it's a wonder. And what he spends at the hotel!—even so, I want to make no kind of move I'll be regretful for later. Because after the soldiers have passed through, and the colonel and the general, and even Mr. Vidor—who's from France himself, I always thought, or Belgium, one of those Continental places—when they are all gone, there will still be the townsfolk here, and myself, and Mr. Bok and the Poppy, why that building's been here long as the town, almost, since the days of old Mattison, now *there* was a fine gentleman, he and I used to play whist together.... And we will all of us need to pick up what pieces we find, and put the town to rights again, and move on. So that is why I am keeping an open mind.

"It would be good to have a fire, here, even just a grate and three coals, anything to keep the stiffness from his fingers. Carving is a devil of a business, one slip and the whole head is ruined.... Swearing softly and happily, Istvan repositions himself beneath the ceiling's straying light, planing knife nimble in his hand, sculpting a new puppet, a kind of toby-dog to pop up and bark when required. When the knock comes, he whisks the head under covers, but "Ah, Lucy-Belle," as Lucy slips inside, still cloaked against the cold. "My good angel, tell me you have what I'm needing.—Oh capital, darling," unfolding the paper parcel, coiled wire and tiny shiny beads. "Do I ask how you managed, or just offer my endless gratitude?"

x"It's bad out there," says Lucy soberly, stripping the holey gloves from her fingers, two pair for each hand, contrasting holes mated to keep as much skin covered as can be. "I had to go 'most to Archenberg for the beads, the milliner's sister's place. And the Palais is closing up in earnest, I saw that turd Faulk bundling mattresses onto a cart. Josey—one of the girls there, she's my friend from before—Josey says the soldiers are taking over their building, to use it as a house-in-town. I saw two of them pissing in a corner of the yard, so may be it's true."

"Really," Istvan's musing frown, threading a bead on the wire. "We should offer the brave boys a citizens' discount.... Say what you think of this, now," peeling back the coverlet to show the face-in-progress, as Lucy settles on the bed to see, companionably close but dreaming no more of growing closer; those first fantasies of arnica and romance superceded not only by apprenticeship but observation, Istvan and Mr. Rupert, and of course the open secret of their new pleasure has permeated the house; impossible to hide a thing like that, with Mr. Rupert glowing like a boy. Although Lucy has kept prudent on the subject, not taunting Decca though she longs to, Decca who feigns an ignorance so all-encompassing and black that to speak of it at all would invite apocalypse so "Have you a name for him?" Lucy asks, fingering the puppet's forming face, wishing she knew the way to draw a soul from a stick of wood, and bad wood, too, half of what they have is barely fit to burn. May be it is like music, how Jonathan can coax a pretty tune from anything, a pair of spoons, or Pearl's rusty old pennywhistle, like music too in that the hands' skills come only with practice and more practice. Such strong hands, and supple—and she sighs a little, gives the puppet back to Istvan as "Vanities," he says, "idols, some church folk call them, they think our small friends here are vessels for wayward souls, or homes for demons." He smiles gently. "I shall call him the Erl-King, what do you think? And the new show—not a word to Puggy yet, mind—is to be called 'The Knave of Hearts.'"

Lucy gathers her gloves and cloak. "Will Pan Loudermilk be in it?"

From the coffin closest to the door comes a rustling, chuckling, muttering noise, as if someone is knocking, greedy and keen and "Hard to keep him out," says Istvan, with a tender wink. "Or in... If our master's about in the hallways, darling, will you tell him that I want him?"

Lucy gives him back the wink. "The whole world knows you want him. If I see him, I shall say."

The whole world? Well, he thinks, as she slips from the room, let them know, if only some are kept in darkness, darkness is the watchword just now as the performance comes to term. Lucy is in charge of the girls, trustworthy Lucy the godsend to take Puggy's place, Puggy who has been tasked only with talking up the show while concealing its content—

How can I tell what you've not told me? Jesu! Why not tie the fucking blindfold and be done!

Mystery makes the best drummer, Istvan soothes, and it is true that Puggy has drummed up a mighty interest, not coincidentally amongst those who will be sure to take the Poppy's side, the long-time tricks and supporters, as well as several in the hotel whom Istvan has himself informed. Omar has been advised that he must be on the muscle and ready for anything, if he feels he need hire a bravo or two then he must do that without delay. For his part, Jonathan works to score the evening, a dark and tinkling tune suitable for Messalina's music box, perhaps, or Lilith's panpipes in the dark of the garden.

As for Rupert, ah, his Mouse has been in the thick from the start, just as he used to be, everything but take to the stage himself: suggesting, correcting, defining, even scribbling a line here and there: *We will spin them one story whilst they watch another, and let them parse it out for themselves. Are you up for a tumble, messire?*

Are you? Jesting, teasing, light at heart enough to leap to the roof and touch the stars, oh this time they shall revel, whip up the yokels while they put that old masher on stiff notice.... The knife pares patient at the wood, the nascent lines of the face that is mostly mouth, mainly hunger, this other knave of hearts scraped and whittled and back into the sack until he will be ready for the light.

All week, the town has heard from the hills the growing mutter of the guns. The stream of departing citizens has swelled, then slowed, the remainder having chosen apparently to wait out the storm, at least while conditions are bearable, in the hectic air of making do: Water the tea, use ash to wash the spoons, stash every stub and penny, bear grease will do for pork fat in a pinch. The livery is still open, the train still runs, even the Gaiety still plays although on a somewhat reduced schedule; the champagne at last has run dry. The Palais sits abandoned, unchosen after all as the soldiers' garrison, inhabited only by twos and threes as a parlor for the Alley whores, whose population has fared hardest, being used and used and used to death.

At the hotel, amenities are scarcer, tempers shorter, the cuisine noticeably more tedious, the same dishes reappearing three nights out of five. As the mayor collects his evening's guests for the show at the Poppy, unattended this night by Mr. Franz, he must dodge a fracas in the very lobby, apologizing to the trio he leads: "Gentlemen, this town is chasing its own tail. And 'twill be darker before the dawn, won't it, General?" as that worthy nods, stern and gracious in his fresh-pressed uniform, the last of the laundry's starch; but not more gracious than the mayor himself, burying the hatchet in the company of not only the General but Mr. Arrowsmith and Jürgen Vidor, all four up front and center as Decca, white-faced in black velvet, her very best dress, herself serves them pheasant and baked hen, the best cullings of the wine, after this they will be reduced to gin and raw whiskey, the first of the worst shortages but one would never know that from her welcome, making a point to press the mayor's hand as "We are so very pleased and honored that you have chosen to be here tonight," she says, as Jürgen Vidor lifts his glass: "To *rapprochement*, gentlemen," including in his toast the General, who returns his nod in a friendly fashion; Jürgen Vidor, it has been noted, has left his bodyguard behind once more, unneeded at the Poppy, a neutral state of *cordon sanitaire*.

Safe himself behind the curtains, Puggy watches the byplay, Puggy in the know at last and a little whey-faced himself: "I thought you said," to Lucy, trussed tonight in feathers and beads, "that that old cunt Vidor was down on the mecs?"

"Istvan says so, yes."

"And we're getting our scratch from him?"

"You'd know more of that than me."

"So why in the fuck are we flouting him? And the mayor, too?"

Dabbing at his neck, he is sweating already. "Is Mr. Rupert going soft in the head as he grows harder in the prick? Why don't we just burn down the building and be done with it? and kick ourselves in the bollocks whilst we—"

"Guillame," says a voice in his ear, a whispering, chuckling, insinuating voice that frights him forward half a foot, Pan Loudermilk's voice and Istvan's merry gaze behind it, done up like a parson in pious black, white plague mask and roundhead hat and "O ye of little faith," he says to Puggy, "must I sic the Bishop on you? Mr. Rupert is a certified genius, trust him if you trust nothing else.... Have you our maestro's cue?" to start the introduction, Jonathan Chopin to play a sweet étude as the plates are gathered and cigars ignited, the General smoking thin Indian cheroots like Rupert's; where is Rupert? His chair is empty, as all notice but none remark.

It is not until the prelude floats into its last glissando that he appears from backstage, swift and dark and flawless, signet ring winking in the tallow light, to take his seat between the mayor and Jürgen Vidor, who immediately makes some trivial remark, mere pretext to lean closer, that Rupert answers with a noncommittal nod, turning then a grave and courteous smile to the mayor, who replies with one as friendly: "I'm surely looking forward to your young ladies tonight, sir."

"I greatly hope the performance will please you," as Jonathan's piano takes up an eerie, chiming waltz, Laddie wandering onstage alone, his dark suit and bright linen twin to Rupert's, his hair brushed back to resemble the same. Mr. Arrowsmith and the General exchange a look. Rupert's gaze is straight at the stage, self-possessed, perfectly at ease. Jürgen Vidor's hand opens and closes gently on his knee.

"What price love," says Laddie, half speech, half song; he does not have a voice for singing but can place the words as an actor does, giving them weight, aiming them into the darkness before him as from behind him Pearl appears, ethereal in pale gauze that barely shields her nakedness, hair loose down her back like an angel's: but no angel ever twined so naughtily about a mortal man as she does Laddie, nor pressed angelic lips so close to skin and flesh.

"What price bliss?" asks Laddie, louder, and here comes Vera, bare legs and dark lace, she makes a swooning face as she wraps her arms around Laddie from behind, while aiming a sly ankle at her rival in gauze, a martial gesture that tweaks a laugh from the audience: it is a full house tonight, expectant but unsure. Soldiers line the wall by the doors, but as yet have been quiet, or quiet enough. Omar watches them, flanked by perspiring Puggy and a likely boy from town, all of them armed: Omar with his truncheon and a knife inside his vest, the boy with a stout stick of hickory that can break a bone if used correctly, Puggy with a tiny nickel-plated revolver with two bullets that is mostly for show. Even Velma is armed, with an iron meat-fork abstracted from the kitchen, though just now she is busy with the slops. Decca stands straight as a ramrod, arms folded, as if she herself is a weapon ready to be used. Last night she hardly slept, her eyes are dry and tireless. She watches Rupert; she watches the stage; she watches for Istvan, whose feline high spirits have disturbed her all week: *When do you go?* she asks him again and again. *It is dangerous here for you, can you not understand?*

It is dangerous everywhere, his smiling shrug. *There's a war on, yeah? Stop fretting, we know what we're about.*

"We"?

All of us. Jesu, stop.

Now the girls turn their attentions to each other, dark and light in a tight embrace, as Laddie advances to the lip of the stage, to address the audience directly: "What price would you pay? For a saucy kiss?" but before anyone can answer, to heckle or support, a lean figure glides forward—parson's black, plague mask—bearing before it the grinning form of Pan Loudermilk, newly spiffed in cravat and top hat, savior and demon, knave of hearts and "Gentlemen!" it, he, cries, to the scattered burst of welcoming applause, "won't you give ear to my little song?" as Jonathan's waltz sprints into a barrelhouse scherzo, and the taunting tenor rises in the dark:

"A gentleman needs a bit of fun (A bit of fun! A bit of fun!)

For he works all day from sun to sun (He works so hard, he needs his fun!)

So when the time comes for to play (Let the gentleman have his say!)

He needs a taste of fluff afore he's done!"

It is extraordinary, but two voices come in rapid counterpoint from the little man, the higher melody, the deeper parenthetical growl, as if the brain speaks its rational mind while the body replies in a voice overriding all morals or conscience, the irresistible voice of the blood. At the center table, Jürgen Vidor, silent, grips his glass. The General smiles at Mr. Arrowsmith, who nods in connoisseur's agreement. Rupert, absolutely calm, leans to murmur one soft word into the frowning mayor's ear.

Now a lamp flickers at stage right: Lucy, bewigged in red, bangled and feathered, Miss Lucinda in blue and gaping bodice linked elbow-to-elbow like a special chum, standing over Jennie arrayed topless on the chaise, as Laddie, Everyman now, canters over to mime greeting, to shed his topcoat, to climb willingly aboard the pliant Jennie, her half-mast eyeballs spinning with dope though only those onstage can see. The audience claps in time, now, to his thrusts timed to the song itself, as the verse repeats—"A bit of fun, a bit of fun"—and Pan Loudermilk seems to lean forward on his own, independent of his anonymous handler, to meet with his carved and gleaming eyeballs the heating gaze of every man in the house:

"But who's to say what fun is had? (Such special fun! This lovely one!)
Can anything so sweet be bad? (She's slippery-tight! It feels just right! I could go on like this all night!)
O Missus may frown, but when Mister's in town (here at this house of greatest renown)
He aims to frolic randy as a tip-top lad!"

Laddie pounds away at lolling Jennie while Lucy, leading Miss Lucinda, beckons the other girls to the opposite side of the stage, her gestures broad and comically vulgar, if Laddie is Everyman, she is Every Madam. Now the mayor's chuckle, nodding in time to the music, the General and Mr. Arrowsmith, too; even the soldiers are laughing as they advance, not as members of the army but as men wanting to see, to get close to those two bare girls squirming away, busy with each other until Laddie, beaming, gains his feet again, steps away from the chaise to be claimed by the eager pair, red lips and rouged tits, he is fairly overrun.

And Pan Loudermilk, avatar, accomplice, grins upon them all, the girls, the soldiers, the ones up front in the place of honor, men of business and repute who nevertheless like their bit of fun, too, his wicked, glinting gaze seems to say, to know, it is amazing how alive he is though he, it, is only a chunk of wood manipulated by a man, a chunk of wood that nevertheless seems to see straight into one's mind, heart, soul, prick stirring in the trousers, a master of revels who revels in license, whose mocking voice soars in tandem with Jonathan's drummed finale:

"So let us each to each incline (A bit of fun! Tonight for one!)
What's yours is yours and mine is mine (Although our tastes may yet entwine)

A bit of pink, a touch of stink (and wash your prick, sir, in the
sink)
And trust the Poppy's flowers to be kind!—Now get in line!"

—this last command delivered as if spontaneously to the soldiers
swarming as though they may try to gain the stage, passions aroused,
the line between lust and frustration a thin one: yet because they are
admonished not by a man but a toy they can laugh, and in that laughter
is time enough for the curtains to safely close. The effect is perfect, and
perfectly timed, and given a last fillip by Rupert's rising to his feet to
announce "First toss half-price for the military!" that brings a gleeful
shout in return: they are docile, now, ready as children to receive their
treat.

And resuming his seat, Rupert turns in that same motion to the
mayor, one arm on the back of his chair and "Of course you follow my
reasoning to restore," Rupert says, serious and leading, under cover of
the noise. "Do I now have your assent as well?"

"To have 'em back? The puppets, you mean?" Already the mayor
is nodding, ready to be given words to frame the thoughts he thinks he
has, the rationale so "I believed from the start that you would agree,"
says Rupert. "It's why I asked your forbearance, to see the playlet fully
to its end. To say the truth, sir, I feared that the total absence of those
toys would lead to a different kind of trouble—you heard that applause!
But your own, how shall I say it, difficulties with the other—"

"'Twasn't me so much, you know, as Mr. Franz. He's young still,
young and hot-headed, he's—"

"This time we sought to keep the focus on the young ladies particularly, I think our Pearl did particularly well, don't you?"

"Oh, Pearl was capital!" as Rupert tips the whiskey to the mayor's
glass, none for himself tonight as Jürgen Vidor marks, Jürgen Vidor
who, after the puppet's first appearance, watched nothing but Rupert:
his faint smile, his absorption, his attention to the plague-masked figure's every move, the glance they seemed to share as the curtains
met.... Jürgen Vidor drains the dregs of his wine, reaches for the gin,
juniper reek as the General nods briefly in his direction, meaning
what? These soldiers with their hierarchy, their unthinking habit of
command—

—and "Mr. Bok," the General genial. "May I borrow his ear a
moment, Mr. Redgrave?"

"Why certainly," as Pearl, beckoned by Rupert, emerges to stop
by the mayor's side, damp gauze exchanged for pale muslin that hides
little more, the mayor rising, beaming, as Rupert pushes back his

chair to follow the General but "When you have finished with General Georges," says Jürgen Vidor, in an odd and arid tone, "I would converse with you, Rupert."

Rupert meets his eyes straight on. "Of course, Mr. Vidor."

Jonathan's piano dances into life, a jaunty jangly tune to drive the shared air of hilarity, of an unnamed crisis averted safely for now. Gin flows like water, whiskey like the wine unmissed. The line for the girls is expansive, the men joking as they wait of the cackling puppet, the ribald song: "A bit of fun! A bit of fun!" Omar, truncheon back in his belt, joshes the would-be bravo boy, who has been visibly affected by the antics of the girls. Puggy hustles backstage as Istvan emerges unmasked, his gaze at once seeking Rupert who moves toward the door beside the General; as if the gaze is a touch, Rupert turns to look, to smile at Istvan who smiles at him, extravagant, exultant, neither marking Jürgen Vidor who watches them both.

Mr. Arrowsmith has been watching as well; now he lifts his whiskey glass: "To amicable relations. To the just rewards of commerce, sanely conducted…. You are shrewd, Mr. Vidor, to give the mayor room enough to turn around."

"The mayor's wits could turn safely in a thimble, Arrowsmith. Let us offer one another the courtesy of truth, shall we?"

Mr. Arrowsmith pauses; he sets down his drink. "Georges' presence tonight has calmed the waters considerably—and it's rumored that he will quarter here. In truth, is that your doing?" Jürgen Vidor stares at him, but does not reply.

When Rupert returns, alone, Mr. Arrowsmith has gone. Jürgen Vidor splashes his glass again with gin. "Sit down." Music swirls around them, voices, smoke. "That performance—I thought I had made my wishes plain, Rupert."

Carefully, Rupert takes his own glass, pours a finger of whiskey, drinks. "'Your house. To do with as you decide.' And it seems it was a prudent decision, since the mayor's more than placated—"

"*Yours*, yes. Mayhap you have evolved past my patronage." The gin is gone. "I can always disburse my funds elsewhere, you know."

"Certainly you may." The man's stare is locked to his, disturbingly familiar, like being handled in an intimate place; still Rupert will not look away. Disburse the funds elsewhere, yes, old masher, old monster, go ahead. An orphan learns early what it is to be without, to own nothing but hunger and sweat; but there is more at stake here than mere money, far more, and far more dangerous. Still he pushes back, carefully, inexorably. "Your aid is yours to offer as you will, to whomever you will, though we shall always be grateful for your past generosity."

"We? Meaning Miss Decca and yourself?"

"Who else?"

Silence. Jürgen Visor's cheeks are mottled, a measled flush. "What did Georges want of you?"

Rupert seems to weigh whether he will answer, or answering, tell the truth. Finally "He seeks to quarter himself here," he says. "With some of his men."

"And you agreed?"

Whether Rupert would have answered once more, or not, told the truth or not, becomes moot as Istvan, crossing the floor, pauses smiling at their table, standing very close behind Rupert, like a man-at-arms, a lover, a familiar, neither deliberate nor wise. "A very good evening, gentlemen," he says, with a flourish of a bow. "I trust you enjoyed the show?"

Jürgen Vidor looks at him, looks him up and down and "Felicitations," he says. "Your wooden wonder was a wonder to behold." His own smile stretches, shows itself as false, means to show it. "How exceedingly—boyish one becomes, with such a plaything in hand."

"Many thanks," says Istvan; the pulse is beating in his throat. Rupert has gone very still. "I do seek to please."

"No doubt why you tarry: the Poppy is a haven of pleasures. Is it not, Rupert?" A precipice pause, his smile becomes a crocodile's, one finger leveled to point—"I'll have your boy"—past Istvan, to Laddie quick and graceful, heading toward the bar. "And a better drink than this filthy bootblack's gin. If you *please*."

Istvan can feel it, Rupert's anger coiled in his stillness, feel it when he pauses for a steadying breath and "I have some brandy that I will gladly share," Rupert says, "it shall be brought to you directly. But Vladimir—Dr. Adderley has forbade him, just now, to receive. You must choose another."

A moment's long silence, very long, Istvan's hand drops discreetly to his side, nearer his pocket and the gutting knife until "That one," Jürgen Vidor pointing this time at Jennie, oblivious and drifting, breasts bobbing loose in her chemise. "Send her up with the bottle. Alone." With the barest bow, barely civil, he leaves the table, leaves Istvan to let out a hiss and "'Only the devil hears wishes,'" as his hand rises to Rupert's shoulder, a claiming pressure. "Don't you be alone with him tonight.... Is that true, about Laddie?"

"It was." Rupert frowns, lines deep in his forehead, as he beckons briefly to Jennie. "Jesu. She's barely awake, and not at all to his taste, but still. I'd rather he have none of them."

"I'd rather someone shoot him in the fucking face.—Oh thank you kindly," as a passerby thumps his shoulder—"Damned good show, sir!

A bit of fun, eh?"—and hands him a shot of gin that he downs at once, a little smile growing, irrepressible, as he turns again to Rupert: "You liked the show? We did well together, yeah?"

"Very well."

"Just like before, yeah?"

"Yes." Rupert's smile is slower, but sweet to Istvan when it comes, as he rises from the chair to stand face-to-face, Istvan's gaze a boy's when he murmurs as sweetly, "Shall I come to you? Later on?"

Madness even to go near him, with Vidor there in the house—but Rupert's look in return is one of helpless heat, and cherishing, calamity and love: what Jonathan calls the kismet. *If you're going to drown, do it in deep water,* yes, deeper even than the sea. "When I can, I'll come to you. Wait for me."

Unseen by either, unnoticed all night, Decca watches from beside the bar, her face as white as the plague mask, her hands hidden like foundlings in the black folds of her skirt. Her thoughts are of fire.

The acquisition of a new familiar must not be done in haste. First was mourning for the lost, disjointed Marco, irreparably cracked by the burghers' sons, singed by some unknown heat, his coffin-box scorched too and Jesu, Istvan fuming, up to his wrists in wood shavings and sticky gut, why not just throw it all up and make my way as a broadsman, yeah? I've fingers quick enough for any cards. Or as a God damned highwayman, just take what I want, and miss all this, this—

Have some brandy, bébé, soothingly from the goddess on the chaise, a slightly raddled goddess, true, but with her bluebell eyes and curls deluxe, aided only a little by the dye-pot, Lucienne is a comely vision still, and still much in demand on the avenues, especially by those who prefer their ladies plush. Istvan does not, prefers nothing at all these days, these nights, these many many months since, bereft, he packed his kit and left his sister to await an advent that he now knows will never come; never. Waiting at the window like Ag used to do, like an urchin, a fool, a baby crying for the moon, for Mouse who has taken his impossible wants and unfathomable rules and has gone. Gone away. As if he had never been.

But that last is not so, Istvan knows, can feel with every furious morning, every endless drunken afternoon, like a sea with no shore that no vessel can navigate, waking always back in port, the journey again unmade. Nights he is reckless and rude, even to his patrons, especially to his patrons, those lordly men and wetly smiling women who engage him for the entertainment he provides, the theatre, the drama, and not all upon the makeshift boards he fashions from whatever drawing room he finds himself; sometimes it takes place on the cobbles, sometimes in the beds, sometimes on the marble sills where panting aldermen wheeze for him to hurry, hurry, catching at his hair, a souvenir of passion, as he goes. Sometimes the aldermen's wives enclose flowers with their billet-doux, rosemary for remembrance, blue violet for constancy, yellow tulips for hopeless love: what a joke! as he flings the litter on the floor, sifted first for the cash barely tallied before it is spent. Never has he made more lucre, nor ever will, yet never feels it earned or even honestly stolen: instead it falls

102

on him like a grimy rain, barely noted; he is a ghost, playing behind glass for lesser ghosts barely glimpsed. Only Mouse is real, has ever been, through all the cold boyhood nights, the young men's journeys, the play upon play upon play; and Mouse is gone.

But life, like the theatre, plays nightly. So: Dressing like a marquis, drinking like a disappointed king, he plays, with a sneer so close to the surface that only those who strive to cannot see it. Some enjoy it for what it is; some enjoy a private sneer in return, O mark the airs of this gutter-bred *artiste*, with his gift for mimicry, for venery, for mockery and mingled voices! Very well, let him play. But he had best enjoy his vogue now, before some irritated man-at-arms or spouse in red flagrante brings a close to his fantastical run.

In the end it is Lucienne who saves him, gives him a place to cool his spite, ease if not end his pain. He is not in love with her, will never, he knows, be in love again, who the fuck would choose to? when it ends like this? Every dark man he sees, every baritone whisper... He aches from aching, lies exhausted from his inexhaustible rage.

But if one is to live at all, in the end one must do something to make the time pass. In his puppets—wounded Marco, the tattered, stately La Duchessa, the grinning unnamed baby who can both shit and cry—Istvan finds the only respite possible: the calm of creation, the maker's ease, refining their garments, their accoutrements, their simplicity of operation; he can (and does) sit by the hour, two, four, an entire evening given to the motion of an arm, a fluttering finger behind a fluttering fan, the way an eyeball rolls in its socket, smoothly, so one sees not the gesture but the impulse behind it. He refines his skills, he suffers his mistakes to make them better. He is learning, with the mecs as his pupils and pedagogues both.

Which is why the demise of Marco twists the knife more deeply in the wound. Repaired a dozen times since the foul attack, he breaks again, and again, once even in performance, calling forth the kind of laughter no performer ever wants to hear: the illusion suspended, the actor cracked onstage. The singeing and burning (and how the fuck did that happen? when he is so careful to lie down nowhere near fire?) has compounded the frailty of this faithful toy and avatar, and the grievous day comes when, the past night's performance as near disaster as he can bear again to come, Istvan, who now is Dusan, tells himself the truth of what lies in his hands: Marco cannot be fixed, to play again as he was. Marco is gone.

This second bereavement brings back the fury of the first, though more brokenly; even for a young man, he is weary, Istvan-Dusan, these terrible months have burned him out like a rocket in the black *night's sky. Which is why, perhaps, it is possible for Lucienne, who finds him owl-eyed drunk in the Place d'Armes, yelling at the disinterested constables, to gather him up like any other stray, and take him home, to her bosom and her bed.*

She is wise in the ways of strays, she does not nurse him so much as let him nurse himself, come back to himself in this place of safety, where he may bring all his traps and smelly glues and strange small weapons, knives and tools, and tussle and curse the exigencies of his trade, declare a funeral for Marco one day then change his mind the next, sorting for the thousandth time through the pieces until finally, carefully, Lucienne asks Can you not salvage a portion of that one puppet, say, whatever portions may serve?

To serve what fucking purpose, Madame?

To build another.

His howl—I am not a God damned cannibal!—*but she has cannily planted the seed, the idea that there can be life in the ruins. And sure enough, he begins to collect what he needs, the wood and the wires, the scraps of silk and leather, the pointy white pebbles that Lucienne dislikes to see, why she cannot say, but* They are his teeth, madame, *says Dusan, his own teeth white in a sardonic smile.* Wooden or not, he needs to eat, yeah? To bite?

As Dusan's work overtakes him, she sees more of him, and also much less: present he may be, fingers in the glue, but absorbed in his toil he ignores the world, accepts no invitations, forgets to sleep, or take nourishment above a glass of tea—

Pea soup, just a cup, bébé, you'll be ill if you don't.

Stop mothering me, Madame.

—and certainly to feed his passion, at least with her: though she has glimpsed a boy or two outside their lodgings of a morning, when she returns from her own assignations, tall dark surly-looking boys who slouch away when she calls to them; Dusan's attempt at another sort of puppet, to assemble from what is at hand what is not.

He is far more successful with his new toy, though this one, this Pan Loudermilk, bears a weight the fallen Marco never did, serving as it, he, does as the hiding-cask of Dusan's heart. More accomplice than mere tool, as the entertainments Dusan devises grow from lusty slapstick and of-the-moment japes to hot little, cold little, morality plays, far more intricate, far more arousing—and disturbing, too, as this Pan seems to honor no limits, to see with his bright blue gaze whatever secrets one would most keep hidden, and to toy, yes, with exposure, as his high, fierce, insinuating voice seems always to hover on the brink of a raptor's cry, and Dusan his falconer equally feral, though his morning coats now cost a fortune and the lover's eye he wears could purchase a small chateau—this last a gift from a patron, a blue-eyed marchioness with a taste for peculiar amusements, in whose succession of country houses Pan Loudermilk is a rousing succès de scandale. Sometimes, in those drawing rooms, Pan's master is Dusan, sometimes Hanzel or Marcel, always with a tale to tell of his one true name, hidden like Rumpelstiltskin's, as he spins the endless straw of his loneliness to gold.

*He uses as well the other puppets, La Duchessa and the awful baby, and putters about with a mournful death's head that one day will be known as the Bishop. The Chevalier he takes almost whole (though headless and without his most distinguishing member) from the workshop of a man Lucienne has introduced to him, a distinguished patron of hers called Laurent—*He has all sorts of dollies, bébé, you must come and see*—who, she tells Dusan in a whisper, has taken a real interest, might even make a protégé of him* If you are only courteous, *she pleads.* You can be so sweet, when you choose to.

His smile to her then is courteous indeed, but remote; the farther away he moves from her, into the mysterious landscape of his labor, the kinder he becomes, as if he has transferred all the truths of his heart to the puppet in its black-masked coffin, and need no longer show her what he truly thinks or feels.

*What Laurent feels, when his large soldier-puppet is abstracted, can be inferred, while Lucienne's wrath at Dusan's larceny is heard all the way from the carriage-house where she struggles, restrained by the sniggering footmen—*You let me take the lash for you, you little shit! You bastard!*—to the gardens where the marchioness and her guests, Dusan among them, sip their black-currant cordials, the marchioness coquettish to scold:* What naughty fix have you 'scaped, Marcel? Tell us true, now!

It is true that I am a bastard, *Marcel, Dusan, Istvan says musingly.* Born to a poor lass seduced by the silver moonlight, born on St. John's Eve. You know about St. John's Eve, my lady? The equinox balance, when the powers of light and darkness hold equal sway?

They certainly do in you, says the marchioness with feeling. Her husband laughs softly. Dusan never sees Lucienne again.

This night be premieres a new playlet, Castor & Pollux, *after the Gemini sons of Leda, brothers from myth, wherein he and his new familiar, himself named from myth, enact a fraternal union of a different sort, with La Duchessa its springboard and a giggling cousin of the marchioness its foil. If few in the audience take to heart the deeper import of the piece—a defiant affirmation of affinity deeper than blood, harder than lust, stronger than any method meant to part it, sung in eerie twain to the tune of Dusan's feet beating time on the drawing room's rosewood floor—*

We are two, we need none other
Cloven not by wife or mother
Even a mistress cannot twist us
We'll just share, like goodly brothers!

—the rest are amply titillated by its lithe, if louche, athletics, not least the giggling cousin of the marchioness, who for not a little time afterward pursues the traveling pair through various drawing rooms, until her mamma, mortified, bundles her off to a boarding-convent in Switzerland, where she relearns virtue, but never forgets her little romp with the wooden man.

This performance becomes a signature piece for Marcel, Dusan, Istvan, one he refines as circumstances suggest: sometimes the wife makes an appearance, sometimes the chastising mother, always the shared mistress; occasionally there is improvised dialogue between the "brothers"; at times the song has musical accompaniment—piano preferred, though strings will do—counterpointed by a satisfied gobble; but always it ends with Istvan kissing his fist to the audience, his gaze aimed far above its head, whether a hundred are watching or only one. There is some speculation amongst his more thoughtful patrons over what that gaze, that gesture may imply, and for whom it might be meant, but no meaningful consensus is achieved, and none seem to want to ask the young maestro directly; he smiles, always, but the smile never seems to reach his eyes, even in the most intimate of moments.

This, too, is discussed by his patrons: There is something of the frost about that Hanzel, *opines one of the Misses van Symans, the elder one, who wears the family rings, the mantle of worldly wisdom.* Very charming he may be, but I should not like to find myself on his dark side.

He has a secret sorrow in his heart, *asserts the other, younger Miss van Symans, who considers herself a truer judge of character, at least the character of young men. Her father's friend, visiting from London, or is it Paris? shakes his head gently and smiles:* Ah, the tender-minded ladies! *as he taps his silver ring—worn on the thumb, a curious affectation—against the sloping side of his glass of port.*

If someone had known to ask the former Agatha, now Miss Decca of the Rose and Poppy, she might have been able to place the gesture's origin, but even if asked she may not have spared the time to reply: she is very busy these days, so busy that she hardly sleeps, puts head to pillow to lie awake, wondering, worrying: Is the roof leak in the parlor turning dire? Is Pamela, that whiny drab, truly down with the ague, or merely shamming? Will the coal man deal fairly with her, a woman alone? To whom can she turn for help?—though she knows without asking this last answer: no one. There is no one to help her, advise her, protect her, no one at all now that Mattison is dying.

For some time now she has been mistress of the house in all but name, her role expanding as Mattison's illness—consumption? no, for he does not pale or cough; it is some other strange and wasting scourge that takes his strength, that melts his flesh—advances inexorably apace. Nearly two years have passed since her coming—odd to think so, each day so like the next they could all be one round of decision and toil. But she has learned a great deal in that time, from him who was her teacher, is now her patient and charge; he has changed the course of her life, has Mr. Mattison.

Who can say why he took such a shine to her? Perhaps her first tears moved him; perhaps it was her youth, or her obvious industry; perhaps he felt his age. At any rate she has been for some time not only his favored pillow but his partner at the desk, in charge of many matters—the housekeeping, the food and slops, the dozen tasks an hour such an enterprise requires—and lieutenant to many more. Disliked from the start by the other girls, who call her "The Lady," mock her aloofness, her frugality, her red hair, equally she disdained them, this cluster of overfed sluts used to doing solely as they pleased, stealing or shamming or scratching each other to bits, a menagerie even worse than Mrs. Segunda's. But a few sharp slaps and a round of robust punishments tilted matters in a brighter direction, and she found that making order soothed her as surely it did the workings of the house. Mattison was delighted by the changes, naming her his lady-at-arms: "Lady-at-arms," *sneered the girls.* What she wants is to be Missus Poppy, the greedy cunt.

To which Decca's reply, had she heard or cared to, might have been a shrug: Marry the master, no, or rather she has no preference, but run the house, yes, of course, so much better than working in its beds, itself a leap from kneeling in the streets; the ladder has many rungs. But her ambitions have grown wider for the business as well, to steer the nights' proceedings more toward the monied and cultured, the theatrical, to at least Have them dress more stylishly, *her murmur to Mattison beneath the midnight counterpane.* Twill ribbons are cheap enough, and dyed muslin can look like silk. That Pamela can sew, if she's pushed to it, and I can certainly—

Ah, but the gents like 'em tits-out, Dec, you know that.

For what looks finer, we can charge more.

Old dogs, his wheezing laugh, the discussion left unresolved: too soft to say no to her outright, soft as well in the bed so that most nights are spent in conversation, he might cup her bum or stroke her hair but their shared passion is for the Rose and Poppy, named, he confides, for his first two girls, Rose a refugee from the streets of Victoria and Poppaea from Someplace southron, *his shrug,* I never did figure out her talk. But she could work a joint like the best of them. And was almost as pretty as you.

His illness, when it comes, moves in jumps: one month a mild aversion to the table, the next a difficulty in keeping down the food; then the wasting, the nighttime sweats, the confusion with accounts— Did we pay that knacker Tomlinson? He's roaring in the streets I owe him coin—*so that is her worry now, too, besides everything else. But having endured so much, more is no real hardship, she knows how to carry weight without breaking. And the pain, well. She has borne greater pains that this, bears them still, wears the scars on her heart where no one can ever see them, or know what, or of whom, she dreams at night.*

Mattison knows, though, and has from the start, taking care to say it gently as she sponges him clean of yet another night's sour sweat: If you never felt for me that way, the heart's way, well, why should you? But you're a trouper always, a good girl. You've always been a good girl, Dec. And that dark lad was a good fellow as I recall—

My brother.

Kindly, I know he's no kin to you, poppet, though you love him. A good fellow, though, and much stronger than he looked. Stronger than me, now, just an old plucked rooster, *waving his feeble arm, as if he will get her to laugh but* Stop it, *she says angrily, fighting the tears that fear can bring; another one, leaving her in the end. Always, all of them leave.*

But before he goes—in rigor, in delirium and sweat—he does her one last service, Mr. Mattison, giving her all that he can—safety; security—in the only way possible, as Decca sits in what was his office, among the papers, the notes and the accounts, and tries to think what next to do. Her brain is infected by echoes, it seems, the rolling wheels of the dead-wagon, the insincere tears of the whores who scattered to the four winds as soon as it was plain that there would be nothing beyond a handful of coin for each of them, those handfuls nearly beggaring what small store was left with "The Lady," *mocking her still as they leave,* the Widow Mattison. High time she started working for her daily bread!

Empty-handed, empty Decca at the desk is another kind of echo: of Rupert, hunched on a fleabit cot at the dreary foreign boarding-house that, despite its drear, is still so overcrowded that his "room" is a closet beneath the stairwell, with space enough only to sit, lie flat, or piss in a chamber pot; and drink; why not drink? What else in life is there for him to do?

He has been here nearly a month, after who knows how many months of the road, less questing than impelled, like a puppet invisibly strung; he knows exactly how a puppet feels, now. After leaving Mattison's employ, for a brief time he was a coachman's road-guard, then a temporary bravo for a dubious businessman, whose import business went up in midnight flames; but until his advent in this city he has called himself a courier, seeking to fund his voyage by carrying messages, bundles, documents, whatever was required, down the road he himself wished to go. The cargo has varied: Once it was a fine morocco-leather case, a jewelry case, filled with worthless old watch fobs. Once it was what no one named as opium, though he knew the thick-wrapped bricks by their dark smell. Once it was a very young woman in gypsy head-wrap, who spoke no tongue he knew, yet none-theless made herself more than plain on the two nights they traveled: she would trade anything, anything at all, for a moment's blindness and her freedom. Untempted, he refused, to find at road's end she was a bailiff's runaway, a nasty little knifer who tried to nip when he turned her over at the gaol: I'd've fucked you, you know, *her snarl in perfect gutter English.* You dim bastard, you must be flat queer. Or busted-broke, *to bring his brief unsmiling amusement:* Or both, mademoiselle.

Courier to himself, at last he carried, was carried here where rumor pointed, then better knowledge, then fact—That Hanzel, of the puppet-shows; that Marcel—here where the end of his journey lies. But truly there is no end, just the road to this room where he sits with his bottle, tangled in his strings, alone with the thoughts he fears to follow, the denouement of a farce so bleak it transcends any thought of tragedy to twist instead to excruciating burlesque, wringing from him a mirthless, furious grin because he has put himself into this fix, has he not? led himself, through months of steerage and toil, merrily across the water, from town to town, led by the nose, the prick, the stupid mind refusing to confront what the blind eyes have come so far to see: Istvan and his puppets, performing—yes; again; still—for the filthy bourgeoisie.

Although apparently he has moved up in the world since last they met, now it is the burghers' masters for whom he disports himself,

*Christ knows how, though in the small placard drawing on the the-
atre door he seems as well-set-up as any margrave or marquis: the
Savile cut of his coat, the haughty tilt of his chin—though no drawing, however expert, can truly render the eyes.... Another reason to
mock at his own folly, lovesick idiot standing stranded in the street,
dumb before that placard as if he were a yokel from the fens, the
sudden shaming urge to put up fingers and touch it, as if he could
thereby touch the face itself. Jesu! and* Now you know, *he tells himself
that night, hunched in a four-table gambling den, drunk to vomit on
whiskey ill-afforded.* Now you know, you have seen, you can go. Go
home.

*But there is no "home" and it is not over, nothing is over, nothing
to do but stay, fight his way back to the boardinghouse past those who
foolishly conflate a drunk with a victim; to wake, wet and wretched,
in time enough to take himself to the show, the tiny, well-appointed
theatre glowing like a jewel as the toffs alight, stepping through the
muck of the avenue, as at the door he finds—another joke! will the
farce never end?—that he may not enter, the performance is by invitation only and he, judging by the provincial hat and wolflike stare,
belongs either to jail or the road. That he could gain immediate, backstage entry with a note bearing his name, with the murmur of his
name, with a mouse wrapped in paper, does not occur to him; those
are ideas Istvan would have had. And used.*

*Instead he turns on his heel and leaves. And walks. And drinks,
gin this time and plenty of it, hateful the juniper taste, the raw swirl
in his belly but he is ready, now, to punish himself, so ready that he
doubles back to the theatre, thinking to lurk outside like a brigand,
clamber the roof like a burglar, use the skills that first he learned,
owned, perfected beside this, this duke of an Istvan, singing inside,
distantly he hears it—singing in a new voice; for a new puppet? But
where is Marco? that he made with his own hands, sanded, polished,
dressed and tended tenderly as a living child, that he and Rupert
played beside so many times, together?*

*O think of it—and he does, there in the chill of the street, cannot
stop himself from recalling all the shows, Marco dancing in a velvet
blouse as he sang baritone, "Paddy's Lament" with a stick in his
belt to quell the boisterous or the furtive, the ones who thought that,
because they were vagabond players, they could be robbed like vagabonds as well. Remember the dawns afterward, too, yawning and
pissing in doorways and on roofs, climbing down into the new day,
the new journey that was the same journey, the same day spent walking, Istvan toting Marco and he trundling the rest, talking, joking,*

planning out the shows, new actions to try, new melodies picked up along the way, arguing this point or that; and pausing, always, at the side of the road, in likely bushes, or deep-shaded ponds, to put aside the world, and be together. Alone together, with the buoyant heat of him, the wet silken lash of his hair, O Christ why think of it now? Why think at all? when nothing will bring it back, those times, those walks, those shows where, for one reason or another—space, or mood, or the possible need to flee a constable untutored in the lively arts—Istvan played alone, he prowling the crowd's edge, usher and bravo both, private audience for whom that most private gesture at the end—Istvan's gaze over the head of the crowd, kissing his fist— was sent, meant, offered and accepted, a way of saying always This is for you, all of this that I do is for you.

When did the sorrow start? When they left the road for the rooms? the cold for counterfeit warmth, flung coins for little folded bills, screeching brats and slippery urchins for smooth and smiling women and men in wool waistcoats who wanted nothing better than to buy the showmen with the show, who saw the show itself as mere prelude to private performance in tandem, dark unsmiling Castor and radiant Pollux, the twins so twain that nothing could part them but themselves?—but why worry that corpse, chew the skeleton bones now that all is over, now that he stands in slush to the ankles with his aching forehead pressed against the bricks of a building he cannot enter, to see a stage where Hanzel-Marcel-Dusan stands unreachable, why even try—

—to find the way that in the end is very easy, just the door past a door that no one thought to lock, a freightway hall that leads to stairs climbing to a kind of catwalk from which vantage he can see, like a blow to the heart, not the handsome placard-picture, not Hanzel-Marcel-Dusan, but Istvan, his Istvan, hair pulled back, a little thin in the face, wearing a faintly brittle air that he has never had before: he looks tired. But the stage setting suits him, its formality, its boundaries, he is clearly in command as, accompanied by a rotund little pianist in the pit, he sings while manipulating, yes, a new, larger, fiercer-looking puppet, half the size of a small man, to match with the new voice: so it is out with the past, then. Out with all the past—

—as Istvan brings the song, some farrago about a shared mistress, to an end, and then, incredibly, in the gust of applause, raises his fist to his lips, the precious private gesture, meant now for whom? Everyone? Anyone? No one? or some special patron unseen by the crowd? Watching, Rupert grips the rusting catwalk rail, feels the

blood surge like iron to his head, a sickening sensation: how many times can a broken heart break? How foolish is a fool?

Before first light, he is gone from the boardinghouse, pack in hand, bottle in pack, its dregs drunk standing on the back of a coach bound eastward, into the sun coming up like a picture-postcard, pink mist and mystic evergreens, some bird's insistent cry like a flute, three notes, sharp and true. He feels every jounce of the coach's wheels, every stone in the road; he feels nothing, cares for nothing, has nowhere in the world to go.

It is by the slightest glance of chance that he finds himself again in Archenberg, breaking his fast in a fourth-rate hotel, listening to some would-be bravo harass a timid drummer, whose meager kit-wagon he saves from harm, using the battering of the bravo to bring a moment's physical enjoyment, as other men exercise horses, or take the air. The drummer is so grateful he stutters, he buys Rupert's breakfast, would pay for his room but I don't stay here, *Rupert tells him.* But thank you kindly.

Where do you stay, sir?

Nowhere. I travel.

Like a drummer, *says the drummer, with enormous sympathy.* Yes, I see. Well, then, young sir, I'll tell you this—you are a young man, sir, with no doubt a young man's taste for, for fun. Take this, *passing him a coin, no, a token, shiny false gold stamped with a star,* to the Gaiety Theatre, the next town over. They have some young ladies there, sir, that will knock your eye out. And they put on quite a fancy-dress stage show, too.

He is about to demur—another theatre, Jesu—but the name, the Gaiety, reminds him, displays in his mind's eye the street it occupies, the street that street crosses, the Rose and Poppy where, if she is not run off or dead, Decca will be. He fingers the star-stamped coin; he thanks the drummer; he drinks the rest of his tea.

And still, yes, the building stands, the Rose and Poppy in a cooling twilight, but the lamp is dark above the sign, blown leaves litter the threshold. The door is locked; he knocks, to silence, he knocks again. Perhaps she is dead, after all, or moved on with Mattison somewhere else in the wide world; absence can no longer surprise him, and perhaps it is better so.

Turning to leave, he is ten paces gone when Rupert? *the voice behind him, Decca's voice flat as a ghost's; she looks a ghost, dressed in black in the doorway, or a strangely cloistered nun, as if she is no longer part of the daily world.* Rupert.

Decca. Hello.

Come in.

The place is empty, that much is clear, or would be but for her, who seems so empty herself that he is reminded, again, of a spirit. She looks less like Istvan now, now that the life has dwindled from her face, or disappeared into hiding. Leading the way through dust and rat-scatter and sheet-draped furnishings, she clears a space for him at the little table she occupies in the fitful tallow light, account book, tarnished teapot, plate with one spoon, asks with a mute's nod if he would take tea, pours, serves until Stop, *he says, to rouse her,* stop that. Where is Mattison? And the whores? What happened here?

Staring at him, this apparition, here, alive, as handsome as ever, though something has gone wrong in his eyes; back without Istvan, how is that possible? Did their paths then never cross? He cannot hear how her heart pounds, as if lurching back into painful life. Mattison is dead. He died in my arms. The girls left straightaway, the trade closed down.

I see that. *He looks around again.* You—how do you live, then?

It's yours, now. The deed is in your name, it is yours.

He stares at her as if she is mad. Perhaps in a way she is. What did you say?

It's yours. He made out the deed to you, Mattison, before he died.

Why the devil would he do that?

Because she had begged him to, there beside the sweat-wet bed, because it was the only way she could keep what was hers, who could own no property of her own; even were she his widow, a woman known to be alone, they would come and take it from her. How else? So she had begged, and he had acquiesced: swearing that they would make the place prosper, she and her "brother," as she guided the scrawling pen. That paper kept her in the building when the solicitor came, and the constable, that paper kept, still, in her chemise, against her heart like a holy talisman, against the endless spooling evils of the world.

Because, *she says now,* he wanted you to have it. *Her voice has grown a little louder, a little more firm.* Because he always said you were a good fellow, and would do well by the place.

Jesu. *Rupert looks around once more, the cobwebs and draped disorder, the musty whiff in the air.* Did they loot it, too, before they left? *But he is not truly speaking to her and she knows it, knows to sit silent, watching him, her hands gripped together beneath the tablecloth: it is like a dream, to see him there, a dream she never had in all of her midnight imaginings. The two of them, together in the great world, yes, always together; but never this, never once had she pictured Rupert come back here alone.*

Finally, guardedly, when the silence grows uneasy: Will you stay the night, then?

It's cold as tombs in here.

I'll make it warm.

He drinks his tea like a man in a dream. She watches, and pours his cup full.

It is not until later, weeks later, when it is clear that he will stay, at least for now, at least until the building is cleaned and repaired, until he has some other idea what to do with the rest of his life, that she speaks, at last, with infinite caution, of Istvan: What news of my brother? *careful not to look directly at him, staring at the mending in her lap, a shirt of his with badly-fraying cuffs.* Did you—

No news, *Rupert says. Lines spring up between his eyes, all at once he looks much older, more weary and more dire.* I know where he is, or was; and will be. We need not speak of him again.

Pearl

We was crying, all of us, crying 'most all the night. Every time I think of her there, folded up in that box, not even flowers to put in her poor hands, I cry all afresh. She was just my age, Jennie, and now she's buried and gone.

All morning there was arguing, sharp-like arguing—you could hear from the hallway, Miss Decca and Mr. Istvan, Mr. Rupert was there, too: *Dead is dead*, Miss Decca says, *a mark is a mark. Needle or pin, stick pin, what difference?*

She didn't take her needles in the face.

She was killing herself at any rate, we do know that.

You have a chilly heart these days, don't you, Ag. You never used to.

And her voice so low and dreadful, she is bloodcurdling, Miss Decca, sometimes. *Chilly? Am I not what life made me? What you made me, both of you—*

And you yourself had no hand in the making? but *Stop,* said Mr. Rupert, and they did. What it all must mean I don't know, but it's true that Jennie was killing herself with the needle, we all knew that, that nice Doctor Adderley come to tell us to be on the watch: keep an eye on her, he said, don't let her spend too much time alone. But we got to be up on the stage or out on the floor, or up receiving in the rooms, so how can we watch? Lucy was a brick, of us all she did her best to keep poor Jennie upright, but in the end—

And that she died with that awful old masher, the one that comes for Laddie; it gives me the shivers. It was Omar found her, all curled on the bed, he said she was dosed, awful dosed. So whatever come she didn't feel it anyway.... She was plenty dosed at the show, eyes rolling back when Laddie hopped atop her, I don't know if she knew it was him or one of them puppets or a trick or what. I didn't see her, after, I was with Mr. Mayor.... Vera always says *He's sweet on you, Pearl, anyone can see that. He asks for you first before all of us, he buys you shandies—*

We got no shandies, now.

I know that, I mean when there's drinks to buy.

115

And Velma says, *Take what you can get, girl, don't be stupid. Get yourself into his house if you can.* But he's so old, Mr. Mayor, and bald, he smells like tinned herring, and his fingers are so fat…. Jonathan's hands are soft, but strong, too, from playing the piano, he can hold three apples in each hand, stretching his fingers like it's nothing. And he's sweet, Jonathan, I don't give a care if he can't talk, he always makes you know what he's meaning anyway. And anyway his music talks for him. Even the angels in Heaven, I bet you, even they never heard what he can play. On anything! Even that old pennywhistle I had since I was a tyke, even that, he played "Lo! the Winter Rosebuds" till we was all a-sighing and crying, it was that beautiful.

He saw me crying, down in the kitchen, because Puggy said *No more "Spinning Jennie,"* but her name wasn't Spinning Jennie, spinning was just what she did in that circus show, and her true name wasn't Jennie either, it was Gail, Abigail, she told me that once. And she was more than just the needle and the fucking—she liked that black-flower tea, when we could get it, and she had a brother named Peter, she said he was a steeplejack, or steeplechaser, something like that…. I said we ought to write a letter to him, and tell him she was passed on, but then Vera got all nasty and said *Oh, can you write? Why don't you write a love note to the mayor?* And that started me back crying all afresh.

And then Jonathan come up to me and hugged me, just 'round the shoulders; there's never no funny business with Jonathan. He is a gentleman, and he treats us like ladies, all of us. Well, except Laddie, you know. And he wrote something down for me but I don't have my letters, so I couldn't read it, and that made me cry, too.

So he—what's it called?—he made a little play of it, made his fingers walk away, waved goodbye, did it again so I understood and *You're leaving?* I said to him, and cried even harder. But then he took my hand, my fingers, made 'em walk as well, wave as well "Goodbye" and *Oh,* I said, *I see,* because I did see, I knew what he was meaning, then. That he and I will go, together. Together we will go! I threw my arms around his neck, I squeezed him double-hard. *When,* I said. He made another motion, up and down with the shoulders, who can say? because now is a bad time, the worst time, with all them soldiers everywhere, even here, at the Poppy! They sleep all over the lobby, you can't turn round without one of them a-staring at your tits.

Mr. Rupert don't much like it, you can tell, even though he never speaks out his thoughts, not to us girls anyway. May be he tells Miss Decca some things, since she is his sib, or half-sib, howsoever. Lucy says he tells Mr. Istvan everything, Lucy says—well, you can't say truth of everything that Lucy says. Mr. Rupert is a fine clean gentleman, I do know that.

When first I come here, to the Poppy, to the city, I was having some thoughts about him, Mr. Rupert, you know, lovering kinds of thoughts—he is that handsome, and nice-spoken, and he never hits. And I was wild, you know, I'd never been nowhere, I thought the whole world was a pig farm and a water trough, and to be in a city this big, with the street-sellers and carriages and alehouses, a dozen alehouses! And the Gaiety Theatre so loud on the corner, the music pumping out so you thought it was holy doomsday! I was scared and wild both. And I thought may be Mr. Rupert would like me wild.... I was that lucky that it was Lorraine's cousin who brought me, Lorraine who used to work here—even though *she* wasn't so lucky, Lorraine, she got the lung-fever and died. Like our poor Jennie. But her cousin put flowers on her, forget-me-nots and white daisies, with her hair brushed back all pretty, and her eyes closed sleeping-like.... Not like poor Jennie. Where could we get a flower, now?

But Miss Decca did give us them ribbons, special ones right from her own room: pretty pink and yellow, I think they was real China silk and *Make her up decently,* she said to Lucy; funny that she gave 'em to her, you know, when they hate each other so much. And Lucy braided up Jennie's hair, and put rice powder on her face, so that was something. Velma said it was a sin to waste the ribbons, *Who's going to see them in the ground?* But Lucy got mad and slapped her, and Miss Decca backed her up, Lucy, I mean; so that was funny, too.

Miss Decca's already mad with Velma, for wanting to put some girl in Jennie's place, some maid called Nancey from the big hotel, Velma said she was a likely girl but Mr. Rupert said *We will make do with what we have,* and Miss Decca narrowed up her eyes at Velma: *One less mouth to feed,* she said, like it was Velma she meant. But we can't do without Velma! She cooks and does all the cleaning, even though we girls help her some; and all the washing, why the bedclothes alone are a mortal chore.... Miss Decca came after Velma in the kitchen, quiet-like, when the rest of us were in the downstairs parlor with Jennie; I was sent by Puggy for the bicarb and whatever gin I could find, and I heard Miss Decca say *You have a finger in the pie, do you? You and your hotel whore?* But I don't know what she was meaning, unless Velma's stealing food, and anyroad she closed up quick and started rating me for walking in without knocking, even though I did knock. And then I cried again.... I guess we could do without Velma if we had to, may be Miss Decca would take over the cooking. I guess we could do without anybody, except for Mr. Rupert. He's the one who keeps us a jump ahead of, of everything. Just to see him there in the lobby, all calm-like, makes you feel better, even with all them soldiers; they give us plenty looks, you know, but they never make a grab on us. Mr. Rupert keeps us safe.

I could do without Mr. Istvan, as nice and friendly-like as he is. Though he did good at Jennie's send-off—Mr. Rupert and Omar and Laddie and Puggy bore her away, and when they came back, Jonathan played so fine, and Mr. Istvan made that Miss Lucinda sing a song he'd writ just for Jennie, about how she was in heaven now, shining down like a twinkling star; I can't feature how he does it, make a lady's voice come out so true…. But I don't like that Pan Loudermilk, even though Lucy and Vera laugh at me: *He's not real, halfwit, he's just a doll.* I know that, 'course I know that. But that first time, when he was fucking me—I know, Mr. Istvan said sorry afterwards. But there in that bed, with his hard hand all jammed up inside me, his eyes looked plenty real, and they look real on the stage, like they can see you; *he* can see you. And that's real enough for me.

In war, even a glancing war like this one, it is less the violence than the sheer disorder that finally confounds, the things one takes in on the streets—a human arm in a garbage pail, still wearing its brown gingham sleeve; piled shoes, dozens of shoes, outside the locked doors of the mercantile; the midwife puffing furiously on a loose-rolled cigarette as she brings a baby in the doctor's storefront window, ashes dropping on the screaming mother's knees; the sporadic percussion of battle, somewhere near, very near, very close, but never right before the eyes—those things create a feeling of unreality so acute that everything is both suspect and accepted, nothing can possibly be too strange to be true.

In the kitchen of a silent morning, the players of the Poppy's latest drama, the house under inner siege, roost as nearly silent: Lucy stirring oatmeal, Puggy sipping tea, Jonathan and Pearl piercing dry bread on the toasting-forks; they have been much together, those two, these last dark days since Jennie died, and the soldiers came, camping in the lobby, spitting on the floors, lingering in the hallways to leer at the girls, who, the General has taken pains to explain, are under no obligation to service them gratis although "Can you work a bayonet?" Lucy asks Puggy. "I'd like to stick that redpoll sergeant—he drinks himself limp, then expects me to make him stand. And all the work I'm to do on the costumes! I don't have time to fuck, let alone to waste—"

"I had a gun," Puggy mourns. "But Omar took it."

"Omar took what?" Omar himself come sour to the table, pouring the dregs of the tea, swearing as they dribble and clog: "God damn it! Is it too much to ask to use the strainer, Velma? Where the fuck is Velma?" as Rupert enters, swift and weary, nodding to Lucy who gives him a smile, eyebrows up at Omar who flushes red in repentance and "I'm that sorry," ruefully rubbing his bald head prickling now with pale hair, his razor has snapped blade from handle, impossible to repair. "I don't know what came over me, I just felt I had to break the gaffer's neck. Did he—"

"He'll live. But I had to go to General Georges on your behalf."

119

"Ah Jesu—my true apologies. It won't happen again," as Decca approaches in her fraying leather slippers, the heel has come off the left one which gives her gait a tilted counterpoint, *click-pause-click* like a broken clock and "What won't? Your silly brawling?" but her bite lacks force; she is tired, too, Decca, rendered nearly sleepless by the cold. The Poppy has become a fugue of cold, and the smell of lye, the soldiers' jackets vigorous with lice, of watery oatmeal, weak tea, and weevily bread. Velma has been bidden to keep a hard lock on the pantry, though at least they will not starve: the General's presence has been invaluable, no need to boil the wallpaper or set nets for the birds outside, one less worry among so many that Decca paces as Rupert used to, back and forth as midnight drains to dawn—

—though how long has it been since she smelled the nightlong smoke from his room? that he now so rarely uses, preferring other quarters: at times they can be heard right through the walls, so reckless is their pleasure; everyone knows now, everyone. Even the soldiers, who snigger or make rude gestures, tight circle and poking forefinger behind Rupert's back, though none will dare to do it to his face, or to Istvan's either. On his own, each is formidable; together they are feared.

No one fears them more than Decca, whose days end and begin with the specter of their bond resumed; but she has other, more impersonal fears to distract her, other appointments to keep—

"—tonight? Miss Decca?"

Omar speaking, to her apparently, Puggy watchful over the rim of his tea, Lucy pretending not to listen, the pushy witch, backstage all the time as Puggy's second, as she has always meant to be—but no way to send her packing, now, they need all the whores they have, could do with another though Rupert says no. "What? What is it?"

"I say, is there to be a show tonight?"

"Why ask me?" looking at Puggy, at Lucy, to Rupert whose face shows nothing but calm, a kind of ease these others have never seen in him before, though she knows it very well, knows why, sees the proof come sailing through the door as if the sun shines just for him: his first glance as always for Rupert who feigns not to smile, his wink for Lucy who fairly simpers, another wink for her whose sudden rage rebels and "Why ask me?" again and louder. "I've no power here, I'm last on the list, behind playacting whores and vagabonds—" as Istvan leans past her unconcerned, hunting by knifepoint through a peck of half-frozen pears—"We've no apples?"—and "For Christ's sweet sake!" she shouts. "No apples, how can there be apples, this is a war! They are making *war* outside, do you see nothing but yourself and—"

"And what?" Mild, but suddenly utterly cold, half turned to her and in that turn obliterating all around them, fox to fox in the dark of the den; he almost smiles, shows his teeth as "Your desires," she says bitterly, backing down. "For whatever pleases you most."

Silence beyond the sullen snap of the fire, no one wants to speak until "We need a holiday," says Puggy, striving for a tone as mild. "May we close, just for tonight?" to Rupert who shakes his head, not tonight but "Tomorrow," he says. "I'll tell the General: a holiday, as you say."

Lucy claps her hands. "Yes! Let Redpoll dip it down in the Alley for one night. And I can get busy with—" Glancing swift at Decca, she lets the thought die, goes back to stirring the oatmeal as Velma returns with some sheep's cheese and, yes, apples, two apples, one of which she sets down in front of Istvan—

—as Decca snatches at the second, storms furious into the hall with Istvan's laughter behind her, Rupert behind that and "Peace," he says quietly, catching at her sleeve, the apple ridiculous in her grip. "Puggy's right, we need a holiday, we're all thinned to the snapping point."

"Not you," she says. "*You* seem capital," and still at ease, warmed by that fire she never has shared, never will share, how many years can one sit shivering by the same guarded grate? "Even though it was you who—" then stops, theatrical, her lips pressed white.

"Who did what?"

"There is no point in speaking of it," eyes bright, voice soft with spite. "She's dead, isn't she?—whom you gave over to him, even though you knew—"

"Knew?" All ease vanished, arms folded tight against his chest; she has hurt him, meant to do so, takes respite in the pain even as she hates to see it, see his face as it looks now. "Do you think if I 'knew' I'd've ever sent her to him? Laddie he would harm, yes, but Jennie I never—"

"Laddie's not the only one," pointing, strange Eve, with the hand that holds the apple, back toward the room where they all sit listening, too quiet not to be listening but now she has begun she cannot stop. "That man wants him dead, can you understand though he refuses? Or are you too bewitched?"

The hallway's shadows make his face a mask, his voice as flat as "Have no fear on that score. Vidor will not touch him."

Why? she wants to cry. Because he knows that way he'll never have you? Instead "You said before you would send him away. Will you do it?" Almost weeping, with anger, with contrition, with despair, he blurs in her vision, a dark form gathered to itself. "I wish he had never come here. His evil toys!"

Movement on the stairs above them, soldiers descending, or the General, or both, to put them on alert, she stiffens and steps back but "Don't forget," Rupert leaning closer, his mouth to her ear, his voice a street boy's murmur. "They are my toys, too."

Turning his back on her, toward the stairs and gone, as she stands still gripping the foolish apple, blighted skin, chilly flesh, dizzy with a feel of bottomless disaster, as if the ground splits to a mouth before her, to swallow her, the Poppy, to swallow them all…. She has lost them both, now. Now she has lost them both.

As it happens, it is the General on the stairs, attended by an aide lately promoted from the unexpected dwindle of his officers lost to casualties; even Essenhigh was hit, though only slightly. And there have been other reverses: the train-way resupplies are less certain than previously calculated, they are having some difficulties with the rations, and morphine for the gravely wounded; fortunately they still have plenty of shovels. And ordnance.

The aide is a punctilious boy, eighteen or twenty, old enough to understand his very fortunate opportunity as aide-de-camp, the spoils of war, but young enough to be distracted by the passing whores in their lacy drawers and ratty peignoirs as "Andrew," says the General, "there are lovelier girls in Brussels. And cleaner." Handing him a folded map-case, pulling on his gloves. "You'll be seeing them fairly soon."

"I am sorry, sir," says Andrew, turning red; he is pale as a pigeon, Andrew, thin-chested but much stronger than he looks. In this he somewhat resembles the redoubtable Mr. Bok, also stronger than he looks, looking deeply out of sorts at the moment as "General, a word," halting him in mid-descent, the three of them filling the narrow stairway. "My people are in need of a day of rest—I'm considering closing, tomorrow. Will that disrupt you?"

"Not at all. Rest is vital. I only wish I could offer the same to my men in the field."

"How goes the effort?" said with an effort; it is obvious he does not much care for military maneuvers or the complications of conflict; for this the General respects him. War is not his business, lust is his business, and he is diligent in its behalf. Although if Hanzel is to be believed, by way of Arrowsmith, they used to tread the boards together, the whoremonger and the showman; well, why not? Is not an actor already a kind of pander, and a pimp an impresario of artifice and desire? What sorts of shows they mounted is anyone's conjecture, but none he would ask of this dark bravo before him, aiming for courtesy though his eyes are dead hard; instead "As well as can be," says the General. "My aide and I," nodding toward Andrew, "are about to meet with Colonel Essenhigh, who himself is just returned from a sortie that—But not to bore you...."

"Nor to detain you. Safe passage, gentlemen," the half bow as correct as a courtier's, up the stairs as they descend and "The men say he's queer," Andrew whispers. "But he seems a fair sort to me."

"Brussels," says the General, "will teach you many things.... Mr. Arrowsmith has a town house there, on the Rue des Orfèvres."

Mr. Arrowsmith's hotel suite is brisk with disorder; as they enter, he is in shirtsleeves, tugging open a trunk burly and battered with much use and "My apologies," as he slips into his coat. "Will you have a drink, gentlemen? Or tea?" that tastes faintly of the smell of burning, the everlasting smolder in the air. "I thought to be finished before you arrived."

The General takes the room's one unpiled chair. "When do you leave?"

"No more than a fortnight, I think. Past—" an event that both seemingly await, though Andrew does not, neither does he mark the pause between them. "How are you finding your new quarters?"

"Unnecessarily cold; last night the piss pot nearly froze. I shall have to speak to the mistress of the house.... Andrew, step downstairs— I find I'd like some whiskey after all." As the door closes: "My horse has the best of it. I may have to relocate to the stables."

"They ought to swaddle you. The safety you provide is beyond price." Mr. Arrowsmith adds a fat cap of sweet brandy to each teacup. "I broke my fast with Vidor this morning—now he's hinting it's been his sop all along, your biding there."

The General shakes his head, as if something, not Mr. Arrowsmith, amuses him. "One gets so deep, sometimes, one can't tell the surface from the scum. *Amour fou!* At least his lucre still runs, but if we must one day do without it, we shall, eh? Other sources," lifting his cup in tribute, "are equally generous.... At any rate the building's nicely placed, and hard to overrun in a fight. And the whores go about in their drawers, so the men are pleased. All in all there are worse places to quarter than a brothel. This hotel, for instance."

"You'll have no argument from me on that score."

Musingly, holding out his cup for more tea, "I'd thought to turn them out, at first, but Mr. Bok is so useful. And then our Hanzel barefaced asked—"

"Ah. I'd wondered. Well, love makes a man bold."

"As was noted at breakfast?"

Mr. Arrowsmith's frown is sudden and surprising, two thin brackets at his mouth and "What disturbs," he says, "is the sheer—rancor.

Cannot one step away with restraint, if not with grace? Must the field be sown with salt and dragon's blood?"

"Dragon's teeth," suggests the General. "Mr. Bok ought not be underestimated."

"Mr. Bok ought not be destroyed."

The General shrugs. "Mayhap he needs a bravo like Vidor's. Who wears his own like a lucky charm."

"He'll need another, now: I saw them bring that giant in last night. Piecemeal.—Yes?" setting down his own tea as Andrew, with a knock, reenters, faintly panting, pink-faced from the cold and "I'm very sorry, sir," setting down the bottle, "I had to go all the way back to the room to get it, sir. I mean, gentlemen."

The General pours into three cups, as Mr. Arrowsmith gives the boy a courteous nod. "You haven't seen the show yet, have you, Andrew? At the Poppy?"

"The puppet show, you mean, sir? With the girls? No, sir."

"*Salut*," as the trio drink, Andrew's stiff-wristed bolt a practiced gesture, though the peat whiskey is more potent than he is used to having; he chokes a little as the General smiles and "Do so," says Mr. Arrowsmith, "front and center at the next performance. It will be something to tell your children, one day."

The day of rest descends on the Poppy like a biblical dove, a foggy, gray-ish dawn where a bundled Velma pokes the fire alive, sets the kettle steaming, as the soldiers in the lobby snore and groan, one blinking trooper left as watch who, watching, still does not see Decca, black silk, black wool wrapper, entering as silent as the night just past.

Outside are the birdcalls, insistent, strange, and true even in the midst of the human skirmish, like an older world calling to itself. Faint smoke rises; a wagon creaks its way up the road, toward the dark of the treeline. Few lights show in the town windows, though the mayor is awake, red-striped nightcap and close to the grate, busily writing a requisition for sundry supplies that he intends to present to the General later in the day, in the company of Mr. Franz, himself abroad in the darkness, trousers askew, back pressed to the freezing wall of the Alley while the girl in his grasp suffers his teeth and swears to herself that she will leave this place before the week is through. Down the street, at the Gaiety, the last of the actresses gathers her bent ostrich-plume hat, her traveling valise, stuffs her reticule with notes and coins not wholly hers; she too had promised herself to flee, and, unlike her unlucky sister in the Alley, will do so this very morning on the passing train.

Likewise, the General and Andrew are already in the saddle, head-ing to Archenberg, attended by two sharpshooters keeping a watchful stride beside. At the hotel, Mr. Arrowsmith still sleeps, his well-worn trunk packed and ready, his suppositions ordered and his plans in place. In Jürgen Vidor's rooms, a hand of patience lies half-played and waiting on the tray, a bottle of Bordeaux, the last, nearly empty beside the bedskirts. The ormolu scatter of trinkets and objets looks dusty, now, the room itself more bunker than traveler's resting-place, the heavy coverlets bunched and twisted, as if his rest has been disturbed.

In Decca's little sitting room all is in perfect, if shabby, order, damask and petit-point, stern cracked-plaster Athena and her vigilant owl. The adjacent bedchamber, though, is a tableau of neglect, the bed-clothes jumbled, a teacup and crusted spoon balanced beside a pile of mending skewered with a shiny needle untouched these last few

126

weeks. The pince-nez lie, closed eyes, atop the room's holy writ, the Poppy's account books, as if she has been reading them to lull herself to sleep. On the tiny dressing table are her silver combs and ancient hairbrush, the selection of jeweled pins, opal and silver, and the blue enamel eye as blind as love itself. Draping the mirror is another kind of silver, a gilt-paper chain so frail it can barely be handled, woven years ago by a boy's clever fingers. A case made for a fine lady's jewels keeps instead a careful collection of bows and silk ribbons, butter yellow, pale pinks and fading blues. Beside it, a tin box painted with a scratched and blooming rose holds several scrawled letters, the paper faint with the scent of old sachet.

Decca herself now sits upright on the bed, eyes closed, numb fingers linked; she might be praying, if ever she prayed, or lost in painful thought. All night she could not sleep, for the cold, the ache of it down her legs and back; sometimes she thinks she will never be warm again. More than anything she longs to go to her brother, to his lover, to send one on his way and keep the other close, to save them, save herself and what she has made, the Poppy rescued from Mattison's grave—for without it, where would they be, any of them? Where would Rupert have ended, where would Istvan have returned, homing bird, raptor rapt to his master's wrist like a hunting hawk? Last night she heard them through the walls again, quarreling whether to stay or go…. She will not go. No matter what happens, she will not go.

Around her, the house is waking, feeling its way into the unaccustomed day: no customers to service, no show to prepare, only the few essential daily tasks, most of them Velma's to accomplish, the rest are free to do as they wish with their leisure and "All thanks to you," Omar's thump on Puggy's bundled shoulder, the head above as prickly-brown as a hedgehog's: he is growing back his hair, for added warmth, he says. "What will you do with your holiday, eh? I think I'll get good and rolling drunk, myself."

"Work is play, if you do it right. Isn't that so, Lucy?" who nods over her tea and toasted bread, wide-awake and gleeful for a day spent sorting through the stuffs and threads and winding strings, backstage where the redpoll sergeant and all the others cannot enter, where she need not stop what pleases her to go please someone else. She has a list in mind of what must be discussed with Puggy—possible skits and dances, props and costumes to construct—who himself has his own growing, budding, convoluted list: shows he would like to fashion, songs he would like Jonathan to learn; it is curious, but the town's chaos has made more fertile the creators at the Poppy, opened wider their eyes and their minds. Perhaps it is because, in war, the lid comes off, all crawls or seeps or bursts to the surface: life struggles more vibrantly than ever just to live since it is so easy, now, to die. And time, forever in short supply, is more plainly shown to be so.

Whatever the spur, Puggy and Lucy spend a happy day together, as do Laddie and Vera, both choosing luxurious sleep, though Laddie takes a noontime break for a saved chunk of smoked hashish, and Vera wakes at tea-time to have a lukewarm wash and try to plait her hair the way they do in Paris, or what she imagines as Paris, a cross between Heaven and a superior chocolatier's. Velma's day is least rewarding, though she has been very quiet, Velma, since Jennie died, and seems not at all to miss her chance at play.

Jonathan, of course, is at the piano, practicing first, then, with Pearl's encouragement, playing tune after tune, old songs recalled from his childhood, nursery rhymes and ditties, and later days at the kirk—"Lovely On the Shore," "Until the Trump Shall Sound"—and then other, more sentimental ballads, concerned with more carnal loves, that make Pearl sigh and sidle closer on the bench, bring sweet tears to her bright eyes: "No Other Love Than Yours, My Charmer," "Cupid's Garden," "Fair Marie" to which Pearl, delighted, knows the words, singing in a faulty soprano that enchants them both:

"Fair Marie, why do you weep, on the Dover cliffs so steep?
I am crying for my lover, gone away.
He was a lord of high repute, in his spurs and leather boots,
And he swore to me that always he would stay.
But one night upon the Strand, as he held me by the hand,
His passion such that I could not say nay,
We stole away to—

—*oh*," ceasing with a blush, Jonathan's fingers stilled to her silence as both see, in the wings, Istvan, arms-folded and smiling, like an older brother watching babies at play. Pearl slips off into the wings, but not before kissing Jonathan's cheek, as Istvan crosses to the bench and "My apologies," he says. "It was such a pretty picture, I couldn't help but peep."

Jonathan smiles and shrugs, a mimed resignation to the moment's loss. Not for the first time, Istvan considers how eloquent he is, this tongueless boy, how much he can convey by expression alone. Between that and his musicianship, he could have a fine career, far away from this sad little town, if only he would take to the road.

So Istvan speaks, in an easy manner, of the places he has visited, the towns he has played, how sometimes one is pelted with flowers and others with shit or pebbles, but always it is "The thrill," he says, as Jonathan's fingers gently touch the keys, the chords, one soft sound after another, in plaintive, haunting counterpoint. "The thrill of bringing it to life, the tale, song, puppet, what have you—that's what draws one on. The ancillary pleasures, well, yes, one does like the lucre, and one does like to travel and see the world, or I do, at any rate.... There is so very much of the world to see, yeah? And a young fellow like yourself must have some dreams?"

Jonathan's hands leave the keys, slip into pockets for scrap paper and stubby lead, printing a note he gives to Istvan: *I would like to play the chello.*

Istvan reads and nods. "I would like, someday, to hear you play the cello, in a proper hall, with a proper audience. The piano, too. For today, I would like to quit this fucking place. But here is where we are.... What do you make of our shows, Jonathan? Is it to your liking, the mecs mixed in?" to bring his instant, emphatic nod, fingers raised like a maestro's, upping the tempo, the volume, confirming what Istvan has guessed from the start: the puppets have changed him, woken in him a new kind of theatrical ambition, who knows how far it could reach? "Did you like that Shakespeare I lent you? 'Now, gods, stand up for bastards!' That's from *King Lear*; you ought to read that one, too. A most unhappy old man, my lord Lear. Many old men are unhappy, have you marked that?"

Another scrap, neatly printed: *Veedor.*

Istvan laughs. "Yes, Mr. Vidor is a miserable old crock. But may be our next show will cheer him. He ought to recognize its provenance, perhaps he will feel flattered."

He claps Jonathan gently on the shoulder, noticing, as he departs, a slim figure reappearing to seat herself again on the piano bench. Up the stairs he goes, silent as a practiced thief, pausing to note the scent of smoke, the voices in Decca's parlor, Rupert and his sister, expenditures and disbursements, yes, of time and energies much better spent elsewhere; though they ought not have wrangled so dismally yesterday, Mouse will be gloomy tonight.... Still he cannot stop himself, always it is Istvan who begins, Rupert who retreats: *Why can you not see? They depend on me, here.*

They do? And what of me?

Not meeting his eyes, head turned away, the curve of his neck a rampart wall. *What of Decca?*

What the fuck of her! She's happy here, it suits her to give orders. But you—

Stop, I tell you. Now is not the time—

When ever is, then? When this shithole's shot to pieces under our fleeing feet? Christ, Mouse, with the mecs we can—

You can, stubbornly, as if to push him away while holding him close: always on the cusp, that unspoken threat of desertion, to bring his own flaring bitterness: *I am your puppet, I always have been. Why don't you make me dance?* And the love then like combat, and nothing resolved…. Half a sigh, half a curse, he passes the smoky parlor for the peace and silence of his Cell, the waiting mecs whose needs are so easy to tend, whose desires are his own, who can wait forever for fulfillment, as he cannot: even Pan, there, in his casket, black silk across his eyes, did ever human clay lie so patient for the breath of life? as *"Fiat lux,"* Istvan murmurs, hoisting the stumpy body upright, the swing of black hair, the eyes rolling to meet his own half-lidded gaze, ah, if only his wider life were so simple to manipulate.

In the quiet parlor, account books open in the uncertain tallow glow, Rupert lights another cheroot, sits back as Decca recites her catechism, the Poppy's financial status: sans most customers, who have either fled or grown too pinched or distracted to spend much on fucking, their money or their time; the surviving Alley whores are doing the best business in town. Supply prices are high, with little to purchase. Their stoutest patron, Jürgen Vidor, has not been seen nor offered a farthing, since—though Jennie's name goes unspoken, though Decca has sincerely begged pardon: *I was mad to speak so, of course you had naught to do with her ending, she was dosing herself to death before Jürgen Vidor ever saw her*: what Vidor did, whatever he did, was not enough to kill Jennie or anyone, only to hurt, perhaps even after she was dead, such the urge to wound the man has…. The way he looks at Istvan frightens her. The way he looks at Rupert terrifies her.

Heart in her mouth all the brief while they met, in the gloaming dawn just past: she creeping like a burglar through the icy streets to the dreary hotel, silent man-at-arms outside the hot disorder of his rooms, burning half the hotel's coal but still somehow a tomb, the cold alive in his gray-pouched eyes that promised nothing, gave nothing, the risk run for nothing, no good done for anyone at all: not Rupert, not Istvan—*Your brother, yes?* How did he know that? And what will he do with the knowledge?—nor herself or the Poppy, either: Will he return there as a patron? He did not say. She could not repeat her former fervent lie, that Istvan would go, soon or at all, though she swore that Rupert would stay, with all the passion of her own wish that it be true; did he credit this? He did not answer, only sat in his dark wrapper and watched, as if her panicked avowals were the gambols of a child, an unpretty, unskillful, unwanted child who ought never have sought so doggedly to deceive; then with a small, fastidious frown, as if they had been exchanging *mots* at a ladies' tea, *You ought always to wear black, Miss Decca. Pale colors make you look a corpse.* Then thanked her for her visit, and sent her back down to the street.

But none of that is mentioned as she details to Rupert, pince-nez, steel nib, their current faltering situation, fiscal and otherwise: the damp has gotten deep into the walls, without heat enough to drive it out, so wood has warped and buckled, wallpaper is fatally ruined by rot. Omar has covered as best he can the shattered windows on the second floor, but those receiving rooms are now unusable. Liquor continues to be an issue, one can only water so much, but the gin at least is holding out. The soldiers are a trial, lice and blood and breakage, fighting amongst themselves and grabbing at the girls, though the General's disbursements of coal and cash will keep head above water for the time being, and the military presence holds worse marauders at bay; it was so wise and far-seeing of Rupert to broker this arrangement but "I did nothing," Rupert says, staring down through the gloom at the ash, "but assent" to the General's wishes; it had seemed that the General might have asked before, certainly Vidor had all but promised so, but then he had delayed—

—until that night, Istvan's night, their first shared show in oh, how long, how happy he was then…. And last night, Jesu, sulking and taunting, always on the brink of leaving, he knows in his heart that Istvan will leave, but when and with whom it is not possible yet to say. Though he has seen their looks in passing, Istvan and the General, recognition, connection, there is something there, he is sure of it. Perhaps that is why Georges came here after all…. But he will not be caught the same way, wrung to agony by grasping for quicksilver; he must just have what he can while he can, all he can, never all the heart can hold though he holds that strong and liquid body as long as ever he may, since it will have to last forever, whatever he can wring from these days. This time he will not follow. No, he will not follow again.

When Decca has finished and set aside her pen, she looks expectantly to him: for what? answers? comfort? He has neither. How tired she seems, worn as a ghost in her mended black silk, why so well-dressed on a day without business? but that is no business of his so he does not ask, lights a last cheroot as "Sleep, why don't you," rising from the foolish little petit-point chair, one of Mattison's last traces, he and she some duke-and-duchess of the whores; how different her life would have been, had Mattison lived. His own, too. "It's supposed to be a day of rest. Or have Puggy read to you, you used to like that."

"He's occupied." With Lucy, she does not add. "Will you—"

"What?" Hand on the door, looking back and "Rest," she says. "You seem—weary." They gaze at one another, through the shadows, the cold. "Or at least eat something, have Velma fix you something, have you eaten aught today? Or only consumed those foul cigars?"

A faint smile. "I'll soon stop, won't I? There'll be no more tobacco. No more of many things."

He exits, alone into the dark hallway, the darker stairs, but he needs no candle or tallow, blindfolded he could find his way from roof to cellar and back again. One building, now his world.... Here the lobby, several soldiers scratching and lounging, the General is apparently elsewhere so they are free to sit and pass a bottle of, what, ginger beer, yellow-brown as soured piss. He feels them watching as he pulls at the theatre door, hears a stifled laugh: one day he may have to react to their silly discourtesy but today is not that day—

—so he passes into the wider, cleaner darkness before the stage, the tables and the bar, all empty tonight, in limbo, and he all alone in this domain he never sought nor wanted, does not want now, if only Istvan knew.... Gatekeeper, man-at-arms, himself alone to keep them safe: as demonstrated by the monstrous visit with Jürgen Vidor, the summons come abrupt as a royal command, to send him, armed and wary, to the ghost hotel, past the idiot in the hall, into his rooms where the man sat like a toad in a nest of leaves, the suite as disordered as his conversation: speaking first of the town, the war, how the outcome has never been in doubt though *There is always suffering,* musing over the rim of his glass, his everlasting Bordeaux. *But we shall see the end of it, you and I.* And then rambling off onto a tale of another town, some vague and violent happenstance endured to a successful end, though *Javier did not expect me to survive, no, nor his fond military friend.* That wet smile. *But I did, yes, I did. Do you know why? Because I am like you, Rupert.*

Every word he says, every breath he sucks, reminding of Jennie, of Laddie, of the pin. The fucking pin. *And how is that, sir.*

Oh, don't call me "sir." Don't call me "Mr. Vidor." Surely we are more sweetly acquainted than that. Pouring; drinking. Wine on the tablecloth, a darkening seep. *You and I, Rupert, we are* sui generis, *part of nothing that surrounds us. And yet, I would see you in surroundings you deserve—in Paris, say, at the Objet d'Art: I'd savor your comments on that seraglio! Or a visit to Monsieur Nadar's studio. His work is exquisite, I would much enjoy to have your portrait made.... Or Prague. You would surely relish Prague.* That voice, the overheated air of the rooms, the tipped and dusty bibelots—all like being in another's darkened dream, and yet the dark has power in the waking world, his own world girdled by this man's desire: *It would be my immense pleasure to—host you, if you would but consent to undertake the journey. And assist those Under the Poppy, as well.* Silence. One hand creeping to settle on his knee. *Will you do it, Rupert? I am asking.*

Those Under the Poppy; could he save them all, save Istvan, by the correct reply? No, he is not fool enough to credit that. The silence like a test of strength, that vain and staring need, until finally his own voice, dry: *My place is here.*

Ah. Here beside Miss Decca—your sister. Or your mistress. But neither of those things are true, are they?

No.

The puppeteer, now. As close as a—brother, yes? Oh so very very close…. But what if one had to choose between them?

A different silence then, the red stillness of the alley, the jungle, two creatures facing one another, eyes and teeth—and his own hand flexing with the maddened urge to be done with it, one swift swipe to end all the feints and threats, part the man's throat, blood and wine in mingled gush—but Vidor hand-in-glove with the General, with Mr. Arrowsmith, what would happen to the Poppy then? Will he live long enough himself, not to care for the God damned Poppy? so instead *I've been to Prague,* he said, and left, rapid down the empty stairs, through the smoky streets, back here to argue with Istvan, hectoring yet again to throw down the reins and go but *Why can you not see?* his own desperation. *They depend on me, here.*

They do? And what of me?

Now he takes a breath, the musty air, rubs at his forehead. If only Jonathan were here, to play some music his mind could follow, instead of these circling thoughts: he was playing earlier, some sprightly air, what was it? "Cupid's Garden," yes, *Come with me to Cupid's Garden,* trickling notes like a silver fountain in the sun, where was that fountain? that he and Istvan saw once on their travels, not real silver of course but it shone in the sun like Paradise, and the water was cold and clean…. Behind the bar, tucked beneath the locked and hoarded gin, is a smaller brandy bottle, filled now with whiskey the color of old gold. Perhaps that runs through the fountains of Cupid's garden, if only one could find the way.

He leaves now via the stage, out a side passage, back to the hall, the stairs, heading it seems for his roost on the roof—then halts instead as if compelled before the Cell, pushing with the bottle's lip at the door, to open it a finger's width on Istvan, legs crossed, hair loose, bent studious as a boy over Pan Loudermilk, the world around him less than a dream as "Working?" says Rupert, on the threshold now; he makes a tired little smile. "Incorrigible. It's a holiday, messire."

Istvan smiles in return, rising to close the door, turn the flimsy lock and "I prefer," he says, "to think of myself as steadfast." Gently pushing aside Pan's body, making room on the little cot. "And every fucking day a holiday."

Black frost crawls the foggy skylight. The whiskey tastes of midsummer, of shining days that never end.

*The father of the Misses van Symans, the Magistrate van Symans, is
not a man much given to hyperbole, but even he will admit that Pan
Loudermilk is unique, not a puppet at all as one thinks of a puppet,
much more a* Provocateur, *as he says chuckling to his friend Georges,
a true will-o'-the-wisp. His folly with the rector—! If he were a man,
we'd have had him in irons. But as it is—*

As it is, yes. How long does Hanzel bide with you?

Van Symans shrugs; the candle flames flicker in echo. Eastertide, I'm thinking, or until Monica tires of him. Or I might carry him
along with us to Paris, *which brings to General Georges an inner
smile: how often the world grants our wishes, if only we will make
them plain.*

*It is in Paris, then, that the General mounts his approach, that
in the end proves absurdly easy: apparently young Hanzel, who in
this city is known as Marcel, has anticipated his growing interest,
is more than willing to further his ends as long as* No harm, *leaning
back amongst the piled traps and boxes, the laces and apparatus of
his vocation,* no harm comes to myself. Or to my mecs.

Of course.

*Dressed like a fop, haughty as a lord, but the street boy is alive
in his face, his eyes, his foxy smile as he lifts one of his dolls, a flaxen-
haired thing with a smooth silk bosom, makes her bob a dainty curtsy,
then abruptly lets her fall, drop to the floor with her head at an ugly
angle, as if her neck has snapped and* Dead, *he says,* I'm no use to
you. And I need my mecs to live, and move—

And have your being.

Again the white smile, slightly wider this time. I see I shall be safe
with you. *He reaches past the fallen doll for a slender bottle, some sort
of green liqueur, it smells of rot and flowers as* The magistrate, *says
Hanzel, Marcel, pouring into a pair of thumb-sized cups,* Magistrate
van Symans, that is, is a man who likes to entertain. Last night, *par
exemple,* he entertained some gentlemen from abroad; their accents,
at least, were purely villainous; German accents. Do you also know
these gentlemen?

Georges takes one cup, waits for Hanzel to lift the other. They gaze at one another, the raptor and the fox. The General smiles. Odd lines spring up around his mouth.

What a pity that we did not meet sooner, young sir. *Salut.*

Paris proves to be a most successful city for les mecs, but success, alas, can sour one on an enterprise: to make the same play again and again, even if it is enjoyed, celebrated, perhaps especially if it is enjoyed and celebrated, breeds subterranean discontent; and as an anodyne it grows so tedious that in the end the only roads away are pain or harder work. Fortunately, the theatre is not confined merely to the space on a stage. One can entertain, as the magistrate does, in a townhouse, in comfort and apparent privacy; one can play for an audience of passing strangers, of those passing as strangers, of others whose motives will never be known, but who can enjoy the intimacy of a story well-told. Hanzel himself seems to savor the byplay of deceit; it is his own notion to carry the General's secret correspondence tucked up inside the puppets, once even as a billet-doux squeezed between the silken breasts of the flaxen doll, lilac-scented and displayed for all to see, if only they had known. That they patently did not, the well-fed, fashionable, purblind audience, is a source of secret hilarity to the master of the mecs, who seems to savor the risk as much as the triumph, the coup de théâtre *of confessional, mask, truth and lie all in one; which may have given the General pause, had he known, especially in the case of this particular protégé, endowed with both malice and talent. But only pause: at more than twice the young man's age he has seen such glee before, shining like marsh gas, a short-lived fire. To take pleasure in the game is a good thing; to toil for that pleasure is absurd.*

Fortunately, what pleases the puppeteer most, it seems, are his puppets themselves. Not only their maintenance and construction, though he is forever tweaking, mending and amending, but their company, their silence, their allegiance; especially the dwarf he calls Pan Loudermilk, who seems to serve as a kind of familiar, almost as if he were alive. The General asks Hanzel that question, once, at the end of another clandestine chat, the magistrate's balcony chilly in the new spring night: Tell me something, Hanzel. Are they real to you, your mecs?

Hanzel glances over from his stance at the railing, the breeze ruffling the Belgian lace at his cuffs; he does not reply. Yet still the General presses: Not to be foolish, nor trespass on your artistry. But the way you converse with them, with the Pan in particular—is it your thought that some—sense—clings to them, these constructions, some life other than that you initiate yourself? *Excusing his own interest, They seem so real, one cannot help but wonder.*

Hanzel smiles, cold and courteous. Puppet he may be himself— for he has no illusions of his own weight in this equation, is wise enough to know his place and keep safely to it—still there are boundaries, places in him that no one now may go so I make them talk, *he says,* and walk. And fuck. They are extensions of my will. You also have such things, sir, you call them soldiers.

The General nods; he asks no more. Later that evening the Magistrate van Symans inquires of the General if the puppet-master seems peevish, surely he is not inclined to banter as he is used to but To play this way, *says the General* sotto voce, takes something from a man, if he does it as well as our Hanzel—pardon, Marcel. He's not a clockwork conjuror, eh?

It's my thought that he is restless, *says the magistrate, sounding peevish himself.* Who knows if he may bolt? And Monica planning her fête around him, peacocks and Salome dancers, the silly woman will beggar me yet.... You will attend, will you not?

If I am able, *says the General, with affable regret, but in the end it is the magistrate who is unable to attend the gala, himself invited to a more private affair involving certain members of the military and select civil authorities, who take a dark view of some of the magistrate's latest activities with visitors from abroad. The General is not present at this interrogation; instead he sits beside Monica van Symans at her garden party, encouraging her to enjoy the entertainment provided by Hanzel, who is in top form, gay and animated, resplendent in a new peacock-blue waistcoat that he later gives, for a smile, to a dark young coachman, who goggles at him in the hay-scented stables as if he were the angel Gabriel himself:* Are you sure, sir? Lord, this is a cracking jacket. Are you sure?

I'm sure of nothing, *says Hanzel pleasantly, pleasantly weary afterward, packing up his mecs to the sounds of commotion in the drawing rooms below: the message has come from the magistrate, there will be weeping and gnashing of teeth but by then Hanzel is on his way, riding not with the General—that would be telling—but anonymous in a hired hack, eyes closed, letting the sway of the coach serve as* lethe, *suspended, like Pan in his coffin, between one night's performance and the next.*

It is indirectly the General's doing that the letter finally reaches him: inside a pale calfskin coin-pouch, cheap paper covered with tiny writing, Decca's writing, though he does not know that at first, feels a moment's strange jagged hope but I had it from a drummer down in the alehouse, *says the General's courier, an older man with a sere, seamed face, dust all over; he seems somewhat offended by Hanzel's indolence and open shirt, there at midday in the inn's upper room.* He said it come from a lady, for you. *Hanzel says nothing, reading.* You get many messages from ladies, I'm guessing. *Still reading, Hanzel gives him the coins from the pouch, inviting his leave only to summon him later:* Does the General send a reply to Archenberg? *and then, at the courier's nod,* Here, *handing back the pouch, the blue lover's eye wrapped securely inside.* For the mistress of the Poppy, one town over; it's a brothel.

I didn't guess it was a church.

You're a funny fuck, yeah? *with a smile of his own, so hateful that that the courier complains to the General*—I don't take marching orders from your jongleur, now, do I?—*but* What has he given you to carry? *inspecting the lover's eye, the brief note it accompanies*—"Sell this if you need to, keep it if you don't. My eye is on you either way" *along with a warning, the scent of trouble on the wind, a troubled question at the end*—*and* Do as he bids, *the General says, rewrapping note and jewelry.* Who is the lady? A madam, he says? If she replies, bring it first to me.

The madam in question had been very painfully surprised by the news of her brother, a surprise curdling almost at once to deep distress. The drummer's advent was coincidental, passing through town with some coin to spend on a bottle and a night with a woman, traveler enough to have stories to tell, yokel enough to wish to share them with Omar, another man of the world there on the door who rolled his eyes at Decca, closing out the evening's till: That foreign-type drummer! I didn't think he'd stop jawing long enough to go take his poke at Vera. On and on about his travels, how he's seen it all, seen a man trained a bay gelding to talk in Spanish, another who makes dolls poke each other—

Dolls?

Dolls, puppets, something like—a young gent abroad, he saw him do some plays a bit ago. Terrible skillful he says, makes 'em seem quite alive—

—as Decca's heart began to race, her glance at once to Rupert behind the bar, a few more guarded questions confirm that yes, the drummer tells of Istvan, apparently now the master of a troupe of toys, calling himself some other name but Istvan all the same. The thought of him wakes aching echoes, What news of my brother? *no news or the same news, all the same it seems to Rupert, he has shut that door and locked it: but if he were to hear once more the name he never speaks, or to see him, see Istvan in the flesh again—*

So: the gathered pouchful of coins—money from the till, her hands shake as she takes it: an odd sensation, as if she pilfers from herself—included with the letter asking how is he, where is he, offering a severely edited version of her own history, admitting to Mattison and the Poppy, saying nothing of Rupert at all. As she writes, there in the dawn quiet of her bedchamber, faint pink light glowing, growing at the window, she remembers other windows, other dawns, the ribbons he brought her, the feel of his hand around hers, leading her safely through darkened streets, and Just for now, *he would say, kissing her forehead before boosting her back to the sill.* I'll be back before you know it, yeah? *Back again to leave again, does he remember those lost days? Does he ever wonder whatever became of her, his little sister Ag?*

In the morning, very early, she rises to roust up the foreign drummer, ruffled and blinking and Will you return, *she asks softly,* to Brussels? *as she entrusts the packet to him, with coin for his trouble, more coin to purchase his silence because the errant puppet-master, she says, is* Our ne'er-do-well sib, sir, and Mister Bok would be so displeased—with me—*She puts up a hand in partially feigned distress.* A man such as yourself, so well-traveled, surely you understand a sad family division?

The drummer nods, unsurprised by life: Oh yes, *he has seen such squabbles before, in fact he himself has a missing sister, married a fool of a tailor who drank faster than he could sew, though the drummer did his best to dissuade her, and their own saintly mother despaired…. And on and on as Decca stands tense as a felon, house noises rising until she pretends to hear Rupert approaching, perhaps it really is Rupert so* I must go, *squeezing his hand around the pouch she watches him pocket, the coins in another pocket, how she hates to trust in this man or anyone, especially in a matter such as this.*

But she is finally rewarded, not by the drummer after all but instead a sour-looking character, booted in mud and stiff with military bearing, either that or a rod up his back passage as You are the madam of this place? *his chilly greeting, her equally chilly response as he is not at all whom she expects—*

—until she sees emerging that same calfskin pouch: and her hands in instant reach to snatch it from him, longing to open it at once, but he stands staring at her as if awaiting some response, does he expect to be compensated? until finally You are very like, *he says.*

I beg your pardon?

You and the jongleur. You are very like.

She examines him more closely, then: he is a clue. You are acquainted with the man who sends this? You are his friend?

Friend, *says the man,* no. Though I do have his acquaintance. *But he will say no more.*

Open at last, the lover's eye startles her: its opulence as well as its meaning, his eye is upon her, yes, as she pins the strange and precious thing inside her bodice, to lie like a secret at her heart. But the rest of the message is past her comprehending: Istvan warning of an "action" brewing, an army's advance: what can he possibly be doing, what patron can he serve who would put him in such proximity, entitle him to use that army's couriers, make him privy to any of its plans? but "I may be your way soon," he writes, though without explaining why. Then, at the paper's wrinkled edge, scrawled as if in haste or pain, the addendum, "Have you seen him?" and this she fully understands.

The courier makes it plain he does not mean to tarry, and the less time he spends, the less Rupert need know—but if Istvan is to come this way, soon he will know everything, both of them will know how she has lied. Never mind that the lies were her only safety, no help for that now, no help for her but to pen instead a kind of truth: Yes, she has seen Rupert, in fact through sheer happenstance he is here; he speaks not at all of his travels so she does not ask, but he has settled in wonderfully, all is well. The pen trembles as she closes with Your devoted, *then cannot recall if she signed the first missive "Decca" or "Agatha," burns her finger on the candle, the fat blob of wax still warm as flesh as she passes the letter to the courier, there at the bar with a swallow of gin, not even a nod as he drinks and leaves. She does not watch him go, as she did not watch Mattison die, only held him in her arms until the thing was done. Nor does she watch the road, for Istvan's advent—how? At the head of an army? Fleeing an army? In some other capacity entirely? Does it matter?*

All that night she sits wakeful, poring over the Poppy's accounts, the book held across her tented knees. At dawn she drinks tea strong as Velma can steep it, sipped scalding hot between her teeth, then goes resolutely about her daily tasks. If there is a certain added shrewishness to her demeanor, a heightened tendency to slap and snap, it goes unremarked, though Rupert wonders somewhat at this sudden ill-weather gust.

To the General, immersed in logistics, steeped in his own brew, it seems he has barely passed on the madam's reply for final delivery before Hanzel is at his door, a different Hanzel than any he has seen before, pale with some emotion he does not even trouble to suppress as I'm off, *curt though he gives a bow, seeming to think that will settle the matter, obviously impatient when recalled by the General's calm questions: By whom has he been summoned? Is there trouble? What news that he wishes to share? but* No news, Hanzel *says*. It is merely time I was about my own affairs.

Of course, as you wish. *No point to detain him, he can always be followed; but this does not smell like betrayal—indeed its opposite, as if Hanzel has been recalled by a master he serves most gladly— though the General is shrewd enough to know, has always known, with both approval and regret, that Hanzel feels no loyalty at all to him.* Still, the roads are uncertain these days—will you have an escort?

I'll have my mecs.

The General smiles. Well. Woe betide the man who halts you, then. Safe travels, Hanzel. I hope your affairs meet all success.

The smile offered in return is so extraordinary—a glimpse into a palace, a prison, a place without a name—it is as if the General sees Hanzel for the first time, or rather not "Hanzel" at all, but the man whose true name he has never learned. That man gives another bow—I am counting on it, sir—and then is gone, leaving a certain emptiness in his wake.

The General toils alone until the evening, until a visitor arrives without announcement, a pleasant man with no accent at all, who accepts a glass of brandy and asks, Where is your actor, then? I had hoped to see a show.

There's no bottling a firefly. Hanzel has gone.

It was Dusan, your gipsy? Well! That is disappointing. I much enjoyed his performances in Brussels.

Perhaps you'll see him elsewhere, *says the General, reaching to take a map case from the shelf.*

False dawn, the bedclothes' musty rustling, Istvan dozing, does he? or no, awake and watching as Rupert sets the silent body of Pan to one side, the knowing wooden eyeballs and "You used to ask me," Istvan's smile, "'cover him,' remember?"

Slipping back beside him, into the fugitive warmth. "Who?"

"Marco. Remember? You'd say, 'Cover him, I don't want him to watch.'"

Somberly, "I remember." His own gaze half turned away. "Whatever happened to Marco?"

"He's here," Istvan pointing back to Pan. "The arm joints, and the feet—all I could salvage, really."

"Salvage?"

"Bits and pieces. They fucking *broke* him, yeah? Past where I could fix. If I had him now, may be I could do a better job of—"

"Who broke him?"

How long to suffer it, yet how briefly told: in the cold of the Cell, Istvan's murmurs, Rupert's stillness, one arm locked around his shoulders, holding him close: "—and made this other, right there in her rooms. She wasn't a bad sort, Lucienne, it's thanks to her I've got the Chevalier. Though she'd not thank me herself, I suppose."

"She cared for you, this woman?"

"Who knows?" and back to the story, the chateaux, the drawing rooms, the jewel-box theatre where "I saw you," Rupert's murmur. "And—" a nod toward Pan. "I watched you sing."

"In Prague? You were—You *saw* me? What in the *fuck*, Mouse!" to bring Rupert's own tale, spooling backward, the words welling up like wrack on the tide—

"—a berth aboard the *Queen Maritsa*—"

"You, on a boat? You hate the sea."

"Yes, and casting up every hour, hung over the rail. But that was before—" that ship and that journey, Agatha peering like a starving cat, Ag turned Decca and "She said she'd had no word of you since. So we fetched up here. Until I left her with Mattison—"

"To go to fucking Prague?"

"To look for you. You seemed—well-tended."

"But you told none of this to me?"

"When, then? or now? I am telling you now."

Istvan's face is white. "And to walk away, as you did before—"

"I was weary of your whoring!"

"And look at you now! Partner in a brothel." Silence. "'No word'? And then to say she'd no clue of *you*, where you were." Furiously: "Her fucking letter, you in the next fucking room, yeah? Who'd ever guess she was such a cunt of a liar? Let me go, I have something to say to her—"

"No."

"Mouse, let me—"

"No, I said. First tell me—" the rest of it, all of it, the two stories made one at last: the deed to the Poppy, the toffs a fortune earned and pissed away, and what of "You and Georges?" Rupert staring down at the creased and rumpled coverlet. "You know him, I can see."

"Not the way you're thinking. I've been of use to him a time or two—I said, not that way! I carried his messages, in Brussels, stuffed up in the mecs. So he owed me."

The relief almost weakening, a sour weight removed but "Men like him owe nothing to men like us. They make certain of that."

"Men like him can never accomplish all they fathom to do, that's why they need other men, like your friend Vidor, or Arrowsmith, or even mutts like me. Like having extra fingers on your hand." Istvan twitches his fingers. "Wouldn't that be helpful. So I mentioned to him—"

"Mentioned?"

"Jesu you're tiresome! I fucking *asked*, Mouse, I called in my chits and asked if, whatever war he studied on brewing, could he keep you and your stupid building out of the stewpot! Since you refused to do the sensible thing and leave with me after I came all this God damned way to get you! Why do you think he quartered here—because he fancies your fucked-out whores?"

For a moment Rupert can say nothing. Finally, deep and soft, a voice even Istvan has rarely heard, "I cherish the gesture. But it is dangerous, to consort with someone like Georges. The world's not your puppet-stage—"

"Nor your God damned fancy-house. And my 'gesture' worked, yeah? You may have soldiers pissing in the lobby but at least they're not using us for kindling. Now let me up, I want to have at Ag."

"No," again and tenderly, arms around him in the darkness, the enormous and delicate stillness of refuge restored, holding him in that quiet until he quiets as well, like boys on the roof asleep at last beneath the braided greatcoat, sheltering both into the chill gray gleam of morning.

And later still, Istvan up on one elbow, light striping bars across his chest, his face: "Think of it, the waste of it. All that time."

"We have time."

That very morning, Istvan's toys, strings, glycerin caps and traps and all are transferred into Rupert's rooms, the hobnailed outer parlor, the tiny bedchamber beyond as clean and spartan as a lonely boy's. The Chevalier and Miss Lucinda stand in comfortable ease against the windowless far wall, the bundled Bishop beneath them, Pan alone at the table like a guest about to dine. Omar helps carry the largest trunk, as Puggy watches, a furrowed frown to meet Lucy's knowing smile: "Now we'll have some larks," she says.

"If we survive."

Downstairs, in the kitchen, Velma feeds the fire, as Decca listens to the footsteps above, to and fro, purposeful and quick; she rations out the oatmeal, she steeps the tea as ruddy-black as blood.

Walter Porter

I sent young Andrew up there myself, I said, Andrew, get yourself in tight with them army officers while you can, this place is drying up like a fly in a windowsill. "War," they're calling it. For those boys up in the hills I wager it is, they die as if it's war for certain. Saw a pair of them brought in yesterday with their heads blown straight off, just neck-stumps left, atop the dead-wagon. Saw another come in this morning all dazed-like, asking after his mother, "Mummy, Mummy?" and wandering around, they had to shoot him when he climbed up the mercantile roof. That's why I wanted Andrew in tight with the officers, because there's no place safer in any battle than a general's berth, wheresoever it might be.

Hunkering at the Poppy, though, that's pure smarts on Bok's part. Keeps the hearth burning, and the building safe as a babe at its mother's tit, since the building's what truly matters anyroad. You can always get more girls, even if they fancies themselves actresses; they do that here, too, girls calling themselves the Jersey Lily and Sarah Sweetheart, flouncing up and down the stage. But without a place to house 'em, you may as well be out in the Alley with the strays, and how long can you last like that?

Figures Bok would get the army in afore we thought to do it, or Faulk, either, who lost his nerve and took that bitch up to Victoria after all. Bok's got a good nose for business, and a brass set for sure; I always said so. That set-to he had with Artie Redgrave, I knew he'd come out on top, and he did. Artie's a fool for giving tuppence credit to that stupid wight Elwin, who must of been dropped on his head by his mother, herself no better than she should be, me *and* Artie both had her more than once.... Anyone who shot Elwin would do this town a mighty favor.

Ought to shoot that jumped-up dollmaker, too, or drive him off anyroad. Frenchman, Dutchman, whatsoever he is, he's the type that likes to stir the pot, then hop off when it gets to bubbling. I knew ones like him, we had one or two here at the Gaiety years back, penny opera or some such foolishness. Come from the road, we sent 'em back up the road, and good riddance. This one too, oh he's here there and everywhere, with Bok over there and the army man here—I saw him myself, gave me a coin to lead him—and the other Frenchman, who I hear's booked himself onto the train; it's got too hot for him here, I'm guessing, or maybe just too cold…. The only one the dollmaker don't consult with is that Mister Vidor, which maybe shows some smarts after all.

That Vidor—I told Artie, I said, watch out for that one, he'll do you down, money or no money. But Artie's too greedy to listen, greedy and dim. That's why Elwin's his deputy, he looked around town for someone to make him feel clever, and Elwin was what he found. Does he know that that Vidor's got a deal set with Rawsthorne and Pepper, them out of Gottsburgh with their sawmills and ironworks? The man drives the munitions cart, his son saw Vidor there in the yards, saw him plain, ugly as he is you can't mistake him. Standing there all a-smiling, shaking hands with Victor Rawsthorne—and *his* son, now, the skinny one, used to bang down our Carrie something awful, it got so she'd run when she saw him coming: *Warn me, Walt,* she'd say. *Warn me when you see that beanpole, and I'll put the "Out" sign on my door sharpish.* Carrie was the last of our girls to go, Carreen O'Brien up on the stage, sings the Scottish laments real pretty, but she'd no mind to end up dead, she said, said she'd flip her skirts for the conductor and keep what cash she nicked to pay her way once the train reached its end, wherever that may be…. Makes sense that a gent like Vidor would be cozy in with Rawsthorne, you got to smash buildings flat before you can rebuild 'em, and to rebuild 'em you need lumber and nails. But you try to tell that to Artie, or anything sensible at all.

Me, I been watching, and waiting, keeping my head down: I'm too old to be a soldier, but old men get shot by accident, too. Andrew thinks I ought to pull up stakes before it gets rougher, and what am I staying for now? I been on the door at the Gaiety since it opened, just about, since that mick Halloran and his brother's time, but my time here is just about through. We're closed down even though the door's still open, without girls there's no reason to come in, and anyroad we're out of drink. Owls in the roof now, and the rats are everywhere…. Andrew's the last of my kin in town, and he'll go with the army when it leaves, which he says will be more than soon: *There's almost nothing left to burn, Uncle,* he tells me, *we've got to be movin' on.* "We," mark it. There's plenty more he could tell, following that general all around, with his gloves and map box and cigars and whatever else, but Andrew keeps his trap shut to keep his post. Well, that's as it should be, the boy's got to look out first for himself.

If I do stay, I may go over to the Poppy. I knew that Mattison, we was never friends but I knew him; I helped bury him, too. Thought I'd seen the end of the Rose and Poppy then. But I watched them bring it back, Bok and his red-headed sister, or whatever she is, who was Mattison's concubine, they may yet bring it back again though this war's stamped us flat to the weeds. Well, the weeds will survive it, they always do. And, like the Good Book says, the chaff'll be blown away.

Hard snow has come to Gottsburgh, and with it a consumptive's wind, cold and viscous, surging in waves. The General curses softly to himself, young Andrew stoic behind him, as they splash and plow through muck and slush, heading for a grand, well-lit hotel, white Doric columns and the scent of brandy, a suite of rooms stoked blessedly hot, where in some hours they will be joined by several compatriots, and, later, by Mr. Arrowsmith, before beginning a longer journey over the water. Andrew carries the map box, lights the General's cheroots, and keeps to himself both his thoughts and his excitement over their eventual destination. Several of the junior officers have detailed the moral elasticity of the young ladies abroad, with thrillingly explicit examples, and he is eager to put this knowledge to firsthand test.

There is no snow, yet, in the town, though one can smell its advent on the thin wind that sifts through the forest, that frame of trees protected from the ax by the gun, the soldiers it shelters; the trees closer to the town were chopped for warmth long ago. The churchyard ground is frozen, so the bodies still requiring burial—many have already been burned—lie stiff in the back of the shuttered mercantile; otherwise the wolves and the packs of stray dogs will make of them a swift and handy meal.

When the wind shifts, it drives off the smell of burning so the smell of decay might rise, astonishing its potency even in the cold. It reaches Mr. Arrowsmith in his rooms, through the windowsills stuffed with rags, and lends a spur of further energy to his penultimate chore; the trunk gone on ahead, his only luggage is an oblong writing case, polished teakwood and mother-of-pearl; this he secures and carries underarm down to the lobby, drafty with the loss of its plundered hangings, the sourly sober desk clerk informing two wary drummers of the last train's scheduled departure. They retreat, to huddle over a bottle they are loath to share, even for coin, even when the clerk threatens. Mr. Arrowsmith, passing, reflects that greed is a sin, though he himself feels a great and simple inner famine for a cup of Assam tea, very hot, drunk in his dressing gown, with his sweet Liserl at his side; ah, well.

148

There is little left to do, now, but make his final visits, and stay alive a few hours longer, until the evening train departs.

One of those on whom he plans to call is out upon the darkening streets: Istvan, abroad on a private prowl. Hair blown and tangled by the carrion wind, bundled like an urchin in raveled gloves and cast-off greatcoat that he wears as carelessly as the opulent outfits discarded on the road back to Rupert, as a snake sheds its skin, to become again the vagabond player, the one-night-only apparition that, like a dream, disappears with the dawn. The *deshabille* suits him, cloaks him in camouflage, frees him to loiter and examine the town *in extremis*, indulge his own hunger for motion: he has been pent, spending so much time in one place—one place? One building, Jesu. No show to mount tonight, and Mouse is busy, Ag he has promised to leave be, so: hand in pocket for a brownish little apple, a pippin apple that he peels with a surgeon's precision on the windy mercantile porch, watching with interest a caravan of limping soldiers traverse the avenue like Adam driven from Paradise, the midwife following after, her face bright red in the cold, trundling like a carter a scratched and painted two-wheeler advertising her art and services; she is the town's sole doctor, now, Adderley and his monocle having been dispatched some weeks before by a stray explosion from the cannon that, like thunder, now call to one another from the hills. Istvan tosses the apple core aside, tugs his collar higher, heads back into the street toward the Poppy, past the hotel. He does not see the two drummers from the lobby, at the door now, step out to follow him down.

At the quiet Poppy, Decca follows Velma into the storeroom, pondering what else might be done to the everlasting potatoes and oatmeal to make them worth swallowing yet again. Her leg aches from the constant sideways gait of her broken slipper: she has tried to mend the heel with bits of wood, but the shoes are fit for nothing but the ash-pile now; it is amazing how long one can make do, but nothing comes from nothing's rind. Velma suggests adding to the oatmeal glue a handful of peas, old as stones and just as tender, and Decca shrugs. There is a finger of cornmeal left, and, sweet surprise, some still-edible molasses: that will help. Istvan used to love molasses, would fling a sticky rope of it into a snow bank, retrieve it frozen, and chew it for an hour…. Istvan, now in Rupert's rooms: What does that portend? Something final is in motion, is already occurring, but as usual she is powerless against it. After leaving Velma, she retreats to her own rooms, turning the penny lock to sit sorting through her things, account books, sachet-tin and ribbons, lover's eye and the deed to the Rose and Poppy, telling each through her fingers like a rosary's beads, like the silver-paper links in the chain made for her so long ago, frail as a sigh though stronger than the time it has outlasted, the other chain between the three in fragments, now, she knows this. She knows this. What to take, what to leave? because that will be the next thing, the knock at the door—

—but the knock that comes summons her instead to Colonel Essenhigh, arriving unexpectedly, snow-coated and tired but glad to have outridden the darkness, gladder still that he need only stay one night in this place that so disgusts him, worse than the war-fields, with its queer innkeeper and unwholesome diddling dolls. There are others the General could have sent on this errand, but the General has entrusted it to him; so be it, he is a soldier above all, he does his duty as he is bidden—though privately, in his darker moments, the colonel suspects the General of having a sense of humor unbecoming in an officer. He inquires of Decca, with an automatic politesse toward women, all women, even madams, if she is well, and she swallows the sudden laugh that clogs her throat, and thanks him instead for his concern: Yes, she is quite well, thank you, and hopes that he is the same.

Making her own quiet way, Lucy, overhearing this exchange of false courtesies, stops to peep in passing—what an ass that colonel is; how ugly Decca looks these days, all stiffened up, as if she has swallowed a whole paperful of pins—then continues up the stairs, down the hall toward Mr. Rupert's rooms; so much simpler, when Istvan was in the Cell, to visit with the mecs, just scratch on the door for admittance—but Istvan is off somewhere, and see, now, Mr. Rupert himself, deep inside himself, step inside those rooms and shut the door. She hears the key turn, turns on her heel, lets out a sigh: Very well, back to her Blue Room, no mecs today—though she misses them sorely, it seems the more she works with them the more she longs to, though the girls mock her, and Puggy teases: *Why, hadn't you any dollies as a child?* But there is so much she could be doing, one idea pops another till she has a fair litter to corral: the queenly costume she would like to fashion for Miss Lucinda, glitter-paste jewels and a new feathered hat—from her own angel's costume, the wings picked carefully apart—and she has a piece of velvet set aside that would look a treat; plus a check of the strings for the Bishop, a freshening brush for the Chevalier, himself locked away for so long, *Your horsemanship is not admired.* And every rummage through the trunks unearths some unglimpsed treasure: like that strange infant neatly wrapped in butcher's paper, the blue-eyed baby puppet that, says Istvan, is no longer able to cry the tears it used to, its lids dried shut in the sockets; but surely it can be mended? How she would relish the chance to try, to use again the fascinating tools, the strong-smelling glues.... A baby, how would one put a baby into the shows? as her memory stirs, the long-ago player and his hook-nosed puppet, the puppet wife and, yes, baby, too! Now, what did that baby do?—

—as footsteps ascend, Omar leading the colonel bearing news from the General, news he will deliver to Mr. Bok with a certain sour satisfaction. Another sort of pleasure lights his eyes as he watches Vera scuttle by in chemise, hair down, from one room—hers?—to the next, arms piled with dress and petticoat and ribbon-trailing hat, graceless yellow and bedizened blue, nothing matching, most of it the property of others, which explains her stealthy haste—though not too hasty not to mark the colonel's regard, to toss him a wink over her shoulder, and flash him half a tit: a working girl needs all the friends she can muster, no matter where she is or where she goes.

In the room beyond the hall-locked door, past Rupert at his desk— gaze fixed on the coins before him, sight a turmoil inside—the silent puppets bide: the tall Chevalier with his wasted prick, the lugubrious Bishop, lovely Miss Lucinda whose feet are fashioned for the dance: if one were to solicit their opinions, what might they say? seeing as they see so little, there in the quiet room, hostage to inaction, awaiting their master's voice? Or, as the General once suspected (himself a would-be player in his faraway youth, a mellifluous declaimer of poetry not his own), are they privy in some deeper way to that master's secret intentions, via art's telepathy, the shared mind of shared purpose played out through the months and years? Are they in some half-formed, faulty manner not living, yet alive?

And thus perhaps most of all the silked and coffined Pan Loudermilk, seeded with lost Marco's parts, themselves so potent with love and betrayal; as Istvan himself once mused, how different is a man from a mec? A rhetorical observation, but one at which Pan, were he capable, might smile, perhaps does smile there in the dark, manipulation after all his métier; how different is a mec from a man?

Hector Georges

Courtesy is vital, especially when ill tidings must be given—and Mr. Bok and his situation surely merit that courteous attention—but one cannot bilocate, no matter the need or desire. It is a bit of a pity, making Essenhigh the messenger, but he is the most expendable of my officers, and at any rate a local man, my future representative there, if he lives. If not, it will be Lieutenant Rodgers, or that large, bowlegged fellow whose name always escapes me, the one Javier calls Pantagruel. Any one of them can sift through the town's ashes, and gather up any clinkers as they fall. And blame the wreckage on the foreigners' advent, an idea already so widely credited it verges on the truth. "Huns," they call them now, and it's a short step from a "foreigner" to the neighbor one dislikes…. War is always a hazy business. And loss tends to foster a grudge.

For now, we are in endgame, in this landscape at least. The men must be out of the Poppy summarily and sent to Gottsburgh; Essenhigh will speed them up the road. The greater withdrawal is proceeding steadily, without undue delay, or so Jack Pepper tells us, though Rawsthorne is impatient to begin his shipments. Well. My young yokel aide is impatient, too: some of the lieutenants have told him that the cunts of Paris smell of roses and dispense champagne, and I thought he would mount up and begone that very evening, blizzard or no blizzard. It is so heady to be young.

Although one need not be a stripling to act as one—witness Vidor's capers, shaming in a man his age. Yet his tantrums do open certain avenues. Vidor and I have skirmished before and elsewhere, not always on the same side; he makes an ugly foe. In London, he blocked my progress, and set me back not a little; in Prussia, he almost cost me my commission. Fortunately Javier was there to intervene…. We'd thought him dead, Vidor, left him for such at any rate. Though here he was a useful ally, for a time. Is that shocking? That is commerce. Why else make war?… Yes, there is the glory, too.

But Mr. Bok—I would prefer not to leave his establishment undefended, retreats are notably chaotic, and his resources are at ebb-tide. And he was a good innkeeper to us, though the men were a trial, I'm a-crawl myself with their merry herds of lice. His sister—no, she's Hanzel's sister; strange, that—at any rate, Miss Decca has an instinct for parsimony rarely met outside a gaol, grudging every mouthful we swallowed though we more than paid our way. She shan't weep to see us go—vinegar tears, and pull her armor-plates tight, that young lady will outlast Armageddon. Women can be so ruthless, it's a pity one can't put them in the lists. I'd send Essenhigh to *her* without a moment's regret. For either of them.

I do hope he's sense enough not to revel in his rôle, Essenhigh, nor try to take advantage, or Mr. Bok might lose patience, there's no love lost between those two. Though it takes a great deal to provoke Mr. Bok, as we have noted. Marvelous fortitude. Yet a certain obscurity of vision—*par exemple*, surely he knows that he is Vidor's Achilles' heel? Every man has one. Hanzel, for instance, is Mr. Bok's.

"Leave off," says Lucy sharply, arrested in her swift pass through the lobby by a grubby knot of soldiers, headed by this boy barely shaving but old enough to have slept for months in a trench in the hills, to reek like shit and gunpowder, this boy who grabs at her sex through her skirt, then fastens on her arm as "Come on, judy," with a lopsided grin; he looks half mad. "Kiss me, I'll make it worth your while."

"Leave off, I say—"

"Look, I'll give you this," reaching into his uniform jacket to draw forth a peculiar souvenir, something shining, something dark, she bends in suspicious curiosity—then cries out at the sight of a severed, brownish finger still wearing its braided gold ring, the boy laughing at her revulsion: "Stuck on a knuckle, judy, so I took finger 'n all! Don't you like it?" but "Leave *off*!" Lucy stamping her slippered foot on his, hard at the instep, not pain so much as sharp surprise that drops his grip, "Fucking whore!"

—but she is at the lobby door, inside the theatre where Jonathan, onstage, fingers the piano keys, making no sound, as if his silence now extends to his music as well. Beside him sits pallid Pearl, bundled in a shabby pink wrapper, head on his shoulder like a weary child's. Laddie hunches knees-up on the chaise, in a brown study, lines between his eyes that echo Rupert's. Puggy, mending a prop basket, weaving colored paper through cracked willow, looks up at Lucy's advent, makes a game smile: "Good evening, mademoiselle," but "An empty lobby," she growls, "*that* would make for a good evening, and those stinking riffraff kicked back to the gutter where they came from. I swear to the Holy Virgin, never will I fuck a soldier again." Crossing to the piano, to Puggy, to the prop box, spangles and feathers, tarnished and limp, she makes a mighty sigh and "Vera's packed her traps," she says, to everyone and no one. "She's on her way up the road tonight."

Their startled murmurs, Jonathan's wide eyes and "The last train," Lucy says. "Bought her ticket with that money she squirrels away, you note she'd never the price of a ribbon or a cigarette, always promising to pay you back later. Well, she's paying us back all right. Off

154

she goes, to Victoria she says, and thence to Paris. Paris! She might as well fly up to the moon."

Puggy frowns deeply. With hair again he looks younger, and, younger, more uncertain, as if his role as impresario has been stripped from him, and no other offered to fill the widening void. "And Velma, too?"

"Velma? Who knows?" Lucy picks at the velvet of the chaise, its blue worn through in spots to the stuffing beneath, like a sky plagued with soiled clouds. Spinning Jennie's old swing dangles empty, its shadow in faintest revolution, weighted by the ghost of a ghost. "Who ever knows, with her?"

Silence then on the stage, as if a performance has dwindled to no conclusion, the actors caught without business or lines and "It's over here for us," says Puggy glumly. "Soldiers and refugees, there's no one left to play to. Unless we relocate to the cemetery. What does Omar say, of Vera?"

"I've not seen Omar. May be he's on the train, too," but Jonathan shakes his head and points thumb-upward, an emphatic gesture and "He's gone upstairs," Pearl translates. "With Mr. Rupert, and that army man."

"The General? He's returned?" but Jonathan shakes his head again, folds his face into a scowl, fingers fanned at his cheeks and "The colonel, you mean," and Lucy, troubled as she is, has to laugh: "You do him perfect, Jonnie. Good for you. May be you ought to hop the train and go to Paris, too."

"Bad advice," a voice from backstage, Istvan approaching hands-in-pockets, his steps uncertain, his face oddly pale. "Roost in a storm, that's what a wise bird does. Lucy-Belle, a moment?" to lead her back into the darkness, open his coat, old brown greatcoat that makes her gasp for its collar is soaked crimson, blood in his hair, blood everywhere but "Hush," in her ear, a hand gripping her own; his is so cold, though he stands upright, in animal instinct to show no hurt. "Not one word. Can you sew?" Her parted lips go narrow, her shoulders firm; she nods. "Good girl. Take me to your room," down the sideway from the stage to the stairs, she his support to the hall above where quiet voices come from Rupert's rooms, Omar outside in the hall with his face to the jamb, listening with all his might so he barely marks their passage, Lucy quick to close the Blue Room door, muffling its click as she muffles her shock to see the wound exposed, neck and shoulder and "They were aiming for my throat, yeah?" Istvan says; he sits heavily on the bed. "Fucking drummers, if that's what they were, fucking thieves. If that's what they were."

Swift she threads her needle, gives him a fat chunk of cork to bite and "This will hurt," she says. "Try to think of something else.... You mustn't move," and he does not, though sweat runs down his greening face and she sweats to see it, knows the pain she causes, does not stop or flinch until the gash is mended; think of something else, yes, and "There," Lucy trembling now that the job is done, clamping a folded square of yellowed silk to the wound. "If I had some gin—or dope, anything—or Laddie might have some smoke—"

"Not to worry, I'd thought it was worse," and then for a moment darkness, how long? and he on his back on her bed, more blood, trickling down his face?—no, water, Lucy sprinkling water to bring him to but "Stop," his whisper, "I'm all right—" speaking again to the darkness, eyes open once more to see Rupert, paler than he. Hoisted upright by strong arms, Rupert's arms, Rupert's voice harsh as Lucy settles him in Rupert's bed: "Omar—the door, Omar, and not to move until I fetch you. Understand? Lucy, you come with me."

It was Istvan Rupert meant to seek, after closing the door on Essenhigh heading off to round up his rabble, content to have delivered the bad tidings—

It's the General's orders, not mine: we're to be on the road by morning, every man of us standing. Ask me, I'd've counseled we not stop here at all. Soldiers—men—don't belong in a place like this.

And did the General ask?—dry as he absorbed the news: never doubting its coming, still he had hoped for more time, a month, even a week, to compose some ancillary plan. Flux is already upon them: Istvan's fury with Decca cannot bide with her presence; his time here too is ended, he knows, knew it in the dawn just passed, silent and replete: they will, they must leave together—with a moment's honest pleasure for the pleasure that decision will bring to Istvan, but how is it to be accomplished? Especially now? Together they might travel swift and safe, they have done so before in dangerous conditions, but what of Decca and the others? Without the soldiers, this building—one of the few in town standing whole and wholly habitable—is bound to be swarmed, unless Omar and Puggy want to spend every waking moment gun in hand; if they had guns, and enough bullets to put in them.... Perhaps they ought all to go, travel in a body as far as Archenberg, say, or even Victoria, and in that city's safety each disperse on separate paths. There are not provisions enough to shutter up and wait it out, and on what kind of desert would they reopen? even in the spring, when the need for fuel is less? No. The best solution is flight. As the army leaves, they will follow. May be that clod Essenhigh will provide some cover; if the General were here, they would certainly reach such an accommodation. Curious to think that Istvan knew Georges in another guise—the puppet-spies, a strange idea. Someday Rupert will hear all those tales—

—as he cracked his door again, on Decca, nearly on the threshold, about to knock? No, only standing, a wraith in the hallway waiting, for what? and weeping, see even in the dimness the shine of her silent tears. It is strange and sad, how little she cries, most girls will sob on a pin drop, but Decca's tears seem to scald, have always been so; why? Strange and sad, to live with her so long, and know her so little, suspect

157

none of her lies but only their reasons, she herself so strange and so sad and *I heard,* she said then, an airless little murmur. *The army is leaving us.*

And he as quiet to explain his plans, they must pack and gather, all of them, they must prepare to go—as her tears rained faster, was she frightened of the journey? They would be fleeing danger, worse to stay here, he tried to explain but still she wept and shook her head, stiff as wood when he took her, finally, in his arms, her own arms tight to her sides, face turned away until *Do you not see,* freeing herself, one hand out to touch the wall, as if it were a living person she grasped for strength, for comfort. *This place is mine. Your name is on the paper, and you've cared for it, yes, I'll never say you haven't. But it's mine, and I'll not leave it.*

Silence then, Rupert surprised that he did not feel more surprise: and a relief that shamed him, how easy it would have been to say "yes" and go, to leave her, Christ knows he and Istvan had done it before, how many times before? so instead his arguments, quiet and stern: she did not understand, a building was not worth her life but *This is my life,* flat, her tears gone dry. *My own life, do you not see? You have Istvan, he has you. I have this.*

His gaze turning cold, then, he could not check it, did not try as he saw that she understood, slowly shook her head and *You said you did not wish to speak of him, you said we would not speak of him—*

And what to say to that? more arguments? when all is finished, the chain broken that held him, too much life already given in the service of those lies, so *We must not be enemies,* he said, holding her gaze. *We have enemies enough out there,* nodding toward the stairs, the doors, the world, as the sudden rush of footsteps made that truth exquisitely clear: Lucy in anxious haste, he must come *now,* Mr. Rupert, hurry! to find Istvan white and bloody across her bed, his blood in surge so hard that for a moment he could not see, only that still face at the heart of a grayish tunnel, when Istvan stirred at last his own head swam. Under Omar's guard in his own rooms, now, safe, now, but too near a thing—

—and Decca after one look thrusting Lucy aside: "I will see to him," to Rupert, as if no one existed but themselves; it is for the last time.

A small blue tin fetched from her own rooms, from its hiding place in the seat of the petit-point chair; basin and bowl from the kitchens, water from the pot barely hot but warm enough to sponge the blood from his skin, his hair, pink floods of it, and she weeps, again, sound-less and in pain: see the crooked pucker of Lucy's black stitching, oh trust that whore to bungle it, if only he had come first to her.... Eyes closed his grimace as the water sluices down his chest, soaks the bed beneath, his sideways mutter—"Stop drowning me, darling"—then frowns, blinks, tries to sit up: "Ag?" as she presses him back, clean cambric, the last of her precious lady's kerchiefs bound to the wound: "Be still. It's I. Please, be still."

From around her neck she takes a wee brass key to open the little blue tin: inside is a supply of laudanum, last souvenir of departed Dr. Adderley. She tips Istvan a generous swallow that he shudders to receive, waits, tips him another. As his taut shoulders ease, she sets aside the basin to wrap him in a fresher coverlet, and cleaner, at least she can spot no moving lice but "Stop," he mutters, irritable now as the pain begins to lessen. "I'm not dead yet, don't bind me…. Ag?"

"I'm here."

An extravagant frown, brows together, lips pursed: somehow the wounding has made him younger, masks overridden by the hurt, parted by the drug and "Ag," he says, "you lied to me." Silence. "About Mouse, a villainous lie. Why?"

Silent still, she does not answer, begins methodically to dry his hair. *You and the jongleur, you are very like,* people have said things like that before but she never has seen the resemblance. He is so beautiful, has always been beautiful, men used to pay to watch him sing and jig, long before Marco, before Rupert ever put eyes on him…. His eyes are open, now, pupils wide: "Why the fuck did you lie? Tell me."

Why did she lie? Which lie? Does it matter? She brushes back his hair. "Do you remember our mother?"

"Mother?" A different sort of frown. "I remember that she liked to sing. And she had a little velvet reticule with peppermints, pink peppermints, for when I had the stomachache…. Give me a drop more of that dope," and she does, wondering which lady in his childhood doled out peppermints from a reticule, for surely their mother had had neither, would have sold both in an instant to keep them from the almshouse, from starving, herself starved to death at last on the pallet bed, squeezing Agatha's hands, calling out again and again for her son, *Where is my boy?* It is in him to inspire love, Istvan, love and blind devotion, they never were alike so "Try to rest," she says now. "I will sit with you, and Omar is outside, no one will pass. Try to rest."

"Where is Mouse?"

"He will be here directly," the last of her lies—or perhaps it is true; either way she will stay, calm and still in her own pain, what is pain after all but her oldest companion? oldest and most trusted—as he winces, he yawns and "I'll not be near you," he says, "not again," and closes his eyes, she beside him, waiting till she knows he dozes to touch his forehead, the pale skin of his temples: *The mudhen hatched a peacock,* their mother used to say. She will care for no one, ever, as she has cared for him, Istvan her very first love, peacock brother perched on the windowsill; but she is not sorry, no. Yes, she lied, but did she not in the end give each to the other, by giving them this place to meet again? And Istvan his road show, Rupert his authority, or at least the chance to ply it, for both of them that chance? Apart, they grew stronger than they would have together. And she is stronger, too, and wiser: she will not leave what is hers, no, and will release what is not, has never been. *This is my life; yes.* That is the truth.

A scratching at the jamb, Lucy's worried face to whisper through the gap: "How does he now? I can spell you." Decca barely spares the stare that backs Lucy from the door, to the outer door, to the hall and Omar's shrug, her own to meet it as she rises on tiptoe to tuck, what, a little mirror, crazed-silver, old but still intact, over the threshold: "To ward off the evil eye," explaining to Omar who nods, privately considering the gesture somewhat late, but surely Istvan was blessed enough to keep hold of his head, whoever it was tried to take it from him. Hear Mr. Rupert, now, closed up with that Mr. Arrowsmith, if he was not tasked to guard he would have been there sharpish to listen, Miss Decca's parlor, not a word can be heard from here but he dare not move an inch, Mr. Rupert would take *his* head and no mistake, Mr. Rupert in a rare killing mood—

—as is noted by Mr. Arrowsmith, himself very grave, watching Rupert cold as stone in the foolish little duchess chair, gaze unnaturally bright and "I had thought," says Mr. Arrowsmith carefully, "to meet with Essenhigh—we spoke, just now, in the lobby—and visit with yourself, and Hanzel too, before I left town. But now this—incident. Did Hanzel name the one who—"

"He's not spoken yet," beyond murmurs, Rupert's harsh whisper, *Who did this to you?*

There were two.

Who were they?

I didn't see much. Just the knife, with Decca's echo in his head, *That man wants him dead, can you understand though he refuses?* And his own stupid assertion, *Vidor will not touch him,* though he had seen it in his eyes, seen it in that room…. Jesu. Once again he is wrong, once again someone else has paid, Istvan has paid…. He looks, now, at Arrowsmith, silent and alert across the damasked table, teakwood case on the floor beside.

"Mr. Vidor," he says, and pauses; Mr. Arrowsmith waits. It is very quiet in the room. His hands lie clenched in his lap; still they tremble. Some of Istvan's blood has stained his shirt-cuffs.

"Enough," Rupert says.

They gaze at one another, Mr. Arrowsmith gives the slightest nod. "I understand. The General will as well. One must do as nature bids him.... May I see Hanzel?" as both stand, Rupert leading the way to his rooms, asking as they go, "You are with us until—?"

"The train departs just before midnight, I believe." Mr. Arrowsmith nods to Omar ferocious on the threshold, arms folded like a palace guard's and "I'll wait here," says Rupert, seating himself on the edge of the cracked-leather chair, hands on his knees, their tremble stilled. "I beg pardon, sir, but—leave that writing box. And keep the door open."

Mr. Arrowsmith gives him a look he cannot read. "Of course. Your caution is admirable, I understand completely."

Decca emerges with the basin and the tin, brushing Rupert in passing—her second love, he has had his farewell—and is gone before Arrowsmith has seated himself beside Istvan who, wrapped and drowsy, manages a mummer's wry smile: "You see me cast in the role of goose, messire. Carved up for the table."

"A phoenix-bird, rather. Still it is a great pity," with a shake of the head, something there of the rueful uncle, the elder brother, something genuine and genuinely fond. "You told me once that you would depart in time. With—" a sideways nod, to indicate watchful Rupert outside.

Istvan shrugs, then starts from the pain the motion brings. "Jesu.— Yes, well, it's he who blocked me."

"No doubt with sufficient reason. Well, one may safely leave matters in his hands, now." Mr. Arrowsmith looks about the half-tidy room, the splashed floor, the splotched and disordered bed, the puppets arrayed outside like waiting courtiers, surrounded by their traps and detritus; he smiles a very small smile. "You are a most dramatic fellow, Dusan." Then the smile fades. "What has befallen you is more than regrettable. A citizen attacked in the street by brigands, this town has tipped into chaos entire. If you need aught in the way of doctoring, I'll have Essenhigh send a man—" A noise past the doorway, the faintest creak of a chair. "Otherwise, I have nothing left to offer but my farewells. Perhaps we'll meet again—in the spring, say, in London? Sir Henry Irving's at the Lyceum."

Istvan shakes his head. Drugged, stitched and white from bleeding, it is still his drawing-room voice. "Spring in London gives me *la grippe*. I prefer Brussels."

"Certainly. On Goldsmith Street."

Mr. Arrowsmith rises on a bow, murmurs in Istvan's ear a word or two too low to carry, gives his uninjured shoulder a brief pat: "Be well, young man." In the outer room he retrieves his writing case, shakes

Rupert's cold hand, noting as he does how weary Rupert looks; he is a young man, too, with many cares, not least of them Dusan. "I can be reached in Gottsburgh," says Mr. Arrowsmith, "should the need require; the General as well. Beyond that, we sail."

"Many thanks." Rupert makes a small bow. "Safe travels."

"The same to yourself." Mr. Arrowsmith smiles. "Perhaps I shall meet you elsewhere, sir, some spot with better weather; Brussels, perhaps? It is pleasant there in the spring."

As Mr. Arrowsmith descends the stairs, he notes the mute piano-boy watching from the landing below, a big-eyed whore beside him; he gives both a courteous nod, that the boy as courteously returns. Behind them is another whore, the saucy one Dusan seems to favor; as soon as he leaves the stairs, she is on them, heading up.

In the lobby it is dire winter, the doors left open to drafts and gusts as the soldiers trot back and forth, swearing, shivering, decamping; Essenhigh is in his element, hardly acknowledging Mr. Arrowsmith, who in any case has done with their shared business, will need only a soldier to escort him to the train, the streets now so patently unsafe. The colonel wades happily encumbered through tedious questions with equally tedious replies, as Mr. Arrowsmith gives a small mental sigh, and sets himself to wait; noting as he does the general decrepitude of the furnishings, the burn marks on the floor, the tomcat aroma of urine, why are the foot soldiers always such brutes? until "Pardon, sir," the kitchen maid quiet at his elbow, the watchful one he has seen before at the hotel. "Miss Decca asks if you will take tea," in the threadbare kitchen hardly warmer than the lobby, but at least there is a door to close.

The maid disappears. The madam stands by the table, pot and chipped cups; silently she pours for him. Sipping, once again he longs for Assam, very very hot Assam. "Many thanks, Mademoiselle. This is just the thing on such a bleak night."

"Bleak to be sure." She pours for herself. Chapped hands and shabby the dress, yes, more patch than silk, still he notes there is indeed something of Liserl in the fineness of the face, the graceful stillness of gesture, a lady's grace; but Liserl's eyes are yet a girl's. This one—Diana the huntress might have such eyes, were she born in the gutter with no string to her bow and one arrow only to employ. Looking at him, now, over the rim of her cup: "You have spoken already to Mr. Bok."

"And to Dusan—pardon, Hanzel. Yes."

"His name is Istvan." Mr. Arrowsmith pauses, with his cup; carefully he sets it aside, keeps his gaze steady on the madam before him.

"They are leaving very soon," she says, "all of them." *Them.* He waits; he knows more is to follow. "You know the law, sir? The—property law?"

This is a surprise. "In reference to—?"

"This," she says, and begins to unfasten her bodice, three hooks, five, to bring forth a worn and much-folded paper, sets it before him; she does not close her dress. The skin of her throat is flushed, like a blush rose. "Will you—review this, sir? There is no one else to ask."

The paper is still warm from her flesh, and smells oddly, sweetly, of verbena. It is beyond all coincidence, but Liserl also favors verbena.... When Mr. Arrowsmith looks up, she is gazing down at the tabletop, eyes veiled, one curl fallen loose and soft against her cheek, red copper on snow.

"I can pay," she murmurs. "For your assistance."

Payment he would not have asked, but—that curl, this cold and ravaged room, it is quite absurd but he feels himself stirring, reaches to touch her cheek, to take the paper and "Have you a room?" he says, softly, a ridiculous thing to ask in a brothel. Already she is rising, leading him to a little chamber just past the kitchen, a kind of pantry with a cot and a stool, where she seats herself before him, hands clasped, the pulse visible in her bare throat.

"Tell me," she says, "what I must do."

Outside the icy and indifferent morning, Puggy commenting how cozy is the room, Rupert's sitting room office when "It's crowded like cattle," but all uncomplaining, himself cheek-by-jowl with Laddie on one side and the Chevalier on the other. "And it smells so much sweeter than the stables. Well, somewhat sweeter. Who in here has washed this week?"

No one answers him, though Laddie offers a tired little smile. Puggy, and Laddie; the Chevalier and the Bishop; Miss Lucinda demure in the far corner, Omar standing yawning beside. Jonathan and Pearl, hands linked, sit at the little table beside the box that holds Pan Loudermilk; Pearl keeps upon it a mistrustful eye, as if, unwatched, its occupant might somehow spring upon her. On the stairs, firm steps approach and "It's done," says Rupert, entering, snow melting on his coat, his bare head. "They're on their way up the road."

No one speaks. Puggy starts to make a joke, then seems to reconsider, lets the pause drift to a silence that grows, and grows uneasy. Resented as the soldiers were, still they were a certain safety; and now they are gone. Everything is gone, soldiers, audience, tricks, food, fuel. All that is left are the folk of the Poppy, there in the quiet room.

Oddly, it is Pearl who speaks at last, for them all—"Mr. Rupert? What are we to do, now?"—but it is not Rupert who answers. From the inner room, bandaged and half-dressed, draped in the coverlet, comes Istvan, Lucy behind him, to drop into the chair beside Pearl who leans away, into Jonathan's reassuring arm and "I'm surprised you ask," says Istvan. His hair is loose around his face, his gaze opaque as a puppet's. "We are players, are we not? What else shall we do but play?"

All eyes turn to Rupert, but for Lucy, who, alone among them, already knows what is to happen, Lucy who dozed all night in this outer room, as Rupert and Istvan spoke together in the bedroom, soft and heated—

You take them on ahead; Omar will help. I'll follow.

Why not together? but Rupert's answer none that Lucy could parse—*See this*—to spark Istvan's reply, feverish, angry, *I'll not slink*

164

like a cur out of town! We've been diddled enough by that fucking masher, I'd spit on the blade at least but *Let me,* said Rupert, in a tone so alien it made her wonder, ever after, if she had truly heard it, if it had not somehow been Istvan burlesquing, playing at the voice of doom.... Sleeping then, another restless doze, and waking to check on her patient, offer him water, ration the laudanum since *Lord knows where more will be had,* carefully capping the flask. *I'm that surprised she had any at all.*

Oh, Ag's full of surprises. Being as she is a foul liar.

I'm not surprised by that, with a smile; Lucy will always be able to smile. *How is your wound?*

It fucking hurts. And the arm's stiffening up, I can feel it.

You'll be needing me, then.

For what?

And her nod at the mecs—*For everything*—brought his faint grudging nod in return.

Now Rupert's gaze takes them all in, one to the next, ending on Istvan and "The Poppy as it was is gone," he says quietly. He looks exhausted but completely calm, a man with his mind made up. "Between the war and our losses—Vera took the train last night—we have little left, here, and less to build on. So flight's our safest course. I had hoped we might travel with the army into Archenberg, but Colonel Essenhigh—"

"Was a cunt," says Istvan. It is not as if he interrupts, rather that he speaks his part, his lines. Rupert nods and resumes: "So we must do for ourselves. As soon as may be, we will go together to Archenberg, and, if we may in safety, on to Victoria. I shall do my best to find you all new positions, or give you coin as I can." He allows them to digest this news, though none seem aback, only grieved, Puggy especially; again, all but Lucy. "You should know, too, that Miss Decca will not join us. She intends to stay on."

Omar frowns. "Stay on how? A lady alone? There's no safety in that," and "I'll talk to her," offers Puggy, "if I may."

"Certainly, and luck to you. I found her unpersuadable.... Any who choose may stay with her, of course. The rest of you, pack up your things."

The room fills with talk, then, and Jonathan's pencil and gestures, the gabble one always hears on the edge of a grave: the trivialities, the minor and essential details attending any death, who will perform what task, is there food enough for the journey, does Omar still have that little nickel-plated revolver? Rupert watches. Lucy watches. Istvan waits, then retrieves from the mounded clutter of the floor the white plague mask, and fits it one-handed to his face. From behind it: "But we shan't leave without a fanfare, yeah?" and from the folds of the coverlet brings forth a dreadful figure, cunningly worked: empty hands and a howl of a mouth, black eyes immovable and "I give you the Erl-King," says Istvan. "He will show us what to do."

Across town, in a habitat as empty and more dismal, Jürgen Vidor has at last readied himself for travel. His packing has been haphazard, the load somewhat lightened by theft: half his trinkets have been stealthily looted, the brass telescope taken, the wax flowers left, the rosewood teapoy presumably burned for heat, the silver Greek god gone as well as the stupid blue eyeball forced on him by Rupert's fool. His clothing is apparently intact, see the fawnskin waistcoat still hanging where he left it, and the burgundy silk cravat, last worn, when? to speak with Rupert, to offer him Prague, and Paris, to give him the life he deserves.... Methodically he turns his patience cards, the creased kings and their tattered ladies, teasing out the aces, ignoring the deuces and treys; it is his way. Pay attention to the larger figures, and the smaller ones will follow in their wake. It is a policy that has always served him, it serves him still.... Worse than a pity that the filthy train has ceased its operation, Arrowsmith urging him to leave like a camp follower with Essenhigh, as if that were a sensible option: *The roads are appalling, you'll want the cavalry at least—*

And how can you know what I want, Javier? Which put the end to that, at least, and sent him scurrying off to his master in Gottsburgh, the both of them on their knees to that merchant Victor Rawsthorne: it is almost comical what lucre can accomplish, what can be bought and sold. Flesh, pain, silence, allegiance, war, arms, lumber, Bordeaux, if there was any Bordeaux to purchase; everything. Nearly everything. Except Rupert Bok. Take away his funding, drive him into Georges' embrace, threaten the peace of his household: still he refuses. There is something almost piquant in such willfulness, such a challenge, who would ever have expected it here in the arsehole of nowhere, this tragic little town reduced to embers and ruin? Life is the strangest game of all.

So now there is nothing left to do but finish out this hand, turn the cards, await the reply that is brought, soon enough, by that nearly wordless creature, dwindled twin to his earlier bravo, this one may not even have language but lucre can buy him, too, a handful makes him loyal as a dog to cross into enemy lines, to bring a reply: *The favor of*

167

your presence is requested, yes, at the last, the command performance at the Poppy, his command, a final sortie. Only a short time left to while away in patience and impatience, as the silence left by cannon is filled with howling dogs and scattered fire, gunfire, who aims at whom? Impossible to tell. No Bordeaux, but still plenty of gin, and his bestial man-at-arms at the door to ward off any last feints or follies mounted by military stragglers, yes, this dungeon hotel is still as safe as houses. And so is he.

There is a certain tonic in activity: see it at the Poppy, now, as treasures are sifted, a cart is readied, blankets bunched, minor provisions gathered past Decca's measuring eye. Wrapped in blue silk and a stained gray woolen shawl, hair in careful upsweep, she is fully the mistress of the Poppy, of the silence and the cold to come, gazing upon them as if already miles away and *Go on,* she says with that gaze, *do as you will, play as you will, I'll not hinder you. Do you not hinder me,* as she makes her own careful preparations, paper and ink, stout new lock on her door, Omar private to install it and "Take this," he says, pressing upon her the little revolver. "It won't stop a man unless you stuff it into his mouth, but it'll give you time enough to scarper…. It's a sin and a shame to leave you this way, miss. This is no place for a young lady, the scavengers will soon take it over. Why not come with, and be safe?" But she resists his plea as she ignored Puggy's dire assertions, and at any rate "You will meet your own dangers, out there," she says, adding the new lock's key to her neck chain, chatelaine. "Safe travels, Omar," and to Puggy, too, busy onstage, the others trotting back and forth, glad to be doing something, tired of waiting for the war to end or worsen, for some unsaid calamity to land on the Poppy like a hawk on a mouse, the way is straight before them: one last show, "The Erl-King," and then onto the road. Pearl already dreams aloud of how it will be in Victoria: perhaps they will have a proper set of rooms, she and Jonathan, bedstead and fireplace, how lovely that would be! as he touches the piano keys, muted chords in the arching emptiness: how large the building seems, now, with no one in it but themselves. Laddie is as quiet as Jonathan, offering no plans at destination, taking little from his room, only clothing and his hashish bag, the blue-framed picture left in place, the boat on the endless sea; though he is the only one to question, softly, as Puggy sorts through the costumes and the drapes: "Why *do* we play, then, if we're closed, or closing? This last showing, what's it for?"

"Ask Mr. Rupert. Or rather, don't."

"But to an empty house—"

"It's my thought that it won't be empty," nodding toward the darkness as if some spectral audience were already in place, for one strange moment Laddie seems to glimpse it too and "I'll be glad when we're gone," he says, and Puggy silently agrees: no fanfare, this show, no matter what Istvan has said, something else is in play here that no one will acknowledge, something to do with Mr. Vidor, and the war. Ask Pan Loudermilk, perhaps he will say.... But he is a born lieutenant, Puggy, his is not to make the plans but to carry them out as well as he may: and the player's heart of him wonders exactly what the frightful little Erl-King might be up to, sequestered in Mr. Rupert's inner room with his puppet brothers and Miss Lucinda, and Istvan, one-armed and pale, but diligent as ever—

—though Lucy goes privately to Rupert, out in the stables, up to his shins in shit and slush, did those bastards never once muck out the stalls? and "It's angried, now," she says, "his arm and shoulder. Swelling to match the fever." Shivering, half-gloved hands tucked into her armpits, though her distress is not from the cold. "I can do what I can do, but a doctor's what we'll want, before—"

"I know." Should he have let Arrowsmith send for the military physician? But would Essenhigh have obeyed? or dragged his feet? Already so much, too much, delay, Istvan ought safely to be gone.... One hand to rub numb at his forehead, his wretchedness so sudden and so bare that on comforting impulse Lucy goes tiptoe to kiss his cold cheek, a sister's warming kiss, a comrade's, and "Not to worry," she says. "Whatever it asks, we'll keep him," with such stout assurance that Rupert has to smile, takes her hand in both his own: "And is he worth all the effort, that vagabond?" to bring her smile in return: "'Course he is. He's our shining star. Yours, too," with a certain daring, watching his gaze become for that instant a boy's abashed, his heart's secret revealed; secret, good Lord!—as he drops her hand, turns again to the tack and "Shortly," his back to her, "very shortly we'll be gone. Hold on."

As she tramps back across the yard, the wind lifts, cold and scorched, yet with a sudden scent of, what is it? evergreen, something fresh and living, and Lucy feels an odd and unexpected glee: not everything is lost, after all, and they will soon be on the road, traveling. Traveling! to Archenberg, and Victoria, and who knows where else besides? Remembering Istvan's litany, *the Capitalia, and the Phoenix, the Theta Grande*—what a long time ago that seems, there beside him on the narrow bed: she had not touched the mecs yet, restrung the Bishop nor dressed Miss Lucinda—which reminds her, she needs to check with Puggy on the tallow, Istvan so particular about the lights onstage—

—as she steps into the lobby, wrinkling her nose, just like the jakes compared to the air outside—and almost stumbles over Decca, crouched and scraping at, what, some foulness on the floor, like scrubbing a stain in a building on fire but "Pardon," Lucy says, nimble to step back as Decca rises to her feet. In the dimness they stand for that moment face-to-face, not madam and whore but two women, still nearly girls, to whom the world has shown itself uncaring; and Lucy wonders briefly if, had they met elsewhere, they might have been allies of a kind. Thinking back to the Palais, the girls there, Josey her friend, where is Josey now? and her sister Katy, gone so long before so "To bide here all alone," she says softly to Decca, "isn't that folly? Come with us. You can always go your own road in Victoria."

And Decca surveys her, curiously noncombative, as if her true focus is fixed elsewhere: "Never mind that. I know what I'm about." Who does she see, Decca, as she looks at Lucy? The girls at Mrs. Segunda's, fighting for scraps? The girls at the Rose and Poppy, their snickers, their sneers: *The Lady, the Widow Mattison*.... Lucy shrugs, is halfway across the lobby before Decca beckons her back: "It's yours to look after them, mind. And it's needed. Mr. Rupert is much too fond of smoking. And he suffers greatly from the headache—"

"I know."

"Coffee sometimes helps it. Or fucking. Though that's another's business, now." Despite herself, Lucy smiles. "And—" Decca does not say his name. "That other—you'll be wanting the rest of the laudanum," leading the way in silence up the stairs to her room, its disorder banished, all trig and tidy, she makes Lucy wait outside as she retrieves the blue tin box: "Here," handing over the remaining bottles. "Make sure Omar doesn't drink it on the sly. And give that other this," a calf-skin coin-pouch, the lover's eye wrapped up in wool, *my eye is on you no more*. "But wait until you reach Archenberg.... When do you go?"

"I don't know," says Lucy. She looks around at the familiar hallway, the opened doors, the emptied rooms: all the tricks who passed through these rooms, through her own Blue Room, can she remember even one of their faces? Six minutes, an eternity; suddenly she is even gladder to be going. "That's for Mr. Rupert to say. Though it can't be soon enough for all of me."

"Where is Mr. Rupert?"

"The stables," as Lucy marches off, bottles and pouch; she will do well enough, Decca thinks, watching her go, perhaps quite well as she does not love Istvan or Rupert, or if she does, it is much leavened with a greed of her own; she always did angle to be onstage, become part of the show. Well, she will have her fill of playing now, and welcome to it. Wrapping her shawl more tightly, Decca descends again, heading for the yard and the stables—

—but Rupert is no longer there, has gone upstairs to Istvan, who lies disheveled across the rumpled bed and "Laddie," flushed and dizzy. "Shared his smoke. It makes a jolly dose, with the laudanum.... See," with a nod, the Erl-King whisked sideways from his bedclothes' hiding place, "doesn't he look a treat?" One-handed to make him bow, that mouth carved open, destined never to be filled. "Puggy can work the Chevalier, and Omar tote the Bishop. But I'll need Lucy-Belle for a right arm. Left arm, I mean." He yawns.

"She came to me," Rupert says. "She's anxious about your fever."

"Not I. It keeps me warm in this fucking tomb. Until I rise... What makes *me* anxious, Mouse, is that I've got no knife. Just lying here, all unarmed," with a wheezy laugh, a breathy noise that reminds of Pan Loudermilk's mirthless chuckle. Rupert reaches for his watch chain, the steel key and "Here," turning from his desk, the narrow secret drawer, to place in Istvan's hand the little white butterfly knife. "Your knife. Did you think it lost?"

"Ah," past a moment's sweet shared silence, Rupert's faint smile, Istvan opening and closing the blade: such a satisfying feeling, very similar to working the mecs. "It can't be lost, remember? Always it will find its way back.... What other treasures have you hidden in there?"

To please him, Rupert turns the locks, springs the drawers to display a sparse cache—the important documents already sealed for travel, others, as important, safely burned—some few spiked papers and tallied receipts, a jumbled handful of coins from several nations— "What gold we've got is in the safe, and precious little of it"—but "Here's something funny," Istvan plucking between finger and thumb a jeweled snake, gold fangs on a smooth black pearl and "I'd meant it for Laddie," says Rupert, taking the stickpin from him, dropping it with loathing on the desk. "To pay for his—efforts. Well, it's his now," but "No," says Istvan, "give it to me. Not to keep, just to use. The Questioning Serpent," on a sigh; those bright and hectic eyes, all night he shivered in his sleep, shivered in the heat, fever can kill as surely as a wound. See him lean against the desk, now, as if standing upright too long is too much for him, his own weight too heavy to bear—

—as Rupert takes him, grasps him, a brief and bruising kiss as "Jesu," in a mutter, Istvan's head on his shoulder, "enough of these God damned maneuvers, I'll make an end myself—" but "No," Istvan's murmur, eyes closed; it is so odd, this fever, like being at the bottom of a well, the events above seen wavering, yet crystal clear. "We both will." Eyes open on a smile dreamy and vicious, the serpent golden in his hand. "We all will.... Send up Lucy, yeah? And tell Jonathan to limber up the keys."

A nocturne floats upon the stillness: Jonathan, solemn-eyed, playing alone and softly on the stage. There is something strange about the music, like a child's voice singing of tragedies, of sins and violations; the tune itself is not Istvan's choice, but Jonathan's—*My grandpapa taught it me. Music has charms to soothe the savage breast*—though he can say this to no one, too much to write out and no time for writing anyway. There was to have been rehearsal, at least of a kind, but no, Lucy sent to say they must prepare to perform this very night as best they may, Lucy herself pale with a chill anticipation that spreads to each of them, all of them with a role to play.... Tallow sputters, but on the piano, the last wax candles in the house shine bright and true in a crack-branched candelabrum, making plain the borderline between the light and the dark, throwing Jonathan's shadow behind him, a dark accomplice waiting by the drapes.

Then Lucy's voice—Lucy herself still unseen—begins to croon, as Jonathan, like that child lured to doom, follows with the music, a simple song about a path through the forest, the fairies above in the trees: "Watching out for you/And watching out for me," as Pearl, all in pearly white, hair loose down her back, wanders across the stage, peering out into the blackness beyond, the faded Chinese screen a warding wall around a single table, a pair of watchers at that table, a ragged man-at-arms stationed off to the side: Jürgen Vidor, fawnskin waistcoat, blood-red cravat, and beside him Rupert, dark coat and white linen, one cold hand on the tabletop. A bottle of gin sits between them, with two glasses, one half-empty, one nearly full.

To Jürgen Vidor, it is akin to a dream, as all true theatre should be: the cellar darkness, the musical mute, that pretty voice fluting nonsense words about good fairies guarding good children, represented by the third-rate temptress in the raveling nightgown.... Theatre, yes, yet no stranger or more fantastic than this night itself, this suspended moment in a dying town, a dead building, his own pocket fattened by a wad of lucre that, when this little farce has finally ended, he will hand to Rupert to purchase the corpse: so little left to buy, yet this last so precious a commodity: Rupert's freedom. It is entirely, almost touchingly, absurd and, were Rupert not so obdurate, a joke they might have pleasantly shared. Very well, he will bear humor's weight alone until the transactional *denouement*, that he hopes will occur very soon: it is villainously cold in here, worse even than the hotel that he has quit tonight, thankfully, for the last time, the traveling wagon waiting outside obtained with a surplus pair of boots, its driver's feet wrapped in rags and chilblains: that they wear nearly the same shoe size, he and the starveling local! A true farce, all of it.

All, that is, but Rupert, whom he has not seen since their last, somewhat disastrous meeting: for reasons unstated and unfathomable, he dislikes Paris and Prague; very well, they will make Italy their destination instead. They will drink black wine in the heart of Venice, they will watch the clouds scud and flutter from the Rialto Bridge, they will visit the tailors and the jewelers, China silks and Japanese pearls—and rings, yes, Rupert tapping his signet ring against the glass of gin, in unconscious time to the fairy song, fairytale onstage where now the white-robed whore confronts, or is confronted by, an eldritch apparition, a skeleton carried by, is it? the majordomo, Omar, clumsy as a bear, its strange bald head beside his own no longer smooth and "You must flee," says the skeleton in a distant voice, not Omar's, but the whore shakes her head and continues on, circling back as the fairy song repeats, as Jürgen Vidor tips the bottle, as Rupert's ring chimes almost soundlessly against the cold lip of his glass.

At the back of the house, Decca watches, wrapped in her shawl, less audience than disinterested observer; they have told her nothing and nothing has she asked, has spoken to none of them since her talk at sundown with Rupert, up in her rooms, pouring him tea drunk standing, requesting, and receiving, all keys but the last, the key to the safe, her own safety then to be assured: *It's already drafted,* handing him the document, her neat and tiny writing, pen and ink set out on the table beside. *You have only to sign it, so. A landhold lease, it's called,* to hold the building in her name as long as she lives, and no one to take it from her, no sheriff or man of the law, even Mattison back from the dead could not wrest it, now, from her grasp.

And Rupert's frown, *How do you know all this?* but she did not answer, he could read for himself the terms and conditions, all quite simple though his gaze on hers was troubled: *I'd meant to give you this,* half-sliding off the signet ring, bloodstone and gold, *to sell if I needed,* she asked then, with a little smile, *or keep if I don't?*

You might do as you like, but my thought was you'd sell it. It's all I've got of value but the gold, and half of that's already yours. His gaze returning to the paper, his question again as he signed—*How do you know to do this?* but she gave him no answer, did not need to, this secretive Decca, Agatha, whoever she is now—perhaps she was always so, Rupert's thought, though not to him? A secret within a secret, her truest resemblance to her brother, may be, her brother whose name she will not utter as he will not glance at her, as if she is already a ghost in this houseful of ghosts, Mattison, and Jennie, and all the girls before her, the dried phantoms of old lust and artifice—

—echoed by Pearl flitting up there onstage, the Bishop receding, replaced by Puggy bearing the Chevalier to tempt her again to flight, to love, Jürgen Vidor watching with mild interest this performance he himself had demanded with his note—*One last hurrah, before the deluge,* yet miming surprise when met earlier at the door: *Why, well-met, Rupert. I was unsure you would accept my invitation*—with his hill-man guard staring at Pearl as if hypnotized by the sight of a pair of tits.... And Rupert's own gaze hooded and on edge, Jürgen Vidor feels it too, he knows, can see: O if there is a God who looks after devils, let him look after them now: one hand near his knife, the other on the glass, the *ting* of his ring as, the Chevalier's rhythmic hoof beats fading, another approaches, black weeds, plague mask, bearing the Erl-King, can Jürgen Vidor spot the resemblance? Or the stickpin fastened to the little breast, gold fangs, black-festered stone as "Who are you?" asks Pearl, pausing in her song, hands clasped before her, as the piano dies to stutters, like a bird with only one song: *te-la-te, te-la-te* and "I am the Erl-King," again the distant voice. "I take the good children, I take the bad children, I like the tang of youth," the gape of the mouth a kind of smile, toothless, sexless, famished, pressing itself now on Pearl, aided by its nimble handler in the mask, Pearl half swooning to her knees as "Pleasure is pain," says the Erl-King, or is it *pleasure in pain?* as the stickpin is applied, its bright point parting Pearl's faded lace, scratching her breast so she moans, *te-la-te, te-la-te*—

—as Decca turns away, the dry whisper of her dress unheard, her passage marked only by Laddie, dark suit and half-clean linen, hair brushed neatly back, himself entering silently from the lobby door—

—as Jürgen Vidor turns unsmiling—"What is this?"—to Rupert, who makes a smile back, lips parted, leaning close to murmur in his ear: "A special tribute, messire—"

"Tribute? Or censure?"

"—to your unfailing patronage, all these difficult days. To one who fully honors his own desires," still smiling, oh Jesu he is not a good dissembler, even in the dark, Istvan can do this kind of thing so much better than he—

—as the thought of Istvan prods him onward, past Jürgen Vidor's grumble, "A somewhat dubious return—" but whatever else he meant to add swallowed in surprise as Rupert leans closer still, to place a hand upon his knee, knead the bone and skin there and "Wait," low. "Watch but a moment, I pray you—"

—while Pearl, bare-breasted, is fully ravished by the Erl-King, the spectacle thrilling the staring man-at-arms, who creeps to the lip of the stage to watch her dress torn from her, her lovely hair sweeping the dust, the plague-masked handler implacable above. The piano, helpless to do more, chants more urgently, *te-la-te*! All eyes save Rupert's are on the tussle, no one marks Laddie standing now behind the screen, now behind the chair, just behind Rupert who rises lightly from his seat as "No," Pearl's voice suddenly shrill, authentic with fear, "*please* no—"

—as "Only watch," says Rupert, his lips to Jürgen Vidor's ear, "for me—"

—while from the opposite darkness comes another figure, somewhat slower, cowled in black and bearing with it a genial Pan Loudermilk, spiffed and grinning, his neck wrapped in gauze and tied in red string and "It will only hurt for a moment," says Pan, stretching out one hand to Pearl who paddles backward with her arms, looses a shriek—

—as Rupert puts a hand to Jürgen Vidor, tilts his head, leaning low to give what the Poppy has always given, the illusion of granted desire—

—as Laddie lifts the creped chin further, to kiss Jürgen Vidor warmly, forcefully upon the mouth—

—while Rupert reaches from the other side, knife in hand, to cut his throat back to the bone: the rush of blood, the reek of gin, and "Caliban and sawdust," cries Pan Loudermilk over Pearl's commotion, "a bit of fun!" while the man-at-arms turns, belated and confused, to see two Ruperts flanking his master: What can it be? Some strange puppet apparition? Nothing in this place is as it seems—

—but past his visible and untouched revolver, he too has a knife, a wolf-hunter's knife that comes so easily to his hand that no one sees it until he is there before the man in the chair, whose wide and dazzled eyes seem to urge him to action, whose blood has splashed the twin men, which one the murderer? But that is too much to cipher now, so he makes a feint at both, Laddie shoved stumbling backward by Rupert who turns, ready with his own knife—

—as the Chinese screen topples suddenly sideways, striking him, Puggy behind it, Omar behind him—

—but Puggy the one who takes the cut, the wolf-hunter's aim less sure than his force, Omar breaks the man's neck with one stout crack but too late, the damage is done. Puggy collapses to his knees, a dreadful gush down his shirtfront, his belly, down to the floor as the players abandon all roles and leap offstage. Lucy rips free the plague mask, Jonathan grips Pearl, who takes one look, then buries her head in his shoulder. Laddie thrusts his own torn shirt into Omar's helpless hand— "Bind him!"—as Rupert, on his knees, supports Puggy, his round eyes already glazing, while Istvan sheds Pan Loudermilk to clamber down, swift and clumsy, to lay his hot hand on Rupert's shoulder, and lever himself to crouch beside: one on the left hand and one on the right, as Puggy bleeds out, *pietà*, in their arms.

Velma Byrd

Brigands was what they told the mayor. Brigands, likely the same ones who hit Mister Istvan, come back all stealthy to cut the throats of Puggy, and Mr. Vidor and his man, and anyone else they could reach before they was chased back onto the road by Mister Rupert and Omar, and nobody to be witness because it was too dark to see in all the struggling. So that was the tale.

The mayor and Elwin Franz come from their bolt-hole, wherever it was, because it was Mr. Vidor killed, the old general's friend, or contrariwise not such a friend after all since no one in the town or from the army made no stink about those "brigands," or tried to find them; they all knew how matters stood. But since there was money to be had, well, the saying is it makes the world go 'round. They shared it out, all of them, the fat lump they found in Mr. Vidor's pocket, and Elwin piped up *They must of known he had this, those robbers—that* made everyone happy. And Jack, who drives the wagon, got to keep those fancy boots, so he was happy, too.

It was a drama anyroad, between their made-up stories and Pearl and Lucy weeping buckets, all sentimental over Puggy, who they dressed up in a cracking suit, brown velvet and a red silk cravat—more of Mr. Vidor's things, I'm thinking, nothing left here is so fine—and set him up for the night for us to pray over, or cry or whatever we would. Omar started drinking an hour past the murders, and hasn't slowed much since, drank Elwin's homemade liquor all the way through the fire that burned Puggy and his velvet to a crisp, a waste, again to my thinking, but I never said a word. The ground's like iron, no way to bury him and anyroad *He'd prefer the flames,* said Mister Istvan. *A far more theatrical finish.... Good night, sweet Puggy prince*, himself half-dead and swaying on his feet, arm swollen up like a club but Lucy milked some pus, she said, and nothing blackened yet, so he should do until they come to Victoria, or wherever they may be bound.... They burned up Mr. Vidor, too, and that chucklehead guardsman, though in a different fire.

Besides that lump of banknotes, there was a kind of letter from Mr. Vidor, but no one read it save Mister Rupert, and Mister Istvan, too, of

178

course; Lucy might have heard them talking of it, Lucy now what Miss Decca used to be, their lady's maid, but naturally she'd never share a word with me *Even if I knew,* all scandalized when I asked her. *That's private. And likely nasty, too, that man was a nasty trick, ask Laddie sometime—*

—who got more than a few of those banknotes, too, and a most lovely piece of jewelry, gold and pearl, a snake curled around on a stick. Just goes to show, even if you're a whore, if you play onstage, you rate with them; if you don't, you don't. Carry their slops and clean their messes, cook their food day in and day out.... And what will Laddie do with the thing anyroad but find a way to sell it, and smoke whatever he gains? Laddie is a fool—and Pearl too, see her moony smile as she traveled off with Jonathan to set up housekeeping, call themselves Mister and Missus, who to know the difference or guess she spent her life as a whore since *We'll leave all this behind,* she says to Lucy, wiping her eyes for Puggy while they sparkled for what she thinks she's going to gain, as if a cripple like Jonathan is able to make a fortune in Victoria or anyplace else. And if she'd stayed, she could have had herself the mayor! Pearl's always been a fool.

Miss Decca's no fool, though, and never was: with that pinprick heart of hers she was made to be a madam. And since that Miss Suzette is gone, like Lucy said, *One dies, one's born,* since Miss Decca says she'll open again as soon as winter's past, now that there's money enough to wait it out, besides the flour and peas and sorghum we had hidden off the pantry, that she swore she'd kill me if I said a word—*It's there in case of famine,* though how we could have been more hungry I don't know, without the army we'd have had to stoop and eat the horses.... Omar for her watch dog and Walter Porter, that old flint, as front-of-the-house man, from the Gaiety's grave; Laddie for a bum-boy and because he reminds her of Mister Rupert; and whatever girls she can scrape up from the Alley, or come homing back to the Gaiety, whichever. *May be I'll bring back the old name,* I heard her say to Omar, pouring him a drink of tea, or whatever was in that cup, the two of them all cozy-like at her table upstairs. *The Rose and Poppy, what do you think?*

Ought to call it for Puggy, Omar's sniveling: does he think it was his fault, that Puggy got chopped? Miss Decca made some noises of how they'd name the stage for him, the Theatre Guillame, and Omar all nodding and wiping his eyes. You'd think he was sweet on Puggy, the way he carries on, or sweet on her, to stay at all; who knows? But she's more money than just her share of those notes, I do know that, I saw the messenger when he come, that hatchet-faced fellow came once before: I do remember, I don't forget a face. Money from the old general meant for Mister Rupert, I think, that I think she kept, stuffed up between her pillows, unless she shared it out and sent it to him, like he shared the gold in the safe with her, but who's to say?

They left in a hurry, I'll say that, Puggy's cinders barely cool, Mister Rupert so anxious to be gone with his will-o'-the-wisp, his sweetheart: all worried for his fever, and the cold outside, and whether he should walk or ride, it truly made a person ill to see. It made Miss Decca white, I know, but she kissed him goodbye all the same—Mister Rupert, that is, not her foxy brother, who sat bundled up with his toys and traps in that cart they cobbled up for him, Mister Rupert and Jonathan, and said nothing to anyone at all, except Lucy—*More dope, Puss, if you've got it*—and she as keen as any of them to be gone, though angry that the puppet dolls were tinkered with, or ruined, or something, going on and on about *Miss Lucinda, who'd do such an awful thing!* as if it were a living girl got ripped. Something about playing makes you soft in the head, I'm thinking.

For me, I never meant to leave, not that they ever asked me. I guess they bet they'd buy a slavey anywhere they landed, and they bet right. But this town is where I plan to stay. When Vera left, it was with my Godspeed, sister or no sister she'd fence your eyeteeth if she could pry 'em out, she was worse'n that junkie Jennie any day. But Nancey didn't go so far, and once the hotel comes open again—and it will—she'll be back as housemaid, eyes-and-ears there as I was, and am still, eyes-and-ears here, for whoever wants to pay for what we see and hear. Though we won't find many as wicked, I'll say, as that old general, or as generous as Mr. Silverfish, or whatever his true name was. That one there, *he* was a gentleman. Wish his like would come again.

"They say," the General sympathetic, "that gingerroot helps, thin-shaved gingerroot held on the tongue," but Mr. Arrowsmith shakes his head, mouth dry: gingerroot, dear Lord. He is at best an indifferent sailor, and the crossing had been more than rough, *mal de mer* from raised anchor to dockside, it is as if he feels the sea inside him even now, days later in his own sitting room. His sweet Liserl, a portrait in pearls and palest blue, serves him his customary Assam, then with-draws with a gentle curtsey for the General, who smiles as she leaves, twists the silver ring on his thumb and "At least you did not suffer in vain," pushing two-fingered across the tiny table a wrinkled dispatch. "From Gottsburgh. Rawsthorne is already kicking up his heels."

Mr. Arrowsmith sips gratefully at his astringent tea. "He ought to be feeling frolicsome, just now. Especially since he keeps half Vidor's cut."

The General smiles his odd smile, takes a seat on the plush settee. "A happy choice of terms…. That fool Redgrave was certain, you said?"

"'I saw his neckbone.' His words. You've asked me that once already, Hector."

"We were certain once already." Again the General twists his ring. "He always was a melodramatic bastard, it's fitting he breathed his last in a theatre. Which is why I'd expected some communiqué, some last poetic fillip. You say Redgrave found nothing at all in his rooms, or on his person?"

"The man is hard-pressed to find the moon in the sky. On that, Vidor and I were in perfect accord. Though he did locate the money." Another restorative sip of Assam. "Why should he not be a fool? It's kept him safe so far." His gaze rises from the steaming cup to the calm beauty of the sitting room, the long narrow windows fronting Gold-smith Street, the ivory settee where the General rests like a wolf on a silken cushion. "Safe from the likes of us, at any rate. Unlike his patron. And Hanzel."

"Come now." The General still is smiling, but it is a different smile. "No evil was ever meant for Hanzel. He was—"

"Bait, yes. To draw his cavalier… Do you imagine the worm on the fishing-hook feels pain?"

181

Now the General's smile has vanished. "You're in a strange humor. We did as we always do, took what was to hand, and used it. And no true harm was done to either, and not a little good. Did we not keep them fed and breathing, all through the scuffle? And Bok took his people safely on to Victoria, then he and Hanzel went their own way, after a stop at the leech's. So all is well."

Mr. Arrowsmith nods. Neither speak for a lengthened moment, then "Did you know," says Mr. Arrowsmith, in a lighter tone, "that his Christian name is Istvan?'

"Who, Hanzel?" The General's smile returns. "Why, it suits him. A gloss on the Greek, isn't it, 'Stephanos' means 'crowned.' Did he tell you that?"

"His sister did."

"The once and future madam? My courier much mislikes her— said she'd offered not a taste of free liquor, even though he'd handed her a bounty." The General shrugs. "She waters her tea, too."

Mr. Arrowsmith leans back in his chair, carved yew, scrolled with willow leaves to match the china's design. "'You are a hard man, my lord, you reap where you did not sow.' She could work that up as a sampler, in her idle hours. Though it's merely good business sense." He smiles slightly to himself. "She does not stint on a bargain, I'll testify to that.... Do you know, Hector, where Hanzel, pardon, Istvan, may be now?"

"I do not, and that's a fact. Though I'd like to. There are many fine uses to which that young man might be put, he and his mecs. And Mr. Bok, too. A stout campaigner," as Liserl reenters, with another graceful curtsey, to invite the gentlemen to walk in to supper, a small but choice repast of clear soup and tender beef, served with a bottle of very old Bordeaux. After their meal, and his gracious compliments for Liserl's hospitality, the General departs with his young attaché, bound on an errand unspecified: to supervise the seeds of a new conflict? or savor the fruits of the last? How would it differ? Either way, the wheels turn, the night wind courses past the carriage windows, the silver ring glints like starlight when Andrew lights the General's cheroot. At length, the young man dozes, for the ride is a long one; but the General's eyes never close.

It is true that the springtime is fine in Brussels, though one must have a certain taste for rain. It softens the alleys and the boulevards, makes a tender scrim of clouds and beech trees, plays a soothing music on the skylight windows of the atelier, a gentle pattering like "Fairy footsteps," Lucy murmurs to herself and to the lady she attends, a resurrected version of the late Miss Lucinda, who retains that other's shiny locks and tresses, though her face is all new, pointed chin and rosy cheeks, and her gleaming eyes weep glycerin no more. Lucy has her own ideas as to who mutilated Miss Lucinda, cut off her feet, slit to ribbons her doll's breast, but she does not dwell upon them; what good would it do, when those days are less, now, than a dream, a memory's memory, and in her new position she has so much to occupy her time. Today, for instance, after she completes this task, she is off to the lace-maker's, then down to Monsieur Alcee's studio, where she is learning the Vienna waltz. It is Istvan's maxim that what one asks of the mecs, one must first offer oneself, and the dance will give Lucy a better feel for onstage blocking, whenever they may return—Miss Lizsette, as she is called now, and the others—to the happy rigors of the performing lights.

The rain falls; she ties the pretty satin bow this way, that way, which is more becoming? so absorbed in the task at hand that when the finger taps her shoulder, she starts, then blushes as "Her industry," says Istvan, "shames us all. The girl would work around the clock, she needs less sustenance than the mecs…. I don't believe you have met my apprentice, messire. May I present Miss Lucinda Bell."

"It is my honor," says Mr. Arrowsmith, bending over Lucy's hand. Their eyes meet: his smile conveys his pleasure at seeing her again, hers a certain sturdy gratitude for being met anew. "Javier Arrowsmith, Mademoiselle. I am acquainted with your master, here, for not a little time. And with *les mecs*," his relishing gaze: when last he toured these rooms, they were empty, piled furniture and dust, and now it is a workshop, a place of foment and creation. See the tools and the laces, the piled props, the strings and glues and puppets on display: here the little Erl-King, there the Chevalier, there the Bishop, a red-hat cardinal now, and, in pieces on the table, a strange infant with fringed blue eyes. "Tell

183

me, Mademoiselle Bell, will you be the one to lure them all back upon the stage? One truly suffers the lack."

Istvan smiles. "She could play alone, if she'd a mind, and thrill the Grand-Place.... Will you take a glass with us, darling?" but "I'm off," Lucy says, with half a curtsey to Mr. Arrowsmith's gracious bow: hat and reticule, becloaked in carmine wool against the rain and "She is lovelier than I remembered," says Mr. Arrowsmith, when the sound of her footsteps has faded on the stairs. "Adapting well to cosmopolitan life?"

"A duck to water. Brandy?" amongst the bottles and decanters, pouring for them both. There is a slight hesitance to some of his motions; he has healed, but will never be the same. Well, of whom could that not be said? thinks Mr. Arrowsmith, accepting the glass with a smile as he accepts Istvan's toast: "To hospitality.... It was kind of you, to help us secure this spot." Though Istvan had wondered privately, as did Rupert, what had spurred that generosity, these rooms at such a thrifty price, the landlord himself had approached them with the offer.... *Hors de combat,* Mr. Arrowsmith's murmur, leaning over Istvan's sickroom bed, was that what he said? And now they and he are neighbors.

The brandy tastes of flowers, an intricate flavor, ripeness veined with a faintly bitter tinge; Mr. Arrowsmith savors its heat. "Ah, no thanks are needed—I simply pleased myself. Now I may most conveniently watch you play, whenever your performances resume." Istvan drinks, and does not answer. "You shall resume, I hope? When you've quite finished settling in?"

Istvan gives a sphinx's shrug, the motion faintly stiff. "'Tisn't only mine to say." He glances at the windows, the silver streaks of falling rain. "And there's no hurry, is there? Eventually... But tell me, what of you, messire? Do you play your games, still?"

Something in his tone halts Mr. Arrowsmith, glass to mouth; they gaze at one another; Istvan smiles. In a chipped enamel letter box, locked inside an iron safe, lies a letter, in Jürgen Vidor's spiky hand, referencing men called Pepper and Rawsthorne, referencing the Poppy as well: *Those walls were mine even as you quartered there, as it was mine to gather what you scattered. Do you recall Prussia? I pray you know me when we meet again.* Unsigned, without a salutation, it was meant for the General, as the envelope, in that same hand, makes plain. First read, through blood and fever's haze, Istvan could not parse it, though later speculation, on the nights when he could not sleep, when his knitting flesh ached and crawled beneath the skin, brought some ideas to the surface, as gold glimpsed through water can be grasped when the current calms. He and Rupert have not discussed the letter beyond the first moment's need to secure it; its uses may yet lie unrevealed, or it may have outlived them as it did its author; still it must be kept, and kept in safety.

Istvan's further speculations, on his own injury and its instigator, are ones he has never shared with Rupert: why tell him, for instance, that he may have cut the wrong fellow? Would it make Jürgen Vidor any less dead, or deserving of death? And how would his avenger feel, to know himself not the hand after all, but the knife? Only once have they reflected on that action, one quiet dawn in a nameless hostel while Istvan lay in pain, and Rupert wakeful beside him, talking to distract him until *The whole foul affair,* in a kind of honest despair. *It's done but not mended, it never will be mended. I wish it was me he harmed, instead of you—*

I don't. And don't fret: we've lucre enough, now, to start afresh, we've the mecs, and Lucy-Belle. It's a charmed ending, Mouse. Even for Vidor—he died smiling. More than he ever offered others.

I've no fucking doubt of that.

Kissed by an angel, did he expire in that belief? And what a shame if he did, why should the old masher be happy in hell? Though Rupert has his own suspicions, which he keeps as private, telling them only in his mind, like blackened prayer beads, as he lies eyes open, Istvan's sleeping head against his arm. How would it profit either of them, to speak such things aloud?

Now "The game of commerce," says Istvan limpidly, as if there had been no pause at all. "Isn't finance a sort of contest? And its practitioners as skillful as any cardsman at feint and toss?" He takes Mr. Arrowsmith's glass from him, refills it and his own. "Cards serve so many uses. I once knew a man played patience when he could not sleep."

"Did it help?"

With another little shrug, "He sleeps now most soundly." Their eyes meet again, this time both men smile and "I had some word recently that might please you," says Mr. Arrowsmith. "Your friend the musician, the pianist, Jonathan Shopsine—a friend of mine saw, or rather, heard him in Victoria. He says the young man plays hymns and tunes for the ladies' church soirees, and his young wife sings along as she may. And they've a child, now."

"But not a cello? Ah well. I would have liked to see him on a wider stage—he's most prodigiously talented."

"My friend said he seemed happy. As did his pretty wife. She does the speaking for both of them, apparently." This time Istvan laughs.

"My friend stopped in at the Rose and Poppy, as well. He says it prospers under its proprietress."

Without interest: "Is that so."

"They've not revived the stage shows, yet. But I understand Victoria's a new theatre, the Golden Dragon," going on to detail the performances observed, singers and plate-spinners and declaimers of Shakespeare and Wordsworth, even a puppet show "Set to the tunes of Tchaikovsky," says Mr. Arrowsmith. "Rather decidedly modern! The puppets are mounted on some sort of flexible rods, and dance about in a glass ballroom, and fight a swordspoint duel as the violins sob. Quite realistic, the spurned lover even bleeds—"

"Glycerin," says Istvan, with a shrug, but Mr. Arrowsmith notes the glint of interest in his eyes. "It's widely used. There's a lad in Paris mixes it with corn starch, he says it evens the flow."

"Paris, yes—Hector's just returned from Paris, that is, General Georges. Has he been yet to see you? It's my thought that he may."

Mr. Arrowsmith watches closely; Istvan's gaze does not change, a calm and friendly regard as "We've not seen the General, no. But of course he's welcome here at any time.—Ah," with a sudden brightening, a moment's lift of the veil, quick footsteps ascending the stairs and "Here's a treat," says Istvan, as Rupert enters, wrapped in a sober greatcoat, a pale china flask in hand.

"A great pleasure resumed," as Mr. Arrowsmith steps forward, and "Well met, messire," Rupert returning the bow, offering his hand as they exchange the usual courtesies, while Mr. Arrowsmith considers privately and anew the feral *gravitas* of Mr. Bok: See him now, hair cleanly barbered, dressed in a finely made suit, one might think him a well-born barrister, a man of commerce, strictly of the daylight world—yet a killer still, and nimble in the darkness, one can see it in his eyes, something in his gaze that calms only when he looks at Istvan. And Istvan, Dusan, Hanzel too, so at home in the drawing room that one might forget, to one's final peril, that he is an actor, a fabricator, a skilled and tempered *farceur* whose smiles may be as counterfeit as his mecs', or more so. And in the frame of this new habitation, as if glimpsing them backstage, one sees the both of them, the truth of them, more clearly still.

But he takes care that none of this rumination shows in his own face, just a mild curiosity as "You've been to the vintner's?" with a nod to the little flask, Istvan laughs and "The confectionery, rather. It's a new vice with him," fondly, "this cocoa. Will you have a taste?"

"Alas, I must be on my way to the jeweler's—my Liserl's an eye for a certain brooch, a beetle made of lapis and pearls. Though a living beetle she'd tread upon, shrieking." Mr. Arrowsmith pulls on his gloves. "The frail inconstancy of women!"

"Of humans, rather," says Istvan. "The mecs, at least, are always true."

"Another reason why I hope to see them very soon. And your-selves as well, gentlemen," with another bow, nearly silent down the stairs, Rupert to the window to watch him step into the street, make the turn for the jeweler's shop and "Elegant company," with a little frown. "What did he want?"

"To felicitate the mecs. And mention that the General was in town.... Here," handing him the flask, "your sweety's cooling."

"The General?" Rupert pours a dark thimbleful, drinks, offers the same to Istvan, who shakes his head, rubs his hands and "It's cold in here," adding coal to the fire; the cold makes his shoulder ache, now; it always will. With his back to Rupert, "He asked for nothing, if that's what you're asking. What he wanted, I don't know."

"What do they ever want. Jesu." Rupert finishes his cocoa, the smooth and bitter sweetness, carefully caps the flask. "I saw that Boulan, outside the confectioner's. He hinted he would like for us to play—'reverse the eclipse,' he calls it. His ladylove's a country house, or somesuch."

"Oh, really?... All my ladies and lords of the landed gentry," Pan's voice come muffled from the coffin, as Istvan makes a mocking bow, all fox now, white teeth, "please to go and pleasantly fuck yourselves, and your lares and penates, too.... Yeah?" in his own voice to Rupert, a fierce little smile as he crosses to his worktable, puts his hand to the Erl-King lying there, one-finger tickling the wound of that mouth and "They've done playing for patrons," he says, the boy, the man, the master. "From now on, they shall play for me. And you," kissing his fist to Rupert, the old, dear gesture to draw a smile, draw Rupert to stand beside him, beside the mecs and "We'll do as you like," says Rupert, and puts a hand to Istvan's shoulder, feeling there, though his hand cannot, the tight pinkish lines of the scars.

In his comfortable coffin, face veiled in dark silk, eyes open or closed, Pan Loudermilk lies waiting, a player from a tribe never stilled so much as gathered, potential as potent as a knife in the scabbard, a poem in the mind, a wind that rises as a breeze in the tropics, later to lash the wintry coastline, and smash its boats and sailors on the shore. Or perhaps that is purest make-believe, as a puppet is only a tool, made of wood, and wool, and wire. As we are blood, and fancy, and bits of bone and dream.

ACT TWO

THE GARDEN PATH

3.

The carven wooden face is antic, the voice decidedly not: a glacial, lyric, haunting little voice, singing a little song about the Garden of Eden, of how the first man and woman learned there to see, then want, then need one another—

"In the green we found our love, and in the light we lost it"—

—as behind the small singing puppet stands a man, old-fashioned white plague mask, top hat and tangled hair, tall and still as if pinned by the light, limelight on this stage that is barely a stage at all, just a flat apron a foot or so above the four cabaret tables, three of which are currently occupied.

Cigar smoke, the faint *chink* of glassware, silence when the voice is silent; a woman sighs. The puppet seems to take a breath, drops into a sharper, minor key: "We lost our love when we understood/Just what the awful cost is.... Do you have love in your lives, *mesdames et messieurs*? Are you certain? It has a certain smell, one can't mistake it, a certain taste on the tongue—" the puppeteer leaning back in modesty's distance, as the puppet begins to whisper of that taste, that scent on the skin, the way the heart pounds when the beloved enters into view, the sensations one can experience that "Are not always so pleasant, are they, *mesdames et messieurs*? That fiery ache, between the knees, the greater ache between—" tap-tapping its own head, to make a little knocking sound, it could almost be comic and there is almost a laugh, the soft gasp of relief—

—but already the puppet has moved on to the torments of love lost, love abandoned, love denied, though "The greatest of these is love granted, held in the hand like a little dove, have you ever held a little dove in your hand? Its little white breast, beating fierce and wild against the palm—" as a miniscule dove, yes, white, frightened and alive, bursts out of the puppet's hand, to disappear into a cloud of paper feathers, a tiny drift of litter on the floor. "So hard to hold, yes, but without it, one is so very dreadfully, sinfully alone, is it not so, *mesdames et messieurs*? And anything may find its way into an empty hand—"

There is no music but one seems to hear music, there is nothing but the man and his accomplice, the puppet and its animator, a sphere of longing and desire as great, and as small, as the world itself, the world of this shabby, quiet, exclusive little venue, the Fin du Monde, its center the stage where the man now bows his head as the puppet seems to lean forward on its own, to offer a secret to the couples at the cabaret tables, a secret it dare not share with the man—

"For only the lover understands
What price he pays for his love's commands
As he strips his heart and courageously stands
At the bloody great gates of the God-damned Garden of Eden."

Silence again, a hush like awe or grief until "*Merci*," the puppet says coolly, "you may applaud," and they do, the women beating their gloved palms together, the men their canes on the floor; one in particular, topped with a silver griffin's head, thumps a martial tattoo. The man in the top hat lifts his masked face to the light, his smile as courteous as the puppet is not, and bows, bows again; when he stands upright, the puppet is gone, he is alone.

"A very good evening, *mesdames et messieurs*," he says, then is gone himself behind the modest drapes that veil a backstage more modest still, a table, a half-filled water pitcher, the door to the alley before which waits a sturdy little half-bald man and "Thin crowd," Istvan says, tossing down the mask and top hat, catching up an opera cape.

"The mayor's sister," says the half-bald man, "is the damsel in red. And her lover beside her, he's the commissioner of drains."

"Well, that suits.... Tell Jardin he still owes me for last week."

"Certainly, Monsieur. Very good show, Monsieur."

"*Merci*," from the folds of the opera cape; Istvan exits into the rain.

Yellow hair in the gaslight bright as brass, golden as the little silk crown she stitches, her needle quick and sure and "I'm that proud," Lucy says, "of our Mickey. You should have seen him climb the rig, without me even giving him the cue. He's going to be a very fine player one day."

Rupert nods through the cloud of cheroot smoke, the scent of strong tea, pouring for them at the wooden seamstress's board that serves as a tea table, as the wide and cluttered chamber is parlor and workroom both. Outside are the streets and darkness, the long windows hidden by close-drawn canvas drapes. She in a gaily quilted wrapper, freesia and rose; he in dark serge coat, little silver spectacles in studious shine; he has recently begun to wear them, to need to wear them.

"Well," he says mildly. "See his teacher."

She dimples at the praise. It is late, well past midnight, but always there is more for her to do, costumes, props, her needle is rarely idle and it pleases her to sit beside him this way, working while he reads; sometimes he reads aloud to her, from the *Telegraph* or the *Daily Intelligencer*, the newspapers in English; sometimes silently, sipping and smoking as she gives him her news of the day.

And together they wait, as they do most nights, for the sound of the door, the rising step on the stairs. Tonight it comes while he reads aloud a review of a recent play, *The Lily of the Streets*, a sentimental entertainment of a poor lass forced into fucking for money, Lucy smiling and shaking her head—

"'—pining in vain for her ultimate protector, destitute young Flora Prudence must endure great heartbreak—'"

"Flora Prudence!"

"'—and the myriad humiliations of disease and daily sin, finally surrendering to the greatest sin of all, self-murder beneath the wheels of a carriage, though still preferable to her coarse and dreadful life on the boulevards. An instructive tragedy.'" Yawning, he folds the paper. "She'd not have lasted a week at the Poppy."

"At least we never spread the venus clap. All the girls round here have it, Otilie says, even the ones in the houses.... Flora Prudence, that's an awful moniker. Who'd pay to fuck that?" as "May be me, Puss," pushing at the door, bright-eyed, hair loose and damp with the rain that has fallen all evening. "Just for a jolly lark." Shrugging off the opera cape, dark velvet puddle on the floor, one hand waving before his face: "It's smoky as Vesuvius in here. And drinking tea? Without a drop of brandy, I'll be bound."

"You've had enough for all of us."

Lucy looks from one to the other, slips her needle into the golden crown, rises to kiss Rupert's cheek, then Istvan's, tip him a little wink. Off she rustles to her own room, from which she can hear the crossing footsteps, Istvan's rapid, Rupert's steady, up one floor to their chamber where "Jesu, Mouse," tugging off his jacket, his dandy's brilliant tie. "Am I drunk?" Kicking off his calfskin boots. "And if I am, what of it, yeah?"

Silent, Rupert drapes his own jacket on a silver coat tree, souvenir of some previous occupant of the building, once a kind of eating establishment, workingman's tables and grub; then a series of mercantiles;

and now the Blackbird Theatre, jewel-box seating with rooms above for Miss Lucinda Bell and her puppet troupe and traps, becoming known in the city for its quaint and surprising children's playlets, and, in some more exclusive quarters, for the occasional participation of its player emeritus, himself known in many cities by many titles and names but in this place as Etienne Dieudonne, his own little joke for the man who stands beside him, now, in shirtsleeves and a frown as "Don't scowl like some awful biddy," reaching to slip the spectacles from Rupert's face. "You know I always come back."

Rupert makes a sigh so small it cannot be heard. "How was the show?"

"Ripping. The mayor's sister was there…. Listen. I saw Denis de Mercy tonight, up at the Beau Royale—"

"Was that a pleasure?"

Istvan's own sigh, then, fingers nimble to unfasten the flat horn buttons of Rupert's shirt, four buttons, six. "He won from me in lansquenet, then spent it double back on brandy. Most of which he drank, not I. And going on and on about the Blackbird, and Lucy's moppets, his own brats are regulars apparently….You know he'd pay us plenty, if that were ever the lure—"

"It's not. Why must you forever—"

"Forever what," though not a question; the shirt slides to the floor. "You're so cold, why are you so cold…. He said he's got a table for us, at the Opera Mauve. And you said you would go."

"I said Lucy should go, if she likes."

"She can come, too; she'll relish it. All the fine ladies in their jewels and gowns…. Do it for her, then, if you won't for me," to bring Rupert's melancholy smile, his own hands rising to draw Istvan closer, to hold him so until "The lamp," turning to make the darkness as Istvan strips off his shirt, until only the fire burns, dull crimson in the grate beside the narrow bed, their orphans' origins still telling, all the years spent sleeping tight to keep the heat, all the years spent in one another's arms, from rooftop to roadside to brothel to here, this room, this city in the dark and drumming rain.

It is an old city, famous for its comic operas, its chocolates, its linden lanes and cheap available munitions; a city of electric lamps and coal fires and horseshit everywhere: the public boulevards, the market rows, the narrow backstreets, even the marble walkways recently installed outside the Elysium, host to one of the city's most venerable traditions, the Opera Mauve that each year heralds the autumn season, where the city's bourgeoisie daughters are traded like cards at piquet, while the great families sit apart, their own arrangements made elsewhere and in private; it is a city with a pleasant face, and deeply private heart.

On this evening the streets about the Elysium are filled with hired carriages; even those who live within blocks would never arrive on foot like country peasants. The men wear capes and swallowtail frock coats, the women lace and dominoes to mask their flushed cheeks, their jewels sparkling, some authentic, some mere paste to foil the footpads. There is laughter for no reason at all, the sound of a tuning orchestra, an avenue of white chrysanthemums and purple asters, and the gorgeous dying blaze of the Chinese maples, heart's-blood red and emperor's gold.

Alighting from a hired barouche, Rupert stops to pay the driver as Istvan and Lucy climb the steps, cavalier and lady, though the trio's truer partnership is not to be displayed tonight. "Step lively, darling," Istvan says in Lucy's ear as they pass beneath the doorway wreaths of blazing candles, glimpsing, here and there, faces he recognizes—though tonight's society, through which he moves as M. Dieudonne, will have incomplete knowledge of his dramatic achievements, in the past or of more recent vintage. "Soon you'll see some fun—half these crocks will be drunk to tears by midnight, and the other half picking their matrimonial pockets.... 'Ware the battleship," as a dowager and her daughter sail past, the girl's curious gaze touching Istvan's for just a moment too long, her mother's hand quick to tug her sideways, toward more suitable gentlemen—though Maman's sniff shows that she knows Istvan is no gentleman at all, no matter how fine his linen, how exquisitely he bows and "The quality," says Lucy, with her own sniff. "As if you'd want that little sardine anyroad."

"Not even as an aperitif. There you are," as Rupert joins them, dark coat and velvet vest, Istvan's smile calling from him the gaze that Lucy sees only at these times, that fleet, sweet, claiming glance—though now, in public, they must be alert, discreet; it is part of the reason, she knows, that she accompanies them tonight, as what the girls on the sidewalks call the agnes, the sacrificial lamb, what in some other towns is called a beard. As purveyors of the theatre, she and Istvan are already socially suspect, though the Blackbird's popularity with the city's children cleanses a bit of the taint. But if the true relations of the three were known, eyebrows would raise and doors would close, even those of "M. de Mercy," says Istvan, with a little flourish of a smile. "And your rascal brother. Well met, gentlemen," to the men who rise, laughing, to shake his hand in turn, bow over Lucy's snow-white glove and "Which of us is the rascal, M. Dieudonne?" asks the older, fairer, thinner of the two. "I note that you didn't name names."

"That's courtesy," says the other, as the dark man behind Istvan extends his hand to be similarly saluted, though no banter is offered him, nothing but a smile and a nod toward a seat: the reclusive Mr. Bok, patron of Etienne and his Miss Bell. It is rumored that Mr. Bok has some highly placed connections in the city, though these are undefined, perhaps indefinable.

What is certain is that he is polite, in a silent way, as Etienne sips his brandy punch and jokes about cards with Denis de Mercy, draws out Miss Bell about her fairy theatre, the playlets of Sleeping Beauty, of Cinder-Ella and "You'll see plenty of those tonight, Miss Bell," Jean de Mercy says, nodding at the passing parade, the girls in their gauzy and intricate gowns, flowers made of ribbons, ribbons made of flowers, hair dressed and powdered with gold dust to make it glitter in the candle-light. "Each of them on the hunt for her own Prince Lovering."

"Or my lord Moneybags," says Istvan cheerfully. "Odd, how often they are the same fellow. See that charmer," pointing with a nod toward a red-headed boy in scarlet breeches and a swallowtail coat striped so violently black-and-white that it dazzles the eye, paired with a bouffant tie of vile green. "Lucky the lass who bags him."

"Lucky indeed. That's Achille Guerlain," says Denis de Mercy. "His father is the Bank Guerlain, old Honoré, you know. Married his own wife when he was fifty and she, what was it, Jean? Fifteen?"

"Twelve, more like," says his brother, winking at Mr. Bok who makes a minor smile in return, concealing his own long-held opinion of the quality folk. Istvan moves among them as if their perks and pleasures were his to dispense by choosing to receive them, his politesse leavened always by a sneer so expert it is difficult to detect, a bubble of clear poison in a glass of excellent champagne.

But Istvan's smile now is genuine as "Watch his didoes," glancing at Rupert, nodding to the boy. "Who does he remind you of?" as the boy hops from table to table with a happy vigor, his ugly tie a beacon, his round cheeks flushed and "Puggy," Rupert murmurs, as Lucy's gaze goes bright with sudden tears, she blinks them gone and "A gentle-man," she says briskly to the table, "we once knew, who said that you could always tell a man by his duds—his haberdashery, that is."

"Young Guerlain's is decidedly Bedlam's," says Denis de Mercy. "It's a foolish affectation, all these boys who worship the poets, those vagabonds from Le Veau d'Or—"

"Look," says Jean de Mercy, as the boy, Achille, is joined by several others similarly dressed, chief among them a dark boy markedly

graceful in his graceless garb, black and severe as a parson's though
with trousers so tight and frock coat so excessive—lapels drooping
like lily petals, coattails that nearly graze the ground—his is the most
extreme costume of all. "I never thought *he* would be here. The beggars' opera, perhaps, but not the Opera Mauve—"

"Or the back-door cafés," sniggers his brother. "Oh! I do beg your
pardon, Miss Bell."

Lucy gives a pleasant shrug, as if she is lady enough not to guess
the allusion, wondering privately what this silly man would think, with
his apologies and gloved-hand kisses, if he knew she had had a back-
door whore for a neighbor and friend, right under the very same roof.
Laddie and his hashish-pipe, his trouper's dogged cheer, what happened to Laddie? to the ones who stayed, the ones who scattered? She
recalls them sometimes as if they were her family, lost as her long-ago
sister: Omar, Pearl and Jonathan, what passes with them now? She had
sent a careful letter, once, addressed to Decca, asking what news, but
received nothing in reply, as if the Poppy had disappeared like a dream
the morning after. Sometimes those days do seem a kind of dream to
her, all the tricks, all the time spent staring at the cracks in the ceiling, waiting for some fat bastard to come off…. And just the other day
she stumbled over a little box of scarves and spangles, souvenir of the
Poppy's stage, she almost showed it to Istvan but in the end tucked the
box away once more. Living in the past is not wholesome, and every
day brings dreams and troubles afresh.

Untroubled, now, though, Istvan, is he? nodding and jesting with
these toffs though watching, always, Rupert, who sits drinking little
and saying less as the gossip goes on, Denis de Mercy wagging his head
over "Benjamin de Metz, he's always been a trial, Madame his sister
lets him run entirely to the bad. That business with the tutor—" Rolling his eyes. "I'll speak no further, before Miss Bell. But Caroline—my
wife, that is—she says that her maid saw him battling-drunk outside
the cathedral just last week, shouting at a constable—"

"And drunker still in the Exchange the next morning, I saw him
myself.—Oh, a waltz," as the orchestra's strings grow louder, the melting strains of "Cupid's Garden." "Do you dance, Miss Bell? Would you
favor me?" as Lucy smiles and rises, hand out to Jean de Mercy as "My
brother," says Denis, "is a direful partner, M. Dieudonne. Your lady will
have broken toes to show for her courtesy. More punch, here," waving
at one of the servers, as Istvan looks past Lucy's empty chair to catch
Rupert's eye, the song a memory he means to share—

—but Rupert is looking elsewhere, out toward the floor where the
boy in black and his compatriots now stand in arms-folded mockery for

the twirling couples to avoid, deliberately disrupting the dance, until a woman in black and white approaches, to tow the boy through the crowd that parts to give them space, past the tables where "Good evening, Madame," says Denis de Mercy, instant to bow as she pauses, her brother silent beside her, hand to mouth chewing a knuckle. Pale in his black fantastic dress, dark curls and dark smudges beneath his eyes, handsome as a classical portrait, *Youth in the arms of Vice*; and she severe in her black-and-white, black silk and white décolletage, diamonds icy at her throat, the face above intelligent and cold, unattractive, alive.

"Good evening, M. de Mercy. Where is your lady?"

She has a curious voice, deeper than a woman's should be, a curious glance for Istvan and Rupert, who stand silent as Denis de Mercy babbles how his Caroline has *la grippe*, is desolate to have missed the ball "as well as yourself, of course, Madame, and Master de Metz," making a bow that the boy does not return, so thoroughly indifferent—to him, them, the table, the room, everything that is not himself—that he gives no notice, reaching instead to pluck a flower from the centerpiece, a fat red rose and "For you, Belle," he says to the woman; he sounds half-drunk. "Your favorite."

She does not speak, no one speaks. He drops the flower, takes up Lucy's half glass of punch, drinks it down, reaches for another almost full but "Pardon," says Rupert, putting his hand to the glass; his signet ring gleams black and gold; their fingers nearly touch. "Ask the waiter, there is plenty. This one is mine."

Still no one speaks, everyone watches, those at the table and those surrounding watching Rupert and the boy, Benjamin, who seems in that moment to have grown younger; cheeks flushed, his eyes have lashes as lush as a girl's.

"It tastes like watered piss," he says.

"That it does," says Rupert, with a very brief smile. "I prefer whiskey."

"So do I," says Benjamin, his own smile sudden and suddenly sweet, withdrawing his hand and everyone smiles, then, everyone but Istvan as "Very well met, Monsieur," says Isobel de Metz, extending her hand, gloved past the elbow, not the current style. "You are—?"

"Rupert Bok," while Istvan beside him bows in turn—"Your servant"—and "Dieudonne," muses Madame de Metz. "Have you a brother, M. Dieudonne, or some relative in the city? I seem to know your face, if not your name."

"Not in this city, Madame," with a charming shrug and "You must come and dine one evening," she says, to him, to Rupert, Denis de

Mercy not to be of the party, Denis de Mercy bowing again as she leads her brother away, the young man's gaze lingering on Rupert and "You should have been a schoolmaster," Istvan says, "you have such a way with *les bébés*."

"Unpleasant boy," says Rupert dryly.

Madame and Master de Metz now mount a narrow staircase concealed by a sweep of bog-green drapery, rising to one of the petite private balconies, a tempting array of refreshments and "Have that dinner, Belle," says Benjamin. "Before I go to Paris." He takes a little glass of whiskey, dark as amber, drinks it down. "I swear I'll be good."

She reaches for her Fabergé cigarette case: silver roses, pink pavé diamonds; he lights her cigarette. "You said you would be 'good' with Mr. Petkov," exhaling a long, voluptuous stream. "And see what happened."

"Oh, horseshit. Is it my fault that I am loved?"

"It is your fault that you are naughty," but he has gone, back down to his friends, Achille and the others, the piss-watered punch and a series of young ladies serially wooed and then ignored, but by then Rupert, Istvan, and Lucy are back in the barouche, headed home: Lucy's fine slipper has cracked its heel, Rupert is silent, Istvan too, unusually so. Upstairs, Lucy. yawning, bids them goodnight, Rupert unspools his tie and "From where does she know you?" he asks Istvan on the bed. "That woman, that Isobel de Metz? Not the shows at the Calf—?"

"Perhaps I fucked her once." Rupert gives him a look. "Or perhaps I rode her to the races, she's ugly as a horse at any rate…. Come here," without a smile, mouth to mouth, strong, clever, agile hands until "The lamp," Rupert's murmur, Istvan stilled and waiting: why must it always be dark, now, when in the days before anyplace would do, dark, day, only let them be together? But afterward, when Rupert sleeps, Istvan's hand rises to his shoulder, his own landscape of scarred flesh, a different sort of keepsake than Lucy's box of ribbons but a souvenir of the Poppy all the same. In the darkness he kneads the skin, the scars; he thinks of the boy at the ball. When he sleeps, they are children again in his dreams, he and Rupert and the toybox of familiars, the puppets and stage on which they staged their days and their lives.

Lucy

The first rooms we had together were nicer, though they were that small, Istvan and I seemed ever in each other's pathway. Still, there was a pretty view down into Goldsmith Street, and the chocolate shop around the corner, where Mr. Rupert—Rupert, that is—liked to go.... Funny how easy it is to call him so, slip back into the old days, though it's my troupe now, my puppets, mainly—though Istvan lets me burrow in his toolbox—and my helpers, when I was once the helper, wasn't I? And barely knowing a chisel from a planing knife, or cotton wool from gut! but sometimes you just must throw yourself in the water and swim. It's what I tell Mickey and the rest: before anything else, a player needs dash.

Well, we've plenty of that, here, at the Blackbird. I've always loved the blackbird's song, so cheeky and brave, I never thought twice about what to call the place. Rupert's name is on the papers until *You marry, or they change the law here,* nodding to the broker, who had a round little head, fringed like a winter cabbage, I remember that. *Name or no, the place is yours,* putting the keys into my hand: I remember that, too, their weight in my fingers, as if they were struck from solid gold. All that night I never slept, just kept opening my eyes to look at the keys on my night table, reach and touch them, I was that thrilled.

Even still, sometimes of a night when the children have gone, I walk from door to stage and back again, relishing it all: even the cracks in the plastering, that bare spot in the drapes where the candle burned, knowing that the thing is mine, cracks and spots and all. What a fine feeling it is! I never dreamed the world could turn this way—from where I started, to have a place like this, my own theatre, my own shows—I wish Katy could see it all, somehow. May be she can, as an angel in heaven; and our Puggy, too, smiling down.... Like that funny boy at the ball, in his horrid coat, how like he was! It made you smile just to see him.

That's how Mickey is, a friendly mug on him, and he's got the gift of turning eyes, he makes you want to watch what he's up to onstage. He needs watching offstage, too—I caught him once smoking in the prop room, hard by the paints and glues, and didn't I give him a hiding!

Boxing his froggy little ears and *Burn it down,* I said, *and you'll eat your fill of the cinders,* and he looking up with his swimming eyes and *Then you'll be Cinder-Ella for real, Miss,* which made me laugh. And he said sorry and sorry, and promised to do his smoking elsewhere, a promise he's kept, or at least I've not caught him again.

Istvan teases me about them, my "children's crusade" he calls it—Mickey and the others, and I've got several girls now, my Snow White and Rose Red—to hear them sing, la! *Such* voices, and purely natural harmony, they are sisters after all. At first their papa was reluctant, but once he'd seen the plays, and how I kept the children—no ballet-girls' whoring as they do in Paris, selling them after shows for the highest bidder, none of that with my girls! Or my boys, either.—When he saw, he said that since the good God had given them their voices, they ought to put them to some proper use. And since he is a freethinker, and the girls were unchurched, the Blackbird was the next best thing.

So the girls are my chorus and orchestra—though I'm training Didier on the penny flute, and Mickey can do anything I ask him, or sham it well enough to make it go—and the boys are my puppeteers, and stage runners, and prop makers, and scene painters, even ticket-takers, though they are slow to learn to cipher, so are a bit too easy to cheat. But we *are* making lucre, enough to pay for fuel and food, pay our way so I need not go to Rupert for money—though never has he grudged it, no, he offers more than ever I'd ask—and Istvan, too: *Buy your moppets some toys,* he'll say, and drop a purse in my lap, Lord Bountiful; it pleases him to give, to scatter joy here and there as the mood strikes.

His own joy is still the stage, like mine, but where he chooses to play, well. Help me he does, with a rôle here and there—he was Mister Quivershanks in our pirate-play, and Holy Doomsday in the Christ-mastide show, didn't he make the toffs shiver! One lady even sent us a subscription, she said his dire performance brought her back to Mother Church. And of course the children love him, Mickey especially thinks he hangs the moon.

But these other fancies, like the café shows, that Golden Calf where the "artists" go—artists, bah, half of them never made more than trouble in their lives. Daub a picture, or gin up some larky poem—it's all larks, there, for most of them, and home in the evenings to Missus and the *pot au feu.* Istvan never could belong there, he deserves a proper stage.

He had one back in Brussels, playing twice a week, though not like the Poppy, no piano and no girls, just himself and the puppets at the cabaret. Most of it was comic, sharp jokes and slapstick, the joke on himself most of the time, as if it pleased him to play the fool. May be it did—we'd all had a sticky time of it, getting free of the war. And him being cut that way—it took some doing to get his arm back, his reach; even now, if you knew him then, you can see a little hitch in how he moves.... I remember that awful day, sewing him up, how he never made a sound, and how Rupert looked to see him bloody on my bed. You can't forget a thing like that.

But Brussels gave them a way to heal, or it did to Istvan; and me, why, I was like a bird popped free of a cage, I'd never seen such a town or had such fine work to do. Rupert liked it least, I think, or may be it was all the time he spent with Mr. Arrowsmith, with business and the like. He went to the bank, and the chocolate shop, and Istvan's shows, some of them, sat clapping in the back, though he never took a part.

Istvan's shows here, now, have shrunk decidedly—no more Chevalier, no more Bishop (who was a cardinal for a bit, Red Hat and Bloodybones Istvan called him), and no more of my own favorite, Miss Lucinda, or Lizsette as we called her for a while. When I asked him why he'd shuttered her, he shrugged and smiled: *There's a real Miss Lucinda now, Puss. We don't need two.*

Pan Loudermilk—he doesn't use him, either, in favor of that new puppet, Feste—Feste half the size, Feste is all smile but there's no smile in his playing; I have to say, Feste makes me wonder what is churning up in Istvan's mind. Though when I ask, he claims he's purely content: *Whatever more could I want?* With his arm round my shoulders. He knows I'd go through fire for him. But only so much will he tell me, trust me with, just that much and no more.

He and Rupert, now—I don't know that Rupert likes it here or doesn't. He keeps so much to himself, all places seem to be the same to him, though it eased him somehow to be away from Brussels and Goldsmith Street—and wasn't Mr. Arrowsmith sad to see us go, asking did we need more space, or a helping hand, was there some way he could be of service? But Rupert and Istvan both had it in their minds to be away, and when the two of them are set on something, there's no balking them, the thing will be done.

Before we left he had a dinner for us, Mr. Arrowsmith and that girl Liserl, I liked her fine though she never had aught to say for herself, just oh yes and smile and see to the wine. And Mr. Arrowsmith making toasts—to them mostly, but for me, too, he always liked me more than a bit—as the friends of the Muse, or the Muses, who must follow the pipes of Pan wherever they led: some high-table talk like that, but it pleased Istvan to see Rupert happy as he was happy that night, saying afterward how *Your worries were gossamer, Mouse, unless the General pops out of my kit-bag, so!* making that little toy hop out from the sack, that dreadful Erl-King who was never used but the once...."Mouse," it is a private name they have together. They are very private, and here, why, one has to be, it's not like the days of the Poppy, where all that mattered was keeping clear of the shooting, and no care for who lay in whose bed. Here it makes a difference, from who will speak to you, deal with you, even who would want to harm you; they do that here, yes, we heard more than one story of how the men were beaten, who care for gents, or even put in jail, though the brothels are still chockablock with boys *and* girls; the back-door cafés, as Mister Lord Silly would have it.... What a dizzy gent he was, to be sure, and his brother even more so, I thought I'd have to lead that waltz myself.

That was a funny night, that Opera Mauve. Istvan was all for it, but dead-quiet after, something got under his saddle, I think. And Rupert gone along only to please him, for those sorts of things don't please *him* at all. Like this dinner we're to go to, at Milady de Metz's, some toffy townhouse up past the court and counting-rooms, the sort of neighborhood I'd never step foot in. Not that it's a risk, quite the opposite! There's a constable on every corner, it's the safest street in town. But Rupert's got no joy to go there; it's Istvan who wants it. Me, I'd just as soon go out to the gaiety district and watch the cancan, and the black girls who dance *le voudou* with the fans.

"You needn't go," for the third time, or the fourth? Rupert to Lucy as they climb into the cab, Istvan rolls his eyes and "It will be a fine meal at least," says Lucy. "Otilie said that they roasted a whole Russian ox, once, just to have the marrow bones. Otilie's a maid there, did I tell you?" though neither are truly listening, Rupert silent, Istvan too antic for real enjoyment, poking Rupert with a finger: "You're not her nanny, what ails you?"

"I'd see her someplace sweeter," thinking of the ball, the women there who deliberately cut her, society ladies and their daughters too refined for a lowly actress, he saw it himself though Lucy feigned to ignore: the quality, Jesu, but "Pshaw," says Istvan, "she's dined with plenty worse. Like that rogue Pimm you see of a Sunday—just what are his intentions, miss?"

Lucy laughs, a girl's sunny laugh, she tosses her head and "Him? Oh, he's just a fellow I met down by the milliner's, nice fellow, just someone to pass the time. He makes those replicas they sell in the arcades, little country houses and such. And churches—he made a little Notre Dame with windows of real colored glass, and when you open the door, it plays a *Te Deum*, like a music box…. Anyroad I'll have you two to protect me," smiling, "won't I?" but now Istvan is frowning, brushing two fingers against her bodice: "Why are you wearing that?"

Blue and gold, the lover's eye from so long ago, Decca's parting charge: *Give that other this* in Archenburg, but in Archenburg or Brussels he would not take it so she took it herself, another kind of souvenir, beautiful and slightly sad and "It's my nicest piece of jewelry," she says now, besides a pair of wee pearl earbobs, she wears those too, her very best for the dinner ahead but "I'll get you something nicer," says Istvan. "And you can toss that—bone away."

"Whyever for?"

"Because it makes me fucking ill to see it, Puss, that's why," which ends all comment save Rupert's reproving glance, the horse's hooves and carriage creak the only sounds until they reach the appointed avenue, the ageless canopy of oak and linden, the new electric streetlights a-twinkle like fairies in the trees; no crowds here, no passing beggars or street-cart men, nothing but the evening calm and a lovely expectant hush, the indrawn breath before one opens the treasure-chest; as the carriage slows, Lucy softly claps her gloved hands.

"It's a palace," she says.

It is: a city palace of luxurious restraint, of black marble doorposts and black glass chandeliers, a footman in dark livery to bow them in past two sentinel vases, carven like pillars and tall as men, made taller still by stalks of white lilies and creeping white vines, some strange sort of ivory ivy as "Otilie," Lucy's whisper and wink, the plump little maid behind the maid who takes their wraps: piled brown curls and a grin fit for the boulevards, especially when she looks at Istvan.

"Please," says the other maid, an unsmiling blonde, "step in to Madame," who tonight wears silk, a dusty damask color, carnelians in place of the diamonds though she is gloved, still, white elbow-length as at the ball; when she sees those gloves, Lucy glances at her own wristlets in quick dismay. Madame de Metz notes that glance, Madame misses nothing. Greeting the men, she turns from them, her lips an inch from Lucy's ear and "If I had hands like yours, my dear, I'd have their portrait made. Never hesitate to display them."

Linking her arm through Lucy's, she leads the trio into a brightly lit drawing room, the gleam of a grand piano, a trove of extravagant *objets*: paperweight eggs of chalcedony; an embroidered book of saints on a silver stand; a pair of taxidermied swans, could they ever have been real? with dead glass eyes, one mounting the other, miniature wings a-spread; an intricate golden clock, at each hour a sign of the zodiac, the Scorpion sits at twelve. And on every table are crystal vases of roses: lush peach and sentimental pink, as well as other, odd, faintly poisonous colors: a pistachio hue, a deep and garish yellow, a tarnished red with tiny, fisted blooms.

"So many flowers," says Lucy, leaning to sniff the yellow ones, drawing back in surprise: "Oh, it's nasty," she says. "Like a musk lily! Or swamp-rose, some folk call them."

"Swamp-rose," repeats Isobel. "I don't know that term, you'll have to educate me, Miss Bell…. Roses," to the men as well, "are my avocation. I admit I am vain of their beauty."

"You have much to be vain of," says Istvan, himself resplendent enough tonight for any vanity: cuffs immaculate, a burnished burgundy vest, a pearl-and-opal stickpin that, on closest examination, shows a vein of black at its heart, like the changeful pupil of a winking eye. Rupert, as usual, is sober in black, as usual silent too, standing beneath the great painting that dominates the room: an allegorical study of a half-robed woman, an older man, a much younger woman, and a naked, smiling boy with an arrow in his chubby palm. The man's eyes and the young woman's are the same, deep-set and pale blue, Isobel's eyes and "My father is fond of the classics," says Isobel. "It's much in that style," of epic romance, the man embracing with one arm the bare-breasted Grecian figure, as the girl stands by, while the Cupid boy looks out dimpling at the viewer, arrow on offer, as if to ask *Who's next?* Behind the figures a garden stretches, green and endless. *"Venus, Cupid, Folly, and Time."*

"It's quite a monstrosity," from the door, Benjamin's bright face above a flaming scarlet tie, though the rest of his outfit is more demure: a forest-green frock coat, dark trousers, only the deeply pointed shoes speak of the dandy. "Indecorous, too, at least where I'm concerned.— Your servant, Mademoiselle," to Lucy, polite too his bow to Istvan, who returns it as politely. Last of all his gaze turns to Rupert, his dazzling smile; he knows precisely how handsome he is.

"Good evening, Monsieur."

"Good evening, Master de Metz."

Tonight he is not drunk, not bent on disruption, aiming it seems to please on every level: joining the conversation, lively though not overwhelming, witty but never quite cruel. Lucy laughs at several of his sallies; Isobel watches him, lips faintly pursed; once or twice Rupert smiles. Istvan quizzes him on the modern writers, and he quotes some of the least shocking verse of the most shocking poets, the few whose genius shines "even at the Golden Calf," says Istvan. "Where so much, alas, is dross, I've found."

"Why, you have been there, M. Dieudonne? The poets draw a young man's crowd."

"I try to stay current," with a chilly little wink, as Isobel summons drinks before dinner, another maid arrives but "Allow me," Benjamin swift to pour a whiskey, himself serving the glass to Rupert: "To make up for my behavior at the ball," with what seems real contrition. "Truly, I was abominable."

"Truly," Rupert's shrug, "I have seen worse."

"I'd show you better," in a murmur, as the last member of the dinner party arrives, announced without enthusiasm by the blonde maid: "Madame Fernande," massive in blue shagreen, full of complaints about her coachman, the roads, the night, the malicious ineptitude and delays of life; she and Isobel briefly embrace, Benjamin, after a theatrical pause, coolly kisses her hand.

"You're barely in time, Fernande," says Isobel briskly. "I had given you up for lost."

"I nearly was, in that foul *rue* of the beggars. They swarmed the carriage like flies," as Benjamin offers his arm to Lucy—"May I take you in to dinner, Mademoiselle?"—then passes a remark to her, under-breath, that makes her bite her lip to check a laugh.

Hors d'oeuvre, the soup, the fish, rabbit *au pain*, artichokes in aspic, course after course begun at once but not before some sleight of hand, the place marks switched so Rupert and Benjamin are side-by-side, Istvan and Lucy opposite, which makes "Me," says Isobel, "head of the table tonight." She glances at her brother, who offers a sweet smile. "You, Fernande, can be the *maman*."

"I will hope," grumbles Fernande, "that your fare tonight includes some game. I am famished for boar." Lucy bites her lip again.

As maids glide in and out, platters and plates, Isobel leads the dinner conversation, its rippling flow somewhat impeded by Fernande's sour manner, and interrupted once or twice by verse, Benjamin quoting poetic *mots*—"'A grog-café/Is where I'll stay/and 'ware the sepulchre.' He means his father's house," pleasantly to the table. "Is like a tomb."

Istvan steeples his fingers. "Why, even our Lord was known to frequent the tomb. Though only for the week-end, it's true."

Fernande scrapes up the last of her foie gras. "All those poets are nancy-men. I saw one declaiming at Elise's, he should have been wearing a gown…. Aren't you bound for Paris yet, Benjamin?"

"I was to go with Pinky, but," glancing to Rupert, "I may stay with Belle awhile."

"Pinky," Fernande repeats scornfully. "Honoré should send that boy into the military. Pity we've no war nowadays."

"War is where you make it," says Istvan. His voice is mild enough, but Lucy's face changes, a sudden cloud across the sun and "Will you dance with us, Fernande?" asks Isobel, "we've music tonight," but as it happens Mme. Fernande cannot stay for the entertainment, she departs directly after the dessert—sculpted caramel flan—while the friendly young pianist, woolly hair and a rented tuxedo-coat, encourages Istvan to take Lucy as a partner, Benjamin beating time to merry Strauss as "Monsieur?" Isobel rustling up through the dimness, past the long French doors where Rupert stands smoking a cheroot, in the deep green silence of the garden. "The music is not to your taste?"

"I cannot dance, Madame. I never learned."

"I hated my dancing master," she says musingly. "He was so much lovelier than I." Rupert is surprised into a smile, Isobel continuing at once—to forestall any possible demur or compliment, though this M. Bok does not seem the man to reach at once for the lie—"When I was younger, they called me '*jolie-laide*'; now I am 'handsome.'" Taking out her Fabergé case. "In our family, Benjamin has all the beauty."

He leans forward to light her little cigarette, its golden tip shining in the flare of the match. "You are a smoker, Madame? I think I have not seen a lady do this, at least not here."

"Is it common, where you hail from?" He shakes his head, he says no more, the silence rests between them until "Will you sit?" on a pretty little bench concealed by a sweeping draft of willow leaves, a half-size willow; everything in this garden is altered somehow, bound or trained or made smaller, its color sapped or enhanced. The bench itself is carved like two hands clasping, a lovers' bench. "This grotto is my plaything, Monsieur. I have always loved the garden, since I was a girl in my father's house.... My brother—half-brother—comes to me from that house. He is meant to be its head, schooled to be so, though that schooling is taking some time," with no mention of the scandal that Lucy shared in the carriage, *Otilie says she heard the boy and his teacher were diddling, the fellow nearly went to prison.* "Seventeen is a difficult age."

Rupert recalls himself and Istvan at seventeen: they were men, they had seen a deal of the world, primarily its darkness. "Most lads his age are lads no longer."

"True enough." Isobel draws deeply on her cigarette. "Your presence seems to have a good effect on him, Monsieur. He admires strength. I hope you will dine with us again, and bring your colleagues—I am simply enchanted with Miss Bell, I must visit her Blackbird Theatre. And M. Dieudonne—"

—as "*There* you are," Benjamin flushed from dancing, swift to part the willow leaves as Isobel rises, retreating up the path as neatly as a clockwork trick, is it a trick? to leave Rupert alone with this boy who "admires" him, what can that mean? He leans close now, Benjamin, to chatter of the music, to offer a quick confiding sip of "Absinthe," from a silver flask, "'the green fairy.' It gives you visions, they say."

"It would be wasted on me," says Rupert, but not unkindly: yes, this is a boy, pampered and perhaps unhappy, who seeks visions in liquor and pleasure in mischief; with a boy's beauty, yes—that skin, and those eyes, strange gray flecked with amber-green; only Istvan was handsomer, as a youth. "I'll take a whiskey instead," leading him back toward the townhouse, its view of the bright drawing room like an arcade tableau, *The Quality at Play*: see Madame de Metz nodding to the music, Lucy spinning round in Istvan's arms, smiling discontented Istvan, why did he accept the invitation? here, or to that foolish ball? The quality at play, yes, and see where it led them before. Why does he play at children's games on Lucy's stage, then with Feste at night, at the Golden Calf? What does he want? though he turns the question on Rupert for the asking, *And what of you, Mouse? Where shall you play?*—with an inward sigh, the boy beside him going on about something or other, some silly poet's song of angels flying through the night "Like those," pointing, where? up astride the lintel of the door, a carven pair of robed creatures, wings rampant, arms entwined but "Those?" says Rupert. "Those aren't angels. May be they are, what is it, kobolds, the bad spirits of the house?" trying for lightness, to raise a smile—

—which he does, but not in amusement, instead Benjamin is amazed: "You are the first, the *very* first, Monsieur, to ever see that! Except for me."

Paused at the threshold, looking back at Rupert who holds open the French door, another man now pauses in the doorway opposite, as in a glass inverted: a pudgy youngish man in a jacket somewhat too small for him, thin blond hair brushed slick to his head. He makes no move to enter the room, stands watching in dry diligence until Isobel notes his presence, then bows to her, a stiff little bob, looks again to Benjamin who does not see him, bent now on fetching "Whiskey," beaming at Rupert, "for you and for me." When Rupert looks again, the man has gone.

One last dance, then several sentimental little etudes round off the evening, Isobel warm to bid them goodnight, patting Lucy's hand: "You must come again, I insist upon it. All of you must come again."

And Istvan's automatic grace—"We would relish that"—gazing sideways past his lashes at Rupert, who is looking at Benjamin, who bows them out and gone and "A fine lady," Lucy's smiling verdict, as the carriage rolls away. "She says she will come to the theatre, too. I'll hope that she does.... That Mme. Fernande, now, what a gargoyle! And Master de Metz, what is it, Benjamin, was jolly, wasn't he?" into the silence, she looks from one to the other: Istvan keeps his gaze for the window, Rupert makes a tired little nod.

"It's good you had a fine time, Lucy."

In the drawing room, quiet now, the maids snuff candles and carry out the plates and glasses, the pianist takes his leave. Isobel looks for Benjamin, who is nowhere to be seen, *absentiéste*, so she will save her compliments for the morrow, though as ever his behavior owed nothing to her; tonight it was M. Bok who held the reins. Dark M. Bok, who behaves so truly the gentleman he is not, and his colleague, yes, the very charming M. Dieudonne, and the clever young lady who is lady to neither, no matter what they may enact.... She steps back into the sanctuary of the garden path, the susurration of the willows. Each night that passes marks the evening's chill more fully; soon the rains will come and the flowers will die, the bone-white asters, the fleshly sedums starred with frail pink—

"Isobel," rising from the lover's bench, a man's voice, she nearly drops her cigarette. "Pardon, not to alarm. I thought I would take in your handiwork, while I cooled my heels."

His voice has not changed, his voice will never change: mellifluous, and cordial on its surface; he had ambitions, once, to be a player, a poet, to alter the world with his words. His silver hair catches the faint filtering moonlight; he still wears the silver ring on his thumb, her father's ring.

"I did not know you were in the city." She hears the tension in her own voice, the girl in it, girl on a garden path. "Or I should have asked you to join us. When did you arrive?"

"I would have liked that," says the man, the General, in mufti or not he always seems martial, fixed for battle; he does not reply to her question. With the tip of his finger he strokes a drooping little blossom, already withering from the cold to come. "It's pleasant, though, to come upon you here. Like Lilith in the gloaming."

"Will you take wine," she says, turning back for the French doors, cigarette burning close to her fingers but she barely notes it, keeps her attention on the General who follows at his leisure, accepts a bit of brandy, speaks of this and that, of friends in common—Letitia van Symans, Honoré Guerlain—of how "The city's changed since last I visited. More hectic, more—modern." Tapping his ring musingly against his glass. "All those café men on the boulevards! And the theatres, why, there must be half a dozen that I've not seen before. Do you go much to the theatre these days, Isobel?"

Her name in his mouth, how does he contrive to make it sound so? "When I may, yes. One enjoys a well-made play."

"Your man said you had some stage-folk here tonight, along with the beguiling Fernande."

"Yes—a Miss Bell, quite amusing, she makes puppet plays for the children. And her partners, M. Bok and M. Dieudonne—"

"Bok?" His gaze changes. "You had Rupert Bok here?"

"And M. Dieudonne, yes." Wary now, what has she given him? "You know them?"

"Oh indeed," with a smile of private cheer, "I had the benefit of watching them play some years ago. You say they've a young lady with them—a redhead, is she?"

"No," slow, she drinks before she answers. "Miss Bell is a sturdy blonde." How does he know these guests of hers, what does he want? what does he ever want, come in the dark like an apparition, like Vulcan rising up from the ground—or no, it was Hades who rose from the earth, to take young Persephone unaware. The gates of Hell, the

gates of Eden, were they made of the same material, made to last forever—as he does, in thirty years he has not changed: that raptor's
calm, the lines around his mouth when he smiles and "Puppetry," he
is saying now, "is a discipline, and quite satisfying when it's done correctly…. Your brother, was he at dinner tonight?"

Is this the true direction, then? Her heart sinks, then settles, a
soldier's at the first warning shot. "Yes, he is here in the city for a time."

He sets his brandy aside. "A pity, that business with the tutor, the
boy should have sense enough to keep out of such scrapes. Isidore was
grieved, I know."

Hades: and Vulcan, yes, at his forge, misshapen thing pounding
with a hammer; yes. "It's very late—would you care to stay, Hector?
You can speak with Benjamin in the morning, if that's your wish."

"No, no, I've a rider outside," bending to kiss the hand she extends,
the glove and "*Au revoir*," with a pleasant nod, "sweet dreams," and
then is gone, to the dark, to his rider, the man on horseback; while
upstairs, the faithful lady's maid must spend a long half-hour massaging
Madame's temples with violet water, trimming the lamp, fetching more
matches for Madame who will sit half the night smoking, knowing she
will not sleep, watching the moon bless the garden, listening to the
rustling of the wind.

Isobel de Metz

He came to me out of the garden, if I live a thousand years I never shall forget that sight: down the path tugging his little stick-horse, collared like a pierrot, so infamously dirty I thought him a servant's child, a dunghill bloom as one sometimes sees. Then the nurse came running, dismayed and frightened, and I knew whose child he was.

From the very first he called me Belle, sometimes Bella when a sweet mood strikes him; always a creature of moods, whims, always pleased to bow to his own passions. Screaming when I took him from the nursemaid's cottage, then clinging to me in the carriage like a little monkey at a fair, arms around my neck, breathless with pain and loss. I held him all the way to Paris, my arms went numb as wax, I never moved once. I would have kept him with me forever.... And Hector, *mon Dieu: Isidore was grieved, I know.* Enthroned in his chair, arms clamped to its sides and *He is your brother, Isobel, why can you never seem to manage him? It is well that you have no children of your own.* While Charlotte sniffled in the corner, perhaps she fears a disgrace on the family name. "Manage?" Myself I dealt with Petkov, paid him, sent him packing with a warning to keep his trousers buttoned in future, and he on the verge of tears himself, asking might he send a note, just one note, to the young master, if it could only be permitted—?

Be wise, I said. *The coach is downstairs.*

Only a note, Madame, I beg you, only to say goodbye, hanging onto my sleeve like a stage tragedian, one does not know whether to laugh or cry at such folly. Love! *I love him, Madame,* and Benny off drunk and lolling in some abattoir with that silly Pinky and a purseful of whores, girls, boys, whatever the broom swept up. *Do you think the young master will visit you in gaol?* I asked him. *Don't be an ass.*

The young master, yes, he will reach his majority soon. Then what? Paris? Or Chatiens? Or some roadside idyll, like those poets he so adores: *I shan't be hidden away in the country, Belle, whatever he expects.* What *does* he expect, Isidore, watching sidewise like a scorpion, like his famous zodiacal clock? He thinks he loves him, Benny: Benjamin the last-born, beloved of the patriarch, like some story out of the Scriptures. If it were worth the wondering, one might ask what makes Isidore what he is, a man who buried his first wife without ceremony or display, gave their daughter to the backstairs servants to raise, saw her twice between that day and the day he married Rachel: there in the doorway in his bridegroom's finery, staring down at me and *You must mind my wife now, Isobel, if you are to stay.* Her idea, of course, to have me there at all.... I recall how lovely she was, golden hair so rare for a Jewess, and those beautiful brown eyes; she was always kind to me, she had no need to be but she was kind. And Benny was her heart's darling, a perfect infant, perfectly formed. If she had lived.... It was I who taught him his letters, who gave him what manners he has, who suffered him when he raged, who held him when he wept—he would permit no one else—who found for him all that he needs, has ever needed. If Rachel had lived, he would never have been mine.

And mine, still, to try to manage, Petkov only the latest of his sallies—that riding master, what was his name? Awful, to have the stables so disrupted. And the poor German, the one with the yellow beard, the servants said he drowned himself, though I suspect that was merely servants' chat. Still, the fellow was quite despondent.... Which will not be the case with Mr. Entwhistle, *there* is a Calvinist and no mistaking. Excellent references, but the man told me he had never tasted liquor in his life, as if that were a boast to be proud of. And what he meant by peeping in at the dancing, I have no idea. Perhaps gathering evidence of our moral collapse? Benny loathes him.

It was a lovely evening, that dinner, and Benny was a delight, all he can be when he means to: even dressing the part in his schoolboy attire, cologne on his hair, on his very best behavior for M. Bok, who took his eye at the Opera Mauve—that little comedy with the punch— M. Bok and his friends whose presence Fernande deplored: *Bad enough they were at the burghers' ball, must we have them in the house as well?* Fernande, who used to bring the butcher's boy up the back stairs to satisfy her taste for meat. *That's the young lady who plays with poppets, is it not? Poppet herself to the both of them, no doubt. All players are whores.*

Perhaps they cohabit in filial affection, as you might with, say, a serpent? I shall have whom I enjoy at my dinners, Fernande.

Benny's enjoyment was quite plain, though I fancied M. Dieudonne was somewhat unimpressed. *There* is a cloven fellow, M. Dieudonne, handsome as a player should be; what is his true name? I am sure I shall recall it with time. Miss Bell is a good little girl, obviously pleased with her circumstances, and why should she not be? A servant once, no doubt, she has that busy air, perhaps a housemaid who found that there were better things to do in the world than serve tea. I shall certainly attend one of her shows.

And M. Bok, yes, there is a man who knows how to be silent. Much different from his colleague, but just as striking, one can see what Benny sees in him. If he would have only a bit of Benny, only enough to get us through this season, get us safely off to Paris, that would ease my mind considerably. Especially now that Hector has returned.... If there were a God, there would be no Hector, I am morally certain of that. Perhaps I shall quiz Mr. Entwhistle on his theories of original sin.

The streets around the theatres, the so-called Gaiety District, are busy every night, all night, for all the men and their ladies, out for an evening's play at the grand arcades. Linked by alleys and walkways, three floors of wood and sheltering glass, one may stroll for hours through the crammed shops, *lèche-vitrine* as the saying goes, to seek or buy whatever takes one's eye or fancy: false golden earbobs, painted picture-fans, translucent fish swimming in metal pots carried all the way from China. One may watch dwarves leap from ladders into the arms of giants, take in a cyclorama, eat burned pork, gamble on dice, have a shave or a scented bath (although the water in the basin ought not be examined too closely), read the latest novel, have one's stars charted and future revealed, while dodging hurdy-gurdy men and little boys who will steal the spectacles from your face, then sell them back to you for thirty pence. There the bourgeoisie rub elbows with the working-men, a swift commercial traffic of men in silver spats, girls in black stockings and spotted veils, carpet-knights and governesses out for a lark, vendors of cigars and half-pint flasks, of the little papers of powders that make a man feel young again, at least until the first light of dawn. The carriages that come and go are hired hacks, weary horses, stoic drivers who swab out the seats when the night's journeys are through; the music that blares and sputters through the cabaret walls is brassy, strident, a Siren with a ribboned tit and no shame at all: *Come in, boys, come and see!* the dancers and the shows that run well past midnight, where nothing is promised that is not revealed.

The Veau d'Or and its several brethren occupy a different land-scape, not so far but still a world away: where the music is stranger and more muted, the girls less on display, though nearly everything is still for sale, even the poets whose howls and sighs are produced for art's sake alone. Here the drinks are of sloe gin or whiskey or shared absinthe, and the watchers poetical themselves, praised for their praise or censure by the poets they heckle or applaud; sometimes they even climb the steps to duel onstage, spooling out couplets on the spot, political, scatological, pelting one another with rhyme until a winner is declared by the crowd, or, in case of a tie, by the master of ceremonies,

215

occasionally paid for his partisanship, though just as likely to give in to spite or whim. It is a pocket universe, this poets' haven, and one in which few questions are asked of its visitors, and much ill behavior is tolerated if one has talent enough, or cash.

Such as the young gentlemen holding court in the corner farthest from the door, in their gaudy waistcoats and jongleur's shoes, a parade of bar girls flitting past to flirt or play at being scandalized, sipping drinks and twirling curls: these boys throw money with both hands. Most generous of all is the redhead in the eye-popping coat, red and blue in a pattern less plaid than outright war, his tie askew though "I've done it up several times already," he confesses to the girl on his knee, a little blue-eyed creature with cheeks as pink as a doll's. "Fact is, it looks a hangman's noose. Will you tie it properly for me, Miss—Miss— what is your name?" and "'Ware, Pinky," burbles another boy at the table. "May be the tie is telling your fate! You'll be hanged by morning for drunker—drunkenness."

"Or spreading the clap," chimes another, bringing forth a happy litany of all the possible crimes of which the redhead could be accused, the boys laughing, the girls laughing, everyone laughing but the dark young ringleader, half-mast gaze fixed fully on his glass until "*Merde!*" his sudden shout at the stage, where a lanky fellow in a yellow jacket shares his opinion of the current civic administration, in endless quatrains. "You're finished, sit down!"

"Shut up, toff!" shouts a friend of the speaker's, another shouts at him: "*You* shut up! He's been up there half the fucking night!" and "Finish, Antoine!" a bawl from the crowd as Pinky gently shoos away the bar girl, leans on one elbow and "Benjamin," he says to his friend, "drink your drink, be easy. He might not even play at all tonight, who knows?"

"I know," though he drinks, no green fairy this time but pale Irish whiskey, it makes his eyes gleam. "He plays here of a Tuesday, I know.... I know where they live, too—at the Blackbird Theatre. You can reach the roof from the building behind."

"You climbed the roof? Without me?" to bring his friend's shrug, not a planned expedition but an irresistible urge: "I had to." Had to see, to follow their departing carriage through the quiet streets, to scale as quietly that steep slate roof, gripping hands skinned bloody, agile as those long-ago days in the country garden, climbing the trellises, the elms, their vast green loneliness, a loneliness so intense that it had, sometimes, no feeling to it at all, only a kind of flavor, the taste of grit between the teeth, the tang of unripe apricots. "Her rooms front the street, theirs are a floor above. His," as if to himself, draining his glass, conjuring again the memory: Rupert in the drawing-room, the dark presence of him, the line of his jaw, his infrequent smile when the talk managed to please. And then, on the shadowed path, *Those? Those aren't angels*: to be able to *see* that, to say it—Of course one must follow after him, there is no question to the thing at all.

And of course Belle, if she knew, would doubtless frown, and bring up Petkov, as if that could compare! It is an insult even to think it. Petkov was a comedy, just something to pass the time—he knew a great deal of poetry, could recite it by the hour, did recite it by the hour, in fact, on those canal-boat rides, mildly pleasant in a way—the swirl of the water, the man's accent making that old warhorse Shakespeare sound new: *That in black ink my love may still shine bright*. But only tiresome in the end, as they all turn out to be, sighing and pestering, just as well that Belle sent him off when she did.

And that other fuss, about the moral code, penal code, whatever was that all about? How is it a "vice" to dally with these fellows—if anything it is a kindness, never he who begins it after all, is it? And if the talks and walks and boat rides, if all of that is so reprehensible, so predictable, then why keep engaging tutors, or riding masters or whomever it may be? Though where Belle found this new one, awful pink-eyed Englishman or whatever he is, Mister Entwhistle with no sense of taste or humor at all—Droning on and on about the duties of a gentleman: *You must always remember your station in life, Master de Metz, you must seek to do the greatest good possible for those under your authority*.

Widening his eyes, a mockery of interest: *You mean as my father does?* That ended *that* lecture.... The old man, with his endless unanswerable letters, his tomb of a chateau, and Charlotte the Harlot with her smiles and sweaty hands, no wonder her houseman looks so fatigued. If Belle knows, she feigns not to; of course she hates the old man heartily.... What an ogre he looks in that absurd painting. The first act of the new master of the house, whenever the old man finally condescends to die, will be to burn the thing in a bonfire, a fine big bonfire, so one can see the flames for miles. Perhaps the house, too.

Until then he has other tasks to take his time—such as today's, the insipid round of calls to return, he and Belle at the Chamsaur's, *Adele is quite accomplished on the pianoforte, is she not?* Thumping out some Chopin, rolling her eyes; if they think he is going to marry that idiot, or anyone like her, they had better think again and then once more. Whoever he marries must be cut of a different cloth, she will have to understand that he is as he is, that he must have what he needs—not fools like Petkov, but—passion. Passion is like air, or whiskey, without it he cannot live. Will not live.

But love—love *is* passion, yet so much more, so very much that he had begun to wonder if he would ever know it, or if he was destined to roam forever like a vagabond in a poem, wandering, searching the world with empty hands—Until that night at the ball; until now. Now he knows. It is not a feeling, it is a world, as it says in "Seven Questions": "Is love a sea? Yes. Is love a sky? Yes." Oh yes. And it has no end, it winds like a path around the heart, a garden path with dark angels in the air, a path where every turn leads to the same destination—

But what to do about it? besides follow the carriage, peer at the windows, and think, and drink, and sit here at this table with his journal in his pocket, waiting for the clod Antoine to finally, finally step offstage, so the night's real performance can begin: that of M. Etienne Dieudonne, provocateur and puppeteer, his rival.

Backstage, such as it is, Istvan adjusts his mask, not the relatively genteel plague mask but a new, cheap black domino, to go with his black beadle's garb, anonymous and unadorned. It is noted that M. Dieudonne is moody tonight, less approachable than normal, although he does share out some gin, a better quality than that served by the Calf that is "Fit only to pickle onions," he says, taking back the bottle from the bar-girl, taking one last long pull. "Or as a morning douche."

"Good advice," says the girl, leaning to kiss his cheek, then smudge away the pinkish lip-rouge mark. "*Bonne chance*, Monsieur, they're a quarrelsome crowd tonight."

"We'll see about that, yeah?" not to her but to the slender figure he brings forth from some hidey-hole in his cloak, a face made for mirth, a pair of rolling eyes that stare, now, as coldly as the puppeteer's as together they take the stage, to the hoots, grunts, and general disorder that generally greets each new performer, the attention of the audience a gift to be won—

—but the man onstage seems not to know that, or, knowing, not to care, speaks now exclusively to his puppet friend, mouth against the tiny carven ear that is ever so slightly pointed at its tip, like a lynx cat's or a devil's, murmuring to bring the puppet's murmurs in return, its sighs and its snickers, impossible not to want to overhear and so despite themselves they quiet, table by table, until the room is still, until one can plainly hear the puppet's croon, a little song with lyrics that at first seem familiar—

"The philosophy of vice is seldom very nice
Unless it's watered well with cum and tears.
A little spot of sorrow will serve us till tomorrow
And light the glow of memories throughout our elder years."

—a neat pastiche of a popular poet's latest broadside, "The Philosophy of Vice," in which the pursuit of disorder, well-fueled with liquor and visits to the cabarets, is celebrated as a gateway to life-changing enlightenment. But as the puppet continues, demure in his master's hands, that master's head tipped sideways, white line of teeth showing in a foxy smile—

"In the wild cafés we gather, work ourselves into a lather
Announcing fierce pronouncements while we suck our fucking gin.
Conversant with anarchic views, yet purblind to the daily news,
For what's the fun of suffering when suffering's not sin?"

—a backwash mutter starts on the floor, half chuckle, half grumble, the scruffy poets acknowledging the truth of the puppet's taunt, but the bulk of the audience—the *haut monde* couples slumming, rings turned inward to hide the stones; the students from the Academy; the toff boys in the back of the room—growing more and more dismayed as the song rolls on, mockery upon mockery, naming names—"*Esprit de corps* is opéra bouffe, the Golden Calf's a golden youth—" as verse by verse, the devotee's pursuit is revealed as ridiculous, a posturing idiocy of the sheltered and the dull, to whom real risk is anathema, a silly child's-play of rebellion revealed—

"—on the very lip of Chaos, as the dragons sent to slay us
Are really Papa's coachmen, and sometimes Mama's whores,
Dressed as sluts the serving-maids are more than willing to give aid
And lick the crusts of toffee from our fingers and our floors."

—but if they cry out their protest, the patrons and the boys, they thus admit the insult, admit that they are, yes, those very play-acting idiots: a twist that twists them in their chairs, turns them finally in frustration on each other—"Be still!" and "Your hat, take off your hat I said!"—until a shoving match breaks out, two men too drunk to do real harm but their ladies shriek and the poets laugh and the master of ceremonies, Jardin in his black slouch hat, must come scurrying onto the floor to quell that fray—as yet another erupts, a wine glass flung, a table overturned, a growing pandemonium that seems to please the man onstage: he and his puppet share a smile, their last courtly farewell lost in the crowd's noise: then they are gone, with no act entering to follow them, just the hectic limelights shining on the emptiness onstage.

"Is *that* your light-o'-love, de Metz?" cries one of the boys, overcome with laughter and confusion, Benjamin turns on him a furious glare—as here he comes, side-skirting the melee, toward the table where the boys all sit up straight at his approach, even "Master Cupid!" as if surprised, *sans* puppet now though still in his domino. "Was it a proper young man's show, do you think?" Pausing, as if awaiting the verdict that does not come, only Benjamin's stiff bow as Istvan takes his leave, stopping off at the back bar to buy a round for all the bar-girls, and a little taste of whiskey for the cab ride home.

"This is a pleasant spot," says the man with the cane, leaning back in the dappled light: a *patio,* as the Spaniards have it, flagstones and a table and chairs, sun enough even in this cool late afternoon to make for an enjoyable tea, Assam tea served very hot and "Just a step from the city, all the joys of the countryside," agrees the General, lighting a black Indian cheroot. "You chose your lodgings well. Or was it your lady's doing? Is Liserl here?"

"No," with calm regret. "I think I did not tell you, Hector—Liserl had not been well for some little time, a malady of the blood, her doctors said." His gaze is not for the General now, nor for the patio, but the middle distance, and a distance even further afield. "She went very swiftly, in the end."

"Why—my condolences, Javier. She was a lovely little sprite." He is surprised to have this news so belatedly, but that is Javier these days, every card played so close to the vest one barely sees the cards at all, though on closer inspection there is, yes, a new weariness in his eyes, a faintly haggard air. "Does Isobel know?"

"No need for that," says Mr. Arrowsmith. The breeze stirs the potted orange trees, their leaves still bravely clinging, glossy green. A bird calls dreamily, four descending notes. "I've not seen her, nor mean to while I'm here."

"Then you don't attend her fête?"

"You do, naturally."

"Yes," with a frown, "I do, and you ought as well."

"Ought?"

The General's frown disappears, replaced by an expression of such neutrality it could mean anything, or nothing at all. "Yes. Time is not our ally here, our colleague in St. Petersburg has wired me twice. And I've just the courier in mind—Hanzel is in town."

"Dusan?" The tea's steam rises. "I'd thought we'd seen his soles for good in Brussels."

The General waves a hand. "Bah—players are inconstant, it's their nature. And as I told Isidore—"

"Isidore. I spent one full day, sun till sun, with Isidore. And his lady." Moist hands, moist glances, scented like a Cheapside strumpet, he could have had her then and there in her little boudoir-sitting room, the creature is so bold; desperation will do that. She may well whelp a child, but it will be the coachman's. And Isidore—threescore-and-ten, three wives, and what to show? One sadly maimed daughter whom no man has ever offered for, called "Madame" now though forever "Mademoiselle," and one rakehell son with no taste for the ladies—though the boy has the proper provenance, as well as his late mother's beauty, and so carries the full burden of Isidore's dynastic hopes.

The General seems to echo that thought, saying now how "Family is much on Isidore's mind these days—too much, I think. I've offered to look after Benjamin, take him into my service perhaps. The military is a good place for a youngster so dissolute, it will put virtue into him—what's that smile about?" as Mr. Arrowsmith salutes him with the cup: "You'll have a fine skirmish on your hands—with Isobel, I mean. She'd no sooner see him with you than back with Isidore. Why does she loathe you so, do you know?"

"Who can parse a mind like that woman's?" who even as a girl was subtle as a snake in the grass, in the garden, yes.... Never pretty, Isobel, not even in those nubile years when every girl wears some luster, the gleam of fruit ripe upon the tree; no other gleam about her, no money— the boy had been born by then, the heir—so no suitors, all she had was her mind to offer, and that saber tongue, what man would reach willingly for that? Though she was lean as a willow-sprig, wasn't she, and shook like a bowstring on that darkened garden path.... He was a younger man then, his tastes a bit perverse, but the vigor of her had its own appeal, the silent urgency of her denials; she cannot have been fully a virgin then? or perhaps, after all, he was her first, the first in a very short line. The idea is amusing. She remembers, he knows. He remembers, too.

Now "Isobel," he says, with an avuncular shrug. "Isobel must understand, the boy is fairly grown, this playhouse life of his must come to an end. He may never be Isidore's equal—who is?—but it is with him that we will have to deal in the years to come, you and I—and still you smile! Now what?" but "I salute you," says Mr. Arrowsmith, raising his cup again. "You plan to live forever, I think, Hector."

"I do," says the General, with a smile of his own. "Not in my skin, though I've some years still to accomplish. But at my age—our age, Javier—a man must do as I've done so often in the field, and send the scouts up ahead."

"Like Benjamin de Metz?"

"Benjamin, yes, and others. It's well to play on every stage one may."

The two men regard one another across the table; the sun continues its retreat; a silent manservant brings candles, and takes away the dregs of the tea.

"Tell again about the dragon," says the young man in the suspenders, comfortable over his cup. "I can't fathom it out, how you got that behemoth to work, Miss Bella-Bell," as Lucy shrugs with pride: "It took a bit of work, but work's not what truly made it go."

Alone together in the little backstage pantry, the Blackbird quiet now in the lull between the day's work and the evening's, she and Pimm with their tea and the biscuits he brought for her, delicate iced biscuits shaped like flowers, from the Tea-Rose Bakery in the heart of the arcade where he hawks his little fabricated country houses, planed pine strips and tiny twists of metal, real-glass windows behind which paper dolls the size of a thumbnail dance their motionless gavottes: *Every man a king with a Pimm's Chateau.* It is a weekly ritual now, this tea-and-biscuits, to which both of them have grown much attached; as well as the walking-out on Sundays, sometimes down to the arcades but more likely up toward the river, the long and pleasant promenade, to take the air, to wander past the statues of this king and that saint, their noble heads bespeckled with pigeon shit and grimy verdigris, to talk of many things and nothing, to place a gloved hand upon a well-brushed woolen elbow; it is purely wonderful, how much a person can enjoy these simple things.

A simple life, indeed, can be the best, being only what you are. A whore, like a player, must be many in one: temporary relief, container of secrets, punching bag—though that was never Lucy's lot—and midnight crying-pillow, and surely she has had her share of those: the ones who aimed to spill their sorrows as well as their spunk, the ones who wanted her to play at being wife, or confidante, stroke their foreheads for them, tell them everything would be all right. They are what she misses least, though the fucking was no treat, stinking armpits and gravy-stained beards, bodies like sacks of split grain pinning her to the mattress; but her good nature felt the strain most with the snivelers, the ones with wife and kiddies safe at home, work enough to put frolic's money in their pockets, yet still they whined and bemoaned. As if her own lot as a whore was one to cherish! Sometimes it made one sour on all the men, though she tried not to feel so—it is the worst fate of all, to have one's heart harden up that way, the private heart that belongs, always and only, to the girl in the bed, and never the customer above her. She is glad, so glad, that she has kept her heart whole, one never sees where the road will lead, and who here knows she was once a dollymop? No one. And if the mistress of the Blackbird Theatre is not most men's first desire, what of it? See Pimm, now, more gentleman than any titled lord, never once has he even tried to kiss her, let alone angle for a fuck. And a kindly heart he has as well, she has caught him sharing out shillings for her troupe, once or twice a bag of chocolates, a posy each for Snow White and Rose Red. He is a good man, is Pimm.

Now she swirls the pot, pours a jot more tea and "It was Mickey really," says Lucy, "he gave me the idea. 'Instead of making the dragon move,' he says, 'why don't we move the castle?' and so we fixed the backdrops to hike back-and-forth, while Didier and the others bobbed our serpent up-and-down—"

"And out front it looked a treat, like he was roamin' the country-side, looking to devour. That little Mickey's a real actor, isn't he?"

"To the manner born," says another voice, Istvan's voice as he steps into the pantry, unshaven in shirtsleeves and stiff black slippers; he politely swallows a yawn. "The boy will teach Shakespeare a thing or two before he's done.... A thousand pardons for the intrusion, don't get up—and greetings to you, Mr. Pimm—"

"Sir, your servant," says Pimm with a formal air, setting down his cup.

"—but I'm hunting a particular planing-knife, that I thought was in my kit but isn't. The one with the warped handle, have you got it, Puss?" to set her rummaging—"Did you look on the long table? My workbox?"—until Pimm rises, somewhat stiffly, bows more stiffly still and "I'd best be off," to Lucy. "Sunday?" as she nods, his nod to Istvan—"Good day, sir"—and gone, the door closed rather emphatically behind and "He's not averse to me, is he?" Istvan asks, to bring Lucy's dimples: "May be just a trifle. He knows how thick we are together, you and I."

"Like sibs," with a quick squeeze round her shoulders. "Mind, I've got my eye on him. As an elder brother should.—Oh thank you, dar-ling," as she produces the warped little planing knife, the thing is older than the two of them put together, yet its blade still fresh as new after a sharpening: Toledo steel, the finest in the world. Applying the knife to a little apple from the bowl, scoring the peel in one long red rind as "I've a mind to tinker with some wormwood," he says, with another yawn, as Lucy regards him with folded arms: "Out late, weren't you? At that silly Calf."

"Now you do sound like my sister," with less enthusiasm, though still he smiles. "Not to worry, I think Jardin was a bit annoyed. I shan't be asked back, perhaps," and "Good," she says frankly, pouring the last of the tea for him. "I don't care a fig for Jardin—I hear he's a rare cheapjack—but it's never been the right place for you."

"What place is?" half joking, but the question is real: and no one of whom to ask it, no troupe now, no traveling at all—pent up in one place, worse even than the Poppy—and no onstage partners but this one last mec, Feste, worked up in a dream of darkness as a kind of, what? confidant? or toy? And certainly not Mouse, who once was partner, troupe, and all, though "When we came here," he says, apple down to take the cup, cupping it in both his hands, "it was my thought that we—he and I—" The oldest, dearest dream of all, he and Rupert and the shows at last resumed, the two of them together on the road, playing as they used to, as they ought, always ought to do.

But instead it came to be everything but: Rupert playing at minder with Lucy—as if she were Ag come again, even still, here, now—and at businessman with Arrowsmith, Mouse the money-trader, who would ever have fathomed *that*? "Purse-string fingers," he says, low, shadows on his face that Lucy has never seen before. "Stocks, and gold, and who the fuck knows what else—What business had he, wasting himself on foolishness like that?"

"He did it for you," says Lucy softly. "For all of us," landing the way they had, as exiles, Istvan healed so slowly from his wounds, she so green and the puppets still idle: it was a godsend, that selling and buying, and the building given them for a pittance, Mr. Arrowsmith not patron so much as friend; wasn't he? So disappointed when they decamped to come here—and what truly lay behind that move, who can say? She never asked; she went where they led her. Was that wrong? "How else were we to live?"

"As we used to," to himself more than to her, he and Mouse hand-to-mouth on the road or drowning in ducats, there is no middle ground and need be none, are they burghers or old women, to count pennies and fear the winter's cold? Christ. "And don't say he was skilled at it, of course he was, he can be anything he chooses. See him at that ball, recall? Anyone would think he was a landed lord—"

"Or at the dinner," watching him, the light in his eyes when he speaks of Rupert; she knows so little of their history, truly. Once they were twain, on stage and in life, then parted in some unknown way, then reunited at the Poppy like two hands folded together, meant to be together, together still though parted also, she feels that distance between them though she cannot give it a name, would not dare to, has rarely even offered the comfort that, shyly, she does now: a hand on his shoulder, her cheek resting just a moment on his own bent head, like sister and brother, yes: she loves him. "Lord enough for Lady de Metz, that was certain—she took a shine to him, I'm thinking. And that Benjamin, too—"

—as he pats her loving hand, pushes his cup aside: a sideways smile, the mask resumed as "Did I tell you I saw him? the boy? Out with his little cronies, at the Calf you so deplore." Sharing the cream of the evening's lark, she shakes her head with a savoring smile, imagining their faces and "That boy," she says, "was friendly-like to me, but he's got a tongue like an awl, doesn't he? Poke a hole straight through you to get to the joke. And monstrous idle, all those rich young men—"

"That's why he's time to dally with groomsmen and teachers and such. That Petkov fellow—they kicked him right back to his shitheel village after the Happy Prince was done with him, yeah? Blinking his pretty eyes, dropping a trail of coins, what else for a numbskull to do but follow." Swallowing the dregs, cup down as Rupert enters, raising his voice just a notch: "The boy goes merrily on, but it's hard lines for the poor tutor, yeah?"

"Well," says Lucy equably, "may be he should have kept his hands to himself."

"Not easy to do when the prick's in play." Taking up the knife again to strop it lightly on his thumb, teasing the skin there as "We've been asked to a party," Rupert showing the invitation, the de Metz seal in a scented crust of wax. "Some sort of masquerade, I gather—her man brought it. I've accepted on our behalf."

Istvan looks it over for half a moment, tosses it down and "Of course you did," pushing back from the table. "We all know how you love to frolic with the quality. Perhaps I'll dress as a gentleman, that's costume enough."

"What's got into you?"

"Nothing," knife to pocket and gone, Rupert looking after him with such honest confusion that Lucy gives an April smile, a little shrug and "That boy," she says, "that Benjamin de Metz. He doesn't like him much."

"What's in him, to like or dislike?"

Should she say it? when Rupert should see it on his own? Why else would Istvan bother to tweak the boy so in public, make a song to shame him, why else care one way or another about the tutor's disgrace? so, lightly, "He's a bit jealous, that's all," to Rupert's look still blank; as clever as he is! Men! "Of the boy, and you.... When is the party? Am I to go?"

"Not this time," with a frown, the invitation for himself and Istvan alone, what does that mean? And *jealous*—what does *that* mean? "Though there's a little note—here—for you," pale violet paper, ebony ink addressed in a feminine and flowing hand, *Mlle. Lucinda Bell* to bring Lucy's little crow: "She's coming here," passing him the note. "She said she would," to the The Dragon and St. George *under the wings of the Blackbird, I look forward to an entertaining and enlightening afternoon.* "She was uncommonly friendly, to me, I mean, a quality lady like that," but he is no longer truly listening, the notion flickering inside: jealous? Istvan? Who has never once evinced a moment's worry that any other might catch Rupert's eye, and why should he? There is no other. Jealous, foolishness—nodding to Lucy as he leaves, climbs the stairs, the matter dismissed—

—until the night of the masquerade, Istvan busy with a new cravat, oversized, a lush and tropic gold and "What's that neckerchief about?" Rupert reaching for the silver box of collar studs, annoyed at the waste of the evening ahead: saying yes for Istvan's sake, Istvan who seeks as ever to cultivate these people, these de Metzes and de Mercys, when he need not bother, need never bother, they have money enough on their own—but now this pitch-black humor, that unbelievable tie. "Is it your costume, messire?"

"What's yours?" Slipping the rude domino into his pocket, a *bal masque*, fine, he knows how to do that. Pity he cannot bring Feste as well, what fun it would be to pop him out at the table. "The modest parson? The country mouse? Why not go as Castor and Pollux, or is that too out of date?" with a look thrown over his shoulder, inscrutable and cold—

—yet the names a touch to Rupert's heart, Rupert's hand reaching to take him by that shoulder—but feeling there, as he always will, as he hates to do, the scars: the scars he caused, the wounds he made with his own stupid recklessness, just as if he had used the knife, the pain felt fresh and grievous every time—

—and his hand flinches back, slides instead down Istvan's arm, the muscles there tight as Istvan's little smile, a different sort of pain unrecognized by Rupert as "Ready for the show?" Istvan pulling away now, catching up his hat. "Then let's away."

The white lilies and white ivy stand, still, at the townhouse doors, though the evening's cold has crisped the flowers' edges, and tonight they are sprinkled throughout with red, bright holly berries like drops of blood, the motif repeated in the servants' crimson livery, the dozens of red candles burning beneath the black chandeliers, the glossy red rosebud offered to every guest: affixed to the gentlemen's lapels, tucked into the ladies' décolleté or headdress, or tied by ribbon to a bracelet or neckpiece, as Isobel wears hers, red against darker rubies "Like a cut throat," says Fernande, herself in black with dyed ermine trim. "And why masked?" scratching somewhat irritably at her velvet domino. "We all know who we are."

Isobel gives a little smile: "It was Benny's fancy," and thus obeyed by himself and all his friends, all present and semi-decorous, at least no one yet is drunk or brawling. Even that Pinky, in his tri-pronged headdress, circulates amongst the ladies, asking in the current manner *Will she take an ice? Would she care to walk into the gardens?* as Benjamin himself, all in red save his mask and black cravat, receives at the door: *Let me, Belle,* and when she showed surprise, *It's my house, too, isn't it?*

All that's mine is always yours. You know that—but what he wants tonight is not hers to give. The usual guests, Guerlains and Guyons and Chamsaurs, could lure him nowhere but elsewhere, the usual gossip a bore. But now, see him sparkle past his mask, see entering "M. Bok," behind a flimsy little domino, his colleague beside in another even less well made, is it some fashion in their circles to do so? since otherwise their dress is faultless. And both so handsome, too, even Fernande gives an appreciative grunt as "Recalling your little beefsteak?" Isobel sotto voce in passing, coming forward as Benjamin leads the men to her side: "No one here," extending her gloved hand, "could look so well concealed. I am so pleased that you could attend, gentlemen."

The cab ride endured in a silence their arrival has not repaired, a silence stretching until "The pleasure is ours, Madame," says Rupert, since Istvan does not speak first as he always does, only smiles, too bright and too swiftly gone: his onstage smile, what does this mean? Silence again as a servant for the moment requests Isobel's full attention, and the other guests stand watching like an audience, seemingly stilled by their advent, these men the only strangers in the room—

—but not to every guest, not to "Achille Guerlain," as Pinky eagerly advances, hand outstretched. "Benjamin said you might be here tonight." Bowing to them both, his admiring smile is for Istvan alone: "Your song was quite topping, sir! Even though it tugged a bit at the shorter hairs, if you know what I'm saying."

"I rather believe I do. All in good fun, though, of course," as Rupert stands excluded, what song? And what is this boy about, now, this

banker's son? as Istvan cuts his gaze sideways: "Why don't you drink?"
coolly. "No doubt there's whiskey here somewhere—toe aside a rock,
see what you find."

 "We're not all like that, you know," says Pinky, as Rupert's lips
tighten and he turns away, Benjamin, of course, following after, like
Mary and her little lamb, after a brief, correct, and meaningless bow to
Istvan, who returns it as briefly and correctly: mark the boy in his red
velvet and rosebud, like a little treat brought home from the chocolatier's. "At the Calf, that is, some of us have got *some* purpose. Not
I, I've only got a title, the old stick's title, you know, but Hugh—he's
one of our set—he's going to get married soon, and Benjamin, why, he
can do anything he likes. You ought to hear him warble! Me," with a
confidential frown, "I can't sing a note, when I try the windows seem
to shatter. But I had a puppet theatre once, my sisters and I used to
play at Punch and Judy—I was always the Judy, can you fathom that,
sir? My sisters are such awful harpies." A cheerful smile that Istvan
returns, impossible not to warm to the boy, in his mad headdress,
snub nose as pink as if it had been rouged: a player at heart, whether
he knows it or not.

 Any folk may be divided so, into those who play, and those who
only watch. Observe now this drawing room as a kind of stage, its grand
piano ready for the overture, its set dressing sumptuous in red and
black: *Scene I, the masquerade.* There is Lady Guerlain, pretty as a
doll made of feathers and moonlight, ill-suited for the heavy pearls she
wears, the ancient Guerlain pearls stout as a hangman's rope about her
neck; call her the ranking ingénue, and her aged husband a pillar of
the stage, so white and motionless he stands beside her. See the lines
exchanged—vapid, rapid, poisonous and sweet—between herself and
her bosom friends, ladies whose days are spent preparing for their evenings, whose bosoms bear jewels as costly as her own, though worked
in more fantastical and modern styles: black filigree earrings frail as
cobwebs, a lizard made of jade and emeralds, a golden locket formed
into a swollen heart; which of them is tonight's heroine? Any? Or none?
Watch their cavaliers play at rakes and roués, the night's license bought
by the masks they wear; yet they go unmasked to greater freedoms in
the greater world, with the girls of the Golden Calf so favored by Pinky
and his friends, or the dollhouse whores whose breath reeks of peppermint, whose bills of health are tacked onto the walls above their beds,
who pay for those bills with a different kind of frolic, another sort of
playhouse show. In the daytime world, these men are the levers and
traps of a great machine, its motion invisible to many, its gears and
grinding wheels felt most by those too small to flee its passing, those

whose passing it never feels at all; like the circling servants, perspiring in their meaningless finery: call them stagehands, there to serve the drama while tasting none of it themselves, as they do with the drinks they offer, the Turkish wines, the crisp champagne, the scarlet punch that Pinky accepts, now, from a proffered tray, hands to Istvan and "What I do *quite* well," says Pinky, taking another glass for himself, "is drink," as an older man, masked in red, his silver hair brushed severely back, approaches, unseen by the boy. "I can drink like a dromedary, sir, or a soldier on home leave—"

"It's a skill you may need someday, Master Guerlain," says the General, one warm hand out for "Hanzel," squeezing, smiling. "I had some hopes I'd see you here."

"Well met," says Istvan, with a genial smile, his hackles rising as surely as a fox penned in a ditch; another actor, oh yes, this old man for whom the whole world is too small an arena, who never ceases to play. See him in Brussels, insistent as a hound on the trail, and now "You'll excuse us," the General dismissing a disappointed Pinky, leading Istvan from the drawing-room into a more private hallway alcove, his annexation not lost on Isobel, whose eyes narrow in sudden memory—

—though Rupert sees none of it, Rupert on the garden path now, whiskey in hand as "This mask," says Benjamin, as they step past the willow tree, feel the evening's rising breeze, "must be made of sackcloth, it itches so." Tugging it off, an imprint of the strings left at his eyes, a harlequin's mark. "Yours fits you well."

"It's cut from felt," Lucy's scraps she stitched up for him, but he does not say this, has nothing, really, to say to this boy, has no business here at all, if Istvan must be so foul he can come to these soirees alone from now on. *Frolic with the quality,* Jesu…. Though the young man—what is it, Benjamin—played the host well, introducing him to all they passed on the way to the whiskey and the door: men who bowed and meant nothing by it, women who smiled and meant even less. Although Madame de Metz seemed genuinely pleased to see them, *jolie-laide* with that dry little smile: *Your presence seems to have a good effect on him, Monsieur. He admires strength.* Well, why should he not? Strength would be a pleasant novelty, no doubt.

Seventeen—recall himself at, what, seven years, or eight? in the orphan school, monastery, whatever it was, cracks in the bed board, doves on the roof. And the stern Latin-speaking men, *Tacio, recite!* Striking him across the face for every word said wrong, it made him a swift scholar; and swift, too, to slip the gates when nothing more of use could be learned, take to the road he never left or meant to, he thought he would roam his whole short life away—

—until that winter's day under the viaduct, ducking in past the pouring rain, to find that antic, teasing, lost little smile; Istvan's smile. Boots too large for him, no heels and half a sole, wiggling his toes frozen white in the rain and *What's your name?* shivering, smiling. Six pennies in a folded scrap of velvet, some rag of a lady's reticule. And the damp head nestling at last into his shoulder, breath warm against his skin: *Where you going? I'm going, too.*

Now this boy, looking up at him from another world entirely, what can he know of loss? or any sorrow greater than a dry-mouth after drinking? Rupert tugs at his own mask strings, stuffs the silly thing into his pocket as Benjamin speaks of his comrades, of "Hugh," with a lofty shrug, "and Pinky, Achille, that is—they've a positive mania for masking. It's juvenile, really—"

"And you've outgrown it, Master de Metz?"

"Benjamin," correcting. "Benjamin is what my friends call me. I hope you think me a friend…. Your friend, now, he doesn't like me."

Rupert's half smile; he cannot check it. "Why do you say that?"

"Because it's true." Taking from his own lapel the folded rosebud, fixing it instead to Rupert's coat. "You missed your favor, Monsieur."

His hands are still on Rupert, pinning and unpinning the little bloom: long fingers, the knuckles sharp and scarred. Those strange eyes, like water in a country stream, so much deeper than it looks—as Rupert asks, to say something, "Is that one of your sister's roses? Or are you a gardener, too?"

Benjamin's frown comes fleeting—"I grew up in a garden"—with a darkness he himself does not seem to mark, but that Rupert takes in like a sudden scent, at once aware, as an animal is, of a smell he knows and understands—

—as, in the curtained hallway alcove, black brocade worked in martial lilies, two ebony chairs set tête-à-tête, the General and Istvan circle one another without moving, the General's mild smile and "Javier," he says, "was sadly puzzled when you and Mr. Bok decamped. Was it the weather that drove you away? All that rain?"

"Brussels is a likely town," Istvan's tone in answer cordial, both he and the General know what comes next. "And we were desolate to leave Mr. Arrowsmith's—sphere. But we are players, after all. We require motion."

"Yet you've come to some rest now, in the Blackbird Theatre—with your young lady, what is it, Lucy? A favorite of my sergeant's, I recall." That smile unchanged behind the domino, the war in it, the stench of piss in the Poppy's lobby, the drift of snow through broken windows. "I hope you'll like it here. I hope you'll stay. For the plain fact is, you're needed, Hanzel. I told you so before—"

Before, yes: in that quiet sitting room, Arrowsmith on the balcony lighting Rupert's cheroots, talking of finance, of this and of that, as inside, on the ivory settee, the General offered brandy, and tea, and servitude: *The actor mounts the play the—producer provides; call it so, if that sweetens the taste. Come, Hanzel, where's your sense of humor? Or adventure? All the world's a stage, is it not? I can place you on that stage, and make your part well worth the playing. I was a bit of an actor myself, in my youth, I understand....* There is never an end to it, say yes once and they believe they own you forever, why do they think they can buy what was never for sale? and use for a thoughtless tool what breathes, and bleeds, on its own? Istvan would never treat a puppet of his own such. And the General should know better, who himself has such a long memory; perhaps power corrupts the reason, as well.

"—but you," still smiling, "you proved a bit of a slippery fish, eh?"

"Not at all," his own smile so winning it might be Feste's. "A mere minnow in your sea. You're a master angler, you'll easily hook another."

"The wiliest swimmers are the most to be prized. In this matter, time is short. And what I ask is not at all onerous, only to do as you did before—"

—but keep the messages, this time, not carry them, tuck them in a puppet and hold for retrieval, by whom and why? Who knows what schemes he spins now, in that spider-sac of a mind, or to what ends? It must be cold in this alcove; Istvan feels his shoulder ache. "'Before' I was another man. Now I am—retired, let's call it—"

"You appear at the Blackbird Theatre. And Le Veau d'Or. Weekly. On Tuesdays."

And the Fin du Monde, when the deeper urge arises, but this it seems the General does not know. "Retired, that is, from the venues I used to frequent. I've done with the lords and burghers," an ironic little nod, "and the ladies in their drawing rooms; here, tonight, I am just another guest. My play these days is solely to please myself."

"Before those empty-heads from the arcades? Or do you mean your chippie's fairy tales? Credit me, Hanzel, that's a fairy tale itself—"

—dropping his voice as people pass by the alcove, servants calling to one another for more candles in the drawing room, another tray of punch, and where has Otilie strayed off to? as behind the curtains, as if cordoned backstage, the two men stare at one another, the General leaning forward, Istvan's face still and calm as a carven mask: "I do credit you, sir. Credit me, or else accept my answer as pure caprice."

"And that answer is no?"

"To this request, yes."

Now the General truly smiles, the odd, hard lines about his mouth and "Come, it's no request. *Quid pro quo*, why act the virgin now? Do you remember Jürgen Vidor?" as if they recall together the name of a departed friend, a name Istvan has not heard nor spoken for years, a name stored in the mind like a letter in a chipped enamel box, lock box and "Your Mr. Bok," says the General genially, "*he* remembers. Especially the mode of the man's passing. Must it come to that, Hanzel, or will you do for me this very simple thing?"

—as simple as fingers on strings, strings of gut, human gut, human blood on a knife in an empty theatre, a packet of money shared out in the dark—but it was never for money and it was never for them, their intrigues or their interests: it was for him, to save him, keep him safe, too late. To Mouse, those drummers were Vidor's, but there lay another truth in Arrowsmith's bedside gaze, *hors de combat,* drugged as he was still Istvan saw it there, feels it now in these scars he bears. And that same truth lies in the lock box letter, *Pepper, Rawsthorne, Prussia*—

—so "Begging the General's pardon, no task of yours is ever simple." Brussels they ran from, well, let the strings be cut here finally and for all. "I was more than pleased to serve you in the past. But I am only a player now, and I only play for myself."

A servant's voice close by the alcove, a woman's hand on the drape—"Madame, your guests"—as the curtain parts and "Is it hide-and-seek?" says Isobel, both men rising as she steps inside. "Well, I've found you, gentlemen. For my forfeit, you'll come and dine, and resume your play later." Her voice she keeps even, though even a moment's glance shows that this is no play, tension sour in the air between them, what in the world or the world below it could Hector have to do with this puppet-man? as "Certainly, Madame," Istvan rising with a player's grace, his shoulder now aching abominably. "May I take you in, or would you prefer this cavalier?" bowing to the General, who bows in return: "Hide and seek, yes," taking Isobel's left arm as Istvan takes her right. "Or *rouge et noir*, perhaps we'll deal out a hand with the brandy, eh? It'll suit your décor, Isobel. Though to win," his nod serene to Istvan, "one ought not bet too steep against the house."

As they turn for the dining room, joining the straggling stream of guests, at the end of the queue come Rupert and Benjamin, stepping in at last from the garden, both bare-faced, Rupert wearing the little red rose. Rupert looks at once to Istvan, who after one swift glance turns his gaze away, as each takes his place at the table, Istvan beside a baron's lady in a peacock headdress, Rupert masked again next to Benjamin, as the servants carry in the soup of pureed pheasant, the rice-and-egg pastries, a bug-eyed German salmon poached in pepper and champagne. String music is played throughout, by a trio tucked hungry into a nook off the dining room: a bit of Bizet with the salmon, a drop of Liszt with the rosewater-almond sorbet.

The very last guest of all does not arrive until the others have eaten, drunk, stripped their dominoes, and gone, the musicians vanished, even the servants abed, all but the lady's-maid, gulping back her yawn as she unlocks a gate that opens from the garden, at the very end of the greenhouse path, a gate to a hallway to a set of stairs unused now by any except the servants and "Madame," rapping softly at a door wide enough, it seems, only for a child but "Your guest," fits it ably, cane and all, bringing a smile to Isobel, wide awake though dressed in a wrapper, waiting at a tiny table in a room itself as small as a bower: once the chapel of the house, its altar holding only flowers now, roses so purple-red they are black in the candles' glow. On the table are Assam tea and cigarettes, he offers the light but she waves him away, no ceremony, they are very old friends after all.

And it is as a friend that she may lean across that damasked table, press his hand with her own in its glove and "Liserl," she says, "that was dreadful news. You must miss her sorely."

"She was like a little—bird, to me. A little bird with a little song. Now all is silent." Dressed in sober gray, like any businessman upon the streets; no one would mark him, except perhaps for that opulent cane, the griffin's head worked in heavy silver, his hand cups it absently as "It has made me thoughtful," he says, "that silence." She says nothing, their eyes meet, her sympathy, his grief, until "I understand that Hector was here," he says, in a different voice. "By invitation?"

"My father sent him." She does not trouble to hide her bitterness. "To see Benny." The steam from the tea makes a faint perfume, mingling with the bower's scent of roses and cigarette smoke; Isobel herself gone tonight into the smoking-room, a bit of an impropriety amongst the gentlemen, but how else was one to keep an eye on Benny, first with M. Bok, and then Hector? Watch him in his blood-red mask, approaching sidewise like a crab, Benny oblivious and all aglow—until M. Bok took his premature leave, the brief and courteous apologies echoed by his colleague, the jester whose smile had gone entirely false; Hector's spoor again, and "I knew," she says, "I knew I should recall him, that M. Dieudonne. In Brussels, once, Prosper Boulan hosted an evening with some dancers—*filles de joie*, you know, and a puppet-show after. He was called Marcel there, I believe."

"Yes, he has many names. Hector calls him Hanzel; to me, he is Dusan. But M. Bok is always M. Bok, no matter where he goes," watching her over the rim of his cup, is there a little spark, there, to match her brother's? One hears that the boy is smitten. "Your friend the asp, she says M. Bok is very masculine, *tres maîtrisé*," to bring her smile, a spark indeed in that unfortunate face, poor Isobel who laughs as "Fernande, yes," pouring out more tea, the cups rimmed in gold, trimmed with a pattern of garlanded roses, scarlet and deepest green. "She'd gnaw his bones in an instant, though she'd done naught but complain, before, about players at a 'proper' dinner!"

"Then she's never been to the gaiety district? Those cafés where the poetry is declaimed, and modern music played, and little men who are not men may speak of anything at all? That's a pity." His gaze kindly on hers, recalling the girl she was, clever, industrious, always alone, always hiding her crippled hand in that glove, always pleased to see him when he came to visit Isidore, making sure to carry along for her a book—Descartes, Coleridge, some likely English novel—or a bit of lace or Turkish delight, some trifle to please her while they conversed in the garden, walking arm-in-arm amongst the rows of roses she tended, she knew them all, their habits and their names. And here, still, the rooms filled with roses, and she still alone, still doting on her brother, still hating her father, not so much growing older as accomplishing a kind of distillation, as one might do with a cooking sauce, say, or a poison, stronger as it ages, a very few drops would have a very great effect—

—as she tells him, now, about that moment in the alcove, how she came upon Hector and the puppeteer "Tête-à-tête," lighting one last cigarette, "and quite tense. Obviously he knows M. Dieudonne—or, what is it, truly? Dusan?"

"Truly I do not know." *His Christian name is Istvan*, who said that? the sister, yes, the redheaded madam who was a kind of double to Liserl; how strange that was. Perhaps one day he will visit there again. "I do know that Hector keeps many tools in his tool case. Some are more esoteric than others—only a buttonhook hooks a button. If that signifies." Finishing his tea, the faintest chime of cup to saucer, taking up his gray silk muffler against the cold of earliest dawn; no windows in this little room, but having slept so many nights in fields or fortifications, one learns to feel the sunrise coming, as one feels the turn of the tide. "You say there was a dispute of some kind between them? I wonder what was said? Though no doubt Dusan ended by agreeing—Hector does not suffer much refusal."

"Yes," she says, crushing out her cigarette. "I know."

Lucy

She said that she would come, and come she did, dressed up like those nuns you see by the cloisters, gray swansdown hood, black gloves, sitting up in the back with her brother, and didn't she applaud? And laughing like a girl at Mickey's folly with the dragon, when he hops into the mouth and back out again all sooty-like, with his eyes popping out of his head: "Sirrah! It's jolly dark in there, by George!"

And barely we were finished before she came backstage, to felicitate, she said. Her hand on my arm, she's got a funny grasp, but strong, and *Brava*, she says to me, *your comic opera was superb. Wherever do you find your little actors? And your puppets, where do they originate?* And we sat right down at the table and chatted, though I was that flustered, I'll admit, still in my stage cloak, and no one having made any tea we had to drink a bit of gin, it was all I had though she said she liked it; she's a very great lady, Madame de Metz. And the boys and girls all peeping out at her, like mice from their holes, well might they! When have they ever seen such a lady up close?

It isn't what Rupert thinks, that I felt badly when they cut me at that ball; or what Istvan thinks, either, that all's a joke; truly it's a joke to him, lords and ladies and beggars all the same. To me it is—it's the way when you go into the shops, there's the champagne here and the gin over there, and what's the harm in that, really? If you mix it all together you'd get naught but a headache, wouldn't you?

I never thought I'd rise as I have, the Blackbird is plenty high enough for me. Though I recall how Vera used to dream of marrying some flash character, some passing-through fellow who'd take her away with him: *Think of it, Lucy,* she'd say, lying on my bed, feet on the counterpane, smoking another of Pearl's cigarettes. *Riding in a coach-and-four, having servants and jewels, that's the life for me!* And always jealous of Pearl, nasty-like when the mayor made eyes at her. I wonder if she ever got to Paris, Vera, or found her toff protector if she did. All the girls on the streets here, most of them covet that same thing, to get off the gin shelf and into the champagne, as if that's the most that any girl could ever want.

But Mme. de Metz, she sees through that: talking of her brother's friends, how they have no purpose, nothing to fill their days but mischief and foolery but *You, Miss Bell,* she said to me, *you have found the pearl of great price: if we do what we are suited for, happiness follows, it is as simple as that. We need not even look for it, it will trail us like a spaniel in the street. You are a happy girl, I can see. But not always?* with that wise gaze on me like a, what you call it, a saint's, one of those church paintings where the eyes seem to watch you wherever you go. I told her I had learned early on to make myself happy, the way you make a meal out of whatever you've got to hand, but that playing the puppets seemed to fit me right away, fit me *Like a glove,* I said, and tapped her hand—it was a silly joke, and she didn't laugh much, but *Whatever your previous condition,* she said, *you have found your right road at last.* My "previous condition"! I had to smile, then.

We talked for quite some time, there at the table, and she told me some things, very useful-like, things you wouldn't think a fine lady would know: that cold water, iced water, on the hair will keep it shiny, and a dab of quince-seed jelly makes it lie flat; I'm going to try that one straightaway, on Rose Red and her elf-locks. And she was even game to work a marionette, one of the toys I keep for the boys to learn on: she fell into a fair tangle, half vexed and half crowing, *Why can I not make it go as it should?* But pleased as Punch when she got that toy soldier walking, up-and-down, up-and-down, she even got him to make a bit of a bow before the whole thing collapsed and I brava'd right back to her, *You've got a nice touch, Madame!* so that we laughed a bit together, there with our puppet and our gin, it must have made a rare sight. I wish someone had been there to see it, like Pimm, or Istvan.

I don't know where he was, that afternoon; nor did Rupert, who was vexed at being summoned, I know, though he never complained; still, someone had to entertain Master de Metz, I had all I could handle with Madame. Later on, when Istvan showed his face, I tried to tell him what a frolic it had been, but he was in a rare sour humor—*It's a family of dazzlers, isn't it?*—so I let it go, let him go up to the rooms where Rupert was already, pacing and smoking; I could hear them through the ceiling, snapping at one another—

You're busy, aren't you, for a man who says he has nothing to do? Where were you?

No busier than you, my lord, with your new attaché—meaning Master de Metz, who had said that he'd like to learn to play, or something, I heard my own name then: *Give him to Lucy,* Istvan says, *or let him go to the devil. Or*—all happy-like, like he'd found the right solution—*Georges. There's the fellow who will take him in hand, yeah?*

He needs some industry—

"Industry"? You truly are a schoolteacher now. Tell me, what else would you have him learn?

He says that he saw you, at the Calf, with that other boy, what is it, Pinky? What else don't you tell me, messire?

It was there I stopped listening; none of my road, when they get to talking like that. Instead I went down into the theatre, to tidy up, and make sure Mickey'd set nothing on fire, and sit awhile over another little glass of gin, thinking of Mme. de Metz, and happiness. What she'd said had a rare wisdom, though one look can tell you she's not a bit happy herself, except with her boy. Some folk need only the one thing, to make them whole; Rupert is like that. For Istvan it is two things, Rupert and the playing.

And me? I won't ask more of the world, not ever, with six days of the Blackbird, and the seventh spent walking out with Pimm…. We're to picnic on the promenade this Sunday, if the weather is fine. He's to bring a bit of drink, and I'm making us a bean-and-rooster pie.

The jeweler's girl is all fluttering lashes, handing Istvan the little brooch: "Your lady will surely adore it," the twinkling golden goldfish, swaddled in blue velvet and tied with a bow, slipped into his pocket with a wink for the girl who leans, now, across the counter, a quick flash of creamy bosom—"Come see us again, Monsieur!"—as he steps into the street. Joining the widening stream that leads to the boulevard, he threads his way beneath the lindens dropping their leaves, between café men and shopgirls heading out for the evening, redoubtable mamans and their spindly issue hurrying home, constables and the vendors who scuttle before them, tucking away their less-reputable merchandise behind little cups of fresh gooseberries, vials of dubious ambergris, trays of watch fobs made of stamped tin and silver-gilt, colored broadsheets touting other, more ambiguous wares, available in other venues just a *rue* or two away.

Through it all Istvan walks swiftly, easily, hat brim tugged low, gaze in constant motion: a street boy's habit, one he will never lose. Marking those vendors and constables, marking the whores in their Josephine bonnets, marking the marks who think themselves men of the world and so they are, just not of this world, this dark and shining tributary of tobacco-brown mud and mounded horseshit, of the motionless flame of the electric lights just starting to glow before the entrance to the arcades, where he steps in to have a glass of tea, a bite of meat, boots shined and pocket nearly picked by one lad as his comrade wields the blacking-brush below. Istvan's smile is one of almost comradely contempt—*You'll need to be neater than that, my lad*—as he grasps the narrow fingers, squeezing till the boy yelps, squeezing still till the boy lets out a groan, then dropping a coin for the shiner—*"Merci"*—and off again, up a twisty wreck of an iron stairway, barely secured to the buildings it links, rust flakes pattering like rain as Istvan knocks upon a door that opens to admit him—"Hello, Monsieur"—into a room filled with bodies, stuffed with straw and rags or planed from wood.

Every city has this quarter, this limbo district of the players, linked to all other such districts by rumor, competition, and a lively spirit of quid pro quo, and in this world Istvan is a kind of prince, known, yes, by many names, in many venues—from the oldest ones of all, the long-ago street days with Marco, through the drawing-room playlets, to his sojourn at the Poppy, to the Blackbird and the Calf today and even the Fin du Monde, where "Monsieur," says the little man inside the room, making room in the friendly chaos of body parts and horsehair wigs, arms and legs and ribbons, "you're on tonight, I think."

"Indeed. Ah, apologies," noticing the crust of horseshit on his heel, scraping it clean against the threshold. "I just had the fucking things blacked, yeah?"

"There's plenty shit in the streets these days, Monsieur," says Mr. Boilfast. "A man needs to be careful where he puts his foot. Even at the Fin. Oh," digging into a pocket, producing an envelope. "From M. Jardin, with *his* apologies."

"Tardy bastard…. The Calf's a funny place nowadays, does he perceive that, do you think?" with a certain feigned indifference, or is it feigned? With M. Dieudonne, whoever knows? as Mr. Boilfast, majordomo of the Calf, master of the Fin, watches the younger man pick and sort through the piled-up toys, this puppeteer who wears a mask inside his mask but may need to bundle up even further: there are, yes, some odd folk about in the cafés, drawn perhaps by the wealthy boys who sport there, whose money Jardin is happy to abstract, while turning a blind eye to the dangers they may import. Some things are worth more than money—safety; autonomy—but this is not an argument that resonates with M. Jardin.

When Mr. Boilfast speaks, his tone is mild: "I really couldn't say, Monsieur. What hours he has between counting coin, he dices, or gets his pecker pulled. It doesn't leave much time for thinking. But you, you'll be wise, won't you," as Istvan selects a mummer's mask, an antlered stag, so ferociously flamboyant that Boilfast has to smile; Istvan lets it drop and "I leave that to Feste," with a little shrug. "He keeps me honest. Or at least afloat. I'm in some dark water these days, you see…. There's a man, you may know him already. A modest gentleman, bit of a limp—"

"And a silver cane? Pleasant gentleman. Yes."

"He has a colleague—wears a ring on his thumb. Older fellow, military," sharing what he can of the General, saying all he cannot with his gaze. "You'll tell me if you see him? I'd spare you his mischief if I could—"

"Monsieur," with a pained little bow; he is strangely graceful, this plug of a Boilfast, this man with his half-moon head and stubby fingers, and deep, dry, dark-currant eyes, strangely dignified too. "You are one of my *artistes*, Monsieur. Without you, there is no Fin du Monde.

Have no worries," bowing again, straightening to show in his hand
a razor, modest wooden handle, slick hairsplitting blade; he smiles,
Istvan smiles. "Tonight we've some visitors from Venice, a marquesa, I
believe. And a pretty songbird on for dinner—"

"I've a stop or two to make first," plucking up a domino of quilted
red felt, spangled with diamonds made of paste. "We'll meet backstage," and then he is off, down a different set of stairs, narrow wooden
slats as old as the city itself, into the street again and through the dollhouse lane, past the windows where the gaslight shines on a series
of lovely tableaux, lovely girls in lace and petticoats, sipping "tea" or
reading poetry, those who can read, or brushing out long yellow locks,
winding brunette curls about their fingers, giving fraught and naughty
frolicsome winks to those passersby they deem most likely to stop, to
spend, to try to purchase what, like a puppet's gambols, can never be
wholly owned. Some of them know Istvan, nearly all of them wink as he
passes, and he winks in return: this field of flowers, of poppies, yes, and
roses, like the roses favored by Madame, such livid colors, no doubt she
would grow them black if she could. A taste for the perverse, perhaps;
perhaps that is why she invited the General to her soiree, though the
look she gave him in that alcove was not that of a friend. Does she
mislike the General, Madame, for reasons of her own? Those reasons
would be good to know—

—with a sketched smile in passing for the peony in the bouquet, a
chubby, ruffled blonde, blowzy princess who blows him a kiss as he hails
a ride, tipping the driver so lavishly that the man blinks—"Why, many
thanks, sir! *Many* thanks!"—but only because he reminds, in the cab's
dimness, of Rupert, Rupert as a younger man, the Rupert who kept him
safe from the hooligans and pennytop brigands, broke a truncheon on
their skulls a time or two, slept always on the outside, to shelter Istvan
from harm. Rough-shorn head and tense, lean-muscled shoulders, like
this man's, the neatly brushed dilapidated coat, long strong hands upon
the reins and "Many thanks," again as Istvan alights, looking up into
the man's face, the cheekbones coarser than Rupert's, the blue eyes
not like at all. The driver holds his gaze a moment, a moment longer—
"Another turn around the block, sir?"—as Istvan pauses with his hand
on the cab's door, the two men regarding one another in the darkness
of the street before the Blackbird, the empty street, the driver's faint,
cautious smile—

—but "A good evening to you," says Istvan, and turns for the door,
thinking, as he mounts the stairs, of all the moments just like that one,
moments brief as memories fading even as they happened: an afternoon, an alcove, a wool coat rubbing rough against the skin, the smell

of well water, of a stranger's sweat.... Has he been faithful? Why bother
to ask? when it is only the heart that signifies, his own heart always
Rupert's from the first day they met, that dark fierce boy coming out of
the rain, gone from the friary but still half a monk himself, so buttoned-
in, so shy in his desires. Nothing like this boy who courts him now,
bold as Cupid, yes, with a quiverful of arrows, and Rupert caught by
the attention, whether he owns it or not, one can see through him like
glass: that little frown, *He needs some industry.* Under this roof, no less!
Pretty eyes, pretty ways, *he says that he saw you, at the Calf....What
else don't you tell me, messire?* Pushing and goading until Istvan must
push back, hand to *his* shoulder, a grab to a shove and then fighting,
yes, like boys, torn shirt and cracked table, a glass crushed to splinters,
Rupert grappling him down onto the floor, fury alchemized to passion
and lying afterward in the debris, breathing hard, aching like athletes
after a bout as *Jesu*, Rupert's murmur, *you nearly broke my arm,* to
bring Istvan's half-lidded smile: *Better that than a broken heart, yeah?*

And stepping now past the parlor door, Mouse inside with his cheroots and newspaper like some sober magistrate, this man who once
stood off an alleyful of bashers, a war's-worth of brimstone, Jürgen Vidor
and the General and all, looking up with that same unchanging smile as
Istvan reaches, gently, to take off the little silver spectacles and "Why
don't you like my glasses?" Rupert asks, tolerant and annoyed. "You
once said gravitas becomes me."

"You're not old enough for such trifles. Save it for the graybeards."

"Old enough?" musingly; he sets his paper aside. "I never expected
to live this long."

Face-to-face in the lamplight, Istvan's face as open as it can ever
be, gaze cast down and "Leave with me," he says abruptly. "Now,
tonight. We'll do as we did, take only what we can carry, I'll carry Feste,
we'll be miles away by morning.... Oh why that look! Is it so strange a
notion? Why can we never be as we were?"

"How can we? That tramping is for boys; we're men, now. And we
have—"

"Have what? People? Duties? To whom, save ourselves?"

"Have a home," so simply said that Istvan goes silent, a silence
that hangs in the quiet of the room, the mantel clock's clicking silver
pendulum, a carriage clattering through the street below, until "As you
say," with a smile of such compliant carelessness that Rupert rises
from the chair, ready for more—but there is no more, only Istvan pouring out a little whiskey, a generous brandy, taking his seat in the seat
opposite so Rupert, bemused, resumes his own, drinking together and
talking for long minutes of nothing in particular, nothing that matters,

certainly not "The General," Rupert's raised eyebrows, "he spoke to you, at that dinner, didn't he? I thought we were shut of that bastard in Brussels. What was that all about?" but Istvan's shrug makes nothing of the meeting: "Whoever knows? Tapping the knifepoint, to see if it holds its edge…. Do you know, I think the old fuck cheated his partner at cards? I thought sure I saw him palm the king."

"Cheating a comrade? That sounds very like." Shaking his head as he is led without knowing onto a path of safety, of other topics far afield; himself the shelter for so long, well, let Istvan be that shelter now, whatever it may require.

Drinks done, the clock's hands reaching for half-past ten, Istvan handing back the little silver spectacles gleaming empty as blind eyes upon the table, lover's eyes and "Don't wait," he says, rising to stretch, head back, a foxy, feline motion, there will always be more boy in him than man, the eternal, restless youth of the player. "I'm off," into his rooms for a thing or two, for Feste, "for the morning papers," with a swift smile to match Rupert's—"Lansquenet, isn't it?"—who watches him go, out the door, down the stairs—

—to detour, briefly, into Lucy's province, the Blackbird's backstage still lively with Didier studious over his penny-flute, Mickey hanging up-so-down from a ladder "Like a bat!" he calls, flapping his thin arms. "See me, Mister Istvan!" as Lucy looks up from her string-work, a quick smile that widens as he takes from his pocket the blue velvet package, its ribbon untied to let the little fish swim straight into her hands— "For me?"—with such astonished pleasure it is a pleasure to behold. Pinning it at once to her bodice, admiring its gleaming scales, its move-able tail, as cunningly worked as a puppet's joints and "Toss that other away," he says to her, that dead blue eye, souvenir of several things he cares never to recall.

"I shan't do that. But you won't see it again," rising to kiss his cheek in thanks, as Didier blows a fanfare on the whistle, and Mickey topples backward, raises dust, coughs out a dusty laugh.

It is livelier still at the Fin du Monde, a fifth table tugged into service tonight to service the overflow crowd: a portrait painter from the Academie, with wife, mistress, and retinue, out for a night on the town; a cassis-sipping dandy, auburn beard and monocle, with a pretty young poetess in tow; a gentleman in pinstripes, drinking port; and the imperious marquesa right up front, cherry-red lace and rather shock-ing décolleté, demanding "*Dove il spettacolo?*"—where is the show? Beside her several compatriots, two lean and sullen cavaliers and a friendlier fellow, grandfather's belly and bald head, soothingly splash-ing more champagne for all.

The marquesa turns out to be quite a competent singer, trilling a backstreet aria along with the cool and purring Feste, more imperious even than she; they make in fact such a lovely duo that an encore is requested, a sad and lilting little tune the marquesa recalls from her childhood, rewarded at its close by a standing ovation; twenty people can make a great deal of noise. Afterward, flushed rosy as a girl, the marquesa demands the return of the handsome puppet master, he must come and drink with her, he must come and dance, there is dancing to be had someplace, an orchestra, she is sure of it, even in this dull metropolis—

—but already Istvan has stripped off his top hat and domino, spangled red and damp with sweat, as Mr. Boilfast, smile on his face, razor in his pocket, conveys past the shabby curtains the gentleman in pinstripes, carrying a griffin-headed cane. There is not much space between the stage and the street, but the two men have room enough to meet, and talk, like the old and affable friends they are: both devotees of the farce well managed, the *mot* efficiently employed; and enemies of pain without reason, force engaged when wit would do as well, or better.

"You are looking quite well, Dusan," says Mr. Arrowsmith at last, taking up his hat. "I am happy—very happy—to renew our connection once more."

"I'm happy to see you behind the lights. Do you stay?"

"No, my primary business is concluded." He pulls on a glove, pauses in nearly natural recall. "I understand we have a lady friend in common—Mme. de Metz," with a hint of a smile. "She tells me good things about your apprentice, Mlle. Bell. And your *confrère*. Her brother—Benjamin, you have met him—he is quite impressed as well with M. Bok." Out front, one can hear the marquesa calling for the puppet master, *encore, encore,* as the spinet-piano leaps to life once more. "Almost overly so, in fact. Someone could make ill use of that attachment, if he were so inclined."

"Someone with an impure heart?"

"Precisely." Mr. Arrowsmith's smile has gone; Istvan wears one now, a chilly, mocking little grin. "Time is indifferent to ambition, have you ever marked that? And power has no choice, it curdles or it feeds. Regrettable, that even one's closest associates are not immune." The two men gaze steadily, one to the other, until "*Hors de combat,*" says Istvan, very softly, and Mr. Arrowsmith nods.

"I saw the way the cards fell in Brussels—there's much prudence in knowing when to leave the game. And we all play the hand fate deals us. Hector, too." The marquesa is singing again, *tira-lira, tira-la,* like a voice from out of time, a safer, smaller world. "Isobel—that is, Mme. de Metz—knows, always, how to reach me. Never fear to ask her.... Until the next performance, then," shaking hands, shaking his head in private rue as he steps into the alley, to the narrow hack awaiting him, the cold metal seat; he can see the smoke of the horse's breath in the air, autumn is upon them now, winter hard on its heels. In his pocket is a jumbled sheaf of poetry, very bad poetry, very carelessly left where anyone might see it, a maidservant, say, who tidies a young man's rooms—*Your closeness on the path, Maître/Makes my heart spin like a compass needle/Makes my head swim like absinthe/The delirium of desire*—the ardent, silly poetry of a boy in love. First love, perhaps, the most dangerous of all, when one feels his strength is the strength of ten because his heart is pure. But the heart of the impure has its own power, as Dusan wisely noted.... Back beneath the Poppy, Mr. Bok did them a service, sending Vidor on his way. And surely Dusan is not the only available courier, though it is true that his venues make him more useful than others might be, and more elusive; true too that Hector does not brook much opposition, if any, without reprisal, especially in this case, the wished-for scout on the future's dark paths..,. *Eh bien.* No player, however skilled, can win every hand, that is the highest truth of all.

"Driver," Mr. Arrowsmith calls, "stop a moment, pray," beside a brick *pissoir*, where Mr. Arrowsmith steps inside to relieve himself of the poetry, white fragments down a dark hole, as a midnight rain begins, a cold curtain tasting of sleet, the hack driver glad to turn at last for the stable, to dry his horse beneath rough blankets, while in other quarters the disconsolate marquesa upsets her champagne glass; Rupert, weary, pulls back the narrow coverlet; and Benjamin sits in the smoke and clatter of the Golden Calf, chewing his knuckle, scratching line after line into a red-bound little journal: the shadow of stubble on a handsome cheek, dark eyes as deep as the midnight sky, the gleam of stars aligned, like destiny, spelling out one true and special name.

Isobel

Every day brings its own tedium, but today was more wearisome than most. With the morning's tea, a whining note from Letty van Symans, piqued about Benny's absence at her nameday fête, what does she suppose I may do about it? Bundle him in a basket to her door? Then the florist's man came about the evergreens, and Helmut in from Chatiens with the month's accounts: half the day gone in columns of figures, his tiny, crushing boilerplate hand and *Apologies*, from the other side of the desk, smelling of those digestive mints he chews. *I try to trouble you as little as I may, Madame,* but that is simply politesse: who else ought he to go to? I am the man of this house; it is my task.

They think me singular, I know, these men who move about in my orbit, perhaps they wonder that I do not retire to the country, let my father carry all the burden of authority; some of them find our household here a kind of oddity. Like Mr. Entwhistle—references or not, I begin to believe I have made an error employing that young man. Last week it was the stuffed swans in the drawing room, not only their "indecorous" position but Benny's mockery: *Do you think it is like?* with Pinky's mouth all pursed up like Mr. Entwhistle's, he really is a rather gifted mimic: *Why, I can't say, sirrah, I've never fucked a bird.* And then snickering together like children, while the man comes complaining up the stairs to me.

And what is it today? Sitting arms-folded in the chair, that awful coat, does he own no other? with a laundry list, a litany of Benny's wrongs: he is rude, he is preoccupied, he is not attending to his studies as he should—

And why do you believe that is?

Master de Metz is not tractable, Madame, even at the soundest of times. "Sound," his greatest compliment; what sort of experience must the fellow have had, what fear of chaos, when soundness, safety, is the highest good there is? *But now, Master de Metz is utterly distracted with those—players. His involvement there is neither proper nor sound, Madame, and I must protest—*

Your protest is noted, I told him, while trying to indicate—for a tutor, he is fairly dull—how Benny's time at the Blackbird is actually

247

quite wholesome: he is learning how to use a hammer, for one thing, and make himself useful; he spends less time at the cafés, and when he goes, comes back well before dawn, early to bed, early to rise, as bright as a schoolboy, indeed. If it is not Mlle. Bell and her quaint urchins who draw him, well, that is no affair of Mr. Entwhistle's, or of anyone's except M. Bok, who must surely understand what it is that Benny is doing there in his theatre, or here in the drawing room.... We had him solo to dinner last week, as M. Dieudonne was elsewhere engaged: a merry meal, just the three of us with a capon and wine, crystallized violets and some very dry champagne, and Benny afterward at the piano, playing Chopin études, while M. Bok drank his whiskey and parried all my questions: Did he play the piano? No, though he cared much for music. Chess? Never learned. Had he been out to the country recently, perhaps, for the hunting? which brought a kind of smile to him, a coolish humor and *No, Madame,* he said. *I find I have very little taste for the kill.*

We sat silent then, as if beneath a pall, until *Come, Monsieur,* Benny calling softly from the bench, coaxing him into a sentimental waltz, four hands on the keys: M. Bok concentrating on his part, two simple chords, as Benny's hands danced around his, coat sleeves brushing, smiling sideways into his eyes. It could melt a heart of steel, to see Benny smile so. One wonders how long M. Bok can resist.... He speaks so little, one must infer much, but he is clearly a man of probity, unusual perhaps in one who has spent his days among players. Probity, and clarity, a kind of keenness of the heart; Benny would be safe with him. Anyone might be safe, with him.

Meanwhile Mr. Entwhistle grows ever more steely—and yes, I chose him so, I cannot complain overmuch, but still. Pink hands knotted on the desktop, that blond slick of hair falling into his eyes, in dudgeon not only for Benny's progress with the Greeks (not a thing he should worry for! though it is precisely that sort of allusion that Mr. Entwhistle deplores), but other subjects, more tedious and abstract: *A moral foundation is all that makes a man truly sound, Madame. And for a youth like Master de Metz, exposed every day to all sorts of temptations, all the dreadful pitfalls of pleasure and wealth—*

Dreadful indeed.

Indeed yes, Madame! And what I implore you to consider—

—while here came Cook, barging in about the Christmas geese ordered from the farm at Chatiens, too many, or not enough, whatever the dilemma was—as Mr. Entwhistle sat twisting in his chair like a martyr at the stake, then off again on the temptations of feasting and frippery: *It is a Christian holiday, our Savior's birth. One ought to celebrate like a Christian, with prayer.*

We do go to Mass, Mr. Entwhistle.

I know that you are Papists, Madame, with a smile of such hungry disapproval that I admit I lost all patience, and reminded him that his business here is to teach Benny Latin and Greek, not rescue him from the fires of hell: *If you cannot aid Master de Metz in his learning, without provoking him unendurably in the process, then you ought to seek another position, or apply to the foreign missionaries. Is that understood?*

Then the tedious apologies, anyone could see the man was near apoplexy; such a clumsy liar, is untruth not a sin? And once he was dismissed, here came the butler! I had to take myself out into the garden to purchase a moment's peace.

Already the frost has come, to my Belle Étoiles, my favorites, their thick white petals and deep orange hearts; the Lady Beckinsales, the floribundas, all are down to thorny canes. It is so sad to see them go, each year, though one believes in spring's resurrection; at least the asters are still vigorous, and the greenhouse is always my refuge.... Botanomancy, it is called, using the leaves of a plant to tell one's fortune, burning them in a brazier fire, the old missus from the village used to do so. Showing me the patterns in the ash, raspberry and daisy and cabbage-rose, vines and twigs, teaching me to read their drift and scatter: *See what the flowers tell you, child.*

And the head gardener at Chatiens, Axel, such a kindly fellow, he seemed old to me then but would have been, I hazard, my own age now. Always in his smock and sabots, a scarf wound round in the cold, never too busy to stop and answer my questions, praise me when I remembered, encourage me when I did not, the greenhouse doors left unlatched always so *The young mistress may have roses in the winter,* he would say, clipping a little bloom for me to take inside.

How I loved the smell, there, so fecund and alive, and so different from the formal gardens, lane on lane of roses, yes, but all sharp and unwelcoming, like a minotaur's lair, to keep the world *en garde.* Not so in the greenhouse, Axel's greenhouse—I remember the softness of the peony leaves, like flesh under silk, the feel of the moths against my skin, the blind white flutter of their wings—flowers are the procreative organs of the plants, I read that in a book and told it so to Axel, and I can still recall his tender smile: *Why, naturally, Miss. All that lives, loves.*

Well. Love one may, whether one will or no, but from the time I could understand how I was damaged, I understood as well that no one would ever want me so: my father's defect, that fused and twisted hand he never troubles to hide, but it is different, for a woman, a girl. I remember dancing, once, with some guest of my father's, some Viennese gentleman who twirled me round beneath the lights, he had me laughing until *You are not much like your mother was,* he said, so wistfully that as soon as the music was ended, I escaped to the greenhouse. Axel was not there, no one was there, only I and the breathing flowers, and the winter rain falling outside. From then on I had the gloves made specially for me. My father never questioned the expense.

Now the leaves drift and litter the narrow paths, now when I sit to smoke my breath makes clouds like my cigarette's. There is little peace to be found elsewhere. Only yesterday there was a letter from Charlotte, inquiring as to our plans for the Christmastide, and Benny's birthday; we must have some gala, even if he does not wish one, though to have it here will please him far more than Chatiens. He will be eighteen, a man.... And that communiqué from Hector, for Benny, my girl brought it quite properly first to me: some breezy farrago about a horse, did Benjamin prefer a gelding or a stallion? Is that Hector's way of being subtle? *Mon Dieu.* If Benny thinks of him at all, Hector, it is as some antique colleague of our father's, no one he must notice or mind. Especially now, when he is in such a dreamy, lovely, yearning humor: watching the stars, calling me "Bella," sharing a song he learned at the children's theatre—*What's the use of tears, my dears*—and *You ought come and see me play,* he said, smiling over his shoulder until I smiled, too, tears in my eyes that he did not see. What's the use of tears, my dears, indeed. Oh indeed. My precious boy—does Hector imagine I will surrender him without a battle? I am not entirely powerless, even with only one hand.

"Are you coming or going?" Istvan asks of Lucy crisply crossing the Blackbird stage where he sits, whittling at a little wooden dagger, blade to blade. Bundled in a duster, daubs and spatters, her skirts streaked dark with rain and "It was that tutor fellow," she says. "Delivering this," a note marked for Benjamin de Metz. Istvan makes a face—"Oh? Are we his postbox, now?"—as he takes it from her, slitting it with a practiced thumbnail, a smile for her raised eyebrows: "Why goodness, Puss, don't you read the broadsheets? It pays to be informed. Is the man still out there?"

She shakes her head: gone almost before he came, thrusting the paper at her as if she were contagious, what an odd fellow and "I'll play delivery boy," says Istvan, slipping the note into his sleeve. "Are they here, both our noble young thespians?"

Lucy sweeps a hand down her duster. "We're painting scenery for the Nativity show. That Pinky had a good thought, to use slut-wool for the background, the sheep on the hills—"

"The boy's got the breath of the stage about him to be sure. Put him in a costume, darling, don't be shy."

"And," with care, "what about the other?"

"The Happy Prince? We'll give him some work that suits him—dip him in whitewash, call him a statue," with a little wink that carries no real humor, Benjamin a subject she mostly avoids, no longer a joking matter. Not that he knows it, and in some ways it is not at all his fault, but it is a pity just the same: handsome is as handsome does, and there is something sad and cruel about that young man, something lost amidst the beauty and the gold.

It was Rupert's idea, to have Master de Metz at the Blackbird: she did not follow his thinking but he has never asked her for anything, has given her everything, so of course she would not refuse him, would not even refuse it in her heart. But Rupert is not the one who has to manage him! nor watch Istvan ignore and criticize him by turns, toying with him like a tomcat does a kit; there is something sad and cruel about him these days, as well.

251

Still, there is in Benjamin an admiration for Istvan, though neither would ever own it: he is, in life, so much like those poet heroes both boys chatter on about, the ones who defy all the rules and do as they will. Just yesterday Pinky was quoting some poetical nonsense as she sewed, something about dying in the arms of the Muse, it sounded pretty enough but *Have you ever watched a man die?* she asked him, and that took some of the air out of the pillow! Oh, well. There is no malice in Pinky, to be sure, even Benjamin says so: *He wounds only by accident,* with that superior air, but they are fond comrades, one can see, Benjamin as leader and Pinky his lieutenant: both have stopped wearing their gaycoat weeds, since Benjamin seemingly decided he must dress as Rupert does, all grays and blacks, though nothing on earth could make Pinky look grave. They would be a fine addition to the troupe, the pair of them, if only—

—as Lucy breathes a little sigh, Istvan resuming his woodwork, then takes herself backstage to find that Mickey has managed to glue a tin crown to his head, causing much merriment all around, until she pulls out the lye-soap and the snips. As they struggle together, the others finish painting the sky above the rustic stable where the Christmas play will unfold: still weeks away, but there is much to accomplish in the meantime, costumes to fit and devise, music to learn, and lines for a story simple enough: a rich young man arrives by accident at the holy site, burdened by his cares, and is put through his paces by a heavenly spirit. It is to be called *Angels on Horseback,"* Istvan promising to be the angel, as well as help the boys with the marionettes, their ambitions far beyond their current skill.

In a way, those young fellows are the youngest of Lucy's charges, just babes on the stage, though each brings his own strengths: Benjamin's beauty and quite passable piano, Pinky's industry and dash, and his hard work—for he does work, more joyfully than he ever has before; Istvan has called it truly, he has the breath of the stage about him. Much to the dismay if not outright wrath of his father, upright Honoré dour to ask his wife across the breakfast tea if *That boy is fully mad, now? Costume or no, people will know who he is, who his people are. I ought send him to Austria, or into the army; that will scotch his nonsense.*

But Madame Guerlain is more sanguine: *Why trouble yourself? Achille tires of everything so quickly, it will be horse racing next, or perhaps he will marry. Or I'll take him with me to the country, shall I?* Privately Mme. Guerlain resolves to go and see the show, in disguise of course, it would not do to show too much consent; she will call in the vendeuse, and have something bewitching stitched up straightaway.

Perhaps she will dress as an Arabian lady, with silks and scarves, or perhaps those quaint balloon trousers—trousers! Would that not be delightful?

It is a tasty tale in the city's more refined salons, the errant young men and their playacting folly, the ladies murmuring with raised eyebrows of the milieu: Miss Bell the unmarried proprietress, and M. Dieudonne, her onstage partner, so dashing and apparently dissolute. A few have seen his puppet show at the Golden Calf, though none will acknowledge it, and even less the Fin du Monde, itself so louche a destination that no lady can publicly admit to crossing its threshold. There are rumors that Isobel de Metz has become a silent patron of the Blackbird ménage, for did she not have those players to her home more than once? And does she not, perhaps, have her eye upon the manager of the place, that handsome and melancholy Mister Bok? for whom a noblewoman like Isobel would surely be manna from Heaven, though the connection were necessarily secret and short-lived. And tit for tat: *If one were as unfortunate as poor Isobel,* opines one of the ladies, perhaps it is Letitia van Symans, *any man would serve as a likely warming-pan. Especially one younger than she—*

If it's Isobel who'll win him, shrugs bosom-friend Fernande. *You know little Benny cannot keep his trousers fastened, he taught that tutor a thing or two. Oh, don't look so shocked,* as Caroline de Mercy makes a face: How dreadful! Benjamin de Metz, a catamite? *What was his name, that German fellow—?*

—as the gossip is filtered and digested in other, calmer quarters, considered over a cup of hot Assam, savored along with the port: if M. Bok is truly become an habitué of the de Metz home, it makes him useful indeed, in more ways than one, and the whole situation worth watching from very close range. Hanzel will not accept his commission? His mind may yet change on that score. Dusan plays his hand alone? Perhaps there is a wild card in the deck.

And from the drawing room at Chatiens issue forth the weekly letters, Isidore de Metz's long epistles to his son, to his far-flung associates, to those whose allegiance is beyond question, to others whom he would not trust within five paces in a noonday light. He feels the growing weight of age and infirmity, he writes more swiftly; imagining Benjamin here, in this chair, carrying on the work begun before his birth, shepherding the de Metz will into the future, shaping the modern age yet to be. Upstairs, in her sumptuous and lonely bedroom, his miserable young wife sees her monthlies come and go as regularly as the carriages to Paris, wishing she were in Paris, or even at the townhouse with Isobel and Benjamin—and what will happen to Charlotte, when *he* is master? If she has no children to buffer her, what then? It is true that Benjamin does not seem to despise her as much as does Isobel, but one can never tell with him, Benjamin who, if the rumors are true, is involved in some sort of amateur theatricals, and what will his father say when he hears that?

Now the young actor in question watches as Istvan approaches Pinky, busy with his paint brush, to draw him aside for some private instruction, Istvan whose approval was necessary for their addition to the troupe, an approval tendered for his own reasons, unshared with Lucy, unshared even with Rupert whose diffidence in asking—*Lucy could do with the muscle, since you're rarely about these days. But do as you please*—reinforced Istvan's own conclusions. *Do as you please,* well and so he has, these young men a useful blend of rampart and litmus: let Benjamin be kept where Istvan can see him, and let the general see him there as well. Even borrowed power can make a shield.

Though most times it seems that Istvan himself does not note Benjamin at all, moving him about as brusquely as the furniture, ignoring or tormenting him by turns, treatment that is distinctly novel for the heir to the de Metz name. Still he bears what he must from this, his rival for Monsieur—Etienne Dieudonne, with his razor tongue and measuring eyes, the faint lines at his lips, the cold grace of his movements onstage: an arch-player, as Pinky says—for the daily chance to watch Monsieur passing through the hallways, or standing, arms folded, at the back of the house, like a warm shadow falling on his heart.... Miss Bell has said that Monsieur, too, was once an actor, playing alongside M. Dieudonne in some long-ago days; will he play in this show, now, somehow? But whenever he asks, she only shakes her head and smiles: *You must put your mind back to the piano, Mr. Benjamin. Have you fully learned your part, yet? Look, Didier is come to practice with you.*

Yet why else is he here, on this stage at all, if it is not Monsieur's doing? For surely M. Dieudonne does not like him, though he is always friendly to Pinky: see them now together at the table, bent over the puppets M. Dieudonne has just constructed, funny, ugly things nesting one-in-another, a devil in a magistrate in a fishwife in a girl with a horse's head like "Bottom," says Pinky with a grin. "She's from the same family tree, isn't she, sir? That fellow with the donkey's noggin?"

"And she has an uncle, called the Chevalier.... You know a bit of Shakespeare, eh?"

"Why, to be sure. And Kit Marlowe, too—that *Doctor Faustus* is my favorite. D'you know, they say real demons popped up at a *Faustus,* once, drawn by the incantations, and drove all the audience barking mad? What a topping show that must have been!—Now what of that one, sir?" nodding to Feste, who lies well apart from the others, eyes open, half swaddled in a length of violet silk and "I don't use him on this stage," says Istvan coolly, but "May I see?" Pinky reaching with reverent hands, admiring the planes of the puppet's face, the ludic grin, the eyes especially. "This one was cut with a sharp knife! He's a rouser. But he's got a bit of sorrow to him, too, hasn't he." Not a question, spoken almost to himself, he and the puppet eye-to-eye, as Istvan smiles with a master's approval—

—but right there at his elbow "May I see?" from the Happy Prince all studious, inserting himself, as always, where he does not belong so "No," says Istvan, "you may not." A strained little silence, then, an itch in his sleeve—the forgotten note, yes—so he shakes it free, toward Benjamin who misses, must reach to take it from the floor: "You may read your billet-doux instead," some rot about stopping at the Chamsaurs' for his sister, they are dining there this evening, hoopla. Stupid, to send the tutor on a footman's errand, but the ways of the wealthy are often stupid, stupid as this boy who crumples the note and tosses it aside, who gives Istvan a prideful, wounded, liquid look from beneath his curls, that look that makes Istvan want to string him up like a puppet so "The fellow came especially to bring it," bending in one smooth motion to retrieve the note and flip it back, hard, so it strikes his cheek, so it almost stings. "You might read the fucking thing, yeah?"

Benjamin stands frozen. Pinky looks from one to the other, asks in as light a tone as he can muster, trying to ease the air, "Why, who came, sir?"

"His teacher," brusque, "the dry guillotine," the soubriquet so apt that Pinky barks a laugh, even Benjamin is surprised into a near-smile: and his gaze meets Istvan's then, meets and holds in a *frisson* so tense and odd that both are struck, though only one understands, and he imperfectly: as if meeting one's phantom in a mirror, the mirror of time, beauty staring at beauty's experience, ascendant and at final apogee until "Off you go, Cupid," Istvan's tone so brutal that Pinky has to look away. "Off to your tea party…. Are you hard of hearing? I said *go*—"

—as Benjamin turns white, turns on his heel past the jumble of lumber and paint pots, pushing out into the narrow hallway, head bent so he stumbles, tumbles into a body right there in his way— "Pardon!"—but "Hold up," strong hands to steady him, Rupert's kindly frown. "What's amiss, then, Master de Metz?"

"Oh!" with half a gasp, gazing up into Rupert's face, and the sudden spring of tears, mortifying, childish—but to be sent away, then run straightaway into *this*! into his arms, like falling headlong from Purgatory into Paradise.... They stand so for a moment, a long moment in the dim and cluttered hallway, Rupert as close as in one of his dreams: and it would be so easy, here, now, to do as he has done before with others, reach up and caress that cheek, the faint rasp of bristles there, the scent of tobacco and something secret beneath it, astringent, intoxicating, to taste it with his lips—yet this is not some grubby groomsman in a stable, some oaf in a boat, this is Monsieur so "M. Dieudonne," he says, tries to say but finds instead that he cannot speak, can do nothing but look, all his heart in his eyes for Rupert—

—who ought step back, take his hands away, but the boy is trembling so, perhaps he is ill, or he and Istvan, did they quarrel? Looking down into those tearful eyes, the tremulous and seeking smile, and it is suddenly an effort to make a smile of his own, past the swift and primal uprush of appetite: this boy in his hands like a puppet, stringless and willing, willing him to do as he pleases, whatever he desires—

—so "Be careful," Rupert's mutter, drawing back, hands at his sides again and now Benjamin is glowing, scrabbling through his pockets for, what? a book, a red-spined little journal that he thrusts at Rupert, almost pushes into his hands: and kisses his cheek, a chaste, hot, fragrant little kiss, then bolts down the hallway for the outer door, a clatter of boots as Rupert stuffs the thing unseen into his breast pocket, takes a ragged breath, and heads, again, for backstage, where all hands are busy with a toppled backdrop wall, tumbled dust and children's hubbub, his advent unmarked by all but Feste, who lies silent as a puppet must, when flesh addresses flesh.

Chatiens is famous for its skylarks as well as its roses, the gardens' air is filled with song on fine spring days, but the crows gather there as well, staring eyes and black wings, scattered like spent ordnance on the lawn beneath the master's windows, where, in the dregs of a long and sunless afternoon, in ink as black as a crow feather, Isidore de Metz now addresses his correspondence.

The room is a marvel of opulent restraint, dark velvet drapes and spotless floors, an ascetic sultan's elevation of a very few perfect *objets*: a bust of Pompey, carved from black marble, as small as a child's fist; an oil study on an ebony easel of Rachel at the well, gaze in downcast modesty, as a satyrlike Jacob approaches stealthily from behind; and, on the cramped and ancient desk before him, a little golden inkwell worked in a pattern of fleurs-de-lys, scored by time to a luminous patina, muted to a wink by the room's dimness: this last a possession of his grandfather's, the first Isidore, who used it much as this descendant does, to rewrite the story of one part of the turning world.

As each letter is composed, in his fine and fluid hand, he notes its import in a small pearl-gray journal, in a code of his own devising. If it is written, it will be read, that is the rule; so let it be written in a way that no one but himself can ever understand. Not for the first time, he wishes such caution on his associates and colleagues, men like Victor Rawsthorne, and Edgar Chamsaur, M. Boris in the Urals, and Guerlain in his tidy banker's box; letters from each lie on the desk before him, to be weighed in the mind's scales, then answered appropriately. True it is that one needs boldness when that need arises, but it is caution that keeps one's interests most secure. Examples of the opposite are abundant, of valued associates fallen victim to their own foolhardiness or greed: recall the elder van Symans, say, or that munitions broker from Ghent; or Jürgen Vidor, *there* was a regrettable waste. How many of their sorties met with so much success, and profit, due to Vidor's fine management? If he could occasionally be ruthless, he was never hot-handed; and if the man had a craving for certain situations, still he balanced both spheres of his life with great discretion, if not the best of taste—

257

"Beg pardon, my lord, there's a caller. A gentleman from—"

"Have him into the library. Brandy and tea."

—until he abandoned all caution, let his desires take the reins, and was thus dispatched by those desires: cut down and robbed in a brothel, what a foolish, shabby end. There may have been a way of averting such an undesirable outcome, as John Pepper strongly believes, and Rawsthorne, too, no matter what Hector insists, but then neither have ever cared overmuch for Hector, the man or his methods. And Hector was there, it was his affair to manage, for good or for ill.

Arrowsmith was there as well, but kept his own counsel, then and afterward, as he does on so many other matters; he has always been a silent creature but has grown more so throughout the years. As well as less intimate with Hector, who seems, lately, to prefer single combat—

Where is Arrowsmith? I have not seen him for some time.

His mistress died.

And?

Javier—is grown poetical, I think. And he spends far too much time in the cafés. But doubtless he is still sound.

—while displaying certain poetical relishes of his own, increasingly so, if his own lieutenants are to be believed, as well as Isobel's stiff communiques: *Hector Georges dined with us this evening, and sends you his regards. He is making a present to Benjamin of a new gelding, it should arrive at Chatiens very soon.*

Isobel—what a pity that Isobel was never useful as a woman should be; there were many alliances a daughter might profitably have secured. Charlotte is proving useless as well, four years without one quickening; it is perhaps his life's greatest sorrow, he who should have fathered many children, a fine and thriving line of succession, to find instead his wives all barren, or nearly so, and his daughter made barren by appearance as well as disposition; Isobel has nothing of her mother, Dorothea was a lovely woman, far more so than Charlotte—Charlotte is a misstep on several levels—though never as beautiful as his lost Rachel. Rachel, the favorite of his wives, does it not follow that their child should be his favorite as well? And such a child: Benjamin, his only heir, a man could ask little more in a son. If only the boy were somewhat more studious, and a better correspondent, when he bothers to write at all his penmanship is atrocious, and unimproved by the upright Mister Entwhistle, whose own writing skills leave something to be desired: *his* last letter was barely legible, and the news it carried tainted with the man's own opinions and cant.—Though Benjamin is too old, really, to have a tutor at all, no wonder he rebels. He is nearly a man, now.

Isidore sighs, sets down the pen for a moment, flexing his fingers. He uses a boneset-and-hyssop salve for the rheumatism, but it seems in recent months to have lost its best efficacy: the pain is bad, but the stiffness is worse, this cramping that makes a claw of his one good hand. The depredations of encroaching age, as much as he refuses to acknowledge them—the sleeplessness; the sharp new ache in his chest; the weariness that drops like a curtain, separating him from what he would do, wills to do—a pity, that there is only threescore-and-ten allotted to each man; and to some, much less. That is why an heir is so important. That is why Benjamin must come to Chatiens.

Though the move must be accomplished with care: what results can be obtained by force are rarely useful, especially with as proud a boy as Benjamin. Attempting to parse the same for Hector, when last they met at the Emperors' Club: port wine in the mellow half-dark of a city afternoon, how many pleasant and useful hours has he spent there, since the chair became his? As it will be Benjamin's—

I can bring him to you in two days' time. Why tarry?

I do not want him "brought." He must come on his own.

How can that be, when he's so busy playing? Onstage, no less, as I assume you've heard? And Isobel encourages this.

Isobel has always been a fool. I did wrong in allowing Benjamin to grow so attached to her. Immoderately attached.

He has other attachments as well, one of Hector's hints, as if he alone possesses all knowledge, sometimes it is wise to remind him otherwise: *I have that information, yes. My man has been to the theatre.*

You have eyes everywhere.

Yes.

It's a sound principle.

Yes.

He tips the pen again to the inkwell, and begins the letter to Edgar Chamsaur, a brief and cordial missive suggesting that the two of them meet—not at the Emperors' Club, but his own house in the city— regarding an alliance between Benjamin and Chamsaur's eldest, what is the chit's name? Adele, yes. *Other attachments,* that may well be, and must be addressed as well, whether Benjamin will or no; a boy will sow some wild oats, but in the end, how can it signify? Guerlain's letter carries a postscript grumble of his own son's gambols with that load of actors, some he-and-she of the boards, some other fellow who owns the place, *a menagerie your boy frequents with my own Achille,* yes. One day they will shepherd the city, these two and their comrades, it is not unwise to remind them so from time to time. Even the most cherished thoroughbred must learn at last to take the bit.

"Beg pardon, my lord, your guest is in the library."

"I will be there directly," without looking up from his letter that he signs, blots, seals, and notes in the gray journal, then "Helmut," as he rises, "inform Mme. de Metz that we will be traveling. We will spend Christmastide in the city."

"Yes, my lord," holding the door as his master passes to his appointment, the majordomo, alert and cadaverous, then mounting the stairs to the young Madame's chambers, where he finds her snipping the fringe from her skirts in a vain attempt to pass the time. She receives the message with puzzlement and pleasure, rattling on to the silent Helmut, silently chewing his digestive mint, of how lovely it will be, such a journey and sojourn, how there are perfect quantities of things to do before departing, how she has been positively dreading the holidays here, alone in the cold at Chatiens—

"How should you be alone, Madame? The master is in residence."

Silence: Charlotte laughs, an empty little sound, then hangs her head like a child. A pair of crows rise from the lawn, calling one to another in the language of combat and flight. When Helmut has withdrawn, Charlotte takes up pen and scented paper, and fills three sheets with exclamations of delight: how very glad she is to accept Isobel's Twelfth Night invitation, how wonderful it will be to see the two of them again, her children-by-marriage, and most of all how pleased their dear father will surely be, to celebrate with his loving family the birth of their darling Benjamin, and that other birth, of the Savior of them all.

The smell is the same, that oily tallow odor, and the dampness, too, in this workroom where Istvan sits, scraping wood to life, like those long-ago weeks spent with, what was her name? that matronly whore? Lucienne, yes. Living on scraps and tatters, constructing, from the corpse of Marco, Pan Loudermilk, who now lies as still, face perpetually shrouded with black silk, in his traveling coffin, with no shows to offer and nowhere to go. The same fate has befallen the romantic Chevalier and the sturdy, lovely Miss Lucinda, who hang in comradely near-embrace, dangling arms not quite touching; the Bishop has gone into Lucy's employ, to become the sad spectre of Death, banished at play's end by the holy Christmas star, without even a line of his own to speak.... The troupe of puppets-within-puppets, the toys, he made for Pinky and the little lads to use—devil and girl and who knows what else, carved as much to soothe himself as for any larger purpose—but they are a fine size, easy to manipulate, they will do well in this show he has promised Lucy he will play in, a promise he may no longer be able to keep, though it will not do to tell her so. Not yet.

The warped handle of the planing knife lies easy in his hand, and Feste, swaddled in purple like an emperor or a penitent, lies within reach, the both a kind of wordless comfort, as he sits otherwise wholly alone; and this, too, is familiar, this loneliness, from the days of Lucienne: Mouse gone then, disappeared, and gone now, too, into hiding, from himself as much as from Istvan. He wants that boy, and, being Mouse, does not want to want him, and thus makes much of what should be little, a shooting star framed up like the sun. On a stage it would be comical. On a stage.... Instead one must sit and watch as he tries not to watch those curls and graces from the dark back of the house, and deflect enquiries that are simply beneath them both—

That Benjamin—you're harsh with him, aren't you.

Not at all, and no more than the little homunculus deserves.

If he—annoys you, why not dismiss him?

Shall I? Would you miss him if I did?

—and that make an ache between them, a raw spot that pains the more as Istvan begins to see how the path is turning, the way he will very shortly have to walk. If only they had kept on the move, and lived the life they were meant to! when one carried all one's life in two hands, and out the back when the shadows gathered; someday, perhaps, they will do so again. It is something to live for at any rate; and this dream, too, is familiar. Perhaps all life is so, the same joys and sorrows in endless repertoire.

Eyes half closed, his hands stay busy, a new face growing into rapid life beneath the blade, a face all eyes but without a mouth, just a molded slash in the wood; this one will have nothing to say, and little to do, at tonight's command performance, the General's dinner at the Hôtel Violette: a public arena, safe enough though he has tipped the meeting to Boilfast; and to Lucy, too, there at the table with her teapot and her Mister Pimm: *I'll be supping with the quality tonight, yeah? Not a true show, just parlor tricks,* making light of it while making sure she understands; she is quick, she remembers how it was at the Poppy. And Pimm, too, is no fool: whether or not the fellow likes him, still he is shrewd enough to see that what touches Istvan touches Lucy, and the man is clearly taken with Puss. So much the better. She will need a strong hand beside her in the days to come.

Now the light has weakened, darkness is coming on, early winter's early sunset to drive the strollers from the streets into the taverns, the cafés and arcades, or home to onion soup and loving arms. The old-fashioned oil lamp twists shadows up the walls; it is cold in the room, now, Istvan's shoulder waking into its sharp familiar throb. The blade glides down the swift-planed face, the wondering eyes, the hair a scrap of boiled wool, stuck so; tie a bit of ribbon for a cravat, an impudent, gallant sprig of yellow silk; enough.

"Enough," he says aloud, rising to dust away the drift and curl of the wood shavings, flex his arms, slip the planing knife into his pocket where it lies like a comrade beside another, smaller knife, with a scuffed white handle, that never can be lost. Into his rooms for his own toilette, his own brave bright cravat, his hat and a hard swallow of brandy to put heart into him: so weary of this kind of combat, but one does what one must and a show is a show so "Hola," he salutes little Mickey, who waits in the shadows near the stairwell, just where Istvan placed him an hour before. "Any movements on the front, Lieutenant?"

"No, sir," stoutly. "No one but Mr. Pimm for Miss Bell."

"Do you consider," gravely, leaning down so they are face-to-face, "that he is sweet on our Miss Bell, that Mr. Pimm?"

"I do, sir. I seen 'em kissing out on the promenade."

"Indeed. Do you consider," slipping him a coin, "that you might stand by this door awhile longer, and tell me, later, or tomorrow, if anyone at all should come? It's much to ask," head to one side, knowing what the boy will answer, Mickey so kin to him that they might have been comrades on the streets long ago, they *are* comrades and "I can stay all night," says Mickey, to bring Istvan's smile, a smile the boy cherishes as much as the coin to which Istvan adds a second and "If you are here when I return," he says, "I'll take you to the Golden Calf the next I play," a promise so vast that Mickey's eyes pop wide, his grin lights up the hallway—

—as Istvan exits down the stairs, not seeing, as he goes, Rupert approaching, hatless and with a bottle in his hand. With a little nod, he acknowledges Mickey's presence, enters the rooms to leave them again in just a moment, so plainly unhappy with the emptiness inside that Mickey, who likes Mister Rupert, feels moved to remark that "Mister Istvan's just gone off, sir."

Rupert pauses in the hallway's dark. "Did you see him?"

"Yes, sir."

"Did he say—" stupid, to ask a child "—where he was bound?"

"No, sir. But he'll be back," as Rupert turns away, stepping into the theatre as empty now, Lucy busy elsewhere, her brood dispersed, only Mickey about, and why is that?—but too dull-hearted to ask more, and what does it matter at any rate? Istvan was the one he wanted, and Istvan, as usual, is gone.

Up he climbs, through the hush all true theatres own, that dim silence like an indrawn breath, up through the dark, the pulleys' sway, to the dry beams and iron shelter of the catwalk; always the urge, when he is wounded or perplexed, to be up high. Istvan used to tease him for it, ask him if his father was a gargoyle or his mother a bird; and sometimes it was simply for safety, how they roosted on the rooftops, wrapped up together in a coat, fresh in the morning to climb back down and take again to the road.... He can smell it on him, Istvan, that mounting need to be off: and dreads the repetition of the demand, surely it will come, but the question is why, not where or how. To roam as mere travelers would be foolish, would in the end satisfy neither; and they cannot be again as they once were.

He rubs his forehead, yesterday's headache become today's, tomorrow's too no doubt. In some ways all *was* simpler, on the road, though even more wearing—always the need to think and plan at least two jumps ahead—and more hazardous, too: not only cold and hunger were their enemies, Istvan forgets so much.... And the Poppy was no answer, either. This place—in this place they could be safer if not safe, they could live quietly, Lucy too, and Istvan could perform on any stage in the town, all would be overjoyed to have him; or make a theatre of his own if he fancies, they have money enough.

But instead Istvan grows ever more snappish, like a dog chained to a post: out to the Calf and back again with his itch unscratched, toys carved for Lucy's children but nothing for himself—and Rupert dare not ask or urge him, for what would the answer be? *Puppets for what show, Mouse? For what house?* And when they are alone, his moods more unpredictable than ever, by turns tender and fierce, or sullen and demanding, that look in his eyes—No, there is nothing to say, nothing to do but watch as Istvan vents his temper on those lackwits at the Calf, or dabbles in society, even jousting, Jesu, with the General at that party. Madame de Metz, now, she has been more than kind to all of them, to Lucy, to himself, but Istvan mocks her, too, because of her brother. Because of Benjamin.

Tipping the bottle, more whiskey sucked slow between his teeth; something scrabbles in the scenery far below, false stable, authentic rat. Reaching into his breast pocket, Rupert takes out the little red journal, balances it unopened on his knee: no need to turn the pages again, read the poems written there; they are all for him, all about him. Dark angel of the garden, heart's desire, lord and master of pleasures, it is strange and amazing to see himself portrayed with such open passion, such—adoration. *Maître, Maître....* Istvan has often been treated so, to bring his own rage or bemusement; but never before has it happened to him.

And even stranger, in some ways, is to read a tale that is the tale of one's own life, Benjamin's daily doings worked into these dreams, these poems, intertwined with his own—*There at the piano, white keys beside black, your hands beside mine*—it is a kind of magic mirror, like the stage itself, as if they all were characters on the boards....

He has made it his business not to be alone with Benjamin, since those moments in the hallway; no one knows except, yes, Istvan, who sees straight through him and always has, and Benjamin who sees, now, that he is wanted in return, the air between them is ripe with it: grown bolder in his overtures, *Did you read my poems yet, Monsieur?* Istvan would scoff, but Benjamin is his best ally in the argument for fleeing back to the road. Those smiles, these poems, nothing in it but rue and trouble—with another swallow of whiskey, a long one, as if he is parched or in pain. And Benjamin himself is troubled, anyone can see that: the changeable moods, now radiant, now downcast; the chameleon clothing; the way he chews a knuckle until it bleeds, Rupert has stopped him once or twice and now when he sees Rupert watching, he will stop himself, give a smile that shows he understands: *See, Monsieur? I do just as you tell me. Tell me what to do.* Jesu. And a lord's son in the bargain—! Perhaps he ought to take to the road alone, hire out to sea on a tramp steamer, or hie back to Decca at the Poppy, perhaps she needs a good front-of-the-house man again: he is not too old, he has a few swings left in him, and there is a certain honest pleasure to be had in breaking heads.

Below, a door opens, Lucy crossing swiftly from one side of the stage to the other, a rush basket of props in her arms, tin stars made to spangle the Christmas sky; she carries no light, she does not see him, like some angel, yes, or kobold, roosting up above. When she has gone, the stillness seems deeper, the silence that falls between one act and the last. He takes up the little journal, to replace it in his pocket, but instead allows it to fall open, allows himself to read once more—as best he can through the dimness, the looped extravagant scrawls of ink—that the sound of his footsteps approaching is the sweetest sound in all the world.

To be a woman is to be, in a certain sense, a creature in peril, the city is as the world, a man's creation, and without a man's protection, a woman alone turns prey. Still, there are many places where a lady may travel the thoroughfares in safety, at least in the daylight hours: the long stroll of the promenade is one, beneath the blind benevolence of the statues' eyes; or down the intersecting lanes of the public gardens, though these are more deserted since the weather turned, the leafy trees bare and the flowerbeds empty, nothing left on view but the topiary evergreens, dark spheres and squares beside the brick-paved paths, where the groundsmen creep along like sturdy beetles, gloved and hatted in the cold.

The arcades, while made primarily for evening's pleasures, have their daylight traffic too, household maids sent trotting on errands, apothecary girls, and the greengrocers' and market shops are busy with the busy working-class mamans. To find the bourgeoisie and their more noble sisters, one need only cross over to Dressmakers' Row, its milliners' and couturier shops, where, alone or with a bosom friend or two, they meet and gossip in clusters, comparing babies' colics and the distant woes of distant husbands, or the nearer joys and miseries of lovers; and learn that red velvet is the color this season, a brushed and burnished shade more russet than cherry, and that skirts are growing daringly narrow, while feathers have fallen quite out of favor, replaced by flowers worked of beading or sewn so cunningly from silk that one can barely tell them from fresh blooms. And the seamstresses assure each customer before the mirror that this caping, that cameo neckline, this tumble of coffee-colored lace, is exactly what is needed to set off Madame's individual charms, whether Madame is sister to Venus or daughter of the trolls beneath the dirt. There is little a wise needle cannot accomplish, and money, as elsewhere, sews a fine exacting seam.

But no matter the ultimate destination, still Isobel is unaccustomed to solo excursions, so this day she is attended by Otilie, in a decorous bonnet and cape to her ankles. Madame's lady's-maid has been left behind, for what reason Otilie does not guess or care to, but she intends to prove equal to her mistress' every need on this odd trip: watching where Madame steps in the mucky streets, shielding Madame from the ruck and clutter of the passersby, guarding Madame's articles as if they were precious relics—not only for the umbrella handle's carven jade, the black pearls that adorn the reticule's pink brocade, if they were rag and twig she would treat them with no less reverence, for they are Madame's, who has all favors to grant and all sorrows to inflict. All the quality are so, and as such well worth the serving, as long as a girl keeps her mind to her task. It is a shame that Master Benjamin is not one for the ladies, that would have been a nice bonanza, but still he has provided Otilie with a penny or two, backhanded though it might have been—funny that anyone would pay for verse, but he writes such a quantity of poetry, Master Benjamin, and scatters it about like falling leaves. She must tell Lucy Bell about it, whenever next they meet....

Now the rain begins again, just a spatter to start, and Otilie has the umbrella open and in service before two drops can strike Madame; but it comes down harder, a dour diagonal sleet, she moves to summon the carriage but "This way," says Madame, turning instead down a nondescript *rue,* skirts splashing through dead leaves, dog shit, and some unknown effluvia, past a dubious locksmith and a stockman's drinking shop, into a shadowy sort of café: six tables below a tin ceiling, three of them filled by girls not a whit better than they should be, two by workingmen watching the girls, and the last by a younger man in an old greatcoat, amusing himself, apparently, by making his teaspoon talk.

"Wait over there," says Madame to Otilie, pointing without looking to the tea bar where the proprietress, who has, it seems, been anticipating Madame's visit, immediately approaches with a clean pot and cups, one of which is already half filled with brandy: this one she sets before Istvan, who puts his little spoon aside, though not without a final whistle of farewell, noted by Isobel who smiles: "My apologies to have kept you waiting. I see the performance has already begun."

"You are punctual, Madame. I was early," swirling the brandy in the cup, toasting her silently before he swallows. It occurs to Isobel that she has never before seen him in daylight, this M. Dieudonne, Etienne, Dusan, Istvan, whatever his name may be. In a kind of studied deshabille, he looks weary, as if his night had been a long one, his lips are turned down but his eyes are bright; and he owns a singular ease, like a cat asleep on a silk divan or a marble step, the player's ease, all places a stage to him, a throne or the dock the same. "A busy day for you, Madame, I am sure. I am gratified that you and I may meet."

"I as well, Monsieur. This is a—likely place," the like of which she has never entered in her life before, its set-dressing of whores and day laborers, its smell of mildew and boiled milk, but the tea is surprisingly good, strong China tea, and its warmth is very welcome: her feet are soaked, she feels the cold all throughout her body. From the corner of her eye, she notes Otilie dividing her attention between the costumes of the prostitutes and this tête-à-tête; the girl is sharper than she looks, she will bear a bit of watching herself. "And to stop for tea is pleasant; as you say, it has been a busy day. There are many details still to settle for my Twelfth Night dinner, many people will be present, some of whom you know—Fernande for one, and Achille's parents, the Guerlains; the de Mercys. And of course M. Bok—"

"Of course."

"And Hector Georges."

He lifts his cup but does not drink. "The General."

"Yes. He is an old friend of my father, whom you have not yet met—he also will be in attendance," with a brisk sip of tea, a fine bit of acting on her own part, the calamity expressed with such offhand calm. How her heart sank, reading the letter, the de Metz crest come not from silly Charlotte this time but from him, telling her only that he would attend her soiree as well as spend some days at the town house, not deigning to say why, but she knows why: he is coming for Benjamin, he and Hector both. And she alone to stand between them, stand them off with what poor weapons she has—if only Benny were plausibly in Paris! or the dark side of the moon; if only Javier were in the city—but he has gone elsewhere, he has sent his regrets although *You may be seeing me in another form,* a mystery she could not cipher until she was contacted out of the blue by M. Dieudonne: *A mutual friend has suggested that we meet—*

—although he speaks, now, this puppeteer with his spoon and his brandy, not of Javier or Hector but of several shows he has recently witnessed, or perhaps performed, puppet shows of such fine craft that "The strings are at all times visible to the audience, as is the puppeteer, but after a moment or two, both disappear entirely to the eye. And then all one sees is the actor, and the play."

"And if one should endeavor to keep the strings in sight?"

"Ah, but it is not the strings that really signify, Madame. It is the motion. Which is why the puppet is the purest actor of all: he—or she—cannot be distracted, or turned inward, or waylaid by appetite or the desire to shine. For the puppet, it is only the going-forward that matters. Into thin air."

Istvan pauses. A heavy cart rumbles by outside, bearing the sudden reek of rotten fish. At one of the adjacent tables, a whore laughs, the scornful laugh of a pretty girl: "So much the worse for him, then! Does he think he can buy me with a rabbit-fur stole?" The two workingmen murmur together, then chuckle. Otilie waits. Istvan drinks the last of his brandy, beckons backward, without looking, for more.

When the proprietress has again withdrawn, leaving behind the bottle, Isobel leans forward, gloved hands clasped before her, like a child listening to a fairy story, grave and alert. "And the moral of your story, Monsieur?"

"A simple one really. All that moves, requires a hand."

He waits, poised, wanting to make sure she understands, to give him some sign; himself a sign to her: *into thin air*, yes, if one must. She takes a fortifying breath and "Hector," she says, so quietly that he must lean forward as well. "The General, that is—you may have noticed, he wears a ring."

"A silver ring. On his thumb."

"Yes," she says, and then she tells him a story: of two men who once were young together, one the son of a landed lord, the other of less noble provenance. The lord's son was sent into the military, to give him some working knowledge of death and command, where he met the other, an especially adept attaché of the regiment. Both young men found themselves united by temperament as well as circumstance in a particular situation, where deeds of special ugliness were required, "the nature of which I do not know, Monsieur, Javier never told me, he said he did not want such pictures in my mind." Gone into her own story, the black fairy tale of rapine; has she ever spoken of it before, aloud? Did she ever dream she would? "All I know for certain is since that time, Hector has worn that ring, which had been in our family from the time of the Terror. Since that time, Hector has been a special friend of my father's, an accomplice for him, as the scorpion rides the snake."

Now her gaze is downcast, as if shocked or shamed by her own revelation. Gently, Istvan tips the brandy bottle to her teacup, urges her to drink as "I will match that tale," he says, "with one of my own." Glancing to the door, where the sleet has turned to snow, the fat wet splashing snow that clogs the gutters, that obliterates the signs, that empties the streets of the upright and the harmless and "There was a brothel once," he says, "called the Poppy," where many plays were staged, and many strings torn and tautened, humans, like puppets, jerked this way and that by a puppeteer intent not on art but domination, a brothel where, in the throes of war, the General clashed in secret with Jürgen Vidor—

"Jürgen Vidor? He—You know him?"

"Yes."

"You know that he is dead?"

"Yes indeed," but by whose hand? since all that moves requires one: was it the knife that cut him, or the plan that set that knife in motion? Madame, he sees, can parse such details for herself, Madame is not a fool although "That knife," she murmurs. "I will not ask more, but the man who—accomplished it, that man is known to you?"

"Indeed," again; and he allows the silence to hang, allows her to imagine it was himself, another shield for Rupert. "But that is not yet the meat of the tale." Speaking so softly now she must watch his lips to make out all the words, he tells her of a letter, written by Jürgen Vidor, found on his person, addressed to the General, naming Georges as the architect of the deed—although this last is not wholly true, the man who wrote that letter never intending it to be a testament from beyond the grave, no doubt he would have preferred to plant it as a flag on Georges' corpse. Would that both were true. "And it still exists, that document."

"This letter," she breathes. Her eyes are shining: *ursa mater*, consider the banked ferocity of the female! "You carry it with you?"

"Never, Madame. It is in a very deep hidey-hole indeed," thinking of the flimsy blue enamel letter box, the little iron safe with two keys, one his, one Rupert's.

"Hector knows you have it?"

"Not yet." He lets that sink, until her smile begins. "That knowledge has been kept between me and one other since the day the letter was found. You are the third," although that is not strictly true, either, but true enough for his purposes now. "And I tell you," because another sort of hideaway is needed, a place where, whatever else may happen, Rupert will not be harmed, a nest made downy by Cupid's love and, yes, Madame's healthy hatred; what a boon to find her so well-armed, Arrowsmith must have a conscience after all—

—as she nods, reaching again for her tea, elated now and businesslike: of course M. Bok is welcome under her roof at any time, for any duration, her protection will extend to him since "We consider him a most dear and valued friend, my brother and I," with a sidewise glance, does M. Dieudonne know of Benny's devotion? Yes. He knows.

And knows as well of her own soft spot for Rupert, though she does not guess how easily it can be glimpsed, giving Istvan another little inward smile: Why, the whole family wants Mouse! A brother and sister, again, how strange life is. Repertoire indeed... Well then, they will keep him safer if not safe, and it is the most that can be hoped for at this moment, the best that he can do.

Now Madame is glancing at her little timepiece, a golden rose depending at her breast, another glance in summons to her maid as "I must be on my way, Monsieur," she says. "I know we shall meet again soon." Leaning forward, her hand extended, but before he can bend to address it she draws him closer, offers her cheek and "I will tell you one thing more about Hector," she murmurs, as his lips graze her skin. "He once thought, years ago, to be a player."

It is the first time Isobel has seen it, the flicker of Istvan's true smile, the way it changes his face, reveals a private universe unguessed—and calls forth her own in spontaneous answer, the curious, questing girl in the garden, impulsive to ask, "What is your name, Monsieur? Your true name. If it is not too impertinent to inquire?"

She is not lovely, Madame, no one would ever say so, but what intelligence in those eyes, in this request, though "It is most impertinent," Istvan says, and kisses her cheek again, not a social salute but as a man to a woman: the scent not of roses, as one might expect, but lilies, cold white flowers crushed to powder, something alluring and bitter beneath. "And we most truly wear the names fate gives us, Madame, do we not? For instance, one might call you Dido," with a courtly bow as the maid approaches, Lucy's little friend, she gives him a wink as she unfurls the umbrella to shield her mistress, beckoning the carriage that rounds the corner to take them in. The door closes, Istvan sinks again into his seat to call for a bit of cheese, a pale mealy apple, both dissected and eaten on the tip of the little white knife as "'We must be Salome,'" he says to the teaspoon, that replies in a wary voice, "'But the platter is yet empty.'"

Fast broken, he takes from his inner pockets a jigsaw of wooden pieces, assembling them on the table as he drinks: the shattered arm, the cracked belly, the head, expression of surprise both intact and apt, none of them saw that coming, did they? there at the Hôtel Violette? Like a tuppence melodrama, Georges costumed in a businessman's bowler, not alone, as he had promised, but attended by a thug called César, a failed pimp formerly of the dollhouse row who recognized Istvan as well, to neither's pleasure, his presence explained by Georges as yet another reason why Hanzel the courier continued to be so inflexibly desired: *So many of my men are known to be my men, especially in this city* where he has, it seems, new and extra-military ambitions, since *A commission, genially, can prove quite constricting. Especially in these modern times.*

I wouldn't know, I'm not a soldier. Hence my reluctance to take orders.

Refusal, you mean, as César glowered, walrus mustache and fat through the brisket, the unnamed puppet making him a special bow—*Paying for your pink, now?*—as *We ought repair to the rooms,* Georges meaning to lead the way but *I'll not take that order either,* his own smile of open amusement, did the man think him an imbecile? To put a locked door between himself and flight? as all collapsed, then, into something worse than farce, Georges proffering the courier's pouch, the last chance to gain, what? a goatherd's path to a slavey's power, and avoid destruction not for himself but *Your fond companion; we need not say his name. Come, Hanzel, it will give me no pleasure at all to harm you*—

Then that is where we differ, his voice become one the General had never heard before, the voice of the feral creature he has never ceased to be, the puppet's regretful *plié* as *Buy yourself two ropes— hang yourself on one, and on the other, be hanged:* with a stare of contempt worthy of Feste, and Pan Loudermilk, and the lineage of every jester servant only to the jest, a look at which César took great umbrage, the poor puppet taking the blow, the General enraged at the lobby's sudden full attention, and off with a stare of his own, like a shot fired over the shoulder.... Hence the urgent meeting with Madame, hence "My poor associate," *sotto voce* to the teaspoon, indicating the unnamed actor's sad demise. "He died so fucking young, yeah?"

"Not to worry, mister," from a smooth voice at his shoulder: one of the table whores, a slippery brunette with her hat cocked sideways, depositing herself unasked upon his knee. "For a nip of that brandy, I can make you smile again."

"An ocean of that brandy could not make me smile today. And you, dear, have the venus clap," loud enough for the workingmen to hear, the girl off his lap with a snarl, she means to say more but the look in his eye, then, returns her directly to the safety of her sisters, as Istvan sweeps the puppet scraps back into his pockets, drops coin onto the table, and takes himself out into the growing storm, where the lights of the electric lamps glow like fire under water, and the streets run with slush as brackish-black as graveyard mud.

Lucy

He said he'd have his answer whenever I would give it, he said he could wait forever and a day *If only you tell me true, Miss Bella-Bell.* There on the promenade, the whole world out for a Boxing Day ramble, the sun so bright, the breeze so stiff and cold—but I never felt it, my hands all tucked up in the muff he gave me: real ermine fur and a fine silver chain, like something Mme. de Metz might carry, what it cost him I daren't guess! And how he smiled, when he saw how much I fancied it: *I wish I could make the world so for you,* he said. *Everything all cozy-like, and soft.*

And then he asked me, just like that, us sitting there upon the little iron bench: *I know I haven't much, but all I've got is yours if you'll have me.* And I cried, I couldn't help it, the tears just popped, and he hopped up like the bench was on fire, that made me laugh.... It was so lovely. It *is* lovely, to think that we might go on together, he and I, as man and wife.

And right here at the Blackbird, too, for I told him straightaway that, no matter what, I must have my little troupe, with this roof above our heads but *I'd not have it different,* he said. *We'll sell our Pimm's Chateaux in the lobby, won't we?* And we both laughed, then, and I kissed him, right there on the promenade, and he held me tight in a way no man's ever done, tucked up in his arm like I belonged there, like we were made to fit so. We could have sat that way forever. Forever and a day.

But I didn't give my *yes,* then, though I knew it made him that sad, and puzzled-like, he couldn't add the parts together, and whyever should he? I couldn't myself. Only—things seem so gloomy now, the streets all ice like dead mid-winter, the children in a funk since our awful show, that we thought would be so wonderful.... The girls had strung up holly berries and green garlands at the entrance, as pretty as a church, and I had Didier piping away at "O Come the Faithful Shepherds" in his little shepherd suit, all the toff ladies cooing over how sweet he looked. Mme. de Metz was there, in the front row, she gave me a specially lovely smile. And every seat sold, the first time ever. We thought it would be a jubilee.

And then! Lines forgotten, exits bungled, strings gone all a-snarl, with Rosa wailing over her cracked-up crown, crying that Mickey broke it, and a nest of mice in the hay-box where the Infant Jesu was supposed to lie—Thank heaven Pimm was backstage, and Rupert, too, to try to bring the thing to a closing. We skipped the final singsong, Master Benjamin played them out with some waltz: not one he knew well, but the piano pedals were sticking in the damp, he did the best he could. If ever a show could go astray on all fronts—!

And Istvan, our Gabriel-angel, white mask and muslin and cut-paper wings—though he said he wouldn't have the wooden horse, even if it ruined the title, *I'm no equestrian*—and such a distant humor, only Mickey had the pluck to nudge in close and ask him why but *It's not for little ears,* he said, and tugged at Mickey's, then mimed to find a penny in his hair, and tossed it to him to stop his questions. No answers for me, either, when I found those chopped-up puppet pieces, one I thought he had just finished, yet when I asked he only shrugged. He is not sleeping, most nights, off gaming or elsewhere, and wherever he goes, he goes armed. "Supping with the quality," right, it's that general he meant, who means him little good, I'm sure, though he saved us before. May be just to use us later.... And Rupert up and smoking, all pale with his headaches, or reading through that little red book—Oh, we are all wretched now, as if the tidings he brought as Gabriel are turning true: *Change is coming,* to the rich young man, Pinky in a turban and eyebrows and beard down to his belt, and Istvan with gilded hair and folded arms, as if he spoke the lines to two plays at once. *What we have sighted for is come upon us,* not like the birth of a Savior but the end of the world; with his shadow cast before him from a misplaced lamp, holly berries crushed and smeared like blood against the boards, the children dumb as sparrows when the hawk flies over—I've never been so glad in all my life to see the curtains close.

And afterward Istvan disappearing straightaway, none of us saw him go, even Rupert who looked everywhere, until Master Benjamin came to him and bade him stop, and go for supper with himself and Mme. de Metz. Arm in arm, out the door to their fine carriage, back so late I never heard him come in.... That Master Benjamin, he is so much like Istvan come again, yet when I said so to Pimm he only stared: *I can't make that one out,* though it's plain as a pikestaff to me. To Istvan, too, but that's another thing he won't discuss, cold as ice when I tried to broach it: *Leave it, Puss!* so sharp it brought me back to the days at the Poppy, how he used to snap that harsh at Decca. Decca and her lover's eye.... I keep the goldfish in its own special box, the one it came in from the jeweler's, and that tucked inside another, one that looks like nothing in particular, like it might have notions or buttons or such inside. It's wise to do so, hide what's treasure in what's not.

Since that night the children have been absent, mostly, my girls coughing through their singing lessons, Didier crying when I ask him to play the flute. Only Mickey, and Pinky, are the mainstays, Pinky here this morning to take down the Christmas stars, still dangling up above there, I haven't had the heart. He sat for a cup with me, the tea boiled too long but he drank it up, and tried to jolly me with gossip about the Twelfth Night dinner, feasting and wassail and the lords of misrule, but *I've seen a deal of those these days,* I told him, *may be a few too many for my taste. I'll stop at home, I think.*

Then I'll bring you a taste of king cake, shall I? bowing his way out past Pimm coming in and *If only they were all like that,* Pimm says, sitting down where Pinky was, pouring himself a cup, *one shouldn't mind them half so much…. Have you thought much more about my question, yet, Miss Bella-Bell?*

And right back, blunt, I never meant to but it just came out: *No, I haven't. But when I do I think may be I ought say no. For both our sakes.*

Whyever? Say one reason, his voice all flat, all the joy gone out of him; it was awful to see but I couldn't stop: *Surely,* I said, *I'll say two. First is, I come from nothing, Pimm. My father—I come from nothing, you understand?*

What does that matter? I don't care a whit, I—

And I used to be a whore.

I had my hands round the teacup, the tea so hot but I never felt it, my hands were that cold, and my voice like someone else's, hard and far away. *Did you never wonder how I came to be here, never married nor spoken for, with Mister Rupert and Mister Istvan? I worked in a house with them, fucking and pulling pud, I used to dress up when I did it. Costumes I still have now! May be I've got a bride's dress tucked up somewhere, too!*

He just sat there, face white and silent as a stone, until he reached past the cups, knocked the sugar bowl astray, and *Well what of it?* he said to me. He was gripping my hands, I was gripping his, like we were in a boat on stormy seas, trying to keep from going under. *We've all sold ourselves a time or two. D'you think I've always made my way ginning up little wooden houses? No one can ever make me think the less of you, Lucy, not even you yourself.*

The room seemed to shrink, then, and I opened my mouth, but nothing came out, not one peep, until *Yes,* I said, all on one breath, *I will, then, Mr. Pimm. If you will have me then I will.*

My name is Timothy, he says to me, he had tears in his eyes, and *Tim Pimm,* I said, and we laughed, and I cried and cried, and he swept up all the spilled sugar and mopped up all the tea.... We've told no one yet, 'tisn't time for that, and when it will be, whoever can say? First this winter must pass, and whatever blackness hides inside it. Then, in the spring, we shall see.... Missus Pimm, just think of it. Mister and Missus Pimm.

The city streets still wear their decorations, like a lady arrayed for a fête not of her choosing: wreaths the size of wagon wheels, branched evergreens and hanging fruit, frozen pears and apples to drop like lead upon the heads of passersby. The weather has been harsh, slicks of ice around each corner to send cabs astray and walkers stumbling, ankles sprained, umbrellas cracked, even the mayor's wife toppling sideways on the steps of the Orphans' Foundation, as she dispenses warm woollies donated by the Gracious Ladies' Guild: whacking her velvet elbow so she wails, the orphans laughing with an open lack of charity that will send them to their beds without supper, to teach them the virtue of prudence if not compassion.

Now the city welcomes Twelfth Night with unusual fervor, as the finale of a strangely sorry Christmastide, in quarters both high and low. In the homes of the bourgeoisie, the round of visits and gifting come to a dutiful end, gin-wassails drunk and king-cakes eaten, while the street-corner whores hike their stockings and stuff their shoes with oiled paper, to try for one more night to keep the wet from seeping in, as their brothers the beggars crouch on the cathedral steps, rattling their croaker-boxes with a menacing air: *Penny for Our Lord, sirrah! Penny for Our Lord!* as if, should the pennies be withheld, Our Lord might come looking for them himself, and for their scrimpers, too.

And the beggars and whores and the bourgeoisie are all united in the wish that the true new year begin at last, the wheel turn and spin the gray stuff of slush and frozen horseshit, leaking roofs and stinking-wet wool, teething babies who scream and stingy tricks who balk at paying fair, into a sweeter landscape of spring breezes and yellow daffs, clean stockings, sleep, and the possibility of pleasure and ease, or, failing that, at least the first fresh casks of rum to lubricate their various discontents.

In the de Metz household, all are busy with the last preparations for the dinner: the tall white vases cleared of snow and pale with ivy, the stables readied for the carriages of guests, kitchens crowded with beef sent specially from the farms at Chatiens, sweating Portuguese cheese, candied figs round as eyeballs, and countless bottles of champagne, *le vin du diable,* pent like embers banked for later fires. The old master and his wife have already arrived, and Helmut with them, to oversee the details of their comfort, a detail that Isobel accepts with outward calm, though the household staff notes that her temper is, these last few days, quite variable. The young master's is the opposite, dreamy and distant and more inclined to drop tips, while he himself is the recipient of quantities of gifts sent by those who court his favor, and his father's, to celebrate both his birthday and the holiday, Twelfth Night to be a double jubilee.

Now Madame and her raw humor sit in boudoir consultation with the glove-maker, a frail and ageless woman, her fingers small and cunning as a child's to tug and adjust the dark kidskin, worked with gleaming silver thread, white lace, and tiny diamonds in a repeating pattern of roses, as if the wearer's hands were plunged deep into ghostly flowers. When the knock comes, Isobel snaps "A moment!" as she reaches for the muslin pattern-glove, no one but the glove-maker allowed to see her hand as it is, not even Benjamin, who pops his head around the door before she has fully hidden herself, who sees her face instead and "Be at ease," airily, "I haven't come to peep at your claw—"

—until he sees her eyes, his own smile disappearing: "I am sorry," bending to kiss her cheek in real contrition, as Isobel nods the glove-maker out to the hall. "Your dress is magnificent," he adds, still in apology, dropping into the vacated chair. "You look a queen in that silver, you'll be the queen of the ball."

And himself less prince, now, than young king: no more Cupid's curls, his hair cut very short and razored close, bringing Charlotte's gush as they dined earlier *en famille*: *Why, you look so manly now, Benjamin!* with Isidore nodding approval at the new and formal suit, the new sense of purpose perceived as "The old man," he says, restless to rise from the chair again, gazing out the window into the fitful moon and fog. "He says we're to have a 'discussion,' tomorrow, he and I. Must I do it, Belle? What does he want?"

"I imagine," says Isobel, keeping her voice even, "it concerns your majority. Or Adele Chamsaur, since he had asked," commanded, rather, "that she be invited tonight."

"*Merde,*" with a frown, chewing at the raw spot on his knuckle, and then he is gone, the glove-maker returning in silence to finish her task. Afterward, the new gloves lying like shed skin upon the white silk of the dressing-table, Isobel turns to her own task still unfinished, her response to Javier written a dozen times and a dozen destroyed, attempting to answer his own brief letter—*I cannot attend, but I shall be present in spirit*—meaning what? Already this night is the cusp of so much tumult.... She lights another cigarette, she pulls forward another sheet of plain foolscap—

—as in another room, another letter is soberly considered, Istvan in shirtsleeves on the edge of the bed, reading once again in the uncertain lamplight the words he knows by heart: *Obstructing me as you do, I observe that you fear no one's disfavor, not our friends Rawsthorne and Pepper, nor even their friends, so much greater than you or I. Indeed I perceive you precisely, in the shadow of the poppy! But those walls were mine even as you quartered there, as it was mine to gather what you scattered. Do you recall Prussia? I pray you know me when we meet again.* Back into the creased envelope it goes, into the chipped lockbox, into the safe secured with the black metal key itself secured, as Istvan takes a swallow of brandy that neither warms nor heartens him, and rubs his aching eyes. Up half the night at the Fin, he and Feste, feasting on the brink since it will have to last, that show, for who knows how long; he had them screaming anyway, that is a comfort.... And Boilfast a bit of comfort too, that dry offer of sanctuary: *You need to go to ground, Monsieur? For how long?* bringing Istvan's shrug, and his own nod in answer: *Why, you are ever welcome here, stay as long as you please. Can you by chance wield a mop at all?*

And back, then, owl-eyed through the dark, to spend the night's last hours fighting with Mouse, another kind of final performance. Placing the quarrel with cold precision, needling, mocking, shouting so he could be heard by Lucy a floor away: *I didn't take you from one bolthole to waste my life huddling in another. You may be content here, in this—domestic bliss, but I am not.* No one will ever know what it cost him, knowing what Mouse will think, tomorrow, what he must believe, seeing that look in his eyes—*Why can you not be—happy, here? With me?*—and yet turning away, back stiff, arms crossed, as if unmoved.... No wonder one flees from love, when it digs its spurs like this, who in the fuck would ever choose to feel so? If he were not the player he is, he could never do this, never.

Afterward Rupert vanished away, furious and stricken—up to the catwalk? or out on the roof, to roost in ice until the morning?— a silence as cold lasting all the day long; and still silent, now, as he approaches their rooms, to ready for the endless evening ahead. Glancing at Istvan sitting hands-clasped on the bed, he looks pointedly away, turning to root through the clutter on his desk, searching for nothing until "Mouse," at his ear, that murmur, "we'll not be at odds tonight, yeah?" to turn him back, each as helpless as the other, to meet in an embrace that enfolds the night just past, the pains wreaked, the scars like, yes, these ropy, hateful, eternal marks, livid as if just inflicted, displayed anew as Istvan strips his shirt, as Rupert reaches to mute the lamp—

—but Istvan stops him, holds him, stands before him wounded and beautiful, the child in the viaduct, the center of his heart, open to him like a heart broken and still beating, a puppet snapped in two yet still onstage and "Leave it," his whisper, mouth to mouth, skin to skin in love enacted and endlessly renewed, until Rupert draws that tired head down to his shoulder, and thinks that, perhaps, now that the New Year is upon them, they might find the way, he might find a way to make Istvan happy, somehow, once again.

At last "We'd better dress," Rupert's weary smile, "and face the world," looking down to Istvan looking up at him from the landscape of the bed and "This is the world," Istvan murmurs. "This bed, Mouse, and no other," so strangely somber that Rupert feels the shadow, like the passage of a dark wind but "Buck up," he says, trying for lightness, trying to rouse a smile. "We're off to a party—I'll even dance, if you like. Won't that be entertaining."

"Save the show for the stage," as Istvan at last tosses back the coverlets, to rise, and stretch, and splash water on his face, to brush his dinner jacket, to watch as Rupert attends to his own toilette, each move and moment stored in mind: this too will have to last. As Rupert bends to his boots, Istvan reaches unseen to the bedside table, to slip into his breast pocket Rupert's signet ring, and leave behind in its place his own little white knife.

At the townhouse Pinky's is the first face they see, beaming and bright above a costume that owes nothing to his friend's latest fad for propriety: lapels pink and gaping as a calf's tongue, a cravat worked in gorgeous gaudy gold, even the beginnings of a curly beard since "I got the taste for it as the rich young fellow," beaming at Istvan as together they approach the drawing-room. "You know, the one you warned off mortal damnation?"

"Ah, but did you take my warning.... It does suit you," with a smile of his own, all gravity hidden, onstage now until the thing shall be accomplished. Joking in the cab to Rupert, kissing all the ladies' hands, he even throws a half smile to the Happy Prince, lovely as a lamb shorn, and the center of much dovecote fluttering and attention: hand pressed and cheek saluted by dreadful old Fernande—"Happy birthday, godson. Though there's not much of either about you, is there?"—as well as a selection of the faster young ladies in attendance, first among them Adele Chamsaur, nudged on by her mother to offer "Many felicitations of the day, Benjamin." Rouge-pink lips pecking his own, white hand squeezing his forearm, a truly daring neckline for an unmarried girl, but he barely nods in answer, barely sees her, lost in a cloud of impatience and desire: Monsieur his master finally, finally arrived, but how long until they might speak alone, be alone? for he has a gift of his own to give, tonight.

Still it is Isobel who claims Rupert first, after she and Istvan have greeted each other as bosom friends, his kiss, her murmur—"Even you cannot guess how glad I am to see you now"—then linking arms with Rupert, leading him in beneath the black glass chandeliers, the sharpened attention of her guests, the faintly raised eyebrows and remarks passed smirking behind hands. She is queenly to be sure in silver, with diamonds in her hair, diamonds at her throat, the striking new gloves reaching to take from a proffered tray champagne for them both as "I've whiskey for your dinner, of course, Monsieur. But have a glass with me now," as Rupert, distracted, looks between Istvan, laughing with Jean de Mercy, and Benjamin, the center of a group of girls clustered below the painting, Venus, Cupid, folly and time, yes indeed, but with eyes for him alone. "You've been scarce, we have not seen you since Miss Bell's Christmas play. And Benny has missed you so."

"Indeed. That is, I beg pardon," drinking to cover his confusion, looking hastily elsewhere in the glitter and throng, this room crowded with roses and lights, musicians in the corner sawing away at some scampering tune, servants in white and guests in red velvet, to see someone else he knows, dark suit, a darker smile approaching and "Why," says Hector Georges, "here is an old friend, unmet for too long. Happy new year, M. Bok," hand out, the silver ring gleaming on his thumb. He looks just the same, the General, as ageless as a cliff or a skull, they might have parted in Brussels just yesterday, or that strange masquerade dinner a moment before. "But where is your partner, sir? A veritable Jonathan and David, one so rarely sees the one of you without the other."

Isobel drinks down the last of her champagne; her smile shows her teeth. "As you and my father are similarly joined. It is wonderful, is it not, to have such a friend?"

"Indeed it is," looking to her as Rupert studies him in sudden wary unease, the old instincts prickling, now what is this?—

—as Adele Chamsaur stands on tiptoe to Benjamin, trying to hold his attention, a girl unused to failure, but fail she does as he turns away with half a bow, passing by Pinky, who tries to catch his eye and fails, too, shrugging to Adele: "He's changeable as the sea, and just as deep; that's how it is with a poet. We'll be boats in his wake together, shall we? Would she care for an ice?"

"She would rather a glass of Champagne," says Adele boldly. "Perhaps two glasses," and Pinky grins, offering his arm, she accepting with the pleasant grace of practicality: a banker's son here in town is in some ways preferable to one of higher social caliber, for Chatiens is so deep in the country, and poetry is not something she enjoys.

As they wend through the crowd, they pass without noticing a man framed for that passing moment in the doorway, slick hair and poorly fitted coat, Mr. Entwhistle the skeleton at the feast: the decadence and frivol before him tucked away like marrowbones, to suck and plunder later in private, safely confirmed in his own virtue by his meeting, so dark and early this morning, with the man whose approach now sends him hasty up the servants' stairs: Isidore a basilisk in black and spotless linen, a stickpin of diamond and gold his only ornament save his wife, Charlotte beside him too bountiful in ingénue pink, cornucopia breasts and too much lace, her curls piled with pink silk rosebuds to flatter Isobel—

—whose kiss, as they meet, noted by the room around them, is merely perfunctory, introducing M. Bok as a "Friend of our family," while he bows to Charlotte, her smile gone roguish—"Why, where has Isobel been keeping *you*?"—as her husband and Hector Georges exchange the briefest glance. Rupert next offers his hand to Isidore, who for a moment does not move to take it, considering this "friend" of the family, this landless theatre man whom Hector has intimated has some unknown sway with his daughter, some advantage if the shrill Entwhistle is to be believed. At last he extends his punishing grip, Rupert surprised and then unsurprised, meeting the older man's strength with his own: in a way it is a relief, this sort of challenge, this at least he knows how to do.

In the end it is Isidore who draws back first, his bones in agony, his smile serene: "Well met, Monsieur," as Rupert, unsmiling, nods in return. It seems more will be said, perhaps by Isobel poised beside him, perhaps by Charlotte, whose sparkling gaze has not left Rupert: but instead it is Benjamin who appears behind his shoulder, face flushed, taking Rupert by the elbow as "You'll excuse us, Father? Belle? I must show you, Monsieur, you must see—" with a sketched bow for the company, towing Rupert through the crowd that parts with avid courtesy, out the garden doors into the dark—as Isobel draws a steadying breath, as Charlotte gives her a look of new respect, as Istvan, across the room, watching it all, makes a final quip to laughing Jean de Mercy, and slips away alone into the hall.

Outside the music mutes, the path lies treacherous and slick underfoot, droplets unseen on the lean line of the branches until

"Look!" says Benjamin, turning Rupert by the sleeve to watch as the clouds part, just for a moment, to show the moon, a ragged coquette's flash that turns all the drops to diamonds, that lights the angels brushed with ice above the doors, silver and fleet and "Isn't it magnificent?" Benjamin says. "I knew you would relish it. But," as the moon disappears again, the chill rises, "it doesn't stay, does it."

"No," Rupert looking up into the clouds, then down into his eyes, what a tumble of light and dark the boy is himself; but no, not a boy any longer, is he? so "Felicitations of the day," he says. "You've had a pile of gifts, no doubt—"

"Oh, we'll not talk as they do in there, will we? that stupid room, all those people…. Did you ever read my poems?" with such abrupt and naked longing that "Yes," Rupert says, very quietly. "I read them all. Many times."

"Oh *Maître*—"

"No," through a wave of his own longing, thinking of Istvan, thinking of the people in that room. "We'll not speak of it. It is not—seemly, Benjamin—"

"I love you." His heart feels as if it will burst: into flame, into flower, the first time he has ever said those words to anyone. And the first time Rupert has ever called him so, called him by name as "You want me," he says, reaching to touch his master's face, careless of who might be watching, careless of the world. "Don't you want me?"

"Yes, I want you," seizing that hand in a hard grip, half a lover's, half a father's, "but it's not to be, you understand? I'll keep your poems always, but you must not write more, you must—"

"You want me," again, as the moon lights up the dead branches, "and you'll see, *Maître*, we'll be together, you'll see—"

—as inside the music changes to a sprightly march, playing the guests in to supper, a silver figure passing like an anxious ghost before the garden doors and "Come," Rupert resolute on the path, turning so that Benjamin turns with him, to step back into the rooms so over-hot and overcrowded, drenched with scents and noise and colors, it is like walking into a distorted dream, from the simplicity and candor of the dark and the cold outside. Isobel notes their expressions, so opposite that they are just the same—Benny's rapturous, M. Bok's like a door locked from the inside—with all those others watching, her father and Hector most of all; oh *mon Dieu*, if M. Dieudonne was not here she must certainly despair. Dieudonne, yes, God gives; perhaps yes—

—as she links arms with them both, feeling the cold come off their bodies, her smile valiant and composed as "We're about to cut the king cake, gentlemen. Join me at the table," where conversation swirls and flutters, wine is poured and drunk, the candles bloom more hectic than any rose, and the ornate cake, spiced with fruit and almonds, smothered in gilt-paper leaves, is carried in, cut, and passed down the table by the maidservants—

—all but Otilie, who stands in the pantry with the lone guest missing, Istvan who takes from her the pair of kitchen snips: "Many thanks," preoccupied with the draping strings in his hands, cutting a wee knot-and-tangle so the awful little sacklike body may stand fully upright. "Now, have you a twist of ribbon, or—that's it. Capital," and he makes to give her a coin in thanks, but "I'd rather have a kiss," says Otilie saucily: this handsome gentleman friend of Madame's and of Lucy Bell's, too, so why not hers as well?

Instead Istvan laughs: "Are you into the sherry, darling? I'm afraid I'm off kissing just now. Take the money," with a wink that is pure artifice, a little foam on the wave of the player's deep, waiting until she leaves to kiss his fist to the empty room, the old and precious gesture, his last private moment before he enters the dining room, to take his seat between Denis de Mercy and Charlotte de Metz, both of whom are quite happy to see him, with the General across and down the table, Rupert next to Isobel, and Benjamin at his father's right hand.

It is the General who raises the curtain, albeit unknowingly: with a satisfied little sound, displaying to the company "The bean," between two fingers, its chased silver bright as a bullet; all dutifully applaud. "Well! I had no thought to be king of the revels tonight, I keep my ambitions modest. But I'll not disdain the opportunity thrust upon me."

"'Twasn't thrust," says Istvan pleasantly to Charlotte, looking from the serving girl who kept the cake piece separate, to the General, whose gaze turns to him as he speaks. "It was a cheat. As many do, who can win no other way.... May I present," louder, to the table at large, "a little disquisition on tonight's feast? a brief morality play? For it's Epiphany, isn't it, the showing-forth of the light to those who knew it not?"

A pleased murmur rises from the guests, heads turning first toward Isidore, expressionless at the head of the table, then to Isobel who nods, Rupert beside her alarmed and silent, trying vainly to catch Istvan's eye: as Istvan shifts his chair, just enough to make room for the tale of "A man," he says, "who roved the wide world over, traveling every path the earth could offer, working his will as he went. He has one secret, this man: he carries his hunger in a little sack inside his shirt, from which recess it tells him where next to go, it drives him on."

"Is the man alone?" asks Isobel, her voice clear in the quiet, the flicker of the candles, delivering her line with admirable sang-froid—players everywhere!—and "He is," says Istvan, "disdaining all companions save the hunger. Did I mention that the man is a puppet?" taking from inside his coat the deflated sack-and-strings affair, short dangling arms, a gaping, suffering mouth and "Behold our hero," says Istvan. He is relaxed now, nearly smiling, the agile humor of a man on a tightrope, enjoying the danger below. "It is not a pretty sight, is it, *mesdames et messieurs*, a creature so empty?" as the unnamed puppet bobs and snatches at Charlotte's plate: she squeals, and then laughs, a faintly disgusted laugh; the puppet is so very ugly.

But Istvan nudges closer, coaxing her—"Won't you feed him, dear lady? Just a morsel?"—until she slips a sliver of duck in sauce between the lips that snatch and gobble at her fingers, so she squeals again, and pulls away. Istvan rises then to travel the table, the puppet begging from every lady save Isobel: giggling or shrinking they all give in, even Fernande deigning to part with a crust, the sacklike body growing round on its strings as "One would think," Istvan pausing with a tranquil smile, just behind the General, "that he would finally be full, this fellow, eh, *mesdames et messieurs*? That having eaten so, he would be fed? That enough would finally be enough?"

Now Rupert sits very still, shoulders tense, hands loose and palms-up on his knees; Benjamin's gaze leaps from Istvan to Rupert and back again. Isobel is as calm as a nun at Sunday Mass, as calm as her father who steeples his crooked fingers, as Istvan halts the puppet just beside the General's plate, its mouth begun to darken, then to leak, tiny red drops becoming a deepening stain.

"Yet what can nourish one," asks Istvan, the General rigid at his elbow, staring straight ahead, "when all's been eaten and consumed? What is left," as the puppet sags sideways, "for such a hungry fellow," the puppet dropping to its knees, "but to swallow himself up whole?" as the puppet sucks itself into the bulb of its body, like fingers closing into a fist, then vomits forth not the scraps of food ingested but a clot of glycerin-blood, a hard nugget in its center, the silver king-cake bean: and collapses, strings and all, across the plate, the ruined and crumbled cake, as Istvan bows—"*Merci*"—and exits, leaving the body where it lies.

The table erupts. White-faced, the General shoves back his chair, Charlotte bursts into nervous tears, Adele Chamsaur turns in outrage to her outraged mother, Pinky tries to stifle his whoop with a napkin. Isobel is on her feet—"Ladies, please! Ladies!" with Rupert beside her about to bolt, but Isobel's maimed hand grasps his with all her strength, the strange feel of those fused fingers as "Help me, Monsieur," beseeching him beneath the noise, as he tries to think what best to do, Jesu, what in the *fuck* is Istvan's game! If he had a knife in his pocket now he would be very glad—

—as Benjamin appears at his side, tense with excitement, a different sort of tool so "Go," Rupert harsh into his ear, "go find him," while half the servants scurry to clear away the mess, and the other half shepherd the ladies away, as if it were an actual corpse lying there upon the table, instead of a bag of food and strings. Pinky is laughing openly now, helplessly, hands on his knees, so he does not mark his father and Isidore, followed by the General, stepping out of the room, or Benjamin sprinting from the door to the darkness, chasing through the streets after a shadow—

—whose hands are suddenly upon him, yanking him into an icy two-foot alley, slamming him sideways into the wall until "You?" with a mildness belied by that stare, so immensely cold and alien that Benjamin, sagging airless and half-stunned, is almost unsure it is M. Dieudonne: until the laugh, hard and unamused, the hand at his scruff and "Come along," says Istvan. "You can be my bodyguard—"

—through the lanes back to the Blackbird, where Lucy waits by the alley door, tense and ready with a gripbag, startled to see Benjamin in tow but "Sometimes the rôle finds the actor, Puss," says Istvan, stripping off his dinner jacket, throwing on a greatcoat and boots, fast as any quick-change player in the street. Bottle, planing knife, Feste already packed, Boilfast to have his person, Puss the knowledge of the letter box, he is ready to depart except for "This," taking the safe-key from his pocket, holding it in his hand stained still with the dead puppet's blood. Mouse has its twin so he must not leave it here, ought not take it, either, but what else to do? while Benjamin explains rapidly to Lucy that "He told me to find him, Monsieur did, I mean. And so I ran—"

—as instantly he knows, the inner blossom of sheer relief: "Here," catching up a handy length of leather cord, the Happy Prince, of course! with none to suspect him, or harm him, not even the General would dare do that. "This key—see it?—this key will keep your master safe. Miss Bell knows what it's for, so you don't need to…. You keep it with you, understand? Can you hold the thought in your head long enough to do as I say?"

"I am not a fool—"

"Yes, you are. But you are the only actor I have now, Cupid, so you must play on this stage."

"Don't call me so, 'Cupid'—" not in protest, but quietly, as if what Istvan does is wrong for another reason; Lucy excluded now, they look into each other's eyes until Istvan says, in a different tone, "Fair enough. I shall call you Puck instead. Will that serve?" Knotting the cord about Benjamin's neck, the swelling on his face just beginning, scraped cheek, a growing purple smear beneath the eye. "Soon as you can, swap this twine for something metal, something that cannot be cut from you in stealth. Never lose it, never take it off. And don't say that you have it, to anyone, fond friends included. To him especially, yeah?"

"No," says Benjamin very soberly, almost frightened, as if he is just glimpsing the depth of this commission: *Treat me like a man,* his gaze had said to Istvan, *and I will be one.* Now immediately he must. "I'll tell no one, I'll never let it leave my sight, nor be seen.—What's passed? Where are you going?" but Istvan shakes his head in dismissal, so Benjamin tucks the lacing safely inside his shirt, fastens his coat like a shield before it, makes a brief bow to pale Miss Bell and "Farewell, then," to Istvan, shaking hands; his grip is cold. "Safe travels."

"The same to you, for his sake. Go on then," with a moment's irrepressible half smile, whoever would believe such a farrago onstage? *The Rivals United,* like a ten-pence tale—

—but pierced, again, as the door closes on the boy and Lucy begins at once to weep, hands to her face in the dark and crowded emptiness, this theatre their safety, absent Mouse his only home, but "Come, Puss," in a softer tone, "aren't you the one who sewed me shut like a trooper? And shouted those soldiers to a standstill more than once? Not to mention the dragon Ag? Come now, don't cry."

"I liked the war better! At least then we could see who was shooting at us!" Big drops rolling down her face, she kisses him like the sister he will never see again, Ag lost to treachery and time, Puss his true sister really—as she tucks into his pocket the little oval mirror, crazed silver and chipped glass, to keep him from the evil eye. "You'll send me word, soon as you may? May be through Otilie?"

"I will do that. Watch him for me."

"I will do that," bravely, kissing her hand to him, holding the door as he goes—and then she breaks, slumping down on a pile of boards, a cracked old sideboard salvaged for another use, improvised like a gilt-paper scabbard, or a princess's gown from ribbons and gauze, or, yes, a handful of wood and strings to hold the world at bay. However will this play out, this awful farce of which Istvan has told her, in the end, so very little? Will Master Benjamin do as he is bidden, will he be true? And what will Rupert say, when he returns? How can she face him, how can she say *He's gone*—

—as a door bangs, far backstage, she hears the sound of running feet, small feet, Mickey and Didier with a basket swung between them:

"Miss Bell! Miss Bell! Didier's mamma gave us strawberry wine, she says we are to share—" Stopping short when they see her, round eyes and frayed jackets, like two little chickens strayed from a ragged flock; her flock. "Miss Bell, you're crying?"

"Why," she says, wiping at her eyes, "I'm playing," making a smile as they rush to stand beside her, one on either side, her little cavaliers. "Playing that my heart is broken.... Now you try, Mickey. Show us your tears."

4.

Isobel

Still it seems a sort of dream, a fancy repeated into a memory, certainly I have relived it a dozen times in my mind: watching Hector's face, first abused by that puppet, in front of them all, then thrust past his armor—by me! Oh, how much I owe M. Dieudonne for the opportunity! Cloistered in the alcove, he did not want to be there but I insisted, I drew him in, my hand upon his sleeve—*There is intelligence you must hear, Hector*—and then slowly, carefully turning the knife, repeating what I had rehearsed: *He says to say that he has now quit the map, but that M. Bok's welfare is still his truest compass needle. He says to say that, should that needle turn south, a letter will surface, written in the shadow of the Poppy, a letter concerning yourself. He says to say that this is the first rope, but he hopes you will find the fortitude not to use it.*

And what do you know of the Poppy, Isobel?

I know what I have been told, Hector. How his eyes glittered! How much he would have liked to hurt me! Truly, it was a moment to live for…. And storming off, then, joining the departing stream of guests—never did a dinner end so swiftly—just as Benny returned and found his way to M. Bok, of whose own ferocity I saw that one glimpse, when he rose from the table to pursue M. Dieudonne—whom Benny instead somehow saw, or spoke to, I have gathered, though on that matter he has not chosen to further enlighten me, nor how his face was so sadly damaged.

It was quite the opera, that evening, with all its exits and entrances, its arias, and even a murder, as all good operas must contain. I cannot say what happened to the victim, I shall have to ask the maids—it would make a fine souvenir, that starveling puppet! Though not, apparently, for Charlotte—up half that night too spooked, she said, to sleep, imploring me to sit *For just another moment, please!* in the west bedchamber, while she drank her witch-hazel tisane, and shuddered about *That dreadful toy, all bloody-mouthed and such! It gives me the red horrors every time I close my eyes.*

Why not read, then? Or say your Pater Nosters? Sometimes one forgets how young she is, nearer Benny's age than my own. Mobcap over her silly curls, curled up on the bed like a parlormaid.... And like all maids, her first concern is always romance: Who is this Rupert Bok, how did I know him, was he friendly somehow with M. Dieudonne? So awful what happened! but such a handsome man, that puppeteer, and M. Bok, did I not think he was handsome, too?

Yes, I said. *He is very handsome.*

And he is your friend, she said, wistful and hungry; poor Charlotte needs a friend, or a man, or both. And my father, of course, is neither, stepping in then like a different kind of horror: he makes cold any room he enters, certainly he chilled Charlotte to total silence, and released me at last to my own thoughts.... Charlotte was not present at our Spartan breakfast, a plate of cold meats and rye croissants, a cold white draft of sun and *I am much displeased, Isobel,* like some gargoyle over the tea, gray-faced and staring at a spot above my head, as if he could not bear the sight of me. *An honored guest insulted at our table, by a common tramp of a player—it is a disgrace. The city will talk of nothing else, the city loves a scandal. And the whole contretemps lies solely at your doorstep.*

The thought of Hector gave me courage; how amusing! *Why, how so?*

How so? For allowing that—actor access to our home. And to your brother, for whom, it seemed, he had had a tidy plan, to put his hand to Adele Chamsaur's there at the dinner, it was to be a grand surprise; but himself surprised instead! It is another debt I owe to M. Dieudonne. On and on he went, blaming and berating me, but I kept my calm, I drank my tea, I even made a smile worthy, I think, of the footlights, as I told him that we shared a deep wish for Benny's happiness, thus uniting us as *Family,* toasting him with my teacup, the tea's heat almost a pain through the thin morning-glove. I should have stripped my hand bare and toasted him with that, too.

By the time he had his interview with Benny, the bile was exhausted, and he was all dry paternal regret. Bumping along in the carriage, up and down the promenade and *I was never so cold,* Benny's grumble to me later, as we sat that night in the quiet house—Isidore and Charlotte gone back to Chatiens, Helmut trailing behind—with the candied figs and a bottle of champagne between us; there is so much champagne, now, in the cellars, we shall have to have a wedding to make use of it all. Or a funeral. *He winced at every turn of the wheels, but still stopped to talk with everyone we passed, Pinky's mother, and Letty van Symans—you despise her, don't you?*

When I think of her, yes.

Pretending nothing at all had happened, as if that would make it so.... And then whining to me about the Chamsaur girl, with a shrug so man-of-the-world that I had to hide my smile behind my cigarette. *You were just right, Belle, what he wanted was to talk of my majority, of what I must do*—that turns out to be, in practice, amazingly, blessedly little: he need not go to Chatiens, at least for now, but he must quit the theatre, a kind of public atonement and cleansing; and then seriously consider himself the master-to-be, and so marry, though not Adele Chamsaur after all: *What a wife she'd make! She acted quite the whore at the dinner, worse even than Charlotte. Besides, it's Pinky she really fancies.*

And whom do you fancy? I asked, to be mischievous, but the look he gave me then was so lovely, and so bruised, that I repented, I pressed his hand as *A wife is one thing,* he said. *But passion*—and then he stopped, hand to his chest, his heart, and said no more. That strange evening has gifted Benny, given him a new sort of gravity, as if he realizes that life can sometimes be *très sérieux.* It suits him.

And, as for passion—I have already spoken to Miss Bell, or rather she spoke to me. Lighting in the east parlor like a brave curbside wren, wearing a pearl ring *From my fellow,* she said, blushing when I inquired. *I'm affianced! though we've told no one yet,* so I gave her my felicitations, and promised to keep her little secret. Such a good heart that girl has; it is one of life's rare mysteries, or victories. I hope that "fellow" values her as he should.

Her own concern was for her partners, first M. Dieudonne in exile, and she needing a conduit for news, asking me diffidently if she might send word back-and-forth through the maid Otilie. I've a better candidate for emissary, self-appointed, in fact, and though I did not name Javier I told her to be easy, as *My friend is both discreet and efficient, you may safely leave all communications in his hands. As for M. Bok, I promised M. Dieudonne I would look to him.*

I did, too. Her eyes filled with tears, then, but she refused to let them fall. *He is in a rare funk, it is dreadful to see.*

Send him here.

I don't know that he'll come, Madame. With Istvan gone, he listens to no one, now.

Send him here, Miss Bell. We shall look after him. And so we shall, both Benny and I.

The building lies quiet around him, like a beast that has swallowed up the night. Lucy's light still burning, silently sewing, but no newspapers tonight, no need to wait up, no one is coming. Istvan has gone.

He has not drunk so much for many years, so very much with so very little effect: bottles of whiskey lined up like soldiers, whiskey like water, but still too shallow to drown.... Like a lad indeed, that tabletop assault on the General, like a child thumbing his nose, just as he used to, making voices pop from rubbish bins to taunt the night-watchmen— but to what end? Why attack the man, when he has himself retreated? To speed his own exit? and make return impossible? If so, then well done, Master God-Gives, Marcel, Hanzel, Dusan, whatever the fuck his name might be now.

Rupert sets aside the half-drunk bottle, kicks down the rumpled coverlet. An epiphany, yes, a showing-forth of the truth: and the truth is, there is no use to lie here alone, in this dank midnight, waning moonlight cold on the windows of this colder room, no use to be here in this place at all. Lucy does not need him, she has the building's deed, and that Pimm fellow to stand beside her. Istvan—Istvan does not need him. Istvan does not want him, else why would he flee this way, not a word said, no goodbye, no chance to argue.... Arguing, yes, the night before the ball, recall the look on his face: *You may be content here, in this—domestic bliss, but I am not.* "No you are not, messire," aloud to the room as empty as these thoughts, hateful thoughts he cannot master, Istvan his own master, yes, and that is the most hateful thing of all: to love so well someone who does only as he pleases, and in the end pleases no one but himself.

Benjamin tried to stop him, and was battered for his pains; Lucy watched him go like dumbshow—*He only said he must be off,* that sounds like him—but "Why not at least tell me?" again aloud, a mutter so dreary that it rings half-mad; well then, he is mad, so. As mad as this room all scattered and stuffed with his things, he took so little in the end, not even his puppets, Jesu, everything abandoned this time, except Feste, apparently. And the knife on the night table, oh, what a touch, messire, what a theatrical clue! as Rupert weights it in his hand, drops it on his desk, remembering that other desk, that other secret drawer like his locked and secret heart. Well. This is one dance he will not do again, no. "Not even for you," as he pulls on his boots, splashes his face, takes a long sour piss and then departs, pocketing his own knife as he goes.

It is amazing, how the skill comes back to one, the way of moving without a ripple through a crowd, through streets he would once have known as fully as an alley cat, though in this city he does not: no habitué of the gaiety district, paradise of dicers and *voudou* girls and kangaroo boxers—he stops a moment to watch that, "The Aboriginal Giant" in chicken feathers and ivory bones versus some tubby brawler in a loincloth that barely covers his shriveled jewels—and purveyors of vices both sanctioned and not. There are a dozen grog-shops a dozen steps apart: he steps into one, a four-table den called the Crocodile's Smile. The taste of whiskey has begun to sicken him, so perhaps he ought to try a different flavor, may be the stuff that Benjamin offered, the jade fairy or whatever he named it, that milky-green absinthe—

—which tastes even worse, like licorice and pond water: amazing that anyone would drink it, visions or not. The bosomy girl who serves him gives him a wink that he stares into a frown, then into the silence of retreat; he has spoken to no one since Lucy, this morning, urging him diffidently to have a bite of meat, to drink some tea. He tried, to please her, but found there was no pleasure in him, no words in him either, nothing left to do but walk the streets like the prowler he once was. But already it palls, this world grown small and overlarge all together, like a telescoping trick, some bit of stage business and he, stupid, blind, bewildered actor, kept out of the joke, or made its dupe—

—on this street called Dollhouse Row, how did he end up here? with the whores posing and preening behind their plate-glass windows, like chocolates in the case at the chocolatier's: a resourceful way to present them, the tricks can just walk by and point with a finger, or a cane. Like this fine specimen here, yellow cane and long floppy coat, a sapphire stickpin as big as a pigeon's egg, joshing with a friend as they all but block the way, but "You!" pettish and overloud, as Rupert tries to dodge; perhaps the man is drunk, perhaps a fool, anyone who walks the streets wearing such a jewel must be a fool. Rupert ignores him, makes to pass again but "Are you deaf, too, sirrah?" raising his cane to bar the way. "You've stepped on my coattails, so you must be blind—"

"I never touched you," Rupert says; he smiles. He cannot help it, he smiles, he waits for what he knows is coming, and so it does: the man offers an insult, raises a hand—

—and before the man understands what has happened, is on his back in the gutter, blood leaking from both ears, cane broken across his ribs which are broken, too, several on each side; his friend has run off shouting for a constable, none of whom are in evidence just then. All the whores are studiously fanning themselves, or turned carefully sidewise to the windows, none of them will say she saw a thing—except perhaps the pudgy one, pink cheeks and lush blond curls, who blows Rupert a kiss in passing. To her he gives the slightest nod, and she breaks into a smile, one tooth missing, and throws him a quick thumbs-up—

—as he turns without noting—perhaps the man was right, and he *is* blind—into another café, or cabaret, the Gilded Something-or-other, and orders a brandy; the taste is a memory, it wounds him; he drinks another. Now the glimmering lights above, the candle at hand seem to have merged, become one dizzy glow; he is drunk, finally, thank Christ. What fun it was, beating that fellow. Perhaps he ought to do it again, perhaps to this man buzzing at his shoulder, murmuring at his ear like a bluebottle fly—

"*Maître?*" and turning his head, he sees that it is Benjamin, puckered brow and "*Maître,*" again and sweetly, hand on his arm, "let's be away. Come, it's very late—And you have blood on your jacket, are you harmed?" as Rupert looks into his eyes, what strange eyes this young man has, he opens his mouth to tell him so but realizes they are walking, he and Benjamin, that strong young arm about his shoulder, they are walking together into the darkness, they are climbing together into a cab—

—where that shorn head rests upon his shoulder, confiding hand against his own; is he never to do as Istvan has done so often, Istvan who has gone, now, how far? And for how long, forever? He need not pursue, only take what is before him, here, now, Benjamin asking softly, "Are you very cold? You're trembling."

"No," says Rupert. His voice sounds strangely to himself. Silence; the cab's enclosure; Benjamin's warmth in the cold, all the warmth in the cold, and his mouth—offered; accepted; as simply as that—tastes of summer wine, lips parting like a bud in sudden bloom. His body taut and fevered with wonder, his murmur—"*Maître, Maître*"—and it is a matter of moments really, endless moments, Rupert's breathing harsh against that unmarked skin as "Did I hurt you?" into the darkness, only the darkness until Benjamin's little laugh, breathless, "Oh no, never, *Maître,*" head back against his shoulder, the smell of his skin like all the promise in the world.

❧❧❧

The first things Rupert sees are flowers, white blooms mounded in white china cups. Gray-striped silk curtains bunched sideways, carelessly, out of the way, books piled like bricks, black drawings tacked up like scrawls on the wall, a window pale with morning light. The next thing he sees is Benjamin in shirtsleeves, scratching in his journal-book, meeting his gaze with a smile so luminous that he must smile, drowsy, in return—

—until he fully notes where he is, how he lies, remembers the night just past; and closes his eyes again, ah Jesu—as Benjamin now stands shyly over him, a cup of tea in hand: "I don't believe that you take honey—?"

No, better that he put some poison in it; but one cannot say so to that look, that smile, and none of this is Benjamin's fault in any way. *He* is the one who should not be here, in this opulent room, silken sheets and flowers, his clothing flung to a corner though "I've left your jacket for the laundress," says Benjamin, "it was rather stiff with blood.... Whatever were you up to, last night?"

"Last night," Rupert says, and stops. He takes the tea. Benjamin watches him swallow, head down, this apparition, this god in his bed; it is beyond believing, it is all he has dreamed of and more, so much more. To find his master so, at the Golden Calf of all places, and then to take him home.... He never slept a wink, up past dawn in a torment of happiness, feverishly writing it all into his journal as Rupert lay in exhausted sleep beside him, Rupert who now meets his eyes: "Last night," again, as Benjamin feels inside his shirt the key dangling on its chain, symbol of all he would do to keep Rupert safe, nothing in the world he would not do so "*Maître*," says Benjamin, "you need say nothing, you need do nothing. If you stood up, now, this moment, and walked out that door, if you walked away forever, I would keep the memory of you forever, I would never trouble you again." His hand has found Rupert's, holds it tight. "But if you let me, I will love you."

"Benjamin—" slowly, wearily, past the waking pain, the mutinous desire, the terrible hope in those eyes, this boy no more a boy who seems somehow so terribly to need him—

"If you let me—"

—as beyond that stillness the house fills with its daily bustle, the servants up and down the stairs, curious to note Otilie perched yawning on a stool, stitching wristbands, just outside the young master's bedroom door; set there sentinel just past dawn by a most serious Madame—*No one is to knock there, no one must disturb*—as she returned to her own rooms, to add a postscript to a longish letter, seal and send it swiftly on its way.

The cardinal virtue of age is simplicity: the graceful whittling-down, the letting go. Mr. Arrowsmith sits considering that principle in the exclusive confines of the Emperors' Club, where so many he has known throughout the years—ones he has served, or who have served him, ones with whom he has together pulled in harness—sit at various stages of their varied campaigns—for kings are not born, despite the common man's romance; they are constructed, made by men like these men, men the common man never knows or sees—the shrewdest among them understanding that time is an arc, not an arena, and must be respected accordingly.

There by the dining table, for instance, is old Herr Konstantine, for whom Mr. Arrowsmith apprenticed long ago: pouring his tea into the frail china saucer, puffing to cool it like some careful grandmamma. Or M. Tillits, a great friend, once, of Jürgen Vidor's, whose joy now in life is racing horses, he boasts a stable of twenty-two and plans to breed many more: *They are more biddable than men, and far more loyal. My pony, Sans-Souci, would come through gunfire at my whistle.* For gunfire, yes, one needs a valorous mount, but in these larger wars, fought on the tilted battlefields of the mind, wars of words as ordnance, betrayals and overturnings, the outcome for which one plots and struggles is not, in itself, an end: there is no end because life has no end. See this current strategy, to install in several places of power those deemed worthy by de Metz and his brethren in Paris, in Petersburg: have they not done the same many times before, in those cities and in others? How many of those men are still useful today? How many are still alive?

Jürgen Vidor himself was a proud guest of this assembly, though he never held a chair, and dined here on many occasions, between his visits to Le Lapin Vert or whatever hellfire club he rejoiced in at the time. A cloven man, yes, but useful, a tool unashamed of his office. And a corrective, too, to men like Hector; to Hector directly, once or twice; that time in London, say. Did Hector ever wonder, one wonders, whose hand lay on the haft? It was a pity to have had to let him go.

He sighs, and shifts his leg. His cane lies aslant against the chair's peacock-blue brocade, his own cup of tea sits cooling on the mahogany table beside. The windows give what light there is, which, on this gray February day, is little; Candlemas, Epiphany's paler cousin, and what a night *that* was. It was all he could do to keep his distance, devotee of the theatre as he is, and though Isobel's account was stirring, what a pleasure it would have been to be there: watching Hector's discomfiture, and Isidore's own surprise—how often does that happen?—but best of all Dusan's flair and flourish, the man is a true artist, it is a rare joy to see such a one at play. And for such stakes, too. He has few regrets in life, but this is surely one of them, that the dice did not roll so he might have seen this command performance with his own eyes. Ah well, one day he shall have the full account from the horse's mouth, *sans souci.*

Meanwhile its ripples are still being reckoned, between Chamsaur's crushed matrimonial dreams and Isidore's change of tack, Hector's disappointment and, to Mr. Arrowsmith's mind, rather childish and outsized rage: *To make me the butt of his foolish entertainment—I would have expected better of Hanzel. And to confuse an opportunity—a rare opportunity! with an order*—never noting that Dusan, of course, saw matters rather differently. Yet does Hector himself reckon where his pique originates? The scout on the path, the protégé, the heir: had he sons of his own, none of this might have happened. Or had he followed Mercury instead of Mars—fancy Hector upon that smaller stage, Dusan might have made a protégé of *him*. But as the path now lies—

Still opportunities are all around us, eh, Javier? And now that Hanzel's—*gentleman is in residence with Isobel, it makes matters much easier.*

What matters? How can either of them matter, now? You've another courier, the work continues—

I never threaten what I will not perform, though of course the performance is ultimately aimed at Isidore: the young man, Benjamin, the crank that turns that wheel, and if M. Bok turns Benjamin, and Dusan turns M. Bok, reaching for one, he will have all. If the wheel turns his way.

Meanwhile *I thought you were taking Benjamin into your service?* just to ask, just to see but *I'd not have him now,* which could mean anything, the statement's opposite, it could even be true; with Hector, who knows? Mr. Arrowsmith sips his tea, he ponders the slant of the sun, he watches M. Tillits rise in greeting to a fat man in pale spats and his thin associate, men unfamiliar to Mr. Arrowsmith; it is a sign, surely. When new counters reach the board, others, older, must depart; yet another decision deplored with heat by Hector—

I told Isidore you had grown poetical.

Did you? Then you may share this as well, call it a poem if you will. I have left the agora, I have retired.

And so our matters are to move forward without your help, is that it, Javier? Without your contacts or your—lubrication?

That would be the meaning of retired, yes. We are not the young men we were, Hector. You yourself have found some, call it flexibility, within your commission, have you not?

I do now as I've always done. But you—

I no longer nurse the urge to risk all for commerce—

"Commerce"! Is that what you call this?

—and to live for it is even worse. I aim to be a private citizen, and enjoy what private pleasures I may—

—such as this moment's, drinking not Assam but robust Darjeeling, watching the dust motes dance in the dying sunlight, and calling to mind a fragment of a poem in Greek, what was that poem? learned so very long ago from his tutor, Mr. Carstairs, fluffy hair and old suspenders, the nervous kindness of a man dependant on the good will of others. Mr. Carstairs, how long has it been since he recalled that name? Dust motes in the sunlight, yes.

Now M. Tillits is nodding, Herr Konstantine is nodding, all the gentlemen in the room are nodding to the man just entered, Isidore wrapped in gray and shadowed by a strange attendant, that odd blond fellow from Isobel's house, some sort of adjunct to Benjamin. Mr. Arrowsmith gives the man a courteous bow, which he returns much too vigorously, causing Mr. Arrowsmith an inner sigh. Unwrapped, Isidore looks equally gray, a deep, waxen weariness to cloak the energy of his gaze, his claw-hand beckoning for more tea, as he introduces Mr. Arrowsmith to Mr. Entwhistle under another name.

Afterward, alone again in the early twilight, Mr. Arrowsmith summons a waiter, perusing the evening's bill of fare: "Deviled chicken, and the hare, the roasted beets, yes. And Assam tea."

"Will Monsieur care for a cordial, or champagne?"

"Champagne," says Mr. Arrowsmith, surprising himself. "And stationery," on which he composes a brisk but consoling epistle to Miss Lucinda Bell: unsigned, but making reference in the postscript to a pair of ladies known to them both, one always a queen in this newly shuffled deck, call her today the queen of hearts; the other only a memory, as Liserl is becoming a memory, of red hair and the soft scent of verbena, call her the lost queen, though her name is still a bona fide, and, come to consider it, both queens are cut very much from the same bolt. Liserl... Liserl was never a queen at all, nor would she have chosen to be one, as the violet on the path yearns neither for the rose's thorns nor the poppy's intoxication. Oh, dear Liserl: he lifts his champagne to her name.

In the growing dusk, as the chill sets in, the streets exchange the day's traffic for the evening's; a timid moon, as it rises, gains confidence to compete with the fires and lamps. Concertinas wheeze, beggars yawn, a pair of shopgirls in matching bonnets scuttle past a ragman's cart. The windows light up on Dollhouse Row, as the girls in their petticoats and sausage curls settle in with teacup gin for the long night ahead. One of them lingers, just beyond the velvet curtains, to repeat a funny tale to her new friend, of a customer she mislikes, the girls call him the Spotted Monster: "Out front a-pointing with his cane, he was aiming at me—again, and I'd just had him that Tuesday last!—when he rubbed the wrong fellow the wrong way," a tall dark fellow with a gloomy air, dressed like a toff but "I never knew a toff could hit. And my, didn't the Monster catch a beating! He's not been back since," smiling so wide she shows her missing tooth, inviting Istvan's thoughtful smile in return—"I wish I had seen it"—as the girl nods: "I wish he'd step in some night, that dark fellow. I'd give him a fancy pull for free."

She enters into the lighted window, onto her stage, as Istvan turns away. How strange that Mouse should walk this very street, just a peep past the curtains, close enough, almost, to touch—or then again not strange at all, he is out on the town, now. Glimpsed in fact that very afternoon, abroad in the marketplace: Istvan in costermonger's cap, hunkered down beside a cart full of cabbages, knees up and watching as they passed, together, Rupert looking restless and somber, though Puck has improved his haberdashery somewhat, Puck so dizzy with love he almost walked into a lamppost; well, Mouse will have that effect. Watching until they disappeared into a tobacconist's, fighting the pull in his heart like the pull of the tide, an undertow, so he must scramble from his cabbage-throne to tuck himself securely elsewhere, quell the pain with third-rate brandy and a five-minute farce, the brandy bottle at war with a soiled serviette, and the whole grog-shop crowding round and clapping, tossing pence and cigarettes, just like old times.

It is the kind of thing that Boilfast strenuously deplores: *Monsieur, when one hides, it means that one is not seen* but *I have to live,* his own mild answer, and to live means to play, even if only stealthily: and so he does, upon a double stage, in fact, since he knows that he is being watched. If the General is quiescent, it is not on this front, Istvan observed not only by clumsy César—whom one would think had his hands full with bravo duty, squiring the General through town, but no, still time enough to skulk and peer around corners like a tuppence villain—but by several more skillful, and rarely the same one twice; perhaps these are not the General's men, after all. No overt threat has yet been offered; and Boilfast remains diligent at the door, he knows his customers and their friends, and his razor is very sharp. Istvan himself keeps the planing knife ready in his pocket; no one will ever cut him again.

Stepping now past the draped windows, he continues down the hallway, to a prim little parlor where the tricks make their arrangements: pink-striped divans and lace-fringed lamps, the daily papers, little dishes full of candy so old even the mice refuse to nibble. This evening Jardin waits there, in his slouch hat, paging through a theatre broadsheet; he gives Istvan a friendly nod as he passes through to the door. The players' network intersects with the whores': it reminds Istvan rather fondly of the Poppy, though the level of artistry is admittedly low. And the wilting regulation of it—that smell of peppermint, the cunt inspector once a fortnight, the licensed bills-of-health upon the wall—must be an enemy to mystery, and thus the more theatrical forms of desire. Except perhaps for a nervous bourgeois.

In this conduit state, screened by both Boilfast and Madame, afloat between worlds, Istvan owns that narrow quantity of freedom, as well as an air of glamour, the leading man in a sad romance: his circumstances, though not fully known, are much guessed at, and he is much pursued. On Dollhouse Row, backstage, there is always someone willing to tip him a drink, lend him an ear, or more. As now, at the Fin, in the early flurry before the evening's show, one he will only watch: a dandy in measle-red plaid, bright monocle and brighter smile inside his auburn beard, offering whiskey: "The weather's foul, isn't it? Warm yourself. Or let me," with a little wink, reaching past the bottle to put his hand atop Istvan's, who smiles, and shakes his head, takes his hand away.

"Ah, Etienne," shrugs the man, "you know me and I know you. Why all these scruples, all of a sudden?"

And Istvan shrugs in return: nothing wrong with this fellow, it is he who is oddly, helplessly chaste, his silent unwilling gift to Mouse, whose own nights are doubtless much different. Still "I've taken the vows," he tells the red-bearded dandy, who returns a philosophical nod: "I thought I smelled incense. Well, *dominus vobiscum*," lifting his glass, as Boilfast emerges with a bucket in hand, beckoning to Istvan: "A moment, Monsieur?" slipping him a folded note, unsigned as always, on finest stationery, assuring that *All is quiet in the garden, and in the blackbird's nest, though winter will own its squalls. But we shall hope for finer weather, you and I.*

"Good news?" asks Boilfast, beginning to swab some unnamable stain.

"Spring is coming," says Istvan, freeing Feste from his coat.

The cab is a useless extravagance, Rupert would much rather walk, but "I promised Miss Bell a drive," says Benjamin. So off they go, through streets still so slick and cold it may as well be deep midwinter, though in the greenhouse the crocuses have already raised their heads, soft purple and glowing saffron, nurtured *By Belle herself,* Benjamin had murmured, he and Rupert standing together in the chilly green. *She likes to make things grow. Like me.... Belle is my sister and mother both, you know, my own mother died when I was very small.*

He has begun to share these details, little stories of his past, that brief road to this moment where his master is beside him, these days the happiest he will ever know. He gives them as gifts, like the sealskin gloves, the black China silk mufflers, the silken top hat Rupert will not wear, as he will not wear the rose-gold intaglio ring, carven with a Greek warrior—*But you do favor rings*, Maître—though Rupert has not worn his signet ring for some time. It has gone missing, casualty of a life lived nowhere, adrift between the Blackbird rooms avoided and the townhouse where he never will belong, ought not even to be, a kind of insanity—

—as he ought not be here, bumping along in this silly cab, beside Benjamin whose cold fingers find his own, while offering another little story: of the gardens at Chatiens, a long-ago day spent hiding amongst the paths, kicked and chased by the nurse's nephews—"They caught me by the goat pens, and rubbed shit in my hair"—until he clambered up a chestnut tree, hiding so long that he fell asleep, wakened by the cries of the frantic nurse "Who never cared a whit for me," head nestled now on Rupert's shoulder. "She was only afraid of my father. Everyone is afraid of my father.... It was wonderful, being in the trees."

"Yes," Rupert's murmur. "One feels safer up there." Idly he strokes Benjamin's fingers, touches the scars on his knuckles: to prompt yet another tale, of trailing their carriage after that first dinner, silently scaling the roof—"Our roof?" in real surprise, looking down into that smiling face. "That's slate, it's the devil when it's wet—"

"I know," with a proud little laugh. "I almost lost a finger on the drainpipe. But I had to see where you lived.... I have loved you for so long," his whisper becoming a kiss that continues, as Rupert reaches backhanded to drag the little curtains closed: more insanity, this endless passion, some days he feels almost drunk with lust. All that young need, and greed, met and matched by his own desire not to think, not to remember—

To go under the poppy, I learned that on a boat.

It means to smoke opium?

It means to forget.

—what cannot be forgotten, only muzzled, muffled by the feel of this mouth against his own, breathing his breath—until the cab slows, and they draw apart, Benjamin flushed and smiling to lead him arm in arm into the Blackbird's foyer, where Lucy, wrapped in a pretty new shawl, rosy wool and bountiful tassels, peeps out to watch Pinky and the children crowd around them, shaking hands: "We've not seen you for weeks," says Pinky, observing his friend's brilliant gaze. "You must give us all your news."

"Where's Mister Istvan?" Mickey asks. "He promised to take me to the Golden Calf."

A silence falls. Lucy takes a step forward, Pinky bends to whisper in Mickey's ear, as Rupert turns away, climbing the stairs with Benjamin following, up into his old rooms, their rooms, empty and dank and unfired. Still in silence, Rupert crosses to his desk, shuffles through the papers left there, the few letters, nothing he cares to see—as Benjamin examines the box of collar studs, the volumes of Shakespeare, a drooping opera cape hung on a silver coat tree, a blazing gold cravat he himself might have worn a month or so before. Beside a straight-backed chair lies a pile of wooden limbs, scraps and detritus, a skein of wire as pliable as gut and "Did you ever play the puppets?" asks Benjamin; he rolls an eyeball in his palm, gaudy green, back and forth. "There's so much you've never told me…. Miss Bell said you trod the boards, in another town."

"No," without looking up from the bank draft, the banker's fulsome letter. "Not the way you're thinking. And leave those—toys alone." The white knife still lies where he dropped it; he ought not have come back here, certainly not with Benjamin, whose arms are around him now, embracing him from behind but "No," again and bleak. "Not here." He slips the banker's letter into his pocket, then catches sight of a narrow traveling case beside the desk. "Wait for me downstairs," he says, bending to unlock the case last used when they left Brussels, he and Istvan and Lucy, the mecs in tow. It seems so long ago—

—as Lucy approaches down the hallway, something soft said to Benjamin—"They're all clamoring for you"—and then to Rupert, halfway around the door: "Some letters came, I put them on your desk." She steps into the room, to his side and "You look a bit tired," she says lightly, shocked and trying not to show it: not only tired but desolate, and overdressed, those toff's weeds do not suit him. "Are you taking care? Or smoking too much, and burning the midnight oil?"

"I keep gentleman's hours," with a humorless smile, turning to see what her eyes cannot hide, though she tries to distract them both with chatter about Pimm: he is making himself a little workshop backstage, Pimm's Chateaux to become Pimm's Theatres, with little paper puppets to replace the dancing gentlemen and ladies. "And Mickey is making finger puppets," she says. "We'll sell the lot in the lobby, before and after the shows—"

"Mickey misses—his friend."

"Yes," after a pause. "They all do," and herself, too, though she knows Istvan has been back more than once, slipping in and out like a cat through a window, her worktable rearranged, a certain tool gone missing; as she knows he is well, or at least that he is observed to be well, from the notes she gets and carefully destroys. No one has come to the Blackbird, the letter box sits unmolested in the safe; her silent hallway quiz to Benjamin, miming a key, brought his fingers to his chest, his nod in return, Benjamin whose key is Rupert, Rupert who now opens the traveling case to find inside a sachet of dried mouse, a yellowed note card advertising an evening's entertainment, "*The Hour of the Flesh*" and "That's apt," he says, dropping both to the floor. "I've had my hour, I ought be on my way."

"What do you mean? You're leaving?"

"Why not?" with a shrug. "You're safe with Pimm. And I'm worthless here, I do nothing of value—"

"Monsieur Benjamin would not say so."

"Monsieur Benjamin." He rubs his forehead, he stares at the floor. "Monsieur Benjamin is heir to a great name, and a very great fortune." He rubs his forehead again. "Each day a boy blacks my boots, a girl tends my coat, another brings me water when I want to shave, whiskey when I want to be drunk; I sleep on silk." He puts some papers into the case, a clean shirt, the little white knife. "That teacher creeps about the house sniffing in corners, he's halfway behind every door I pass. And letters come like clockwork from the country house, from the old man, that old mummy who thought to break my hand. Meanwhile I play about in the gardens, or Mme. de Metz tries to teach me chess.... Jesu," looking about the room, as if it is already a memory, as if she is a memory, a sweet one he must still forego. "I used to have industry. Now I may as well be a puppet in a fucking box."

And what to say to that? so she says nothing, only reaches to press his hand, as he takes her into his arms, holds her as he once held

Decca, another woman who found her own way, and "Mr. Pimm, now," he says. "He'll help you keep what's yours."

She closes her eyes, she breathes the strange flowery scent of his new waistcoat. He is a good man, it is dreadful to see him so, dreadful that she cannot speak truly, say at least what little she knows. "We're to marry, in the spring. You must—you must stay for the wedding at least, you must give me away—"

"Marry! Why, felicitations, Lucy," kissing her cheek, a kind of relief in his eyes that makes her bite her lip. "I'll stop at the broker's today," as Pinky's knock comes gaily to the door: "Excuse me, milady's chariot's below for Miss Bell?"

"I'm there directly," Lucy calls back, as Rupert gives her the smile he used to, in the days of the war and the soldiers in the lobby, the stink of piss and pus and gunpowder and "He'll come back," she says, as if compelled. "You'll see, he'll come back to you," and rushes out, face red, before she can say more: leaving him with the half-filled case, its key slipped onto the ring beside another key, black metal for the safe he checks mechanically, the gold intact, yes, and the box with its strange letter, what use for that anymore? *I pray you know me when we meet again,* well, there will be no meeting in this world, and the General will have naught to do with them again; with him. May be he ought to burn the thing before he goes, may be he ought to burn it now—

—as he takes from his pocket the matches, bends once more to the safe but "Aren't you coming, *Maître*?" Benjamin diffident in the doorway, so he closes the safe again, closes the traveling case, tucks it under his arm and follows Benjamin down to the cab: where Lucy, Pinky, Mickey and Didier wait to take a turn around the promenade. It is a festive ride, the sun striking silver the statues of statesmen and saints, the pigeons wheeling, the vendors crying rabbit-fur muffs—"Rat fur," says Mickey wisely—and pocket-stones to heat and slip into one's coat, black paper sacks of steaming chestnuts, and chocolate almost too bubbling-hot to drink, a taste of it carried back in a china thimble-cup for "Bella," with Benjamin's flourish of a bow, Isobel in pale lavender silk beside the fire in the east parlor, sable-cuffed gloves and writing letters; she lets her pen fall as they enter. "The man said it would give you sweet dreams."

She sips; she smiles her thanks; she notes Rupert pouring himself an unusually large whiskey. "We've a simple bit of venison tonight, Monsieur, I hope it's to your liking. Benny, you dine with the Guyons, I believe." A one-act charade, but one that Benny will accept, as he will also accept—whether he yet understands or not—the Guyon girl,

Christobel, as his wife. The letter from Chatiens has come, the *fiat* has been issued, but overall it is a very suitable choice, much more so than Adele Chamsaur. Isobel has met the girl on several occasions, and while she may not be a beauty—too pale, and much too tall, almost as tall as Benny himself—she has lovely eyes, and is quite accomplished, a reader of more than silly novels, she and Isobel once had a lively chat about, what was it? Voltaire, yes. The Guyon name is an old one, and Mme. Guyon is the sister of M. Guerlain, so that connection will be well-attached. As for Benny's connection to M. Bok—it is well that he is dining alone with the Guyons. The gossip has grown dangerous— Fernande asking archly if Isobel will wed M. Bok, to keep him in the family—and loud enough to be overheard at Chatiens—

—where Benjamin has been summoned by a letter he has not yet read, left lying on a pile of others on his desk, beside the heap of unfinished poems and his red journal; into which, before he leaves, he scrawls a quick summary of the day's events—the clutter and chill of his master's old rooms, how he longed to take each object into his arms, everything bright with Rupert's luster: *The piled-up scraps of puppets, that's I before I loved him*—then lets the cover fall. Hat and gloves and down to the carriage, but not without a moment's pause in the parlor, to whisper once more to Rupert, Isobel watching their faces, their eyes. She cannot feel envy of Benny, but—to have someone look at her so, someone like M. Bok, what must that be like? as "I shan't be late," says Benjamin. "I won't stay for the dessert, it's always something rather foul—"

"Why not consider your hostess, for once," says Isobel, with such asperity that both men stare at her: then Benjamin offers a cool bow and departs, while Isobel reaches for her pink pavé case, an unpleasant flush across her cheeks. Rupert says nothing, he lights her cigarette, he lights a cheroot. Finally "Shall I read, Monsieur?" from a book of essays, "A Map of the World" that maps no world he knows, but it is a pleasure to sit and listen to that low, commanding voice reading of long-ago princes and their stratagems, queens and their intrigues and discontents. A servant comes to draw the drapes, replenish the logs; another sets with daily silver the small fireside dining table, pours the wine, brings the meat. Outside, the wind rises, pressing against the long windows as if seeking the weakest spot for entry; small things creep unseen in the frozen garden, hunting one another through the dark.

After dinner, Isobel nods invitingly to the chessboard, an old and starkly carved set from the Indies, red jade versus ivory, but "It's a waste of your time, Madame," says Rupert. "You need a proper partner—I still can't tell the damned bishop from the knight."

Something in his tone, the cast of his gaze, brings her softest smile, very rarely seen: "Oh, Monsieur. What difference if you play a certain game or not! And as for bishops, I am sure you know one when you see one."

Rupert shrugs. "I've never met a cleric, unless it was in these rooms." He nods at the book, the map of the world, her world, and Benjamin's. "The landscape I know best—" Looking now not at but past her, at the draped windows, the roads to the fields to the wilds he understands; he almost smiles, a wolf in a brocade waistcoat as "I am a traveler," he says. "A traveler, and a brawler, and a bravo, a front-of-the-house man—if you know what that is, Madame, which I most truly doubt—alongside men whom you'd not allow inside this house, or even near it, if you were wise. And in the days of the Poppy, we—" but there he stops, the name gone silent on his lips.

That silence lies between them like the firelight, the drifting haze of smoke until "Monsieur," says Isobel, "I am well-acquainted with the lords of this city, and of many other cities; I have watched such men come and go since I was a very young girl. Bishops, yes, and mayors, military men, men of industry; viscounts and dukes. Once even a king." Her gaze stays locked to her gloved hands, tightly clasped in her lap; the fur trim trembles. "And I tell you that never have I known a finer man than yourself, Monsieur. Most truly, I tell you so."

He stares still at the draped window, he does not see her, no one sees her. But in this moment, opened like a rose, Isobel is beautiful.

In the dimness of the hallway, Mr. Entwhistle stands listening, tense as a cherubim at the gates of Eden; he too has had a letter from Chatiens. On the stairs, Otilie pauses to watch him, then deliberately drops the heavy tongs she carries, to make them clang, to make him jump, to make his presence known to the ones in the parlor. He throws her a look of loathing as he hurries past—

"Jade!"

"Spy!"

—as the butler opens the outer door to admit both the wind and Monsieur de Metz, back early but not too early, having dutifully consumed Mme. Guyon's dessert—*The mayor's lady gave her cook's recipe for* tarte tatin, *she had it from Louis Vaudable himself!* as Christobel Guyon rolled her eyes to make him smile—and promised more than once that he would return. Otilie lingers, tongs back in hand, longing to tattle on the awful tutor, but already Monsieur is stepping into the parlor—

—as a moment later, Madame steps out, having kissed her brother— "You'll tell me in the morning all about your evening, Benny"—and smiled to M. Bok, retiring then to her own rooms, where her lady's maid sits waiting with the violet water: surprised instead to find herself dismissed until the morrow, Madame saying only that she is very, very tired.

And in Benjamin's chambers, Rupert sits with one last cheroot, as Benjamin tosses down his jacket and tells the story of his night: the meaningless pleasantries, Mme. Guyon and her gluey dessert, M. Guyon and his careful inquiries—*Your father is quite well? Your father is a true friend of mine, and an old one, we were in Ypres together years ago*—with Christobel calm in white bridal lace, placed across from him at table since "They want me to marry her," he says. "No one has yet said so, but I know."

"Is she likely?"

He shrugs. "She's not a fool. Or a strumpet, like Adele Chamsaur. But I'm in no hurry."

Rupert considers him, the cropped curls begun to grow again, the faint shadows of his cheeks, the shadow of the man he will be; a man that he, Rupert, can never know. Very gently: "You ought to wed."

"You say this to me?"

"For—safety's sake. For your own sake. What we do—"

"What we do belongs to us. No one else."

Monsieur Benjamin is heir to a great name, and a very great fortune. "If you say that, then you don't know the world."

And Benjamin smiles back at him, cravat in hand, safe as Adam in the garden. "What other world is there than this, *Maître?*"

In two long steps Rupert is beside him, bending to kiss him, claiming and relinquishing, a master's kiss. A little flurry, Benjamin hasty to shed his shirt, bunch it in one hand as they come together, as the moon recedes and the gaslight glows, the wind trembles the window-glass left bare, a pair of charcoal drawings fluttering like falling leaves. Footsteps pass the room, pause, return to pass again. On the carpet, unconcealed by the fallen shirt, its silver chain gleaming, lies the black metal key.

Lucy

Thank Providence it was Pinky here with me when they came. The children were with Pimm, at the arcade, and we were onstage, planning out the props for the new show, "Jack-in-the-Box." A potato crate with a flat false top, a broomstick length for Rosa to crank, and Mickey will pop up in the motley-and-bells: *In French, you know, it's "diable en boîte,"* Pinky told me, *a boxed devil. Which suits our Mickey to the fingertips.*

He always calls him so, "our Mickey," as it's always "our show." How much he brings Puggy back to me! Once or twice I've even called him so.... His own dearest wish, he says, is to apprentice to me—to me!—and learn to play the puppets proper, though his father would never allow it: *The old stick gives me a fairly slack leash, but it's just so long and no longer. One dark day he'll make me tuck in my tail, and marry, and go roost at a desk in the bank,* with a tragical roll of his eyes. *Still, he's not a thorough pharaoh, like Benjamin's father. It was a treat to see Benjamin, wasn't it? It's been an age. We talked a bit of, of M. Bok. You know.*

Yes, I said. *I know.*

He says they'll go to Greece, soon. As a surprise. Most thoughts he has show right upon his face, again like Puggy, and I could see his worry, though I kept my own worries to myself; some things I don't tell even Pimm. *He's happier than ever I've known him, but—Miss Bell, you see, I'm not the swimmer he is. I splash about in shallow waters, I don't go out into the deeps. But Benjamin—*

It was then we heard it, *tap-tap-tap* like knocking, but already he'd let himself in: the General, bold as day down the center aisle, and climbing onto the stage, with some curbside thug there at his elbow, the kind Omar would have pitched right out into the street. Except for the bowler hat, he looked just the same: bowing to me all affable and kindly-like, as if we were old bosom friends. *Greetings, Lucy, you're looking very well. And in a theatre, quite the likely setting.... I'd have a word or two with your M. Bok.*

I could feel myself puff up, like a cat does when she's cornered, while Pinky set his hammer down, then straightaway picked it up again, so I knew he felt it, too. Whatever the General wanted of Rupert, he could have had elsewhere, and he'd know well and good before he came that Rupert's elsewhere himself these days. So why did he come? Standing ramrod-straight with his arms crossed, as if his army was right behind him, and that bravo looking me brazen up-and-down, like he was totting up an offer; no one can do such to me, not ever again. So before I said a word I stared at him, I stared his gaze right back down into the boards, and then I told the General, *He's not about just now, sir. You can leave a message if you wish, I'll see he gets it.*

I'm afraid that won't suit. Shall I step up myself, and see if he's in his rooms? Achille, you'll excuse us, now.

No, sir, from Pinky there at my side, agitated and too loud—they've no sense of trouble, these toff boys, but is that their fault? And frightened or not, he stood his ground like a trooper. *I do beg your pardon, sir, but I'm here just now to visit with Miss Bell.*

Truly? Well, you wouldn't be the first young fellow who did. I recall she was a favorite of my sergeant's, he said she gave rare value for the price. And he smiled then, a smile that put me back into the Poppy and the war, the soldiers—his soldiers—grubbing and grasping as you passed, that boy with the mad eyes and the stolen ring—*Stuck on a knuckle, judy, so I took finger 'n all!* And his bravo laughed a little, as if he had been right about me from the start.

Pinky looked at me, I felt it, felt the color burn in my face but *I recall you, too, sir,* I said, and I stepped up to the General, I stepped so near I could smell the bay rum on his cheeks. *I told you true, Mister Rupert's not here, so you may give your message to me. Or you can walk out, sir. It's yours to decide.*

The stage seemed very small, the two of us so close together, like we were players acting out a scene. I swear I did not know what I would do, if he made to go upstairs, where that safe is, or if his bravo tried some move—I can't guess how Pinky would fare in a close-up brawl! He was pale enough with the threat he got—*Your father will be most unhappy, Achille, he mislikes disobedience almost as much as I*—but it's he who saved me, I've no doubt of it at all. He's a toff boy from a toff family, and the General well knows that. If it had been just Pimm and me, or I alone—

They left straightaway, then, the bravo turning back to spit on the floor, and Pinky dashing to bolt the door behind them, then crashing off into the pantry for water, or smelling salts, or who knows what, he brought back a cup of ice-cold tea and *Miss Bell!* all anxious-eyed, as if I might faint dead away. *Miss Bell, what a, what an extraordinary thing! Are you quite all right?*

I took the tea, I made a smile—he's used to frailer girls than I, that's certain—and *Surely,* I said, but I didn't meet his gaze straight-on. All around us was quiet, just the little scrabblings of the mice, and the carts and cabs outside, and our box for Jack as raw as any prop we ever fixed up at the Poppy…. *Rare value for the price,* yes, I only did what I had to do, in the bed or on the stage. But I'm no more at the Poppy, whatever anyone may say. This is the Blackbird Theatre, and I am to be Missus Lucy Pimm.

Meanwhile Pinky was still a-stir, crossing back and forth, looking toward the door as if they might burst back in at any time, until *You're acquainted with M. Georges,* he said, then stopped and flushed beet-red, as if he had done me a wrong. I looked him in the eye, then, and *That old boxed devil,* I said, *yes, I've seen him a time or two before.* And I rose for my hat and gloves, because word had to be given to Mme. de Metz: for Rupert, and for her messenger to Istvan, whoever that may be.

But Pinky stopped me—*Please, let me go for you, Miss Bell. You know I am your servant, whatever may happen.* And the look he gave me then was so dogged, and so true, I swear I felt Puggy there, smiling down on us both. Rare's the theatre without a ghost, so may be Puggy is ours, and who better? I'd have him on the boards with me any time— the one who put me in a show to start with, who showed me all and everything he knew, and who perished in a tragedy brought about, yes, by this same General and his friends, these men to whom we're naught but scenery on their stage. So I wrote up a note on the first scrap I found, and *Give this to Mme. de Metz,* I said to Pinky, *straight into her hands and no other's. And be careful…. Leave the door unbolted, mind. Pimm will be back directly.*

Off he jogged, and I sat right down with my sewing, to settle my mind: stitching on a doubled line of bells, gold and silver all a-jingle, it will make a merry sound on the Jack's motley-cap. After a while I emptied out that sorry tea, and poured myself a jot of gin, to lift in toast to Puggy: with his bald head and wobbly French, his relish for the spangle and flash, Puggy who taught me that an exit can be an entrance, too. It all depends on where the audience is looking, and with a bit of tit or fire, you can make them gape wherever, and howsoever you please.

The morning's rain feels almost Biblical, running through the spouts and gutters, floating what seems all of winter's muck all at once through the streets already splashing and congested with the clash of black umbrellas, vendors hunched beside their awninged carts, cabs on every corner, a river of bodies heading in out of the wet. Everything is washed with gray, everything is sodden, though Mr. Arrowsmith notes with some admiration the bedraggled greens in the tall white vases at the townhouse—only Isobel would attempt a flower in this weather—while he raises his cane to knock—

—as the door swings open, on the butler and Benjamin: "Pardon," the young man stepping back so Mr. Arrowsmith may enter. Mr. Arrowsmith offers his hand with his own apologies: "Pardon me, rather, I'm fairly damp just now. You're bound out into the deluge, I see," and apparently for longer than just the day's rounds: now Mr. Arrowsmith notes the dark gripbag the butler holds, notes as well the young man's marked pallor, the strong odor of liquor as "Yes," says Benjamin, hat in hand. "I'm for Chatiens."

"Ah? Safe travels, then. It's a short journey, when loved ones await—"

"No," rudely, but with a bitterness unconnected to Mr. Arrowsmith; he does not trouble to bow. He and the butler pass into the rain, to the carriage pulling up the drive, a man already waiting inside—while the saucy brown-haired maid approaches to close the door, to take Mr. Arrowsmith's dripping hat, and conduct him to the east parlor where Madame waits, Madame rising when she sees him, offering her cheek: "Javier," with a tired little smile. "You are so blessedly prompt."

As promptly he sits beside her at the little table, takes a cup of tea, the hurried note she sent still tucked into his breast pocket, along with the scrap from Miss Bell, whose handwriting is somewhat scrambled, but the gist of the communiqué is clear: Georges has moved his counter, the round of play has begun. The timing may not be fortuitous—in Mr. Arrowsmith's pocket lies another letter, from a colleague in the Urals, suggesting delay in all matters where Isidore is concerned, *The man is most unwell*—but things are as they are, the major actors are

311

fairly in place, although "In my last missive from your father," says Mr. Arrowsmith, lifting his cup, "he said nothing of Benjamin coming out to the country—?"

"He's been asking for weeks," says Isobel; this morning she looks her age and more, dry-eyed in a house gown riotous with peonies, another attempt to force a flourish where the ground is hard. Pushing aside her untouched teacup, she lights a cigarette, smokes a moment in silence. "Benny rarely reads his letters, but this time Helmut came especially to fetch him. I'd thought at first it was regarding the marriage—"

"Yes, I saw Guyon at the club. He's quite delighted."

"—but Helmut was so insistent…. And Benny is so—cheerless. Something else is amiss," something dreadful that he will not tell her, as he will not say where M. Bok has gone, or why: sharing only his blackest humor, the drunken, echoing silence from his rooms, turning so viciously on her gentle inquiries—*Stop badgering, Belle! One more word and I'm in the river*—that in her own distress she must turn, alone again, to Javier.

At least Mr. Entwhistle has been jettisoned, with unexpected speed, in a scene both grating and comic; as if the day had not brought enough to carry…. Seeking as always the sanctuary of the greenhouse, trying to think what to do for Benny, trying not to worry for M. Bok, as she sadly, calmly trimmed and snipped, examining the canes, the nymph-rose just an amber stick, though in the summer it blooms like a wanton, petals as lush as a young girl's kiss. The little shears felt cold in her hand, Axel's gift from many years before: *From one servant of the garden to another, Miss*—old shears, very silver, very sharp.

Then up loomed Mr. Entwhistle, grim and grimly energetic, a sheaf of papers in his hand: *Mr. Rupert Bok—I have feared it exceedingly, and now I know. He is a criminal, Madame, a foul criminal! M. de Metz is in great peril.* Asking *How so?* without great interest redoubled Mr. Entwhistle's outrage, the man was like a hayrick set alight: *How so! That Bok is—I cannot even speak of it, before a lady. He is* unnatural. *What he does with M. de Metz—*

How is it that you are so well-informed on M. Bok's state of being? Or, for that matter, my brother's?

This, Madame! These—infamous verses, shaking Benny's poems in her face.

She did not read them all, a sample was enough: the poems were very sweet, very silly, very damning. *That is a serious assertion. So serious it may well demand recourse—a duel, say. Would your rectitude rise to that challenge?* as the man's martyr's ardor flickered visibly, like a bonfire in a cold wind: *Dueling is against the law, Madame.*

Yes, it is. Pack your traps directly, Mr. Entwhistle. I abhor cowardice. A manservant escorted him out within the hour, rumpled and outraged as the head of John the Baptist, while she burned the poems in a yellow cachepot, along with a handful of crushed stems and dried petals, looking by rote for patterns in the ash: *See what the flowers tell you, child—*

—though she tells none of this, now, to Javier, sharing instead, in light of Hector's visit to poor Miss Bell, a different tale, Mr. Arrowsmith astonished to learn at last of the lock-box letter: "Dusan himself gave you this information? Dusan has this document?" Recalling a quiet sitting room on Goldsmith Street, Georges on the ivory settee, turning his silver ring as he spoke of Vidor's passing: *You say Redgrave found nothing in his rooms, or on his person?* Ah, but there was nothing left to find, was there, as Dusan was so clever! even while in real pain and disarray. One can almost share Hector's disappointment at the loss of this courier: a player so nimble does indeed merit a broader stage. Now "I am more than pleased to learn this, Isobel—though it could have been told me sooner," with not a little reproof. "And it must be kept very close between us, no one else must know—"

"Hector knows," with a brittle smile she cannot check, her quiet recital of the Epiphany moment, while outside the rain continues to fall—

—as the carriage to Chatiens sways and gallops, making excellent time despite the weather. Helmut in a mackintosh pores over bills of lading and receipts, Benjamin in the opposite corner hunches over a bottle of whiskey, a bottle from which his *Maître* has drunk; if he closes his eyes, he can pretend to taste him there, try to drown the last moments between them. That hateful, fragile dawn, Rupert gone already from the bed, and he half-awake and reaching by rote for the key: and finding nothing. Unease, then fear, then panic as he tumbled naked to the floor, rooting through a mulch of half-made poems and books and broadsheets, oh God it must be here somewhere, he stripped it when he stripped his shirt—! All these weeks, he has been so careful—*Never lose it, never take it off—*

—putting, at last, his hand to its shape, almost laughing for sheer relief as he slipped the chain safely back about his neck: only then seeing Rupert, silent as a spirit at the door, how long had he been there, watching? And crossing to the bedside: *What is that? Let me see.*

And then Rupert's frown, a terrible frown that said in an instant everything that was to come, a side of him that Benjamin had never seen, remote and utterly resistless—that key, M. Dieudonne's key, how did he come to have it? *Don't lie to me, Benjamin. Don't lie*—while he tried his best to dissemble, calling on all his skills as an actor, a lover, to hide what in the end he could not hide, while the black key dangled on its chain between them, like a puppet on slack strings—

Where is he? He gave you this, you must know where he is.

I swear to you, Maître! *I would tell you if I did!*

—while seeing, too, like a deadly blow, Rupert riven by the need to find M. Dieudonne, a living, driving need, a need he has never, ever shown for Benjamin: a love that finally brings the tale entire, he white-faced and naked, still, trying to hold onto Rupert's cold hand but *All this time,* beside him on the bed, already gone forever. *You knew, and never told me. All this time.*

But it was for you, you mustn't—What was I to do? I gave my word! the tears burning on his cheeks. *It was for you, all for you*—but no tears, no words could keep Rupert there, his *Maître* pulling on his coat, taking up his traveling case, gone in silence from the room and the house without one look behind him: as if their love did not matter, as if Benjamin did not matter, so nothing matters now, nothing, nor ever will again—

—as Benjamin takes another obliterating swallow, aims his blind gaze at the window once more. Helmut raises an eyebrow, but is wise enough to keep still, it is not his place to enquire. The old master, ill or not, will sort things out, and just in time, too, judging by the look of the young master, twisting on the seat as if on a red-hot brazier. What a pity, that one so gifted by fortune should prove instead such a wastrel and a fool—

—as Rupert, now bearing both keys, traveling case in hand, walks, as a traveler does, through the gush and spatter of the streets, boots wet, gaze set, heading for the Blackbird Theatre. The last day and night he spent in a lodging house, one of several clustered by the train station, trying to marshal his thoughts, to piece together what is known and what can be guessed, and decide what he must do next. After the first shock, Benjamin's lie seems less dire: he was a tool, not an accomplice—though it was rash beyond belief for Istvan to entrust him with that key, if the General is in fact involved, and for what unguessable stakes? The key for the safe must mean the letter in the safe, Jesu he almost put the match to it.... God damn Istvan, for telling him nothing, for leaving him so entirely in the dark! *He said the key would keep you safe, he said Miss Bell knew all about it.* Lucy—Lucy plays on this stage as well, what else might she know? He will find that out within the hour.

He will find Istvan, too, indeed he will, if he is in this city at all, though Benjamin swore that no one knows precisely where he is, swore it with tears.... Benjamin. Yes, it is right to leave him, time to leave, especially if he is to marry; but he himself ought not have been so— harsh. He is used to Istvan's vigor in combat, the boy just dwindled, like a leaf in flame.... Istvan, still in the city, in hiding, or in trouble? Or both at once? As reckless as any boy, yes.... Thinking of him all the long night past, there in the topmost room, how long since he has stayed at a place like that? Packed with men both noisy and furtive, up and down the stairs all night, the faintly sickly smell of unwashed bodies, splashed liquor, weariness and dust, and the hum and screech of the train arriving, the train departing, leaving behind more men to climb the stairs, to call to one another in German, in English, in pidgin French, in some music of a language Rupert had never heard before. He gave up on slumber, sat instead smoking and watching out the window as the rain swept in, swallowing the dawn as it swallows the noon, gray sheets like a scrim behind which anything might travel. *I am a traveler,* yes, did he not say so to Mme. de Metz? Belle, Benjamin calls her. He must send some word, to Belle, and to Benjamin, as soon as he speaks with Lucy, as soon as he finds Istvan.... Istvan, he would like very much to break his neck, more perhaps than ever before, and that is saying something. *Save the show for the stage,* oh, messire, there will be a merry reckoning! once Istvan has been brought to ground, once they are together, safe together, once again—

—as from nowhere a hand clamps onto his shoulder, another on his arm, a hold he breaks at once by instinct, a street boy's old instinct but the constables take him again: "You're Rupert Bok, sir," not at all a question as he bucks in their grasp, as they march him in lockstep past a pair of peering whores, into a closed police cab, rolling off quietly down the alley into the rain—

—as in a lodging house not so far from the one Rupert has just quit, Mr. Entwhistle neatly repacks a greenish leather bag: some few clothes, his shaving kit and writing case, but most of the cargo is books, Scripture, and the Latin and Greek grammar: more successful with the second than the first, may Our Lord forgive him, but he has done everything he could for M. de Metz. It had seemed a gift from above, to be summoned from the orphan school by a family so in need of his services: the young man and his ignorance, Madame with her mockery, he had been warned of both by the old lord: *My daughter considers herself the final word where my son is concerned. Let her think she has engaged you, but know that your toil is for him, and for myself. You will keep me informed of all his progress.*

And without stint he has done so, reporting everything, believing, always, that Providence had arranged at last a way for him to leave this foul city, with its "modernity" and depravity, to teach the children the young madame was sure to bear: the reward a good and faithful servant most deserves, the chance to be of even greater service, and spend his days in sound employ. Why else was he so closely monitored by the old lord? Why else take him to that supper club, if he was not to be taken in due time to the family house?

From the first he disliked Mr. Bok, as a bird dislikes the snake, with his vagabond watchfulness, his whiskey and cigars, his puppeteer friend (*there* was an imp from the darkness), and Madame doting on him like a, like a paramour, anyone could see he was unsavory company for a young man. But once he discovered what truly passed between the man and M. de Metz—! Those disgusting "poems," and the young man kept a journal as well, a red-bound journal, though that did not come to hand, even though he searched so diligently…. Could any matter be more grave? Could any father fail to reward the hand that saves his only son?

But instead his report on M. de Metz and Mr. Bok was met with silence, a strange unbroken silence, until that gore-crow, M. Helmut, landed, to tell him—to *dismiss* him—*Your service is at an end.* No use to argue or appeal, though he tried both, tried as well to involve Mme. de Metz in her brother's welfare—and met, there, with talk of a duel! With shears in hand, as if she would start the carving herself! Is it any wonder that he turned to the last help at hand, the civil authority? Though the true Judge will weigh Mr. Bok in the scales, as He weighs all hearts and hopes and actions, all unjust, hateful, ungrateful actions…. He made sure to state, as he signed the citizen's complaint, that this was no ordinary evil, that the folk involved were of very high degree. Let the whole city know that vice occurs at the heights as well as in the arcades and the slums. Let everyone know that the proud de Metz family harbors a sodomite as its heir—

—as the day's clouds drift at last from steel to silver to a ghostly ivory, revealing behind a sun as worn and wan descending on Chatiens, as the long velvet drapes are drawn, as sad Charlotte dabbles at her dressing table, as at his desk, eyes hooded, face the color of dried clay, Isidore waits for the sound of the carriage wheels, and sets aside his pen. Beside the stack of letters to be posted and his own gray journal lie several crumpled sheets: Benjamin's handiwork, to be dealt with this very night, though far sooner would have served far better for them all.

As it is, matters have been swiftly arranged between Louis Guyon and himself, the formal engagement is ready to be announced. In some ways, that Twelfth Night disruption proved quite fortuitous, the earlier connection not as sound as one would have hoped—note Chamsaur's endless, womanish wails at its dissolution—but one cannot continue to propose marriage contracts that come to no fruition, one will be seen as insincere at best.

And it is time—for many reasons, some of them owing to simple propriety and custom; others, more complex, known to Boris in the Urals, to the councilors in St. Petersburg, to Guyon and Arrowsmith here in the city, all of whom share his own hopes for the future, and his recent conclusions on Hector Georges; and one reason glimpsed only in the dark house of his flesh, where pain claims more space, more boldly, than ever before—for all of these reasons it is time and more than time for Benjamin to become the next master of the family, take up the mantle he was born for, and marry, scotching once and for all whatever filthy rumors may already have begun to fester.

If that incompetent Entwhistle had done the task that he was set, instead of pursuing his own agenda—if traitorous Isobel had not winked at her brother's escalating folly, allowing such proximity—daily proximity! *Drink me like whiskey,* Maître, *cover me like the garden in snow....* It is infamous. He takes his son's writings, he folds them in half, in quarters, each motion painful and precise, as one pounds nails into a coffin lid. They have planted a pretty garden, yes, one he must now thoroughly uproot. This time there will be no leniency and no delay: Isobel will be punished like the unfaithful servant she is, and Benjamin will do exactly as he is told—

—as outside the tired horses shudder and blow, the muddy carriage rolls to a final stop before the chateau doors. Helmut tucks away his accounts, and unbends his travel-stiffened legs, to disembark and shepherd Benjamin—the prodigal son, drunk on whiskey and heartbreak—past the ancient archway, into his father's house—

—as miles away, beneath a black and ragged sky, Istvan wakes, yawns, rises from an afternoon's thin sleep to piss and contemplate the evening's toil. On a pair of flat-bound boards beside the monkish bed, amidst a small scatter of tools, Feste reclines in his purple weeds, while beside him a new courier has taken shape, a puppet's puppet, a dark little *diable en boîte* with long carven fingers and a little red keyhole for a heart. He has no name, yet, and no function, but the urge to make him was very strong, the work itself a fine companion on these long and aimless nights, the nights that whisper that pain is the only constant, and winter will never end.

When the quiet knock comes, Istvan wraps himself in the coverlet, yawning still, as Boilfast pauses on the threshold, to give him news of a dollhouse girl who watched a man arrested, that in itself is no news but "The man was Rupert Bok," says Boilfast. "The girl is certain, she says they called him by name. She knows nothing else, what charge, nothing, she only saw him taken. Now, Monsieur, before you act, consider your own situation, consider—"

"*Merci*," with a smile so feral, so utterly remote, that Boilfast shakes his head, saves his breath, and withdraws as quietly as he came. Istvan—calm with rage, a player released—pulls on clothes, packs a kit with a pair of puppets, several tools, and the planing knife, slides the signet ring onto his finger—too large for his left hand, he must wear it on the right—and slips out into the midnight streets like a fox into the alley, an urchin to the gutter, a man on urgent business who hails the first cab passing and pays the driver triple for double speed, all the way to the fine avenues of oak and linden, to a silent house where the butler conveys him at once to Madame, awake in the tiny chapel, startled and then so grateful to see "M. Dieudonne? Oh Monsieur, you have heard, you know—"

"I know," as the butler, politely refused the kit case, bows to the unlikely visitor, bows to Madame, and seats himself, with a silent sigh, on an unpadded chair outside the chapel door. What angels fly in the darkness, what lost saints, pass unseen as the butler dozes, and the two friends murmur and confer. Downstairs, in the empty drawing room, the four figures in the painted landscape hold their eternal postures of desire, the hands of the zodiac clock continue their patient march through time. Outside, beyond the draped windows, gray clouds crowd through the night's last sky, giving way as if in ambush to an absurdly brilliant dawn.

Isobel

M. Sellars is a little man, he barely reaches to my chin, though his coat was very fine indeed for a police commissioner's; perhaps Hector provided it, it has that somewhat military cut. Hector—I heard his voice in everything M. Sellars did not say, his evasions, his extreme *politesse*. Perhaps to a police commissioner, a civil servant, Hector seems a Jove-like patron, a powerful man with powerful connections.

I am very sorry, Madame: he must have said it fifty times, there in the parlor with his hat on his knees. He was very sorry that he could not conduct me to see M. Bok; his current status—not a prisoner, he is not in the common jail, thank God, but "detained" in some custodial location—made such a visit impossible for a lady of my stature, indeed for any lady. He was very sorry to cause me or my family any distress, and yes, he would certainly be my servant in the matter of an advocate, an advocate would indeed be allowed to see M. Bok as soon as an arraignment was accomplished, if it was accomplished; but when that might be, he could not yet say, he was very sorry.

You must be overwhelmed by sorrow, I said. *There is an easy anodyne: let M. Bok return at once—today—to his friends.*

I am very sorry, Madame, but there is still the matter of the allegations—

Made by an unhappy servant, already dismissed; they have no merit. Unless you yourself mean to suggest that my brother as well should be detained—?

He actually blushed, then, M. Sellars, and looked away, into the eyes of M. Dieudonne, in whom he found no resting place. M. Dieudonne is as self-contained as always, but his gaze—there is something frightful there now; certainly M. Sellars was not its match. Perhaps M. Bok is his tether, his better angel…. The sole virtue in this nightmare is the fortitude of both M. Dieudonne and Miss Bell, each of whom are a comfort in differing ways. M. Dieudonne I have installed here, for the immediate moment, though he chafes—sweetly, but he chafes—at the imposition. Miss Bell, herself sorely distressed, is still stout in assuring me that M. Bok will be freed, that M. Dieudonne will find a way, that Benny will return—my dear, my broken-hearted boy, still missing, no

319

one knows where he is. First the terrible rift with M. Bok, then his flight from Chatiens, from our father—

—who himself has come into the city, though not to the town-house: ensconced instead at the Emperors' Club with Helmut, in one of the private suites where I was summoned, to sit in that half dark like a Gorgon's cave, and hear that Isidore had in no way moved against M. Bok, was as disturbed as I by what had happened, though for a much different reason: *The man no doubt belongs behind bars. It is the evil of the scandal, the damage to the name—*

It will break Benny's heart.

Oh, the look he gave me then; even Helmut turned away. *You are my daughter, I cannot alter that. But I have altered my will so that you shall inherit nothing beyond my name, itself an ornament you do not merit. And when this matter has been settled, Isobel, I shall sell your town house and you will come to Chatiens, you will live out your life as a servant in my house. As for my heir, my son—*grasping for the little cordial cup, his hand as twisted as his love, whatever passes for love in that dungeon of a soul.... He would or could not speak further; Helmut gave him water, then led me into the hallway, leaning close, reeking of those mints he chews: *The journey here was difficult, Madame. And this is a most trying time for your father, most trying—*

Where is my brother? What happened between them, to send him fleeing?

Your father has agents everywhere, they will find the young master. And that was all, he would say nothing else of Benny, instead returned like the dog he is to Isidore: *He must not be subject to more distress, Madame, truly. His health—*

Never fear, Helmut. My father will live forever, it says so in the Scriptures.

I left then, silent through the hall, the dining room—and how they stared, all of them, though pretending they did not; M. Chamsaur, M. Guerlain, there will be plenty of that in the days to come. I was nearly through the lobby when someone halted me, *Isobel* like a sigh at my ear; it was Javier.

He had a cab outside, he put me into it, as tenderly as if I were made of china, as if I might break; sometimes, yes, one would like to break, to give in and shatter from the weight; but that is a luxury for kinder days. Instead we drove to and fro on the promenade, past the tinkers and the chocolate vendors, while he gave me still more ill news: Mr. Entwhistle had at last been located, but would be unable to recant his accusations, as *He was crushed by a train in Valrohns,* said Javier.

*A simple accident, it seems, they found his grip bag on the tracks....
It is a pity.*

*Oh, a pity indeed. Perhaps Hector will pay for the funeral?
Though I suppose it's my father's debt—he never expected a servant
to act on his own initiative.*

*Prompted by the spirit, yes. One wonders what spirit. When we
spoke at the club, he seemed useful still, if somewhat excitable. But
the task now is to move the counter correctly, and obtain the correct result for—Isobel?* Ah, Isobel, for indeed I was weeping: for Benny
gone into hiding or worse, no word from him for a full week now, no
sign. And M. Bok in some foul "custody"—released he will be, there
is no doubt of that, but angry, and abused by his connection to our
house…. For the moment it was more than I could master. I hid my
face, I felt the tears seep cold into my gloves.

Then Javier took my hand, my good hand, and pressed it in both
his own: he has never touched me so before, even when I was young.
Take heart, he said, looking into my eyes, and in that moment I saw
him as perhaps young Liserl had: a man of both gravity and gaiety,
whose own heart might contain a multitude of tenderness, alongside
a certitude of force. *Your cavaliers—I speak, of course, of Dusan and
myself—are planning an entertainment. Quite diverting, on several
counts! And you may invite some others if you please.*

Shall we have Hector?

Most assuredly.

And I remembered what M. Dieudonne had told me: *It is not the
strings that really signify, Madame. It is the motion.* Perhaps this
motion will draw us back together, Benny and me, and if Javier will
look to my father, and M. Dieudonne safely see to the strings… I felt,
then—I cannot say what I felt, it was a singular sensation: as if I had
swallowed an elixir, or some very strange champagne, to make me put
back my head against the cab seat, and quote, in a voice I did not
know I had: *"What would it pleasure me, to have my throat cut/ With
diamonds? Or to be shot to death, with pearls?"* That is from The
Duchess of Malfi…. *Tell me what is in your mind.*

*Perhaps you, too, are a player at heart, my dear! Dusan will
have to put you on the stage.* He knocked on the window, to make the
driver turn the horses. *It is time for you to have another dinner party.
Dusan suggests it be a beggars' ball.*

It is a mask such as the street children sell, a rough-paper boar's head with tusks of chicken bone, the ears crooked and peaked like a cat's, the whole tied on with a gaudy ribbon: "I tried to dress in a tradesman's disguise," says Pinky, out of breath, "but I hadn't the proper coat. Or hat. What do tradesmen wear? Miss Bell, you simply must stop laughing."

Lucy tugs the door closed behind him as he pulls off the silly mask, to show a smile beneath for both Lucy and Pimm, there in the musty Blackbird; the pantry ceiling has sprung an unknown leak, one can smell the seeping water but not trace its source. Pimm salutes him with the thick-clawed hammer—"Pleased to see you, sir"—then returns to his handyman's duties, up the ladder that Pinky helps to steady, steadied himself by Lucy's smile in return: "We've missed you," Pinky nearly as scarce these days as lost Benjamin since "I daren't be seen here— the old stick is still livid, M. Georges has been to see him, you know.... Any word?" She shakes her head. He bites a knuckle, Benjamin's gesture, then passes up to Pimm a greasy little coil of wire.

It is the talk of the city, this scandal, though the spoon, as they say, is not quite long enough to stir the stew, what news there is is sadly incomplete: Is young de Metz really exiled by his father, or run off on his own, or merely on some disgraceful binge with a new lover? as the former one, that dark fellow, has been detained, some say for the usual reasons where Benjamin de Metz is concerned—the old tales of the German and the riding master bruited once more for spice—while others insist the familiarity is not so much with the young master but the mistress of the house, and perhaps the account books, as well; with a man from the streets, of such indeterminate provenance, what perfidy could surprise?

Old de Metz is in the city, but staying at his club, bespeaking some larger friction with Isobel de Metz—whom no one has dared to ask directly, not even Fernande; though Isobel's demeanor is not one of dejection, or even defiance, but instead a glacial assurance, so perhaps there are other factors in play. Certainly the Guyon family has chosen to brazen it out, Christobel Guyon seeming not at all dismayed to be on the cusp of marriage to a man gone missing or fully beyond the pale. Instead she openly takes the air with Mme. de Metz, the two of them seen together shopping on Dressmakers' Row, being fitted for similar new gowns (narrow skirts, sleek tobacco-brown silk and green garniture, like the palest, frailest tendrils of spring on the earth: very *nouveau*).

And—if the latest rumor is to be credited—another man has now taken up residence at the townhouse, though his presence is too intermittent for absolute fact. But he has been glimpsed there, surely, a smiling shadow in a top hat, the puppeteer from the Twelfth Night affair, if you please! Whether old de Metz resents, deplores, or even knows of this new outrage to propriety, he has done nothing to prohibit it; perhaps that is due to his failing health? And now Isobel mounts a party, a masquerade, a "beggars' ball"—to show off her newest acquisition? To announce her brother's departure? or his engagement? or some madness of her own? So the tongues wag on.

There is other talk—more private, and taking a much cooler view—of de Metz *père et fils*. It has become an article of faith in many quarters that Isidore is not well, though how long he can function, and in what capacity, remains a subject for intense debate, the young heir still too much an unknown quantity to factor, especially now. What is not debatable is the drift between de Metz and Hector Georges, who has fashioned himself into another sort of paterfamilias, assembling a civilian cadre of those who find the usual routes of change and fortune too slow to travel, and seek, in the modern way, to bring speed to the process. Chamsaur is his ally here, it seems; and Guyon an adversary. Others, in other cities, take sides, or take note, all noting that a lynchpin indicator, the calm and solitary Arrowsmith, seems to be remaining neutral in this contest, holding to his stated posture of retirement. One evening he dines with old de Metz at the club, the next with the daughter and the Guyon girl, at the Guyon home, then with Georges and Chamsaur and Guerlain, who is allied by blood to the Guyons, but through the bank a closer friend to Georges, and what greater friend can there ever be than lucre, itself always independent of the fray?

And if, after these dinners, Arrowsmith climbs into a cheap barouche, to sit in a club where young ladies perform in damp gauze and feathers, and let the gentlemen buy them drinks, one may take that for a mark of an aging man's foolishness, or loneliness, the little mistress still unreplaced in his affections if not his bed. If there are meeting rooms as well in these kinds of clubs, very few of his peers have ever seen them; though Jürgen Vidor was one who knew, and Hector Georges another, habitué of the Poppy as he had been. Matters were somewhat more straightforward in those days: there was a war on, of course, with all the clarity that open bloodshed brings, and many unusual alliances were temporarily formed.

Still a man like Mr. Boilfast, say, is equally at home in situations of war and peace, or ambiguous combinations of the two: as is Mr. Arrowsmith. As is M. Dieudonne, Istvan privy to their backroom conversations, night or day, stropping the planing knife on a length of leather, drinking whiskey from a china cup—

"—while he sits in a fucking box, doing what? Improving his French? It may not seem a proper jail to you, but to Rupert—"

"Everything that can be done has been done," says Mr. Arrowsmith: because for this moment it is true. Though Commissioner Sellars has proven surprisingly intractable—he has bet his all upon one horse, never the wisest plan—still he shared readily the address where M. Bok was being held: a dull brick building in one of the duller *rues*, backed by a tannery and a disused ironmonger's, an outpost where the municipal overlaps the military; Georges' new territory, in short. There are several other guests in that building, none of whom are known to each other, none of whom signify in the current situation other than M. Bok. But for every guest there are three guards, and every window is grated in iron—

—like the little iron safe, now safely removed to a new location, where both Boilfast and a fellow of his acquaintance, a sad lean man with delicate fingers, examined it for possible entry, coming at last to the sadder conclusion that *A cheap box like this, you can't fire her,* said the sad lean man. *Any good screwsman'll tell you, the cheaper the box, the faster it burns.*

And the items inside? asked Mr. Arrowsmith, to which the sad lean man did not even bother to reply, beyond *Getcher a locksmith, sir,* as he shared with Boilfast a look of professional pity; though that had already been tried, several local fellows protesting that the mechanism was as old as Methuselah, and *Made elsewhere,* said the last of them, perhaps justifying his failure. *Mebbe in China or somesuch?* to bring, when consulted, Istvan's distant shrug—"We found it at the Poppy, we used it at the Poppy"—more distant still when Mr. Arrowsmith references the original keys: "M. Bok has one, I understand, but we ought not draw attention to that fact by trying to retrieve it. The disposition of the other," eyebrows faintly raised. "Was that entirely wise, Dusan?"

"It was at the time." More whiskey, into the cup. "How does Puck stay so well-hidden, do you think?"

"Perhaps he has gone farther than Paris," says Mr. Arrowsmith, a fear he will not voice to Isobel, though he knows it gnaws her heart with every hour that passes: the boy could very well have drunk himself into a broken neck, a robbery, a tumble through the darkness into some sewer or creek, one can drown in a bowl of soup with proper assistance.... He was last seen by the majordomo Helmut, who gave his tale with Isidore there beside him, that man in pain so great it is painful to behold: *The young master became very quarrelsome—he was intoxicated—and went to the stables to sleep, he said. I left a lad to watch him, but within the hour he had gone*—which will complicate matters unpleasantly, if Isidore should die before the young man is located: for Guyon and many others; for Mr. Arrowsmith himself. And if Benjamin is dead—

Now to Dusan he emphasizes that "Many people are looking for our young friend, and he will be found; there is no doubt of that. So be easy, and concentrate on your part—"

"I know my part," softly, seemingly only to himself, though both Mr. Arrowsmith and Boilfast share a look, Mr. Arrowsmith gently rapping his cane, the griffin-headed cane, to draw Istvan's full attention: "The players take the stage when the stage is ready, you of all people should know that. Especially a performance of such delicacy," to elicit Istvan's nod, his shrug of apparent assent that neither can fully believe. Boilfast politely withdraws so Mr. Arrowsmith may speak to Dusan alone, and try to impress upon him the scope of the business in which they are together engaged: "You see only the hem of the skirt, here, there is a deal of struggle in play—"

"I'll not ask your aims, only do you know them yourself?"

"Peace and plenty. As always." Istvan says nothing. "For today, I have a colleague in the Urals who keeps me current, and another in Cologne—"

—though Istvan himself flies closer to home, a triangular path between the arcades, the town house, and the Blackbird, an open path, his pursuers having been recalled since Rupert was taken. It was at the Blackbird, in fact, where Otilie—in a rather alarming bonnet, red plaid bows and painted silk—shared the name of a young lady whose sister is a kitchen maid at a kind of private gaol, hard by a tannery, whose goodwill she, Otilie, was prepared to access *For a friend,* with a sultry gaze at Istvan. *Or are you still "off kissing just now," sir?*

With a bawdy wink straight from her days in the Blue Room, Lucy made her exit, and what passed between the two no one can reliably say, though Istvan reflected, while refastening his trousers, that it was a singular way to break his fast, and one he will not repeat.... Only for Mouse.

Otilie proved as good as her word and prompt with the proffered introductions: see Istvan in coat and grocer's apron, riding a delivery cart piled with leeks and onions, beside a delivery man who, for a bit of money in his own pocket, allowed him to stand in the alley beside that cart, while he himself delivered to the kitchen maid he is fucking a little blue muslin bag, no wider than two fingers, inside which lay a ring wrapped in newspaper, a signet ring that she—for her own bit of coin, and a promise of the delivery man's undying love—dropped into the lap of a man sitting in silence by a grated window, a man who felt the ring as if it were another's touch, felt it like a charge through his body, felt it so intensely that for a moment he could not react, could only stare out the window to the street, where a figure stood waiting beside a cart, a figure who kissed his fist to the man at the window; his pure stillness, watching, was almost frightening to see.

This quiet-type gent knows how to talk to a girl like the kitchen maid; nothing but polite in the days he has been there, unlike lots of other gents, who swear or threaten or think that because she serves their grub and empties their slops, she is theirs to diddle or let loose upon, oh yes, these toff-type gents are less a gent than her own Henry, or the fellow who carts the wine for the constables downstairs. And this one is handsome, too, though he wanted a bit of a shave and more than a bit of a wash, blood, still, on his shirt, in his hair; and a darkness in his eyes that had little to do with missing sleep, though he does not sleep much at all. And suffering awfully for a smoke, he told her! though it is not permitted her to bring him or any other of them any such thing, and he ought not smoke anyway, it is a filthy habit for a gent to have.

But she saw how happy the ring had made him, this nice gent, and delivering the ring made her lover happy, which made her happy, so to continue the happiness she accepted back from him the little blue bag and its new freight, two black metal keys, that she then delivered to her lover, who handed it off to the man at the cart, who offered in return a bow so perfect, and so perfectly sincere, that for that one moment the kitchen maid knew exactly how a princess feels, with her Henry beside her transformed into a prince.

So when, in the dusty backroom, Istvan reaches at last into his breast pocket, and draws forth the double keys, it looks so much like pure prestidigitation that even Mr. Arrowsmith has to laugh: "Your mind is a *wunderkammer*, Dusan! But your timing—I wouldn't think we'd want more drama.... This second key, you did not have it from young de Metz?"

Istvan shakes his head. It does not matter, now, where poor Puck has gotten to; unless it matters to Rupert, which it will; Mouse is that way. "'Cast your bread upon the waters...' I don't question fortune, when she bends for me."

Now the key is inserted, the antique tumblers turn, the safe is open, and the letter—in a hand undeniably Vidor's, see the heavy ink, the oddly slanted T's—is read at last. Mr. Arrowsmith is visibly pleased: "For a confession, it is a bit oblique, but the thing is well made, and can be put to many uses. You may safely—very safely—leave this weapon in my hands."

Istvan's smile is very gentle. "Do you know the story of Hansel and Gretel? They dropped crumbs in the forest, to find the way back out again, but mice came and ate up all the crumbs. Better they had used a compass, yeah?" As gently he takes the letter back. "This is our way out of the forest, Rupert's and mine."

"You do not trust me?"

Still smiling: "No."

"Quite right," says Mr. Arrowsmith, with a smile of his own. "You are a natural diplomat, Dusan. Though we are colleagues in this matter nonetheless, and I am still your patron on the stage." He refills Istvan's china cup, he pours a drop for himself, though normally whiskey is not his drink. "But greater care must be taken with this—instrument, surely we agree on that?"

Istvan nods: "Here's a lockbox," producing the dark little puppet with the keyhole heart, its body engineered, with the help of Pimm's carpentry, to fasten without keys, a cunning trick of counterweights. The letter, rolled into a tube, fits neatly into the puppet's body, while the black metal keys are strung on two different chains, one of them Mr. Arrowsmith's watch-chain, as an empty sheet is substituted for the letter in the safe.

The two men toast each other, then, as Boilfast rejoins them, Boilfast who takes no whiskey—"I grew up nipping gin"—but shares in the quiet celebration, as well as the news of the beggars' ball: "With all in costume," says Mr. Arrowsmith. "Even I, though I've no experience at masking." Istvan laughs softly. "Perhaps you will be kind enough to assist me there, Mr. Boilfast?"

"I'll send a girl later to rig you up, sir."

Istvan empties his cup, offers again the ennobling bow—"At the ball, then"—and departs into the day: watery sunlight, the smell of boiling cabbage and a passing herring cart, two shopkeepers arguing in a storefront with a third, one waves a wooden paddle like a chevalier's lance: "Do you think I live on air, messire? Cheese costs me what it costs you!" Istvan tugs down his hat and travels swiftly uptown, to the Blackbird, knowing that Mr. Arrowsmith will have a man or two on watchman's duty for him, now; so much the better. And better he be seen roosting at the town house, not in this suite he much prefers: as he gathers his own costume and a tool or two, considering, for a silent moment, Rupert's desk, and pen, and sober cravats, his own cape still hung on the coat tree, though the little white knife, he notes, has gone missing. Well, no matter, it will be recovered—

—as he assures Lucy and Pimm, down in the musty pantry crowded with living ghosts, Pinky just gone "in his mad disguise," says Lucy, with the last wisp of a smile. "He might as well be sporting a sandwich-board. Or going to your party.... We miss him sorely. And with our Jack show ready to play—" The scenery has been painted, along with the potato crate, gay diamonds of ochre and gold, its long crank handle stirred with barely a push: more of Pimm's skillful handiwork. The children's costumes are made, as is Pinky's, that must be worn instead by Pimm, her master of ceremonies, now, though the role does not entirely suit him, as the costume does not entirely fit; both will have to be altered. And she has engaged a boy from the *école*, the music school, to play with Didier in place of Benjamin, Benjamin still missing, Pinky so distressed. "He's been barred from us, you know, by his father—the General stirred him up, he says. Poor boy."

"Don't ever fret for the fucking quality, Puss. Especially the quality at play.... Have you any apples, there?" poking through a sack of winter fruit, as Lucy produces a granite-hard pear, and Pimm packs away his sack of nails, his hammer and chisel, every tool its proper place.... It is a pity one cannot sell tickets to a hanging, especially when the man hangs himself, but there will be an audience all the same: Madame, of course, and Mr. Arrowsmith; and the spoofing toffs for camouflage, a beggars' ball, indeed. Feste may join him onstage, beside this newest colleague, primed up now for business, what is his name? No matter, it will come. Puss he may not have, alas, but Pinky should be on the premises, and may be even Puck will surface, who can say? since the Fates, themselves so vagabond, have been known to favor the lost. And Mouse... In his mind's eye he sees a figure at a window grate, silent and contained; in one guillotine swipe he chops the frozen pear in two.

Rupert rubs his forehead, where the headache throbs; he turns the ring on his finger, watching the gold catch the light. It is afternoon, one can tell by the sun and the noises in the hallway; soon the day's guard will give way to the evening's, their chaff and bluster—"I broke the gaffer's face for him, that's what I did!"—rising and falling like boys' in a schoolyard; some of them are hardly more than boys, several with their faces broken by Rupert himself, one fellow's teeth left a gash in his hand before they scattered on the courtyard bricks. They never expected him to be able to fight, nor, when the fighting was finished, to be so still, just as they expected no weapons, then too many, but never just the pair of knives.

They took those, of course, as they took his traveling case and his billfold, though they left his spectacles and keys alone, noting, as he mopped the blood from his face, that those keys would do no good on the doors around him: one for this room, another and stouter for the hallway, and a third, with bolts as well as locks, leading to the courtyard and the street. They left him alone, then, too, to take the measure of his hurts, and discover for himself that, beyond the pallet for sitting and sleeping and the pot for pissing, there was nothing in the room to make a weapon of, and nothing to do but sit by the window and wait.

At first he had thought himself snatched for a ransom, something to do with Benjamin or Madame, though they called themselves constables who took him, and wore uniforms with little round pins; and struck harder than any footpad would have, harder than they needed, perhaps they thought he truly was a toff. It was not until the third morning, when the General came, that he began to understand his captivity, though the General spoke less in riddles than in jokes, as if they were old friends bound together in some silly mishap soon to be rectified: *I try to stay out of churches, that's where the rascals congregate. Like the bishop and the chambermaid, isn't it? Or your friend Entwhistle.... With what did they charge you?*

No one has charged me, carefully, using his swollen mouth as an excuse to take his time in answering. *They took me from the street and put me here.*

And no one has mentioned, say, venery? Gross indecency? Winkingly, one man of the world to another. *No one has mentioned Benjamin de Metz? Where is Benjamin, by the way?*

He felt the blood, then, beating in the raw spots; thought first of Istvan, then of Benjamin, Benjamin in tears on the bed. More carefully still: *How can I know that? Ask Madame de Metz.*

Madame de Metz is distracted just now—and soon to be in mourning for her father, he is not long for this world. Perhaps he ought to consult that Entwhistle before he goes, eh?... No, Isobel's no idea where the little rabbit's got to. Your little rabbit, Mr. Bok, your petit-maitre, for whose pleasure you suffer in this box, making it plain, then, what any charges would entail, making plain what those charges would cost: *Not you, there's nothing in you for such scandal to feed on, you're only the instrument. It will hurt your lover—may I speak frankly? Your young lover stands to be destroyed by these charges, his future prospects ruined, perhaps even stuck in gaol himself: a fine return for the family's hospitality! You should have kept to bum-boys in the brothels, Mr. Bok. Or men like Jürgen Vidor, whom you could cut when you were done.*

Then he understood yet more precisely why he was there, and sucked his cheeks to bring the pain, to keep his attention from the keys in his pocket, to keep himself from stupid rage: a long and truthful wince before he answered, most carefully of all: *What happened to Jürgen Vidor happened with your full knowledge, sir. And Mr. Arrowsmith's.*

It was my money you spent, not Javier's.

Money? I took nothing from you—

More fool you, then: your whoremistress had it from my man.... I understand you have a letter that belongs to me.

The General has a singular gaze, Rupert has marked it before but never so fully as in that moment: not penetrating, or fierce, but instead so flat it is like looking into sea glare on the water, no depth on view, only an endless surface. He has seen drowned men's eyes own that same opacity. It is not alarming, rather the opposite, as if seeing what the General will look like when he is dead.

If I had such a thing, would I be here?

You are here because one man is a fool, and another a greater. But you yourself can escape this foolishness anytime you like, and save both your boy and his sister from much grief and shame. Perhaps even your colleague, too, though I confess I find it harder to forgive Hanzel's didoes.... Come, Mr. Bok, you are a man of commerce, of business. What business have you in a pisshole like this, where men I would not allow to lead my horse can batter you whenever they please? Can you see from your left eye at all, by the way? Rupert did not answer. *You might reflect as well that murder is a crime. Especially the murder of a man like Vidor.*

He spoke with care, then, so the words would not slur, so he would be precisely understood: *I never was your servant, sir. Nor—Hanzel, either.*

When the General's face changed, and the door opened, he tensed for the beating, the two young soldiers, constables, with truncheons on their belts—but then the old man entered, Benjamin's father, and truly he did look half-dead, more than half, in his China silk and caped overcoat, as if already bundled for the cold of the grave. His advent was a shock to the General, Rupert could see that, bad eye or no, though he said very little, the old man, and what he asked was like a puzzle, or a poem: Did he, Rupert, know the roads to Brussels well? Did he have many friends in Paris? Finally the old man made a motion, and the two soldiers stepped outside, the General too, though with great reluctance. Broken as the old man is, he did not fear Rupert, who with one hand could have broken him for good, did not fear to lean in close on the pallet and murmur, on a breath like a tomb's, *Where is my son?*

For a moment Rupert felt the laugh in his throat, a wild black bubble: where is the letter, where is my son, for a man in jail he is much consulted! But he sucked his cheeks, he shook his head, he waited for what else might come, as the silence stretched between them, the old man's gaze as if from a mountaintop, staring down at a crawling ant. Finally *You killed him,* the old man said, in that tombstone murmur. *Jürgen Vidor. Is that not true?*

I cut him. He killed himself.

Ah, and the old man even smiled, as if parsing out the nicety of such a statement. Then he made as if to rise from the narrow pallet, as Rupert sat and watched him struggling, like a scorpion on its back, until with one strong hand he brought the old man to his feet. Face-to-face for that one moment, past the veil of rot Rupert saw the echo of Benjamin: there in the high pale forehead, the deep sockets of the eyes; blue eyes, the same shade as Mme. de Metz'.

Then the guards were back, the General was back, they surrounded the old man like an honor guard and then all were gone, and he was alone; and stayed alone, except for the daily visits from the kitchen maid. Until this ring, and Istvan in the alley. And nothing since.

Again he looks beyond the grating, into the indifferent sun, into this district he does not know or recognize, no landmarks, nothing but a landscape of dark tile roofs, the kind he used to climb when he was a lad; he could climb them still, but this grating is too stout—

—as something strikes the window, a ball of soot, soil, something to draw his eye: to a figure on the roof across, for a moment he thinks it is Istvan, and his heart hammers. But no, the figure is too thin, and ragged as a beggar-boy—

—as another clot strikes the window, and the figure waves, waves so fiercely he nearly falls, then rights himself and stands waiting, hand to his mouth—

—because it is, yes, Benjamin: and Rupert puts his own hand, palm up, against the glass, Jesu what game is this, now? as Benjamin sees that he is seen, and waves more fiercely still. *Where is my son?*— this time he does laugh, a short dry cough like a chained dog's bark, as Benjamin makes some gesture he cannot understand, waves once more and then is gone, shinning down a pipe as swift and reckless as the boy he is, still is, and where has he been that his father seeks him so?

Rupert takes a hard breath, he takes his hand from the glass, he stares out the window; he waits. The guards laugh and grumble; the kitchen maid brings the day's bread, takes away the slops. The sun wavers, and begins to fall. The roof is empty. Rupert waits.

The carriage wheels make a comforting sound; strange to travel in a carriage again, after walking for so many days, like a vagrant, like the poets whose work he has loved into memory: chanting lines to himself while he wobbled, half-drunk, half-frozen, past horses in the fields, the muddy lanes, the crumbling brickwork, trickling smoke in grubby inns—*To see the world in a swallow of wine/To see God's face in the barkeep's scowl/To see while blind*—as he has tried to blind himself, those long days and nights; the nights were the worst of it, filled with memories of the bed, the warmth of the bed, the warmth of his master beside him.... He had never imagined there could be so much pain.

And it has changed him, the pain, he saw that at once in Helmut's eyes: his flurried welcome, rushing for barber's tools, for maids and water, for clothing suitable to a meeting with the old man, who is *Much grieved, my lord,* said Helmut; Helmut has never called him so before, "my lord." He has vowed never to go back to Chatiens, ever, until the old man is dead, but as it happens the old man is here, at the club, with the heavy port-wine drapes, and lost hours sifted up like dust in the corners.... The old man had seemed livelier back at Chatiens, if fairly gray around the gills: waving around the stolen poetry—that measly, filthy, hand-wringing tutor—and hissing of punishment and "disgrace," but in the next moment insisting that the marriage would take place directly, to Christobel Guyon, no need to delay beyond *Your own intransigence:* staring at him as he stared at the painting on the easel, the pretty woman at the well, the creeping thing in the dark behind her—like the old man's hand, so repulsively cold and damp, creeping across the desk to fasten on his own.

You are the flower of the stock, you are my heir, Benjamin. And a man such as my grandfather was, born for command. Why do you seek to ruin all that I would give you?

Ruin? Did he laugh, then? He cannot remember, past the glaze of whiskey, the ache in his chest, the empty place where the key had hung, the key stripped from him by Rupert—about whom he tried to speak, through the whiskey and the ache: Yes, very well, he will marry Christobel Guyon. But he will have, he must have passion, must find some way to be again with the one he loves—

—as that cold hand rose again, to strike him hard across the face, very hard, a blow that brought water to his eyes and *You will be the master of Chatiens,* the old man said, *you are de Metz. Never speak so again.*

Now, in the carriage, the de Metz carriage with the crest upon the doors, Benjamin puts his head back against the seat, he quotes aloud, "Is love a sea? Yes. Is love a sky? Yes." He is a monster, the old man. Belle has always said so, well, Belle is right. And a monster makes monsters. Perhaps he stinks of ruin, too, and that is why his *Maître* prefers M. Dieudonne.... He understands ruin, now, has learned it in these past few weeks, a lifetime in which he thought to wander forever, whyever go back? To what? Instead he had the road, and the bottle, he drank and he fucked and was beaten, once, by a pair of toughs, mad because they could not rob him, because he had nothing to steal. What perfect freedom.... They did not know he had already been robbed of everything, except a kind of silence inside, the silent, howling shadow of the pain.

And all was silence, too, when he stepped into the club, the eager hush of scandal, which the man from the Golden Calf had warned him to expect: *You're quite the talk these days, Monsieur,* with that dry little shrug, as if nothing known could surprise him. If the man had been surprised to see Benjamin appear at his back door, dirty and in rags, he kept that to himself, sharing instead, with a chunk of bread and cheese, the infamous tale of what had befallen M. Bok, *which business you might have a thought for, yes, Monsieur? Why not wait here, have a glass of something, while I call for M. Dieudonne?*

But he had no wish to see M. Dieudonne, who if he were a better lover might have taken better care, and prevented this outrageous kind of harm. Instead, when the man stepped out, he took himself to the tannery streets, to clamber up, up, up, yet found no way inside, no chimney-sweep trapdoor as sometimes one can see, no fire ladder or catwalk, nothing. At least, then, let his master know that he was there....

And once that was accomplished, the rest became easy: starting with the town house, the garden stairs to the hallway to the old chapel where Belle stood staring at an altar full of roses, white roses massed as if for a funeral, cigarette burning heedless in her hand: *For whom do you pray, Belle?* He had thought to make her smile, he can always make her smile; instead her knees collapsed, she nearly fell.

It was Belle who told him where the old man was, who spoke to Helmut while he was being shaved and dressed, who said to him in Helmut's hearing *Do as you think best, Benny, and it will be so.* So when he walked into the room at the club, the old man lying on a red-padded chaise, shirt undone, smelling of some disgusting poultice, he did exactly as he thought was best, with the quiet confidence of a man in a dream, a figure in a poem, it all might well be a poem, might it not? A short and tragic epic, by a poet who dies young.

And still the poem continues, each verse leading on to the last: as the carriage halts, now, in this dreary street, before this nondescript building, as he presents the document he carries to the policeman at the desk: waiting through the thrum and consternation, the nervous constable who calls another, more nervous constable, all of them murmuring over the document, the signature on the document, a signature that is itself a key: until the last series of murmurs, from an unhappy little man in a large and braided coat, like an actor badly costumed on the stage. At last the doors open, his master emerges, to be conducted into the carriage—

—where Benjamin instantly sheds his gloves, tears them off, to touch Rupert's damaged face, brush one finger beneath his eye—"This is bad"—trace the lines of his mouth, each in his own silence until "What happened, here?" Rupert asks him, very quietly. "They couldn't free me fast enough."

"I freed you," says Benjamin. His face is cold, bright-eyed, in agony. "I am the master, now.... I could give you straightaway back to them, you know. Or to my father. My father loathes you."

"Your father asked me where you were."

"No one could find me," with a proud little flash. "I did not mean to be found." Of all the things he says this night, this is what Rupert will remember, that lonely pride, the boy in the hideaway tree. "When I left Chatiens, I thought, Why not get drunk? There are many shitful little taverns in the countryside, every shitful little town has one. I believe

I drank at them all. Until I was jailed, for drunkenness. I paid my fine with my boots, isn't that a joke? And walked out of jail in my stockings.... We were both in jail, *Maître*. And I was in hell.... You left me."

"Yes."

Benjamin takes up Rupert's hands, to kiss them, slowly, caught between his own; on his right hand he wears a ring, a rose-gold intaglio ring, carven with a Greek warrior. "I have a berth on a ship to Greece, for both of us. I was to tell you, that day—That key. It was not my fault, *Maître*."

"No. I know that. But you should have told me."

"I know that.... You left me," again. "Will you not leave with me, now? We can go straightaway to the docks, or to Paris, any place you like. We can go anywhere—"

"Benjamin," in a whisper, no one has ever said his name so, half caress and half command. "Listen to me—" while the carriage wheels murmur, a patient susurration, as if repeating again and again the last lines of a poem—

—as the carriage turns down one street to the next and the next, approaching the town house with its tall white vases, dressed, tonight, with white roses, one might say profligate with roses, spilling their massed sweetness onto the cold stone steps. Inside the air smells of more roses, and candle wax, of the pottage pies and mutton bread cooling in the kitchens, and spicy punch, rum punch, served in tin cups as if direct from a street seller's cart. Receiving at the door, Christobel Guyon stands tall and slim as a linden, dressed in a serving maid's black woolens, a frilled yellow mobcap perched atop her braided hair. She smiles at Isobel beside her, who returns the smile with warmth: she has been nothing but strength, Christobel, and showed nothing but sense when told of Benny's reappearance, there in the old chapel as abruptly as an answered prayer: *We shall have many days to ask him questions, Madame, and hear all his answers. Ought we not let him come back to us in his own way?*

His own way, yes. She has seen nothing of Benny since he left earlier for the town house with Helmut, his gaze detached as a statue's, though he did tell her he would set things right with M. Bok; she did not ask how he knew of that trouble, she knew he would give no answer. As Javier has reassured her only of his own continuing toil.... But having Benny whole and safely home again—such a joy may yet bring another in its wake. Perhaps she will soon see M. Bok beneath this roof once more, drinking whiskey in the parlor, while Benny plays Chopin.

Both Christobel and her lady's-maid prevailed upon her to take a bite of food, a glass of wine, and it was well they did so: Isobel feels light-headed still, and unmoored, in her plain black gloves and wimple, threadbare velvet, like a mistress of misrule. M. Dieudonne is already here, in the east parlor's pantry with his players, whence he will emerge, he has assured her, with a spectacle merry enough *to bring a smile to Lazarus at the gates—though we'll spare the dogs licking at the sores, shall we? Such a dreary detail.* Fastidious in his own bright tatters, hair loose across his shoulders, hands wrapped nearly to the fingertips, he showed her the plague mask he will wear, its odd and plunging beak, and the severe little puppet who will *Make his debut this very night,* tugging a string unseen to make him bow for her, a dark changeling toy with a keyhole heart. *I call him Puck, Madame. Do you like him?*

She put one finger to the keyhole, then: what a perfect conceit, the heart as lockbox. *Puck, and Feste—you do honor your Shakespeare, don't you?*

Puck is older than Shakespeare, Madame. And his elder brother is Pan, with a private smile, a smile that showed his teeth, as he bowed her out of the backstage pantry that must, he instructed, be kept quite inviolate: she has put Otilie on that door, who seems glad enough to be there.

Through the chill of the hallway now comes the stream of guests, jolly in their unaccustomed rags. It is not to be a large group, only enough for "Chiaroscuro," in Javier's murmur, "a moving frieze." Swathed up like a mummer, he looks oddly festive; strange, how a mask so often reveals more than it hides. "And I see Helmut has come," which means her father has as well, removed from the club to lie in state, or nearly so, up in the room he had lately shared with Charlotte, herself uninvited to this evening's affair; poor Charlotte. Her last letter was as bewildered as a child calling out from inside a locked room: Benjamin had come and gone like a lightning bolt from Chatiens, and his father was very grieved, and so unwell already that to grieve him further seems a shame—but poor Benjamin seemed caught up in his own tumult, will no one tell her what passes in the family? Charlotte, the widow-to-be, surely even she has guessed that outcome. What a mercy there is no child…. Isobel presses Javier's hand while he passes from her side, Javier so grateful that Benny is safe, nearly as pleased as she herself. And if Helmut is here, does that mean Benny has come as well? As for Isidore, let him stay in splendid isolation; tomorrow, perhaps, she will send for the priest, though one would need to be at least a Pope to shrive that soul. Or perhaps he has repented on his own of his crimes against Benny, whatever wrong he did to send him headlong and away—

—as Christobel beside her continues to receive, a gracious nod, the smile of a chatelaine: to Denis de Mercy, the Guerlains, Letty van Symans—dressed exactly like a bourgeoisie, how destitute of fancy!—and M. Guyon, who salutes first his daughter's cheek, then Isobel's, as Fernande bobs up behind him, round as a turnip in her turnip-bag of a dress; in truth she makes an excellent fishwife. Her glittering gaze seizes at once on Christobel: "Can one be a widow before one is even a bride? Is that the meaning of your black gown, miss?"

Before Isobel can frame a response—this girl is under her protection, now—Christobel gives a tranquil little shrug: "One's a maid before either, Madame. Surely you know that? as you are one yourself." Isobel laughs—Fernande's crusty old maidenhead! As counterfeit a conceit as her gown—and squeezes Christobel's hand, that strong young hand with a grip as firm as her own.

In the quiet of the east parlor's adjunct room, a narrow little servant's pantry, Istvan waits, his shoulder aching from the cold. He glances once more to his new accomplice, Puck with his paper freight soon to give birth to commotion; and vengeance, his vengeance pick-a-back on those others and their complicated politics. His own is much simpler and more useful, and, in a strange twist, a gift from a man who hated him to a man who thought to be his patron still. Whoever writes the play of life has a sense of humor, that is sure.... Apparently the other Master Puck is once more about, according to Arrowsmith, who passed the news in a whisper, before noting that the General is present as well. So the stage is fully dressed.

Feste as well sports a fresh new suit, suitable for any clime; this show is one night only, but if the reviews are good, who can say where the troupe might travel? As for the others, still swaddled in their various trunks and hanging boxes—the sturdy Chevalier, so long unridden; the other Miss Lucinda; the Bishop; and Pan Loudermilk—Feste, in fact, wears Pan's black vest, and a buttonhole twist of his hair—they will be a gift to the bride and groom, to further feather the Blackbird's nest, as Miss Lucy Bell becomes Mistress Pimm, another kind of quick-change, love's transubstantiation.... Let Arrowsmith and the others play the show they mount; himself, he will pass through unencumbered, there is only one companion that he needs.

Past the door voices mingle, ardent guard Otilie's and a man's: Istvan puts his hand to his pocket and the planing knife, but it is only Pinky, dressed as an extravagant burglar, all black woolens and masked in red, and toting a bottle of brandy: "I once read, sir, of a musician, a violinist I think it was, who soaked his mitts in Spanish brandy before all recitals. He swore it kept him nimble."

"No doubt it did. Many thanks." Istvan pours for himself, drinks, raises the bottle Pinky's way: they share a toast. The brandy is French, and excellent, mellow as a long-banked fire. Istvan drinks again as a noise in the hallway, men's voices passing, makes Pinky jump. "Why, what spooks you so? Have you a bad conscience, young man?"

"No, I'm petrified of the old stick—he swears he'll send me off if he catches me near a stage again, though I miss Miss Bell like fury, and the Jack show's near to start. That box is a wonder, isn't it! Open and close with a fingertip, that's artistry.... He doesn't seem to care a whit what I want, my father, that is. Did you find your own father so, sir?"

"I never did find my father.... I am a bastard," when he sees that Pinky does not understand. Swallowing one last splash of brandy, it makes him warm; and he smiles, a calm and pleasant smile, letting the rôle take hold. "It's a shame Miss Bell's not with us tonight, but we shall do the best we may without her. Here," taking from his kit a concertina, chipped buttons and spavined bellows, a veteran of many shows at the Fin. "You'll play the overture?"

Pinky bows, and sets his robber's mask in place. "Your servant, sir."

Just past the door, Otilie hears them stir, and tugs her modest décolleté to best advantage: he gave her a tumble once, that handsome player, mayhap he might again. In the west bedchamber, Helmut stirs a brownish syrup into a glass of red wine, a tincture of laudanum and honey, and gives it to his master to drink, Isidore in spotless linen set upright and grimacing in a dark baronial chair. In the drawing room, amidst thickets of roses, stark white and meaty red, Mr. Arrowsmith and M. Guyon raise their tin cups, while Hector Georges makes a bow to Isobel, who returns him an icy nod, as Christobel Guyon gazes up at the Cupid in the portrait, the arrow and the tumbling curls, the naughty, haughty smile. Unseen by all, one last guest, cloaked and hurried, climbs the servants' stairs, to be bundled at once into Benjamin's rooms, where Benjamin himself pours the wash-water, and hunts for a shirt that might fit, while Rupert sits blinking in the gaslight, smoking a very necessary cheroot.

"*Mesdames et messieurs*," says the merry voice, top hat and plague mask, greeting the evening's house, chairs arranged in a semicircle, like good children promised a special treat. This is an intimate show, here in the east parlor, and much anticipated by its audience, all of whom enjoyed the Twelfth Night *succès de scandale*, and hope for another as memorable if not, perhaps, as grisly. Though not every guest is present, the room is full, with Isobel and Christobel up front in the places of honor, an empty chair set and waiting between them.

"All you joyful beggars, many greetings from myself and my associates," as Pinky, hidden behind a lacquered black screen that also hides the connecting pantry door, gamely squeezes a gasping tune—it could be "Chanson des mendiants," it could be of an on-the-spot devising, it could be Pinky is unsure how to properly work the buttons—from the tattered concertina. Both Feste and the little Puck make their bows, a complicated roundelay of hands extended but overshot, foreheads knocked, at one moment the beak of the plague mask becomes a barrier around which both puppets peep and batter; the audience laughs. "Gentlemen, please, you'll have each other's stuffing out.... Do you know the very moral tale of the fox and the grapes, *mesdames et messieurs*? You do? Why then, we shall play another," to bring another laugh that echoes through the hallway—

—though more faintly in the west bedchamber, with its hermetic air of illness, its fire burning high: the room is hot as midsummer, but Isidore's hand is very cold, yet steady as he directs his several guests to their places: M. Guyon masked in blue, the mummer Mr. Arrowsmith, Hector Georges in his costume of infantry jacket, with one chair kept empty to Isidore's right. M. Guyon begins by praising the joining of the two families, the engagement to be announced that very night, at which the General, domino tossed aside, makes a hawkish smile: "Oh, felicitations. But who will stand in for the groom?"

Isidore sips from his wineglass, the sediment black at the bottom. "What is your meaning?"

"Come, gentlemen, let's not waste each other's time. Will your daughter wed a man in disgrace, Guyon? Mired in scandal and perversion?"

M. Guyon does not reply, looks not to Isidore but to Mr. Arrowsmith, who says mildly, "You are rash, Hector."

"And you have betrayed me. I had a note this afternoon from M. Sellars—But you know what news it brought. I'll not even ask how you twisted the mayor's stones—"

"Not the mayor. The prefect."

"The prefect…. Well. Touché.—Isidore," turning in his chair to face him, turning the ring on his thumb, the old silver ring that dates from the Terror. "We have been allies for a very long time, you and I."

Again it is Mr. Arrowsmith who speaks, still mildly: "We have all been allied for many years, and gladly so. But lately you have cast your own net, have you not? And cast it very wide. You seek not to make kings, but to be crowned yourself."

"In St. Petersburg—" says M. Guyon, but the General speaks over him, still addressing Isidore: "Isobel may have paid off those tutors and stableboys, but this is something different, this Bok is a known and common criminal—a pimp, Isidore, to be plain. As Javier knows well, and as well a killer, he murdered Jürgen Vidor in cold blood. You ought be glad I had him taken as I did, to spare you from the task. Will you now let yourself be foxed this way? When there is so little time?"

Isidore's eyelids droop a fraction, like a lizard's on a rock; he says nothing. M. Guyon steeples his fingers. Mr. Arrowsmith thinks of the puppet show in the parlor, the letter in the little puppet's gut: if he were a man prone to fancies, he might think Jürgen Vidor present now, as he is so palpably in that letter, here in this very room where, no doubt, he once received instruction, once gave news of tasks attempted and accomplished, that odd, stained, secretive man…. Hear the merriment downstairs! Dusan, as always, must be playing his part superbly. It is a pity not to ease his mind at once regarding M. Bok, but good news can always wait its curtain call. And Dusan is unpredictable, even at the best of times, he might slit through the traces and bolt. Only let him keep the gait a little longer—

"—because the sweetest taste, *mesdames et messieurs*, is always just out of reach, as the poor fox found to his dismay—" while Pan and Puck grasp and bob in tandem for a bauble dangled by the giggling Letty van Symans, a fat pink pearl on a golden chain, not really what a beggar wears but the theatre is nothing if not elastic, a thing is what it says it is for as long as it holds the stage: as a puppet is a man is a lover is a world entire: as the pearl swings like a pendulum, as Istvan eggs her on: "That's it, my lady of the ashcans! Make them work for it, the rogues!"

"Use your earbobs, Letty!" someone cries, and "Oh!" squeaks the laughing Mme. Guerlain, as her own earbob is popped free, a cherry-colored stone, by the festive Feste, then flipped back to her by decorous little Puck: everyone laughs, then, even Isobel, whose gaze never strays far from the door.

Upstairs, another door opens, very slowly, like a flower in final bloom: the door to Benjamin's bedchamber, as Benjamin himself steps out into the hall. His face is as white as if he has been bled, his gaze stays fixed as he walks without haste to the west bedchamber, looking back not at all; it is Rupert who stands watching, silent in the aperture, until Benjamin has put his hand to that other door, and disappeared inside. If Rupert sighs, then, it is without sound, a painful inner breath marked only by himself. Then he pulls the cloak closer over the stained suit, the borrowed shirt—from one of the taller footmen, it sits too tight across the chest—and moves in swift purpose down the stairway, toward the happy noise of the audience below.

In the odorous heat and tension of the west bedchamber, the men turn as one as Benjamin de Metz, pale as his father, steps inside, to take the seat at his father's right hand. Seeing him, a tremor seems to pass through Isidore; he closes his eyes. The General turns back to Mr. Arrowsmith, still smiling, a raptor's contemptuous smile, as if there had been no interruption: "You say many things of me, Javier, all unworthy of a colleague. Can you prove even one?"

The room is quiet except for the sound of the fire. The General's smile does not waver. Finally "There is a letter," says Mr. Arrowsmith gently. "From Vidor. It was found after his death."

"You have this letter?" asks M. Guyon, as if on cue; it is on cue. Mr. Arrowsmith displays a little black key on his watch chain: "I have access to it, yes. And I have read it myself. In it Vidor speaks of certain—exigencies, of Rawsthorne and Pepper. And he names the author of his end—"

"Javier—"

"You, Hector."

The General's gaze flickers, and Mr. Arrowsmith knows he recalls a sitting room in Brussels, a conversation they shared—*some communiqué, some last poetic fillip*—as "I'd see that document," says the General, no longer smiling. "Before another word is said."

Isidore leans forward, one hand on his son's, his voice like a saw on stone. "You can dictate no terms here. You took my servant without my leave—"

"Your servant! Your own father," jerking his thumb, "he took me from the butcher's shop, to make of me a better butcher—"

"You took my servant, you yourself must replace him. Unless you choose to make your stand alone."

"You stand," says the General, very softly, with bottomless hate, "on the very lip of the grave. Is this where you choose to make war?"

The older men look one to another, a pause in common before response, but it is Benjamin who answers: his left hand still grasped by his father's, his right is bright with a ring, a signet ring, black and gold and "I am the head of the family now," he says, with a young man's scorn for the grave, for those subject to the grave, for the General there before him, and the ageless certainty of his own command; in that moment he is so powerfully his father's son that even Mr. Arrowsmith is still. "Make your war on me, Monsieur, or do as you are fucking bid."

From downstairs comes a little shriek of laughter, a pair of voices in tandem chanting a little tune: tonight it is called "The Lament of Reynard the Fox" but it is a barroom sally, very old, with very many titles—"Up-So-Down," "The Two Croakers," "Paddy's Lament"—that Pinky, sweating behind the lacquered screen, labors with pluck if not success to follow on the concertina. The squeaks and yips seem part of the merriment, although the master of the show winces inwardly at the wayward notes, as Puck and Feste mingle their verses—

"For what's worth most we'll puff and strain

—Huff and puff and gladly strain—

For the rarest grapes make the best champagne, an oyster barrel full!

And let it bubble to the top

—Keep a-bubbling, don't you stop!—

For fellows such as we need quite a pull!"

—pulling as well at the ladies in attendance, nips and grabs but nothing too ribald, a purely complimentary sauce: even the prim Christobel Guyon is laughing as little Puck untucks the top lace of her gown, irony's wink that she cannot appreciate, why should she? Only Mouse should guess that jape—

—as the music jerks, then smooths and finds its rhythm, the concertina chuffing in a jaunty style such as one hears in the arcades when played well, much too well in fact for thumb-fingered Pinky, Istvan's smile flickering as the puppets swing into a final verse—

"So let poor players have their fun

—A taste of jelly on the bun!—

For our days are short and then they're done—"

—as suddenly Istvan's smile blooms, an unguarded, boyish, joyous smile beneath the cloaking mask, past a stolen glance at the tall figure just behind the screen, much taller than Pinky, playing along as Istvan sings, now, with passionate energy—

"—As done as well are we!"

We thank you for your kind attention, and let us once more gladly mention

It was wise Aesop's true intention

That grapes be plucked, and sucked, for fancy-free!"

—as both puppets and their master bow nearly to the floor, with a wild grace and a spilled flourish of little seeds, or beads? No, they are grapes, hard wizened white grapes, sour enough for any fable, that scatter and roll across the floor like pearls from a broken necklace, to bring a final laugh as Istvan makes a final bow, then slips behind the screen, past the door concealed—

—to see, in the chilly pantry room, like a magician's trick, Rupert, setting the concertina aside. Bruised and unshaven, the cheap white shirt like an undertaker's shill, as Istvan pulls off the mask and reaches for him, for his face, less a name than a noise: "Mouse—You're wounded."

In answer Rupert puts one hand to Istvan's chest, palm against his beating heart, a profoundly intimate touch, and "Play out your show, messire," as soft as a breath. "What is my part?"

"Your part—your part's to get the fuck away, and me with you." Once more Istvan touches Rupert's face, as one touches a creature in a dream, to prove reality, until, like waking, he pulls himself away, to pack with swift efficiency the puppets and traps to the case, as Rupert checks the movement in the parlor and the hall—"We'll skirt out through the garden"—so "Exeunt," says Istvan, while Rupert plucks from a sideboard serving-case a silver knife, with a bounding stag worked into its handle. As they head down the narrow servants' passageway, low ceiling and smoking oil lamps, Istvan proffers the plague mask, still slightly damp from his own skin: "It's a costume ball, yeah? Put it on. The hat, too."

The guests, still chuckling in wonder from the playlet—however did the fellow make both puppets sing at once? And so dexterous, too, as many arms as branches on a tree!—have all followed Isobel in to supper, a modest one as befits a beggars' gathering: the mutton and the pottage pies, black bread, braised river trout, with a little jest set at each place, an amuse-bouche of golden grapes in sour black-currant sauce, noted by Fernande who says, "I thought you might serve fox tonight, Isobel," with rather more approval than not.

All at once, the pleasant post-show chatter falls into a hush, as Benjamin—unsmiling in black velvet, severe as a tarnished angel—enters the dining room. He is followed by Mr. Arrowsmith and M. Guyon, masked again, the latter murmuring as they find their places, "Will Georges make an attempt, do you suppose? He is still quite capable of harm."

"A patron of the higher explosives, Hector, yes. But I think he will not care to burn.—*Nunc dimittis*, eh?" watching as Benjamin takes a whiskey, takes his seat at the table's head. "He did quite well tonight, our young friend."

Mr. Arrowsmith's calm gaze seeks Isobel's, then, to hold it for a moment, to give a tiny nod that she returns. Raising her voice to carry like a player's, "We've wonderful news," she says, as two maids tug in a gilded trolley heavy with champagne, while the gossipy mutter rises to a high, excited buzz. Isobel takes Benjamin's right hand in her gloved and crippled clasp, as Christobel reaches for his left: the two women share a look, while Benjamin looks at neither, looks at nothing, his shoulders taut as a man's in battle, feeling again in his ravaged heart that last embrace, his *maître's* mouth rough against his own: *Go and be their master.* Go; yes. Nothing in the world he would not do…. Belle's gazes searches his, now, then softens as if she understands, how can she understand? She squeezes his hand.

The servants hustle back and forth between the dining room and the cellars—all that champagne to carry—so only Otilie sees as Rupert, with Istvan a step behind, pushes at the servants' door to the garden, Otilie who halts Istvan with a hand hooked to his arm—"So you're off then, sir? Give a girl a kiss goodbye?"—while Rupert, outside in the darkness, takes his first free breath: the air is cold, yet very sweet, even through the unaccustomed mask. Behind him on the path, framed by willow branches, the empty drawing room glows, the spirits of the house fly on above: *You are the first, the very first, Monsieur, to ever see that! Except for me.* The first, yes; would to God it had not hurt him so. Benjamin… He takes another breath, a deep one, he closes his eyes—

—as "Hanzel," a whisper at his back: the voice is the general's, as is the knife. "Your play's ended, then? I was waiting…. Be very still—I am not playing, now."

Rupert does not move. The knife blade lies colder than the air against his skin; its tip slides in, a red pain just below his jaw. He can hear his own dry breathing through the mask.

"That letter from the dear departed—" The General's arm is like iron, he smells of rum punch and rage. "All have seen it, but no one seems to have it. Do you have it, Hanzel? Or it is just a bluff?" as something rustles on the path, something small climbs through the detritus—rotten leaves, dead branches, potsherds and broken twigs—heaped waist-high for burning beside the greenhouse walls. "Either way, we will find it out together. Walk forward, now. Walk to the gate—"

Rupert takes two steps, four, careful steps, the knife urging him on. Beyond, past the artful curve of the path, a wee whistle echoes, antic and eerie; the knife hesitates; the whistle sounds again. Almost but not quite a child's, a child at dark play in the empty garden, and the General pauses, to peer anew at the man he holds, head to one side: "Hanzel—"

—as Istvan, come up from behind like a puppet through a stage trapdoor, shoves the planing knife to the very hilt between the General's ribs, while Rupert, bleeding from the throat, swivels in his loosened grasp, grasping the stag-worked knife as the General takes a breath of great surprise, does even he know whose blade splits him first? though it is certain that masked Rupert's is the last face he sees, Rupert gripping his shoulders as he sags, as Istvan's voice breathes in his ear, the culmination of a life's work, "*Hors de combat,* you old fuck."

The three, then two, stand close together, as if they confer without words, colleagues in a most confidential alliance. Once more Istvan makes the child's whistle, this time sounding from the head of the path, then a hard little laugh. Dinner music begins to drift from the house, a droll peasant's air, perhaps *Till Eulenspiegel,* as the General is dragged behind the greenhouse and left to contemplate eternity. Rupert pulls off the plague mask and assumes the dropped puppet case, while Istvan unbolts the gate that leads to the stables and the quiet landscape of the street beyond. A portly man, waiting alone past the line of the guests' carriages—is it César? in a military hat?—seems to mark as they pass, but does not pursue as they turn the corner, then another corner, finding in the rising fog an idle cab a street or two away—

—but the driver takes one look and shakes his head, shakes the reins to take himself briskly from harm's way: both men are splashed with blood. So "We'll walk," says Rupert, and they do: beneath the stately lindens to the humbler avenues, ashcans and turnip carts, an infant crying in a third-floor window, down to the arcades, where the night is in full swing, and men in a private hurry are not so much remarked upon, bloodied or no. A mazey little alleyway, the smell of fish cakes and pipe tobacco, a courtyard loud with revelers and a fat girl flaunting tit, a rusted iron staircase to a door that—"A moment"—Istvan unlocks with an even rustier key—

—and then they are inside, and safe, alone. The case is set onto the floor, and the other puppet players, in various stages of life—just-born or dismantled, heads and limbs, rags and straw and shiny glass-marble eyes—watch as Rupert secures the door, Istvan lights the lamp, then tugs a boiled-wool coverlet from an ancient horsehair divan, disturbing a brief skitter of rug-bugs, but they have slept in much worse, many times before.

"Now," says Istvan, frowning, "let's see your souvenir," but Rupert shakes his head: there is blood, yes, but most of it Georges', it is just a small wound after all. "What bothers me is this," tapping lightly beneath his left eye, the dark spoor of the blow. "It was the butt-end of a truncheon—I can't see much beyond shadows, now, except in brightest light."

"What else?" reaching to turn Rupert's face, to trace the last of the yellowed bruising, unfasten the borrowed shirt to find, and mark, each of the hurts, all of the pains inflicted since they parted, as Rupert— slowly, gravely—does the same, until they lie together, scarred and naked and whole. In the landscape of the players around them, actors of all known desires, they reenact their own, the cherished rhythms of passion, the sweet familiar skin: Istvan's fingers quick and tender, Rupert's lips upon the ropy, pinkish scars, that other bleak memento, the old harm made well at last. The lamp smolders and burns out, the courtyard quiets, the coverlet is wide enough to wrap them both, and so it does: like an old overcoat, a greatcoat, containing all the warmth there is or ever need be, against the lifelong onslaught of the cold.

Later, in the earliest pearl of dawn: "All this time...I was a monk, yeah?"

A sleepy murmur of deep content: "You're a liar."

"A monk in my heart, yeah? You, now—And how did you winkle yourself from that jail?" but it is full morning before that tale is told, in a few dry sentences—a visit, a letter, the open door—to make Istvan shake his head: "A trump to Arrowsmith, and all his clockwork plans. Mine, too."

"You," as Rupert feeds the stove, "you and your Twelfth Night frolic, you had me—foxed, at first. Cur fox," with a little smile, with infinite love.

Istvan shrugs. "I did as needed to be done.... So it was little Master Puck engineered that sleight-of-hand, did he? Hey bravo."

On one knee by the grate, Rupert pauses, and looks up. "Give him his name."

A shadow in his voice, upon his face; Istvan sees both. Gently: "Benjamin, then. He did well." Rupert says nothing, stands, and dusts his hands, black rime of coal and the gleam of rose-gold, the Greek warrior; Istvan sees that, too: "A bonny bauble. But where is your ring?"

"This is my ring."

"And this," reaching for him, "this, Mouse, is the world," drawing him back down upon the divan, back beneath the coverlet, until the grimy window shines with noon, the courtyard yawns and quickens, and Boilfast comes quietly with his own key, to share a pint of *vin ordinaire* and several black Indian cheroots, and a tale of a man found dead in a garden, and dumped at the docks, a much-respected military general, whose assailants, alas, had stolen entirely away.

Lucy

Our Jack was quite the day's sensation, even if I say it myself. Mickey looked brave in the jingling motley—you could hear the bells from the balcony, Pinky said—and he and Rosa played it out like troupers: never missed a cue, never lost a line, as fine as players twice their age or more. I told them so, how proud a sight it was, and Pimm gave them the little toys he'd made, each for each: a locket for Rosa, with a tiny carven rose inside, and a jack-in-the-box for Mickey, with a monkey-Jack who popped you in the nose if you cranked it up too close. Pimm was a fair master of revels—only I could tell he had the nerves—and he strutted about some afterward in the costume and cocked hat: *Why, I'll wear it for our wedding, hey? With a cabbage in my buttonhole, and Mickey for my man-at-arms!*

But when the day came, you never saw a sweeter sight than my Pimm, hair brushed clean and flat with quince-seed jelly, a toff's top hat beneath his arm, all spiffed and fine. And when he said "I will" the whole house heard him, I think they heard him in the street outside: for we did it here, of course, with Didier's uncle for our parson, who is a curé in his own village, and Rosa's mamma to dress the stage with flowers, she and I worked half the night to get the garlands hanging straight. It was Mme. de Metz who surprised me, with the servants and the champagne, 'twas Pinky told her when they cried the banns—and Pinky there too, of course, he was the one gave me away.... If only it had been Mr. Rupert. That was my single sadness, that neither of them saw, or were there, though it was Istvan who made me the best bride's-gift of anyone: *All of them?* I said. I cried then, like a child, I couldn't help it, there by the worktable and the scatter of the tools. *You're giving me all your puppets?*

And their accoutrements, too, showing me all the cunning little drawers in the trap-cases, the rods and mending-loops and costumes, the way to lock the trunks without the key, and *Who better to have them, Puss?* with a kiss on my cheek. *They'll have a proper home here, with you and your troupe—though I'd not star Pan and Mickey in the same show, not until the lad is older.* Smoothing the black cloth soft down across that carven face, tucking in the ends like a babe beneath a blanket—it was a sad sight to see, you could tell he was that grieved to let him go.

But when I urged *Take him, at least take Pan,* Istvan shook his head: *We must travel very light, now, Mouse and I. And very swiftly, too—not that I mind. I've had a bellyful of this place,* with the old faint lines of scorn and strain, looking around the rooms as if he saw there only that he had never meant to stay so long.

Then his gaze met mine, and we both smiled, though the tears still ran down my cheeks. "What's the use of tears, my dears?"—it is a song the children sing—and *I've something for you,* I told him then, *or rather, for Rupert. From Otilie,* as he made a face, *her friend the kitchen maid* who'd said she kept his things for him, there, at that gaol; most of them, anyroad. A case with its locks snapped, and some bank-papers inside, a rolled-up shirt, a billfold emptied out—a shame there, but no surprise—though I was that surprised to see the knife, that fine little knife with its ivory handle, you'd guess someone would have picked that up right away. Istvan did not seem surprised, though very pleased; he tucked the knife into his own pocket, and left the rest in the case. *I'll give it him directly—he'd add his thanks to mine, I know.*

How is Mr. Rupert?

Mr. Rupert is fine, though his eye wants doctoring. There's an oculist in London who is said to be the best; we will travel there first, I think.

And then where?

Everywhere. Who knows? with a careless shrug like first I saw him, so long, long ago, there at the Poppy when I thought—I have to laugh, remembering—I thought, Why, I'd like that saucy puppet-fellow, I'll have that fellow if I can. Showing my leg like a voudou dancer...! And wanting so much to know the things he knew, hear of the places he had gone: like a chick peep-peeping in the egg, watching a bird fly by above. A blackbird.

He had to leave sharpish, he said, they were for the road that very night, but after he had gathered what he needed there was time for us to share a glass, and I put on, for him, the goldfish brooch; I wore it at the wedding, too. We talked of the big and the small, of Pinky, Pimm, and Mickey—*I owe him a sport at the Calf,* said Istvan, *though I won't be playing there again. Here, give him this,* taking from one of the puppet cases a thing half a knife and half a kind of buttonhook, with a wicked little blade. *It will carve wood nicely. Just let him be mindful of the edge.*

That ceneral—I heard he took some carving.

Why, I heard that, too, and we had a little smile, because I was glad, and he was glad, and we drank to that passing without needing to say more. And I asked after Mme. de Metz, though he was chary there, saying little beyond *What's here*, knock-knocking on the lip of the puppet case, the good hard pine, *that's what's yours, yeah? Let the rest go diddle itself. Especially the quality.*

And what of Master Benjamin? Though he knew what, really, I was asking. *All's well, there?*

As well as ever will be…. Give a kiss, then, Puss, setting down his glass, picking up his hat: and I did, I did not cry, I kissed him with all my heart: for the puppets, and all the things he had taught me, the stages of the Poppy, and the Blackbird; for himself. And I tucked a pippin apple into his pocket, and I kissed him again: *For Mr. Rupert— tell him farewell. And to have a care for his eye. And to stop smoking so!* which made him smile, a smile I kept until his cab was all round the corner and gone, kept it even while I cried…. I touched the little golden fish on my breast, to make its tail move, then set it safe back inside the lockbox, with the little blue eye, that strange old lover's eye beside my earbobs, the prettiest things I have but for my wedding ring, now, my pearl from Pimm.

Since then, there have been many things I would have cared to share with Istvan: for one, Pinky's announcement of his wedding-to-be. I don't know as his missus will be kinder than his father, but Pinky is like Puggy was, a friend of the west wind, he always sees the bright side of the coin: *Why, it's my thinking we'll go on fine together. She likes a bit of fun, Adele does. And best of all, when I marry, there's money set aside from the old stick, money to do as I like with, and I do like to help, Miss Bell—pardon, Mrs. Pimm, now! My, that was a pretty party, wasn't it?* For not only did he give me away, he poured out the champagne, and gave the salutation, and squeezed the concertina as Didier piped along on the flute: *I'm getting miles better, aren't I?* And he put into my hands another gift from Mme. de Metz, a pair of gloves so lovely I almost feared to wear them, all trimmed and fluted with Alençon lace, bridal lace, with a little stone—Pinky said it was a peridot—to fasten up with a loop at the wrists. They were snug on me, made for some lady with tinier mitts, but didn't they look a treat?

And last week who did I see but herself, Madame in a carriage on Dressmakers' Row: where she spotted me, too, and insisted I take a turn about the promenade. A tippet of purest ermine-white, and a kind of skirt I haven't seen before, blue-shot silk and quite narrow at the hips: *It's Christobel's choice*, showing me the ruching at the sleeves. *She is outfitting me* à la mode *for our journey*—to Greece and Italy and Spain, all the sunny places, though we've had our bit of sun here, too: all at once the promenade is greening, tulips tipped out, the little bushes tight with sturdy buds, everything alive again but *I heard about your father, Madame,* who went in his sleep, Otilie told me, without a damp eye to mourn him, except may be his man-valet, that Prussian whom nobody likes. *Condolences, I am very sorry.*

You would not be, had you known him. But I thank you, my dear.

Sometimes I think it's better they run off, as tomcats do, once the kindling's done.

Your own father is still living?

I hope not! and she smiled, and I did, too, not a happy smile but a true one. She had the coachman stop for a chocolate-vendor, and she drank it up as if she were thirsty; poor Madame, she must often have had a thirsty time of it, with that dreadful old father—and Monsieur Benjamin too, who's to marry in Greece, she told me, to bypass all the wagging tongues, wagging of Mr. Rupert, but we didn't speak of that.

And afterwards, she said, *I will go to Chatiens. The gardens—at this time of year, they prune off all the dead branches, then heap and weave them in armatures and figures, like a wicker-man, and make a fire to welcome the growing season. It's quite theatrical,* with a smile for me, *and pagan,* with one for herself. *As are we all…. I shall miss our conversations very much, Miss Bell.*

I shall miss her, too, that brave and tired Madame, and Monsieur Benjamin—"As well as will be," but for whom?—to set beside the ache for Mr. Rupert, and Istvan. We shan't have a player like him on this stage again. May be someday, when our Mickey grows up…. May be they will come back one day, and see for themselves; it is a hope. I shall keep the room for them in any case, swept up and ready.

For now, I'm that glad Pinky's not to be of any traveling party. Cross as he was to miss the Jack, he's ideas aplenty for the next show—though he can share them only *"januis clausis,"* as he calls it, *see the jolly new words I'm learning at the bank?*—that I've promised to the girls this time, my Rosa and her Snow-White. We'll do something with a princess or two, I'm thinking, something with spangles and some dancing, and a handsome puppet-prince…. They are all gone, now, or going, to London and Greece and whoever-knows-where, but Pimm and I, and Pinky, and the children, we are here at the Blackbird to stay.

From the windows of the train, the fields and hills, the little towns that pass like faces in a dream, the whole glowing autumn landscape of bounty and harvest, might be a scrim upon a stage, or one of those moving-zoetrope affairs, such as one sees at the Théâtre Optique: or so it seems to Mr. Arrowsmith, half drowsing in his comfortable seat. His griffin cane lies neatly to hand, beside the apricot tisane, and the stack of correspondence still to be accomplished, letters from Paris, and Philadelphia, and Ghent; well, there will be time this evening, they will dine in at the hotel, he and Isobel.... His wife, Isobel.

Their bond, of course, is morganatic, and very few are in the know, though the news flashed between those few like lightning. There was the unavoidable whiff of envy, even Guyon chaffed him, if very mildly: *The eminence grise! Felicitations. But I thought you had retired?* to bring his own modest shrug: *One goes where one is needed. Benjamin is very able, but very young.* Privately he considers it a unique gift, that the cards fell as they have, a kind of philosopher's revenge on a world without meaning. How incensed would be Isidore! to whom blood was always paramount.

And yet no one of his line was there to see the ship leave shore: not Isobel, for whom he did not ask, nor Benjamin, for whom he died calling, there in the drip and stink of the town-house bedchamber, not Chatiens, his seat of power. The fire so hot that all three of them were wet with sweat: Isidore, his man Helmut, and Mr. Arrowsmith himself, who watched those terrible eyes close, then open, close again, as last instructions were offered, old debts settled, and *That—man killed Hector, did he not?* in a voice that was the voice of the pain itself, an inhuman little mutter. *And Vidor—he told me that himself.*

He is an upright fellow, Mr. Bok, all things considered.

You knew, Javier? with one manacle hand on his wrist, living or dying he had tremendous strength, did Isidore: but what exactly was he asking? when there was so much to know: what the prefect needed, what M. Sellars feared, what Dusan meant by the second rope. So instead *I served the interests we share, as I will serve your son, now. Your only son. Let the dead bury their dead,* which also was accomplished, with becoming pomp, yet not so ostentatiously as to make the grief suspect; and only Charlotte truly grieved, Charlotte with her red nose and Victoria-veil to her knees; how deeply that annoyed Isobel! The extravagance, the display.... There is much of her father in her, though he will never point that out. And Charlotte's tears were dried relatively swiftly, packed off to her beloved Paris with her trunks and furbelows, and a generous if not excessive widow's dowry to compensate for Isidore's refusal to make her an heir; that last was Isobel's idea, annoyance or no.

All the rest, of course, belongs to Benjamin, his father's major legatee: Isaac to Jacob, for whom the faithful Helmut reserved his Esau moment of sour grief: *He ought have come, Monsieur, at least to give his father peace,* Helmut who ought have held his peace, and saved his breath. Helmut has been packed off, too, though Isobel opposed it: *I love him as little as you do, Benny, but he has served our family very well—*

Horseshit. I'd as soon wear the old man's suits, and so that settled that. It has been demonstrated that Benjamin has decided tastes—in servants, liquor, décor, itinerary—that are his sister's joy to foster; and his wife's as well, apparently, Christobel so like to Isobel that they might be sisters indeed instead of in-law. What the new Mme. de Metz makes of that young fellow there, that M. Gabriel lounging in the seat beside her husband, sharing whispers and a silver flask.... Well. As he has learned from his own brief experience, one must occasionally labor to preserve marital felicity, and silence is often a boon.

Now Mr. Arrowsmith shifts slightly in his seat, sips his tisane, and slightly yawns, glancing across the aisle to where Mme. Arrowsmith—though she never wears that title—sits improving her mind with Diderot, though a mind such as hers needs little in the way of improvement. Does she feel his gaze? and so raises her own, to make a gentle smile that he returns. There is much that is gentle in Isobel, and much that is wounded beyond repair, though he has urged, and will continue to urge, that she consult a surgeon for her poor hand; she still will not show him, not bare without the glove, but one day she will. Or she will not. Nevertheless, he still will try: she deserves the effort, and is so amazed and grateful when it comes.

Now Isobel lets her gaze drop down again to Diderot, but her true attention is elsewhere, roaming the walks and garden lanes of Chatiens: so much to accomplish, she is quite eager to begin. If she had had only herself to please, she would have spent the summer there, content with her sketchbook and shears; but the time belonged first to family affairs, to funerals and weddings.

Her engagement—what a singular moment, an event she had long ago ceased to believe in, let alone ever expect. There at tea with Javier, noting his sudden silence, then astonished by the ring, a sapphire in a nest of diamonds, weighty and imposing, though his proposal was a model of delicacy: *If it suits you, Isobel…?* And when she had accepted—for of course she had accepted—he put the ring upon her, he kissed her on the forehead with great affection and respect: *You have done so well on your own, my dear, it is time for you to rest. I should like to stand between you and the world, for as long as life lets me.* Her own tears surprised her; Javier did not seem surprised.

The ceremony itself was quick and secret, there in a Barcelona hotel: the ambassador and his wife to witness, Benjamin and Christobel the guests, Benny very drunk, afterward, on whiskey and champagne. His own wedding had been barely more public, though it was accomplished in a chapel, a lovely Moorish chapel filled with bright, angelic light, Christobel trembling with emotion, Benny so calm and remote. The Guyons have planned a season full of fêtes and balls and teas to honor the returning newlyweds, now that the time abroad has sponged whatever scandal might still cling…. They disappeared like smoke, M. Bok and M. Dieudonne, though after some time there came a note to the town house, *poste restante*, M. Bok's note thanking her for her hospitality, regretting that he could not tender his thanks in person. The fine, stiff handwriting, the careful wording; as carefully she tucked the note away, she has it still.

Their flight, if one could call it that, came in the aftermath of Hector's death, perhaps a too-cautious reaction—could anyone mourn Hector so much as to avenge him? Did anyone mourn Hector at all?— but there is so much of that affair that she does not know, will never know. Javier has never explained precisely how Hector met his end, or by whom, though apparently there was some sort of investigation, and a brief flurry of public nervousness—if a military man should be found dead on the docks, who else might be in peril there?—but all was soon forgotten in the wake of some newer outrage. The obsequies were quite thrilling, all that somber martial music, and a riderless red-plumed horse marching beside the bier; afterward she sat alone in the parlor and drank champagne, quite a quantity in fact, she had a sad headache next day. Both Hector and Isidore gone, the scorpion riding the snake down into hell—ah, cry the jubilee!

Isidore's funeral was a high church affair—and true to his vow, Benny put not one foot inside the house at Chatiens until that day, a silent beautiful statue throughout the service, the mourners queuing up to make their bows, to press his hand, would they kiss his ring as well? His signet ring…. Later, alone with her in Isidore's rooms, the bleak drapes furled to show the faintly greening lawns, shed light on the stoic bust of Pompey, the painting of Rachel: *Do you fancy this, Belle? You can have the whole place if you want it. Or burn it for kindling.* Restless to the window, as if the day had been a year. *I shan't come here again.*

Do just as you like, Benny.

And the look he gave her then—*I can't do "as I like," but I will do as I will*—was a signpost on the road to come: not the old silly dissipations, but a newer, tainted sort of play. Such as this Edmund Gabriel, the minor son of an extremely minor baronet, Benny picked him up, or won him, at lansquenet in Greece; it suits, the boy is a trinket. And such a universe away from M. Bok as to be a tragedy; but that is a subject Benny never will discuss, though she tried, once, noting very gently that signet ring, but so instant was his snarl—*Am I to have nothing of my own, then?*—that it sent her to full and silent retreat.

It was Christobel who broached it, boarding this very train: not to Benny but to herself, dismayed to watch Benny give the seat that should have been his wife's to the boy instead, leaving Christobel to sit alone but *He has lost a great deal, Madame,* those great dark eyes filled with knowledge; she sees so much more than she speaks of, Christobel. *Not only Monsigneur his father, but his*—cher ami, *as well.*

And that is a suitable replacement? Together they watched the boy's sulky displeasure, the seat has too much sun, he must have another, Benny changing with him; the creature is always pouting over something. *You are remarkably accommodating, my dear.*

What comforts my husband comforts me, Madame. And you, too, which in the end is true: it is how she has tolerated the boy's company while they traveled, though he is always deferential to her, if merely correct to Christobel, who herself is always kind to him; Javier he ignores completely, as if he were a superior sort of servant…. Isobel sighs, now, watching as Benny exchanges the gleaming flask for his journal, an old pearl-gray journal; strange that he would choose to use an artifact that once was Isidore's, but it seems never far from his hand. See him now, busily scribbling away—

—as the boy beside him gazes out the window at the approaching station, one last loop of the journey to take Benny and Christobel to the town house, with Javier; she herself will change trains and go on, for a fortnight, to Chatiens. It is not so verdant in the autumn, but there is great loveliness all the same, and beauty is its own balm and reason: the sketched line of tree limbs, the bonfires heaped to the sky, the smaller fires that bless by consuming all that is lost, and dead, and broken, leaving in their place a space for clean new growth. She will think of Axel as she walks those paths, planning for the spring's renewal, the trees she will have pruned, or moved, the avenue of roses she will have refreshed—and the town house bench beneath the willow, the lovers' bench, she will have that transported as well—

—as the train comes to a steaming stop, Javier rising to consult the compartment conductor, Isobel tucking away her book—"Will you walk out a moment, Benny?"—but he shakes his head, still writing, then gives her a brief, abstracted smile—"I'll see you in town, Belle"— as Edmund Gabriel looks incuriously past her, out the window to the platform, where, in the crowd, two men, both in dark traveling coats, one wearing small silver spectacles, suddenly catch, and rivet, Isobel's gaze.

Christobel sees that gaze, sees the men; she nods to Mr. Arrowsmith, then as if by unspoken consent, resumes her seat and begins, lightly, to quiz Edmund Gabriel—Did he prefer the sights in Barcelona to the sights in Rome? Which would he most care to visit again?—as Benjamin continues to write in the journal. Meanwhile Mr. Arrowsmith conducts Isobel off the train, Isobel who is smiling now, a pained and joyful smile as "Monsieur," with one hand out, to brush, barely touching, the man's sleeve, his guarded regard turning into a smile of his own as "Why, Madame," says Rupert, and bows, and takes her hand.

M. Dieudonne smiles just past his shoulder—"You are coming or going, Madame? You have the look of far shores about you"—as Mr. Arrowsmith bows to both the men, then draws Istvan discreetly to one side, while Isobel smiles to M. Bok: "We are just back from abroad.... You look very well, Monsieur," in the traveling suit well-cut but sober, though with a dandy's fine detail, and the golden flash of a golden ring. And the little spectacles—they suit him, so studious and keen, and mask what looks a scar beside his left eye. Gazing into his gaze, his face, she sees that he has not changed so much as blossomed, in some subtle but arresting way; then it comes to her, that change: M. Bok is happy.

"You are bound for the city, Monsieur?" she asks, but no, it is mere happenstance, this meeting, they are only passing through en route to "Paris," says M. Bok. "There is a show he wants to see there, a Guignol show. And you, Madame?"

In answer she unhooks her reticule to show a silver cameo locket-case, one side the marriage portrait, Benjamin and his bride, the other of Benjamin alone. "We have been up and down the continent," she says, trying for a light tone, "'honey-mooning.' Now they will take up residence, and I am off to the country." M. Bok examines the portrait, and smiles still, but more gravely—"Felicitations, Madame"—as a part of her longs to cry out, to say If only—! He and Benny and herself, upon this trip, upon this train—

—but "I as well am wed," she says, still lightly, "though we have kept it close to the vest, isn't that the phrase?" His smile changes yet again, in honest pleasure as she relates the circumstance, she and Javier, and "Felicitations indeed," he says, and bends to reach again for her hand—

—but instead she raises that hand to his cheek, to touch his face as she leans close to brush his lips with hers: like a girl, eyes closed as if in the deep dazzle of summer, the sweetness of the garden, kissing him goodbye—

—as Mr. Arrowsmith and Istvan exchange friendly, impersonal bows, their business concluded in a final way, though Mr. Arrowsmith asks if "You will be performing in town, perhaps? Or in some other place—say, Brussels? Or Paris?" seeming sadly disappointed when the answer is no: "I am off the boards these days," says Dusan, Istvan, M. Hilaire, a name he lately has begun to wear. "It is a pleasure to be of the audience for once, one can learn a great deal just by watching."

"Ah. And M. Bok watches with you?"

For answer, M. Hilaire only smiles. There is something new in that smile, something ironical and cold, and Mr. Arrowsmith wonders privately what sort of puppet plays a smile like that may breed. Then Mr. Arrowsmith gives his hand to Rupert, as Istvan leans in to kiss Isobel's glove, even though she offers her cheek: "Well met, Madame, and safe travels. It is a great pleasure to see you," though she sees, now, that he is no longer open to her, impregnable inside himself, like a guarded fortress on which the sun shines bright.

She asks, "Will you take up residence in the city again, M. Dieudonne?" and he smiles, as if the name is one of a friend he has forgotten, a friend she now recalls to momentary life: "Indeed no, Madame. We shall be traveling awhile, become mere orphans of the road. Fortunately we know how to be orphans."

"You two, Monsieur, never can be orphaned."

He gives her a look that she cannot wholly parse, though humor is a part of it; then "Your trunk has been loaded, my dear," says Javier, and "I must see to ours," says M. Bok, as bows are exchanged, as all part as if part of a dance, a last gavotte there on the crowded platform, Isobel boarding her country train, Mr. Arrowsmith returning to the other, Istvan and Rupert crossing to a third—

—as Rupert looks back for just a moment, not to Isobel but to the train Mr. Arrowsmith enters, as if he would glimpse through the window that face from the cameo: watched himself by Christobel whom he does not mark, Christobel who gives him a searching look, as though there is a question she would ask him, this living key to her husband's icy heart, this *cher ami*—

—who as swiftly turns away his gaze; it is better not to see, what good could it ever do? They have had their moment, he and Benjamin: alone at the last in the bedchamber, sponging off the crusted blood, tears in his eyes and *Why will you not go with me,* Maître? *Why will you not love me?*

It is because I care for you that I do not go. To dream a dream is one thing, to live it out another; but how could Benjamin know that? He is so terribly young. *And you—you go and be their master, make the bastards bow,* as he took to himself one last time that face, that wounded, open, seeking mouth, then pulled the ring from his finger while Benjamin did the same, signet and intaglio, and watched him walk forever down the hall…. Rupert sighs, a sound unheard in the busy crowd, Istvan taking back from an officious porter a dark calfskin traveling case—"This travels with us"—and lets his gaze go elsewhere, as the train across the platform huffs and churns—

—while aboard, Edmund Gabriel changes his seat yet again, for the distaff side of the train, Benjamin changing with him: and as Benjamin starts to seat himself he sees—his whole body sees—Rupert, there on the platform opposite. A convulsive little motion, his hands go flat against the glass, while Christobel and Edmund share a glance—hers of heartfelt pity, his a puzzled frown—as the train gains greater speed, and pulls away.

Having boarded their compartment, Istvan secures the puppets in their case beneath the seats, as Rupert passes the tickets to the conductor: Paris, yes, and then Lyon, there is another performance Istvan fancies, a troupe of players hardly more than boys, who make quite the ribald spectacle, if the broadsheets can be believed. And after Lyon, Istvan has mentioned Prague, some fellows there who have a puppet opera—What did he name it, to Madame? "Orphans of the road," yes. Since they left that place they have stayed nowhere very long, the soothing constant of constant motion giving both a chance to rest and to recover—though the London oculist said there was naught to be done, his left eye will have that gray gauze forevermore, bringing Istvan's shrug—*I'll see for you*—and his own in answer: *I have my spectacles,* the little spectacles he is never now without, and one good eye to balance out the shadows.

And as they go from place to place, watching what others do, how others' *mecs* make mischief or make merry, they have begun to chart their own and subtler spectacle, two men and their two avatars, two puppets called not Feste and Puck but Mr. Pollux and Mr. Castor, who for now make their feints and dashes in private, as Istvan dreams and Rupert writes: *The dark one tells stories, and the one with the puppets acts them out*, said long ago, years ago, when the stories were always those of others, picked up like jackdaw glitter on the road. Now they will tell a different kind of tale, and he will write it all down, stories not of the mere moment, spent like confetti in drawing rooms or cabarets, but ones that will speak of their own lives, as Benjamin's journal-poems once spoke to him; plays that, if they are skillful and play hard, may find the way to life, and finally last.... It is his task, and he made for it as he never could be for the management, or the finance, though those have been a kind of making for him, each in its narrow way. *They are my toys, too*: he said that to Decca, fierce and truthful on the Poppy stairway, Decca who never had liked Marco, or Pan Loudermilk, or any of the puppets, who had somehow—had she?—been arrayed with the General, if Georges could ever be believed: *He said there was money*, Rupert's murmur one midnight to Istvan, lying in the London hotel. *He said, "Your whoremistress had it from my man."*

More than what we had from his pockets?

May be. If one could credit him.

Him or her. Well, there's no quizzing him now, is there. Fucking Ag—I hope Omar pinched it all for smoke....When next I see friend Arrowsmith, it will be to give back his bit and bridle, too. You and I, messire, we work only for love now, yeah?

For love, yes, and for themselves, as Istvan has always wanted, himself and Rupert and the show: with money enough to be their own patrons, go wheresoever they please and *May be a theatre, too, Mouse, if you still will have just the one roost:* a place of their own, a home where Istvan will play and he will work, industry, yes, together with these actors sleeping now in their calfskin case, this Castor and Pollux, an ironical smile and a keyhole heart, and who in the audience to say which is which? "We'll just share/Like goodly brothers," like Istvan in that theatre, recall it? and he above and pining on the catwalk, thinking that all was over, love, life, everything.... Foolish to call the play at all, for comic or tragic, while the curtains are still parted; always there may be a twist to the story, a *coup de maître*, a masterstroke.

Now Istvan takes the window seat—he always claims the window seat—as Rupert settles in with a *Courier-Dispatch*, he makes a point to read the papers of whatever locality they may visit. This one tells mainly of mundane doings, a robbery here, a grain strike there, and the society columns full of the upcoming Opera Mauve, one of the capitol's great traditions, where families from all over will bring their marriageable daughters and their hopes for greater things. As he turns the page, Istvan nudges him—"Look at that fellow, there, by the hack-carriage—the peaked red hat, there—" a street-singer kicking up his heels, jogging his knees together, like a mec stranded clumsy without strings, trying and failing to interest the passing crowd.

Rupert gazes over the folds of his paper. "Looks like 'Paddy's Lament.' Some kind of lament, anyway."

"He wants a handler," says a voice from beneath the seat, muffled but still antic; Istvan laughs a little, softly. The train begins to move, past the platform and the stringless singer, the hurrying, incurious, oblivious crowd, the lanes that stripe like lines the city and the countryside, to make all a hurlyburly of motion and speed, a living echo of the strands that bind each playing life unto the next. But that greater sense of a greater whole is seen, perhaps, only with a god's eye view, pitched far above those strands and lines, a sight first glimpsed in Eden, say, or in the view one has from the balcony, watching the twist and gambol of the puppets and the puppeteers.

My great thanks:

To Rick Lieder and Carter Scholz, for close reading and invaluable comment, and to Kelly Link, for editorial insight.

To Aaron Mustamaa, Jane Schaberg, Diane Cheklich, and Deborah Newton, for much encouragement along the way.

And to Chris Schelling, uniquely.

This book was made possible by the generous support of the Rappahannock Foundation.

KATHE KOJA's (underthepoppy.com) books include *The Cipher, Skin,* and *Extremities*; her young adult novels include *Buddha Boy, Talk, Kissing the Bee,* and *Headlong*. Her work has been honored by the ALA, the ASPCA, and with the Bram Stoker Award. Her books have been published in seven languages and optioned for film. She's a Detroit native and lives in the area with her husband, artist Rick Lieder, and their cats. *Under the Poppy* will debut onstage at the Detroit Opera House Black Box Theater in 2011.